THE
Marriage
DEAL

BESTSELLING NEW ZEALAND AUTHOR

JACKIE ASHENDEN

THE
Marriage
DEAL

MILLS & BOON

THE MARRIAGE DEAL © 2024 by Harlequin Books S.A.

The publisher acknowledges the copyright holders of the individual works as follows:
CLAIMING HIS ONE-NIGHT CHILD
© 2019 by Jackie Ashenden   First Published 2019
Philippine Copyright 2019   Second Australian Paperback Edition 2024
Australian Copyright 2019   ISBN 978 1 038 90005 0
New Zealand Copyright 2019

CROWNED AT THE DESERT KING'S COMMAND
© 2020 by Jackie Ashenden   First Published 2020
Philippine Copyright 2020   Second Australian Paperback Edition 2024
Australian Copyright 2020   ISBN 978 1 038 90005 0
New Zealand Copyright 2020

THE SPANIARD'S WEDDING REVENGE
© 2020 by Jackie Ashenden   First Published 2020
Philippine Copyright 2020   Second Australian Paperback Edition 2024
Australian Copyright 2020   ISBN 978 1 038 90005 0
New Zealand Copyright 2020

MIX
Paper | Supporting
responsible forestry
FSC® C001695

Published by
Harlequin Mills & Boon
An imprint of Harlequin Enterprises (Australia) Pty Limited
(ABN 47 001 180 918), a subsidiary of HarperCollins
Publishers Australia Pty Limited
(ABN 36 009 913 517)
Level 19, 201 Elizabeth Street
SYDNEY NSW 2000 AUSTRALIA

Printed and bound in Australia by McPherson's Printing Group

CONTENTS

Jackie Ashenden writes dark, emotional stories with alpha heroes who've just gotten the world to their liking only to have it blown apart by their kick-ass heroines. She lives in Auckland, New Zealand, with her husband, the inimitable Dr. Jax, two kids and two rats. When she's not torturing alpha males and their gutsy heroines she can be found drinking chocolate martinis, reading anything she can lay her hands on, wasting time on social media or being forced to go mountain biking with her husband. To keep up-to-date with Jackie's new releases and other news, sign up to her newsletter at jackieashenden.com.

Claiming His One-Night Child

MILLS & BOON

DEDICATION

To my dad. He'll probably never read this book,
but just in case he does... Hi, Dad.

CHAPTER ONE

As one of Europe's most notorious playboys, Dante Cardinali was used to waking up in strange beds. He was also used to beautiful women standing beside said beds and looking down at him. There had even been a couple of instances where he'd woken up with his wrists and ankles still cuffed, the way they clearly were now.

What was unfamiliar was the barrel of the gun pointed at his head.

Dante had never been a man who cared over much about anything, but one thing he *did* care about was himself. And his life. And the fact that the beautiful woman standing over him was holding a gun in a very competent grip.

The same beautiful woman who'd been in the VIP area of his favourite Monte Carlo club and with whom he'd spent some time…talking…because he hadn't been in the mood for seduction—something that had been happening to him more often than not of late. It was a worrying trend if he thought about it too deeply, which he didn't. Because he didn't think about anything too deeply.

Whatever. He couldn't remember how long he'd spent talking to her, because he couldn't remember full-stop. In fact, he couldn't remember much at all about the evening and, given his current situation, it probably meant he'd blacked out at some point.

What he did remember was the beautiful woman's piercingly blue eyes, fractured through with silver like a shattered sky.

Those eyes were looking at him now with curious intentness, as if she was trying to decide whether or not to shoot him.

Well, considering his wrists and ankles were cuffed and he wasn't dead already, it meant there was some doubt. And if there was some doubt, he could probably induce her to give in to it.

He could pretty much convince anyone to give in to anything if he put his mind to it.

'Darling,' he drawled, his mouth dry and his voice a little thick. 'A gun is slightly overkill, don't you think? If you want to sleep with me, just take your clothes off and come here. You don't need to tie me to the bed.' He frowned, his head suspiciously muzzy but beginning to clear. 'Or put something in my drink, for that matter.'

The woman's cool gaze—she had told him her name but he couldn't remember it—didn't waver. 'I don't want to sleep with you, Dante Cardinali,' she said, her icy tone a slap of cold water on his hot skin. 'What I would like very much is to kill you.'

So. She *was* trying to kill him and she *was* very serious.

He should probably be a little more concerned about that gun and the intent in her fascinating eyes, and he definitely was. But, strangely, his most prevalent emotion wasn't fear. No, it was excitement.

It had been a long time since he'd felt anything like excitement.

It had been a long time since he'd felt anything at all.

He stared at her, conscious of a certain tightening of his muscles and a slight elevation in his heartbeat. 'That seems extreme.'

'It is extreme. Then again, the punishment fits the crime.'

The barrel of the gun didn't waver an inch and yet she hadn't pulled the trigger. Interesting. Why not?

He let his gaze rove over her, interest tugging at him.

She was very small, built petite and delicate like a china doll, with hair the colour of newly minted gold coins, falling in a straight and gleaming waterfall over her shoulders. Her precise features were as lovely as her figure—a determined chin, finely carved cheekbones and a perfect little bow of a mouth.

She wore a satin cocktail dress the same kind of silvery blue as her eyes and it looked like silky fluid poured over her body, outlining the delicious curves of her breasts and hips, skimming gently rounded thighs.

A lovely little china shepherdess of a woman. Just his type.

Apart from the gun in his face, of course.

'What crime?' Dante asked with interest. 'Are you Sicilian by any chance? Is this a vendetta situation?' It was a question purely designed to keep her talking, as he knew already that she wasn't Sicilian. Her Italian held a cadence from a different part of the country and one he was quite familiar with.

The sound of the island nation from where he'd been exiled along with the rest of the royal family years and years ago.

The island nation of which he'd once been a prince.

Monte Santa Maria.

'No.' Her tone was flat and very definite. 'But you know that already, don't you?'

Dante met her gaze. He was good at reading people—it was part of the reason he was so successful in the billion-dollar property-investment company he owned with his brother—and although this woman's cool exterior seemed

completely flawless he could see something flickering
in the depths of her eyes. Uncertainty or indecision, he
couldn't tell which. Interesting. For all that she seemed
competent and in charge, she still hadn't pulled that trigger. And if she hadn't done it now, she probably wouldn't.

He'd seen killers before and this woman wasn't one. In
fact, he'd bet the entirety of Cardinal Developments on it.

'Yes,' he said, discreetly testing the cuffs on his ankles
and wrists. They were firm. If he wanted to get out of them,
she was going to have to unlock them. 'Good catch. I love
an intelligent woman.'

She took a step closer to the bed, the gun still unerringly
pointed at his head. 'You know what I love? A stupid man.'

Her nearness prompted a heady, blatantly sexual fra-
grance to flood over him, along with bits and pieces of
his memory.

Ah, yes, it was all coming back to him now—sitting in
his club in Monte Carlo, this pretty little thing catching
his eye and smiling shyly. She'd been innocent and artless, a touch nervous and, despite her strongly sexual perfume, when she'd said it was her first time in a club he'd
believed her.

He hadn't been in the mood for small talk but, as he
hadn't been in the mood for seduction, and there had been
something endearing about her nervousness, he'd sat beside
her and chatted. He couldn't remember a single thing about
that conversation other than the fact that he hadn't been as
bored as he'd expected to be, as he so often was these days.

He was not bored now, though. Not in any way, shape
or form.

She was looking at him coolly, like a scientist ready to
dissect an insect, no trace of that shy, nervous woman he'd
talked to in the club. Which must mean that it had been an
act. An act he hadn't spotted.

Oh, she was good. She was very good.

His heart rate sped up even further, the tug of interest becoming something stronger, hotter.

Are you insane? She wants to kill you and you want to bed her?

Was that any surprise? It had been too long since he'd had any kind of excitement in his life, too long since he'd had anything like a challenge. The closest he'd come to interesting had been when his older brother Enzo had married a lovely English woman and Dante had been tasked with making sure Enzo's son behaved himself. A shockingly difficult task, given the boy had already decided that Dante was less uncle than partner in crime.

Dante had had to spend at least a week afterwards in the company of various lovely ladies simply to recover.

Marriage and children were *not* the kind of excitement he was after. They were too restrictive and far too...domestic for his sophisticated tastes.

Though, given the state of his groin, if a lovely woman could get him hard simply by waving a gun at him maybe his tastes had grown a little too sophisticated even for him.

Then again, it didn't look as though he was going to be able to escape any time soon, unless he charmed his way out. It wouldn't be the first time that he'd used his considerable physical appeal to manipulate a situation and this was a situation that definitely required some degree of manipulation.

And besides. It might be fun.

'Stupid, hmm? Maybe I am.' He allowed himself to relax, looking up at her from underneath his lashes. 'Or maybe I knew who you were all along and simply wanted to see what you wanted from me.'

Her lovely mouth curved in a faint, cool smile. 'I see. In that case, care to enlighten me on why you're here?'

Dante raised a brow. 'Isn't that your job? I'm still waiting for your villain monologue.'

'Oh, no, you apparently know all about it already, so don't let me stop you.' She cocked her head, the light gleaming on her golden hair. 'I'd like to hear it so, please, go on.'

Adrenaline flooded through him in a hot burst. This was getting more and more interesting by the second. And so was she, playing him at his own game. Little witch.

He allowed his gaze to roam over her, giving himself some time to collect his thoughts. If she wanted him to give her the run down on what he thought was going on so far, then he was happy to oblige her. Especially as he was starting to get some idea.

If she was from Monte Santa Maria—and that seemed certain—then the most obvious explanation for his current predicament was an issue with his family. The Cardinalis had once been rulers of Monte Santa Maria, at least until Dante's father had mismanaged the country so badly that the government had removed him from his throne and exiled their entire family.

Luca Cardinali hadn't earned them any friends during his troubled reign.

So, did that mean she was from a family whom Luca had wronged? She looked young—younger than he was—and he'd only been eleven when their family had had to leave, so she was likely to be someone's daughter.

He didn't remember much of his Monte Santa Marian history—he'd tried his best to forget about his country entirely—but he seemed to recall an aristocratic family who'd been famous for their beauty, and most especially their golden hair.

'Well, if you insist,' he said. 'Your accent is familiar—from Monte Santa Maria, if I'm not much mistaken—and, given your general antipathy towards me, it's likely you're someone my father wronged at some point.' He watched her lovely face intently. 'But you're young, so I don't imagine Luca wronged you personally, but your family. And, given your accent again, I would say you're from one of the aristocratic families. Probably…' His brain finally settled on the name it had been looking for. 'Montefiore.'

Something in her shattered sky eyes flared. Shock.

So. He'd been right. How satisfying.

'Guess work,' she said dismissively, her chin lifting, her hold on the gun tightening. 'You know nothing.'

'And you are very good at pretending.' He smiled. 'If you're going to pull the trigger, darling, you'd better do it now. Or do you want the suspense to kill me before you do?'

'You think this is a joke?'

'With that gun in my face? Obviously not. But, if you imagine this is the first time I've woken up tied to a bed, you'd be wrong.'

'This isn't some sex game, Cardinali.'

'Clearly. If it was, you'd be naked and so would I, and you'd be calling me Dante. Or screaming it, rather.'

A whisper of colour stained her pale cheekbones and he didn't miss the way her gaze flicked down his body and then back up again, as if she couldn't help herself.

Excellent. It would appear she wasn't immune to him after all.

His satisfaction with the whole situation deepened, not to mention his excitement. This was indeed going to be a lot more fun than he'd initially envisaged.

Her jaw had tightened. 'You seem very casual for a man who's about to die.'

Apparently she didn't like his attitude. Well, not many people did.

'And if I was really about to die, I would be dead already. But, no, you put something in my drink, dealt with

my bodyguards, somehow managed to transport me to...'
he took a brief glance around the room which looked like
a standard five-star hotel room '...wherever this is. Cuffed
me to the bed. Waited until I woke up, then started talking to me instead of pulling that trigger.' He allowed his
voice to deepen and become lazier, more sensual. 'And,
darling, considering that little look you gave me just now,
it's not killing that you want to do to me. It's something
else entirely.' He let his smile become hot, the smile that
had charmed women the world over and had never failed
him yet. 'In which case, be my guest. You've already got
me all tied up. I'm completely at your mercy.'

STELLA MONTEFIORE HAD never thought killing Dante Cardinali would be easy. He was rich, important and more or
less constantly surrounded by people, which made getting
an opportunity to take him down very, very difficult.

But since she'd taken on the mission she'd spent at least
six months planning how to get access to him and, now she
had, her family was counting on her to go through with it.
Especially her father.

It was a just revenge for his son's death and a chance to
reclaim the lost honour of the Montefiores. It was also her
chance at redemption for her brother's death, a death for
which her parents still hadn't forgiven her, and she did *not*
want to make any mistakes. There was no room for error.

In fact, everything had gone completely to plan, and
here he was, at her mercy, just as he'd said.

So why couldn't she pull that trigger?

He was lying on the bed in the hotel room she'd managed to get him into with the help of the hotel staff, having
told them he was drunk, and he was cuffed hand and foot.
He shouldn't be dangerous in the slightest.

And yet...

There was something about the way he took up space on the bed, all long and lean and muscular, the fabric of his expensive black trousers and plain white shirt pulling across his powerful chest and thighs. Not to mention the lazy way he looked at her from underneath his long, thick, black lashes, the glints of gold in his dark eyes like coins on the bottom of a lake-bed. Completely unfazed. As if he dealt with guns in his face every day and it didn't bother him in the slightest.

And it didn't help that he was so ridiculously beautiful in an intensely masculine way. All aristocratic cheekbones, a hard jawline, straight nose and the most perfectly carved mouth she'd ever seen. A fallen angel's face with a warrior's body, and the kind of fierce sexual magnetism that drew people to him, whatever their gender.

She hadn't anticipated that, though she should have, given she'd put a lot of work into researching him.

In fact, there was quite a lot about Dante Cardinali that she hadn't anticipated, including her own response to him.

Her heartbeat was strangely fast, though that was probably due to the sheer adrenaline of the moment and the unexpected success of her mission, nothing at all to do with the seductive glint in Cardinali's dark eyes.

Not that she should be thinking about how seductive he was when she was busy trying to work up the courage to pull that trigger.

'In which case,' she said, trying to maintain her cool, 'Perhaps you should be begging for your life instead of making casual comments about me sleeping with you. Which, I may add, I would rather die than do.'

He laughed, a rich sound that rolled over her like velvet, all warm and soft with just a hint of roughness. 'Oh, I'm sure you wouldn't.' That fascinating hint of gold gleamed from underneath his lashes. 'In fact, give me five minutes and you'll be the one who's begging. And it won't be for your life… Stella Montefiore.'

Shock trickled like ice water down her back, smothering the heat his sexy laugh somehow had built inside her, and distracting her totally from his outrageous statement.

He knew her name.

Kill him. Kill him now.

Her palm was sweaty, the metal of the gun cool against her skin. She'd practised this, shooting at tin cans in the makeshift gun range her father had set up in the barren hills behind the rundown house they'd had to move into after her brother had been arrested, working on her aim in between shifts as a waitress at a local restaurant—the only employment she could get, as no one wanted to hire a Montefiore. Not when they were such a political liability.

But shooting a can was very different from shooting an actual man. A man who would have his life snuffed out. By her.

She swallowed, her mouth dry.

Don't think of him as a person. This is revenge. For Matteo. For yourself.

Yes, all she needed to do was pull that trigger. A muscle twitch, really, nothing more. And then all of this would be over—her father's quest for blood done, Matteo's death avenged and her role in it redeemed.

You asked for this, remember?

Her father had wanted to hire someone and she'd told him, no, that it was better for one of the family to undertake the mission, to minimise discovery, and that the person who did it should be her. He'd told her she was too weak for the job, too soft-hearted, but she'd insisted she wasn't. That she could do it.

And she could. It should be easy.

But still her finger didn't move.

'You're wrong,' she said, not quite sure why she was arguing with him when a single movement would solve all her problems. 'That's not my name.'

'Is it not?' His eyes glinted, the curve of his beautiful mouth almost hypnotising in its perfection. 'My mistake.' His voice was as deep and rich as his laugh and the sound of it did things to her that she didn't want.

The same things it had done to her all evening from the moment she'd seen him in the flesh and not as an image in a photo or an online video. She'd spent months studying him, reading up on his history, his lifestyle, his business practices and personality. Basically everything she could find on him, building up a picture of a dissolute yet charming playboy who seemed to spend more time in his string of clubs than he did in the offices of Cardinal Developments, the huge multi-national that he owned with his brother Enzo. He ruled the gossip columns and the beds of beautiful women everywhere, apparently.

'The world won't miss him,' her father, Santo Montefiore, had said viciously. 'He's selfish, just like Luca was. Another useless piece of Cardinali trash.'

Yet when she'd stepped into that club in Monte Carlo, sick with nerves—unable to adopt the veneer of icy sophistication she'd perfected to get past the VIP bouncer—and Cardinali had appeared out of nowhere telling the bouncer that it was fine and she could come in, it wasn't trash she'd been thinking of. Not when he'd smiled at her. Because it hadn't been a practised seducer's smile. It had been kind—reassuring, almost—and inexplicably comforting. In fact, he'd been kind all evening. He'd taken her under his wing, sitting her down in a quiet end of the club and getting her a drink. Then he'd sat opposite and talked easily to her about everything and absolutely nothing at all.

She'd been expecting predatory and cynical and he

hadn't been either of those things. To make matters worse, she'd found him so utterly beautiful, so magnetic, so charming, that she'd almost forgotten what she'd come to do. He'd overwhelmed her.

The attention he'd given her had made her feel like she was the centre of the world and, for a girl who'd come second best most of her life, it had been an intoxicating feeling.

Until he'd looked at his expensive, heavy gold watch that highlighted the bones of his strong wrist and said that he was going to have to leave soon. And she'd realised that if she wanted to make a move she was going to have to do it then. One more drink, she'd said. Just one more. And he'd agreed, not noticing when she'd slipped the drug into it.

Cardinali was watching her now and the smile turning his mouth wasn't kind this time. No, there was something else there. A hint of the predatory seducer she'd been expecting, along with a certain calculating gleam. Almost as if he now saw her as an equal and not the nervous, inexperienced woman she'd been in the club, or the soft-hearted, weak girl her parents had always thought her.

It made her heart thump hard in her chest, an inexplicable excitement flickering through her.

'My name is Carlotta,' she said. 'I told you that in the club.'

'Ah, then you'll have to forgive me my poor memory. Someone must have spiked my drink.' He shifted on the bed, as if he was getting himself more comfortable, a lazy movement that drew attention to his powerful body. 'So, are you going to stand there all night talking at me or are you going to murder me in cold blood? If it's the former, I hope you don't mind if I go to sleep. All this excitement is exhausting.' He shifted again and she caught a hint of his aftershave, warm and exotic, like sandalwood. It was delicious.

She took a steadying breath, trying to ignore the scent. 'Don't you care at all which one it is?'

'Since you're not going to kill me, not particularly.'

Her finger on the trigger itched. 'You don't know that.'

'Please, darling. Like I've already told you, if you'd really wanted to kill me you would have done it by now.'

He's right. You would have.

Except she hadn't. She'd told herself she couldn't shoot an unarmed and unconscious man. Plus, he needed to know why he had to die, otherwise what would be the point? But now he was awake and she wasn't telling him why he had to die. She was lying and pretending to be someone else instead.

What was she doing?

You don't want to kill him.

A shiver passed through her. She had to kill him. This was the job she'd undertaken months ago, for her father and for the sake of her brother's memory. For the honour of the Montefiores.

An eye for an eye. Blood for blood.

One of Luca Cardinali's sons had to die and, as his older brother Enzo was untouchable, that left only Dante.

Except…

His eyes were inky in the dim light of the room and they seemed to see right into her soul. There was no sharpness in them, only a velvet darkness that wrapped her up and held her tight.

'Lower the gun, sweetheart,' he said quietly. 'No matter what I've done, nothing is worth that stain on your soul.'

No, she shouldn't lower the gun. She needed to keep everything her father had told her about blood, honour and revenge in the forefront of her mind. She needed to be strong and, most important of all, hard. There could be no emotional weakness now.

And yet…her hand was shaking and she didn't understand why he should be so concerned with her soul when she herself didn't care about what happened to her after this was over.

'My soul is none of your business.' She tried to keep her voice firm and sure.

'If you're preparing to risk it to kill me, then it most certainly is my business.' His dark gaze held hers and there was no fear in it at all, only an honesty that wound around her heart and didn't let go. 'I'm not worth it, believe me.'

How curious. He made it sound as if her soul was actually worth something.

She should have shot him right then and there, but instead she found her hand lowering, exactly as he'd told her to.

He didn't glance at the gun, his dark eyes steady on her instead.

The weapon was heavy in her hand and she didn't understand why she hadn't pulled that trigger when she'd had the chance. Because now that chance had gone. The moment when she could have fired was lost.

You failed.

Shame rushed through her like the tide. How had he done it? How had he got under her guard? And, more importantly, why had she let him?

She'd worked hard ever since Matteo's death to excise all the soft, weak emotions inside her, the ones her parents had despised, and there shouldn't have been any room at all for mercy. But it seemed as if there was some small part of her that was still weak. Still flawed.

Anger glowed in her gut, hot and bright, overwhelming the shame, and before she realised what she was doing she'd put the gun on the bedside table and was bending down over him, putting one hand on the pillow on either side of his head. His hair was inky black on the pillows,

his eyes almost the same colour as they stared challeng-
ingly back at her.

He smelled so good, the heat rising off him making her
want to get close, to warm herself against him.

'What is it, kitten?' Dante murmured, staring straight
up at her, gold glinting deep in the darkness of his gaze.
'Is it time to show me your claws?'

Again, there wasn't an ounce of fear or doubt in him, just
as there hadn't been right from the start. He'd seen through
her. He'd seen through her completely.

Her anger flared hotter, a bonfire of rage. How dared he
find that weakness inside her? How dared he exploit it? And
what was wrong with her that she had allowed him to do it?

Her perfectly executed plan was now in ruins and all because she hadn't had the guts to do what needed to be done.

Because, somehow, she'd let this man undermine her.

Well, if he wanted to see her claws, then she'd show
them to him. And she knew exactly what to do to in order
to cause maximum damage.

Her experience with men was non-existent, but she'd
studied Dante Cardinali and she'd studied him well. Including what she could find on his sexual predilections.
He was a man who liked being in control and who always,
always, got what he wanted.

And it was clear that he wanted her.

Which gave her the perfect leverage over him.

'Not my claws,' Stella murmured, staring right back into
his eyes. 'You can feel my teeth instead.'

Then she lowered her head and bit him.

CHAPTER TWO

The lovely woman who was probably Stella Montefiore, but definitely wasn't Carlotta, closed her teeth delicately around Dante's lower lip and every nerve-ending he had lit up with sweet, delicious pain.

He was hard instantly, his whole body tight, his wrists and ankles instinctively pulling against the cuffs with the urge to grab her, hold her.

He hadn't been expecting this particular move, though really the glittering flare of anger he'd seen in her eyes just before she'd bent her head should have warned him.

She wasn't as cool as she seemed, which was a delightful surprise.

In fact, the whole of her bending over him with that rich heady scent, her silky golden hair falling over one shoulder, her pale skin glowing against the fluid fabric of her blue dress, was a delightful surprise.

He'd been hoping for some fight and he'd certainly got it.

If only his hands were free.

Instead, he opened his mouth and touched his tongue to the softness of lower lip, a gentle coax.

She went still, her teeth releasing him, her lips a breath away from his.

So he bit her back, but not hard. A light nip to see what she'd do.

Her head jerked back and she looked down at him, her blue eyes glowing with anger, her cheeks pink. 'Damn you,' she whispered.

'Why?' His own voice had roughened. 'Because I stopped you from doing what you didn't want to do anyway? Because you're not a killer?'

She didn't reply, merely bent her head again, and this time her mouth was on his in a hard, furious kiss.

That she was inexperienced was immediately obvious, but she also tasted of anger and of passion, and his interest, already piqued, deepened even further.

He'd had inexperienced before, though he tended to steer clear of women who didn't know what they were dealing with when it came to him. He'd had plenty of anger before too, not to mention passion. But not all three at once, and not when the woman dealing them out had been on the point of shooting him in the head.

It made him even harder than he was already.

Still, that inexperience was a warning sign that this woman, no matter how cool and strong she seemed, no matter that she'd had him at gunpoint, had her vulnerabilities. And it was interesting that the mention of her soul had been the thing that had made her lower the gun.

But what had been even more interesting to him was the definite shame that had flared in her eyes after she'd put the gun down, only to be swiftly overtaken by rage. She hadn't liked failing her mission, that was for sure. And yet, instead of shooting him anyway, she'd kissed him.

Yes, that was very, *very* interesting.

Not only was she a woman with vulnerabilities, she also seemed to be a woman of strong passions. Which made for an intoxicating combination.

'Kitten,' he murmured against her mouth. 'Are you sure you know what you're doing?'

In response she bit him again, harder this time, the tips of her breasts brushing against his chest as she leaned in closer. Holy God, her nipples were tight and hard. He could feel them through the cotton of his shirt.

Lust uncurled in his gut, thick and hot, making him catch his breath.

It had been a long time since a woman had made him feel like this, he had to admit. And he wasn't a man who denied himself anything he wanted. Self-control was all very well in certain situations, but when it came to sex he would freely admit to being a glutton.

Then again, she'd had the gall to drug him then tie him to a bed, so why should he give her everything she wanted right now?

He moved his head on the pillow, pulling his mouth away from her. 'Sweetheart, if you want that, you're going to have to ask for it.'

She made an angry sound and tried to kiss him again but he closed his mouth against hers.

The breath went out of her and she lifted her head. Her eyes were electric with anger, her cheeks pink. She said nothing, merely looked at him for a long moment. Then she straightened and took a step back from the bed.

But he didn't think she was going to move away. No, he'd seen something shift in that furious blue gaze of hers. She'd made a decision.

Anticipation coiled inside him, his breath catching yet again.

This woman was proving to be more and more intriguing with every second that passed and he couldn't wait to see what she was going to do next, how she would answer this particular challenge.

He didn't have anywhere to be or anything much to do beyond the usual round of PR work that he undertook on behalf of Enzo's and his company, plus the running of the more pleasurable side of the business, the resorts and clubs he owned all over the globe.

Anyway, he was bound to a bed. He couldn't go anywhere even if he wanted to. Luckily he didn't want to.

His lovely captor stood there a moment, her breathing fast in the silence of the room. Then she lifted her hands and pushed the straps of her silky blue dress off her shoulders, allowing the fabric to slide slowly down her body before pooling at her feet.

She was naked underneath it apart from the scrap of white lace between her thighs.

Okay, *that* was a move he hadn't anticipated her making. Not that he was complaining. Not in the slightest.

He'd seen a lot of beautiful women in his lifetime—more than he could count. But it wasn't this woman's physical beauty that felt like a punch to the gut, though she was indeed lovely: small, delicate and pale, her breasts the sweetest curves, her nipples pink and pretty.

No, it was the way she stood there with her chin lifted and her back straight, proud as a queen, her gaze full of challenge. As if she was daring him to break his bonds and come to her. Kneel at her feet. Worship her the way she was obviously used to being worshipped.

His pulse accelerated, the ache in his groin becoming acute. He almost jerked against the damn cuffs again, but managed to control himself at the last minute.

'Is this a request?' His voice was uneven even though he tried to mask it. 'Because, if so, it's a very persuasive one.'

She said nothing. Her hands went to her hips and very slowly she eased down the lacy underwear she wore then stepped out of it.

Dio, she was golden between her thighs too.

His mouth watered, his heartbeat hammering in his head.

What is it with you? It's not like you to let yourself get all hot under the collar for a woman.

It really wasn't. He didn't care about much of anything these days, but he found he cared about this. He wanted her hands on him. He wanted her skin against his. He wanted to be inside her. Preferably right now.

It was concerning. He didn't want to want anything at all.

He gritted his teeth, for the first time in a long while considering denying himself. Because he shouldn't care if she didn't touch him or kiss him, or get that delicious body on his. It shouldn't matter to him in the slightest.

If it doesn't matter, why are you even thinking of refusing her?

Dante had no answer to that.

He smiled, though for the first time in years it felt forced, more like a grimace than a smile. And he tried to make himself sound nonchalant. 'Well, don't just stand there, kitten. Come closer and let me see you.'

And perhaps she heard the strained note in his voice, because an expression that looked an awful lot like satisfaction flickered over her lovely face. Then she moved back over to the bed, clearly in no hurry at all, and looked at him very deliberately, the same way he'd looked at her. She was flushed now, the pink extending down her throat and over the pale curves of her breasts, and it deepened as her gaze dropped to where he was hard and ready and aching.

And stayed there.

Electricity crackled the length of his body.

What the hell was she doing to him? He didn't let himself get like this, not with anyone.

'I can get hard for any woman,' he murmured lazily, trying to keep the hoarse note out of the words. 'But it'll take more than you being naked to get me off.'

She gave him a brief, scorching glance. 'Who says I want to get you off? Maybe I just want to play with you.'

Sneaky kitten. So this was a power play, was it? She'd seen the general state he was in and thought she could take advantage, clearly.

Well, she could try. He might be finding it a tad more difficult to be his usual cool self, but when it came to bed-room power games he was the master. Even cuffed to the bed.

'Obviously I'm not going to object to that.' He let his voice get lower, become seductive. 'But, if you want to play, you'd better know what you're doing.'

'Who's to say that I don't?' She reached out and stroked lightly over the hard ridge just behind his fly.

More electricity crackled along his nerve-endings, the light brush of her fingertips maddening. Dante ignored the sensation. Instead, he gazed at her from beneath his lashes, letting the look in his eyes burn hot.

She was inexperienced—that kiss she'd given him had proved it well enough—and even though it wasn't some-thing he'd normally use to his advantage, given the circum-stances, beggars couldn't be choosers.

'That kiss for a start.' He let his gaze roam over her, bla-tantly sexual. 'Best to know what you're getting into, dar-ling. I'm a lot for a little kitten to handle.'

A deep-blue spark glittered in her eyes as she stroked him yet again. 'You're very arrogant for a man tied to a bed.'

'And you're very confident for a virgin.'

The deep pink flush staining her skin became scarlet, gilt lashes sweeping down, veiling her gaze and hiding her expression. And he was conscious of a very particular kind of satisfaction spreading through him. Firstly, for guess-ing right and, secondly, for the fact that he was perhaps the first man she'd ever touched like this. The first man with whom she'd ever been naked.

He normally steered clear of virgins, as he wasn't a man an innocent should get entangled with, but he couldn't deny that for some reason he liked the thought of this particular woman being a virgin. He liked it very much.

A virgin with a gun. How…intriguing.

'Don't be embarrassed, darling,' he said, watching her intently. 'Even I was a virgin once.' Though, thinking back, he honestly couldn't remember how or when he'd lost it.

She didn't say anything for a long moment. Then suddenly she lifted her head and moved to the bed, climbing on top of it and straddling him. The weight of her was slight, but the heat of her bare skin seeping through his clothes was astonishing.

His breath caught as the blatant sweetness of her perfume surrounded him, but underneath that was something light and fresh, combined with the musk of feminine arousal.

Pretty, pretty kitten.

She rose above him, the pressure of her body against his groin an agony, the sway of her lovely breasts making his mouth go dry. Her skin was glowing, a sheen of perspiration at her throat, the look in her eyes all fire and challenge.

There was not a hint of shyness in her, or at least none that she let him see.

'I'm not embarrassed.' She reached for the top button of his shirt. 'Why would I be?'

Her naked heat had sharpened his hunger while her refusal to back down ignited something far hotter. Something he'd thought he'd killed long ago.

His determination to win.

He smiled, allowing some of his sexual hunger to show. 'No reason at all. But if you want to play with me then I do suggest learning the rules of the game first.' He paused. 'You don't want to lose on your first try, do you?'

For the merest second an uncertain expression flickered over her face. Then it was gone.

'But I'm not going to lose,' she said coolly, pulling open the buttons on his shirt one by one then spreading open the white cotton, baring his chest. 'I might be a virgin, but I'm not stupid. And a man is only a man.' She pressed her palms to his skin, the heat of her touch like a brand, her blue eyes burning into his. 'Like you said, Mr Cardinali. You're at my mercy. And there's nothing you can do about it.'

DANTE LAUGHED THAT intensely sexy laugh of his, the sound heating everything inside her to boiling point, making her skin feel hot and tight, as though she wanted to claw it off and step out of it.

He was giving her the most blatantly sexual look from underneath his lashes, all liquid darkness and heat, and the feel of his muscular, powerful body made her lose all her breath.

It wasn't supposed to be this way. Biting him, taking off her dress, touching him, was supposed to tease him, taunt him with what he couldn't have. Prove her strength to him and also punish him for making her lose her nerve so badly.

And yet the only one feeling as if all of this was a punishment was her.

She hadn't expected that bite to ignite something inside her. She hadn't expected his mouth to be quite so soft or for him to taste quite so delicious, like dark chocolate, fine whisky and all the seven sins rolled up into one.

She hadn't expected the way he'd looked at her naked body to make her feel as if she was going to burn to ash where she stood. Or that touching the hard length that pressed against the wool of his trousers would feel so astonishingly good.

She hadn't expected the intense throb between her thighs to be quite so demanding either.

Damn him. This was supposed to be a strong moment for her, not one where she felt as though she were standing naked in the path of an oncoming storm with nothing to protect her.

You've only got yourself to blame.

It was true. Sadly. She'd been the one who'd decided to bite him, to kiss him, to get naked and touch him. And now here she was, sitting on top of him, completely at the mercy of the desire inside her that had gripped her by the throat and wouldn't let go.

That wasn't supposed to happen. Sexual desire was supposed to be another of the weaknesses she'd cut out of her life. And yet his bronze skin beneath her palms was so smooth, the muscle under that so very, very hard, and all she wanted to do was press harder, test his strength, spread her fingers out and soak in all his heat.

But the hidden glints of gold in his dark eyes held her completely hypnotised and she couldn't look away.

'Poor kitten.' His voice was rough and deep, the rich amusement in it like a caress against her skin. 'You don't understand, do you? I'm not at your mercy. You're at mine.'

It seemed a ridiculously arrogant thing to say, when he was the one on his back and cuffed to the bed. Yet...

He was fluid and powerful underneath her, and hard, like granite carved direct from a mountain. She could see that power beneath her hands, feel it in the tight coil of his muscles and in the heat running through his body. It was there in his eyes too, an arrogant certainty of his power that made her want to tremble.

She felt that certainty within herself, in the desire that

wound through her, exposing her. In the way her breath came short and fast, and in the relentless throb of heat between her thighs. In the tightness of her skin and the acute awareness of every part of her that touched him and every part of her that didn't. In the delicious, warm scent of him that made her mouth water and her heart beat faster.

You're weak. You've always been weak.

Stella shoved the thought from her head. There was only one answer to that and that was simply to be stronger. She had to be if she was to overcome the insidious dragging need to surrender to him and the relentless pressure of her desire.

Dante Cardinali had seemed to be a simple man. A man driven by the single-minded pursuit of pleasure, a slave to any pretty face that came his way.

But it wasn't him who was the slave. It was her.

'No,' she whispered, both to him and to herself. 'I'm not at anyone's mercy.'

'Prove it, then.' Deep in the velvet darkness of his eyes, golden fire burned. 'Get off me and walk away. Put on your dress and leave this room.' His hips lifted as he said the words, the hard length behind the wool of his trousers brushing up against the soft, sensitive tissues of her sex.

Pleasure bolted like lightning straight through her and she couldn't stop the soft gasp that escaped.

'Do it.' His voice was rough with heat. 'If you think you can.'

She could. Of course she could.

Except he was moving subtly against her and the rhythmic pressure against that aching place between her thighs was making her shiver with delight. She'd denied herself many things in the quest to become better and stronger than the girl who'd betrayed her own brother into prison, and that included physical pleasure. She hadn't thought she'd missed out on anything, but…

Get off him. Walk out. Deny him. That's what you were going to do, wasn't it?

Of course it was. And, yes, she would get off him. Right now.

Except…the heat of him, and the power of his body beneath her, and the gentle rocking of his hips were all mesmerizing and she didn't want it to stop.

You have to do something.

He wasn't expecting her to get off him. That was obvious. He was expecting her to stay, to be at his mercy, exactly as he'd said. And her body simply wasn't going to let her leave. Which meant she was going to have to do something else to prove her strength.

She shifted back on him, shivering at the brush of the fabric of his trousers against her. Then, with shaking hands, she pulled at the buttons of his fly.

He stilled, his big, rangy body tensing beneath her. 'Oh, kitten,' he breathed. 'I'm not sure that's a good idea.'

She ignored him, tugging down his zip and reaching inside his boxers. Her fingers closed around him and she blinked, her breath sticking in her throat at the feel of him in her hand. So long and hard and hot.

She pulled the fabric away from him, staring at the length she held in her hand, completely fascinated.

'Stella.' Her name this time, in a rough and hungry growl. 'I wouldn't do that if I were you.'

But it was too late. Backing down was an impossibility. It would make this entire evening an even bigger disaster, not to mention reveal the depths of her weakness, and she'd already revealed more of that than she wanted to when she'd put down her gun.

She lifted her gaze to his, the molten heat in his dark

eyes making lightning crackle in her blood. 'What did you want me to prove again?' It was another challenge and she didn't wait for him to answer. Instead she lifted her hips and fitted that hard shaft of his against the entrance to her body. Then she lowered herself down on him.

The feel of him pushing inside her was exquisite. There was no pain, only a wonderful stretching sensation and a pressure that tore a groan from her throat.

His smile vanished, his mouth twisting into a snarl, a rough, masculine sound breaking from him as she slid down on him even further.

Then she had to move and she was helpless to stop herself, the urge overwhelming. Rising and falling on him, at first hesitant and uncertain, then finding a rhythm. He'd gone silent, his hips lifting with hers, the fierce hunger on his beautiful face holding her captive.

They stared at each other as pleasure began to unwind in a shining cord, wrapping around both of them and pulling tight. Getting tighter. Then tighter still.

Stella braced herself with her hands on his chest, the world narrowing down to the rock-hard body under hers and the astonishingly good push-pull of him inside her… to the coil of pleasure that was tightening and tightening and tightening.

Her skin felt raw and over-sensitive, the desperation inside her growing teeth. She hadn't thought sex would be like this, that she'd be so feverish and hungry. That she'd be so desperate.

The room was cool and yet she'd broken out into a sweat, her palms damp on his chest. A moan escaped her, because somehow he was dictating the pace now, the movement of his hips faster, her body trying to catch up, chasing some kind of glory she didn't understand and which agonisingly kept moving out of reach.

'Touch yourself,' he murmured, his rich voice rough with dark heat, no trace of the polished playboy in it now. 'Do it now.'

And she found herself obeying him without hesitation, driven by her own hunger, moving her hand between her thighs and touching her own slick flesh. And as she did so he lifted his hips, thrusting up hard into her.

Pleasure suddenly detonated like a bomb, and she cried out, throwing back her head, feeling herself come apart in the most incredible blaze of light.

Dimly she felt his body tense, another roughened growl escaping him, but she couldn't seem to focus on that, not when her whole body was busy being flooded with such sharp, intense ecstasy.

As it faded, she fell forward onto his hard chest and for a second or two simply relaxed there, her cheek against his hot skin, breathing in the delicious scent of sandalwood, salt and musk. It was like lying on a rock in the sun and she wanted to close her eyes and drift, listening to the strong, steady beat of his heart beneath her ear. The sound was reassuring in some way, as powerful and enduring as the sea...

'Kitten,' Dante Cardinali said, his deep voice echoing through her.

The delicious warmth was fading, the feeling of reassurance going out like the tide, leaving her cold and shaking, and not in a good way.

Her arms trembled as she pushed herself up and met the darkness of his gaze staring back.

What have you done? You were supposed to kill him, not get into power games. And you definitely weren't supposed to have sex with him.

Shame flooded through her, crushing her. This was a mistake. A terrible, terrible mistake.

'Stella,' Dante said.

But she couldn't stand being in this room a second longer, surrounded by the ruins of her mission and the evidence of her weakness.

She slid off him, pulling on her dress and underwear with shaking hands, pausing only to grab the little clutch she'd brought with her. Then she moved quickly to the door on legs that felt as if they might give way at any moment.

'Stella,' Dante repeated, more forcefully this time.

But she didn't turn. She couldn't bear to look at him.

She opened the door and fled, the sound of him roaring her name one last time ringing in her ears.

CHAPTER THREE

'What do you think, Dante?' Enzo asked. 'Do we want to go with Tokyo on this one or stick with the New York office's plans?'

Dante wasn't listening, too busy restlessly pacing around in front of the windows of the boardroom in Cardinal Developments' London office. Rain pelted against the glass, obscuring the view of the city below but, just as he wasn't listening to his brother, he wasn't paying much attention to the view either.

He was in England with Enzo to work out some of the details of a new project in the City, which had been hijacked by some disagreement between their people in New York and Tokyo, and quite frankly he didn't have the patience for either thing right now.

Not when his head was full of Stella Montefiore.

It had been over a month since she'd left him cuffed to a bed in that hotel room in Monte Carlo, running out on him mere minutes after the most unexpectedly intense sexual experience of his life, and to say he was annoyed about it would be to understate things massively.

He wasn't simply annoyed. He was furious.

And he wasn't furious that she'd not only drugged him and cuffed him but then tried to kill him. No, he was furious firstly because she'd run out without even a thank you, and secondly because, try as he might, he simply could *not* stop thinking about her.

That brief moment of excitement and pleasure should have been more than enough for him. After all, there were a great many other lovely women in the world, so he shouldn't be fixating or caring about one particular woman.

But for some reason he hadn't been able to stop.

For weeks all he'd thought about was the feel of her tight, wet heat around him and the scent of her arousal, the unbelievable pleasure that had licked up his spine the moment she'd lowered herself down on him.

Of the challenging look in her beautiful eyes as her fingers had closed around him, upping the ante on their little game in a way he hadn't expected. Or the way that look had turned to wonder as she'd lowered herself down on him and the heat and the pleasure between them had taken hold.

He'd never seen that look on a woman's face in bed before and he'd been riveted. Caught too by the knowledge that she was experiencing this for the first time and he was the one who was giving it to her.

Maybe it was simply because she'd been trying to kill him that had heightened everything, including the pleasure.

Whatever it was, one thing had become very, very clear to him: given that she had in fact been trying to kill him, and that he had no guarantee she wouldn't try again, he couldn't simply leave her to run around on the loose.

So for the past month he'd spent most of his efforts on investigating her and, more importantly, finding her. Efforts that had all ended up with frustrating dead ends.

Until now.

'Dante, for God's sake,' Enzo said curtly. 'You're giving me a damn headache.'

Dante blinked then turned around, shoving his hands into the pockets of his suit trousers. Enzo was leaning against the long, sleek black table that dominated the boardroom, his arms folded, his golden eyes disturbingly sharp.

'Are you going to tell me what the matter is?' he asked. 'Or are you going to continue to pace around, pretending to be me?'

His brother wasn't wrong. Pacing was definitely Enzo's speciality, not Dante's.

With an effort, Dante tried to relax. He didn't want Enzo to know about Stella, not yet. His brother was happy for the first time in his life and Dante didn't want anything to worry him, such as attempts on Dante's life from enemies back in the old country.

Besides, Enzo would no doubt start taking charge of the operation if Dante did tell him, and there was no way Dante wanted him to do that. This was his problem and he was going to handle it his way.

Nothing at all to do with wanting Stella Montefiore in your bed again, naturally.

Naturally. He'd had her once. He didn't need to have her again, no matter how beautiful she was or exciting he'd found her. He just wanted her found, any threat she presented negated.

'There's nothing the matter.' Dante consciously tried to relax his tense muscles. 'Why would you say that?'

'Because you haven't listened to a word I've said and you're pacing around like Simon does when he's restless and wants to go outside and play.'

'Though presumably with fewer tantrums,' Dante muttered. He loved his nephew but, as Simon was only four, Dante didn't much appreciate the comparison.

One of Enzo's black brows rose. 'Is that a comment on my son's behaviour? Because if so—'

'Of course not,' Dante snapped, unaccountably irritable.

There was an uncomfortable silence as Enzo stared at him.

'What?' He stared back. 'There's no problem.'

'And our father is alive and well and ruling peacefully at home,' Enzo commented dryly. 'Tell me. And it had better be work related. Simon starts school in a couple of months and the last thing he needs is one of his uncle's scandals all through the media.'

Since Enzo had married Matilda six months ago, he'd got very protective of his little family. Annoyingly so, in Dante's opinion. His brother had never minded his affairs before, but in the past few months he'd turned into a damn prude. It was irritating.

Dante had managed successfully to build a life that consisted entirely of seeing to his own comfort and he was more than happy with the present arrangement. He did *not* want anything to change it.

'It's nothing that need concern Cardinal Developments,' he said, trying to find his usual casual smile. 'Or Simon. It's merely a distracting entanglement.'

Enzo frowned. 'That doesn't sound promising. She's not married, is she?'

'Brother, please. A married woman? It's like you don't know me at all.' There, that sounded more like his usual self, didn't it?

Enzo's gaze narrowed, studying Dante in that sharp way he had. 'You're lying.'

'I'm not,' Dante said with perfect truth.

'She must be very distracting to get you tied up in knots like this.'

Enzo didn't know the half of it, but Dante wasn't going to enlighten him.

It had indeed been Stella Montefiore who'd drugged him and cuffed him. As soon as he'd got out of the hotel room, he'd called his personal assistant and asked her to find out everything she could about the Montefiore family. She'd given him a complete dossier the next day and he'd spent most of the day going through said dossier, trying to work out why on earth Stella had targeted him.

Not that it was all that difficult to find out once he knew her family history.

The Montefiores had been one of the leading aristo-cratic families on Monte Santa Maria until Dante's father, the king, had been exiled.

After that, because the Montefiores had supported the old regime, they'd suffered a terrible fall from grace that had led to Stefano Montefiore sinking everything he owned into Luca Cardinali's plans to retake his throne. The fam-ily had been beggared and then, to add insult to injury, the authorities somehow had found out about Stefano's machi-nations. While Stefano had escaped being implicated, his oldest son Matteo had not. Matteo had been imprisoned, along with various other of Luca's supporters, and then, years later, had died while still incarcerated.

It didn't take a genius to work out why Stella Monte-fiore had been trying to kill him: she and her father wanted Dante's blood in return for the death of a brother and son.

It was a vendetta worthy of a Sicilian.

Except she hadn't gone through with it.

'You know how it is,' Dante said aloud. 'The right woman can be…lethal in certain circumstances.' Though not so much in his case, except for the lethal blow she'd dealt to his self-control.

Enzo lifted a brow. 'Is that a fact? Care to talk about this particular woman?'

Dante looked back blandly. 'Not really.'

'In that case, can I please have your attention concern-ing this—?'

Dante's phone buzzed in his pocket and he forgot about his brother entirely, pulling it out and turning round to look down at the screen.

It was a text from one of the private investigators he'd hired to locate Stella, giving him an address in Rome.

He smiled, an intense feeling he couldn't quite name filling him. It was mainly satisfaction, but there was something else there too. An undeniable, feral kind of excitement.

It had been frustrating not being able to find her, that she'd somehow managed to escape all the people he'd sent out looking for her.

But now, *now,* he had her.

She wasn't going to escape him again.

Seems like you do care about something after all.

Of course he cared when it was about his own life. Though what he was going to do with her once he'd found her, he hadn't quite decided. Probably, if he was feeling particularly merciful, he'd give her a warning that if she made another attempt on his life he'd report her to the police. And, if he wasn't feeling merciful, he might just call the police then and there.

That's not what you want to do to her...

Well, no, of course it wasn't. He wanted to punish her a little too, for how she'd taken up so much space in his head and for the sensual memories that had tormented him for the past month. The memories that she'd given him.

It wouldn't be a painful punishment, naturally, but she'd definitely scream. With pleasure.

'You're looking pleased with yourself,' Enzo murmured. 'Does this mean you're going to listen now or are you going to interrupt me yet again?'

'It means,' Dante said, putting his phone back in his pocket, 'that something's come up. Looks like I have to head back to Italy.'

'I see,' Enzo said dryly. 'Nothing at all to do with a woman, I suppose?'

He gave his brother a brilliant smile. 'Not in the slightest. You won't need the jet? Good. I'm flying out ASAP.'

Enzo snorted. 'What about Tokyo?'

But Dante was already heading to the door. 'You know what to do about Tokyo,' he said over his shoulder. 'Don't wait up, brother mine.'

It only took a few hours for him to land in Rome, but he was impatient as he went straight from the jet to the car his assistant had organised for him.

Dante had never bothered with his own car, or even his own home for that matter, preferring the number of hotel suites in various different cities that he kept for his private use. He didn't like to stay in one place for too long, as he didn't like getting too attached to anything, so hotels suited his impermanent lifestyle.

He gave his driver the address the investigator had sent to him and told the man to get there ASAP. The traffic as per usual was hideous, and Dante tried to curb his impatience but, as the driver turned down increasingly narrower sets of streets lined with rundown-looking apartment buildings, his impatience turned into uneasiness.

The area reminded him of the dirty tenements in Naples where he and his mother had ended up after she'd dragged him away from his father and Enzo back in Milan. She'd told him they'd be going somewhere exciting where they'd begin a new life. A better life far away from Luca's petty rages and selfishness. And wouldn't that be nice? No, he wouldn't have his brother, but he'd have her and wasn't that important? Didn't he love her?

Naturally, he'd loved her, so he hadn't argued. Not that he'd minded leaving his frightening father, but he'd been upset at leaving his big brother behind. He'd hidden his distress, though, as it had upset his mother and he hadn't liked upsetting her. Especially when it had made her drinking worse.

The driver pulled up onto the narrow footpath and gave a dubious look out of the window at the graffiti on the walls of the nearest apartment block and the garbage in the gutter. 'You want me to get your bodyguard, Mr Cardinali?' he asked, glancing at Dante in the rear-view mirror.

Dante snorted. 'Please, Giorgio. I was raised in the gutters of Naples. I think I can handle a few tenements in Rome.'

He pulled open the door and stepped outside, giving the area a quick scan, his unease deepening still further.

The Montefiores had little money these days, but as far as he was aware they were still on Monte Santa Maria. So why was Stella living here? Presumably because it was easier to hide in a slum, but still. Not a good place for the small, delicate, lovely looking woman he remembered from back in Monte Carlo. Then again, she'd seemed very capable with a gun, so maybe she was perfectly able to fight off all manner of thugs.

He approached the address the investigator had given him—a large and rundown apartment block—ignoring the group of surly youths standing around outside the door. One of them said something to him as he went past, but all he did was pin the boy with a look. He still remembered the street-fighting skills he'd learned back when he'd been thirteen and he'd been beaten up for the fifth time while his mother had done nothing, passed out from another of her drunken binges. He'd decided that night that he was sick of being the neighbourhood punching bag and so had gone out to find someone to teach him how to defend himself. That was the last time anyone had laid a punch on him.

The teenagers, making the right choice in deciding they

didn't want to take him on, didn't say anything else, leaving him to enter the building.

It was dark and dingy inside, the lift out of order, half the lights in the lobby out.

He ended up walking all the way to the fifteenth floor, grimacing at the dirty floors, stained walls and huddled shapes of people in the doorways and clustered in the stairwells. It was all too familiar to him. It was the 'new life' his mother had promised him when she'd taken him away. Only it had ended up with her dead a few years later, and him alone to fend for himself at sixteen.

An old anger twisted inside him, but he ignored it, as he'd been ignoring it for years.

There was nothing to be angry about, not now. Things had turned out well despite that. Enzo had come for him four years later, and together they'd eventually claimed that new life for both of them. His mother would have been proud.

On the fifteenth floor Dante scanned the hallway for the number the investigator had given him and eventually found it right down the end. He paused outside the door, aware that there was some kind of complicated emotion burning in his veins. However, since he didn't care to examine his more complicated emotions, he ignored it, lifting his hand to knock hard on the door instead.

There was silence.

'I know you're in there, Stella Montefiore,' he said without raising his voice. 'So you'd better open up, darling. Or, if you prefer, I can get the police involved. I'm sure your father would love that.'

There was another brief moment of silence and Dante found his heart rate accelerating for no good reason that he could see.

He had his hand in his pocket ready to pull out his phone

and call the police when the door suddenly opened, a small, fragile-looking woman in jeans and a faded red T-shirt standing in the doorway. Her golden hair was in a messy ponytail, loose strands hanging around her lovely, if rather pale, face. Familiar cool blue eyes fractured through with silver met his.

And desire hit him in the gut like a freight train.

'There's no need for that,' Stella Montefiore said calmly, looking for all the world like she'd been waiting all day for him to show up at her door unannounced. 'Though, if you're afraid to be in a room alone with me, then by all means call the police.'

STELLA'S HEART WAS RACING, fear coiling tightly in her gut. The hard edges of the door handle were digging into her palm, but she didn't want to let go. Given the weak state of her knees, she'd probably collapse onto the floor without support, and there was no way in hell she was doing that. And definitely not right in front of him.

He'd found her. Somehow, he'd damn well found her.

Dante Cardinali stood in the doorway of her grotty apartment, blazing like an angel sent straight from God, the reality of his physical presence hitting her like a blow.

In the past five weeks, when she'd gone over that night in her memory—and she went over it a lot—she'd told herself that what had happened between them was an aberration. A momentary weakness on her part, brought on by inexperience and a failure to prepare herself properly for what she'd had to do. She'd also told herself that she'd overestimated the intensity of his personal magnetism. But all it took was one look to know that, if anything, she'd underestimated it.

He was so tall and broad, lounging on her doorstep as though he was at one of his exclusive parties and not in a rundown tenement in the middle of the worst part of Rome.

He wore one of those phenomenally expensive custom-made suits he seemed to favour, with a black shirt and a silk tie the same inky blue as the Pacific Ocean. Somehow, the colour made the deep brown of his eyes more intense and highlighted the smooth bronze skin of his throat.

She'd touched that skin. She'd stared into those eyes as he'd been deep inside her...

Her breath caught.

No, she wasn't going to think of that. She *couldn't* think of that.

You have to. Considering that got you into the situation you're now in.

The fear she'd been battling the past few weeks returned with a vengeance, wrapping long fingers around her throat.

How had he found her? She'd thought she'd been thorough in her efforts to disappear. Initially, after the panic of her failure to complete her mission had worn off and she'd had some time to think about her next move, she'd briefly debated the merits of returning to Monte Santa Maria. But had then dismissed it.

She hadn't been able to bear the thought of going home and confessing her failure, of having to deal with the weight of her father's disappointment in her. Of having to tell him that, yes, he'd been right to doubt her. That she hadn't been strong enough to go through with it after all. That he should have got someone else to do what she couldn't.

No, she hadn't been able to accept that. Matteo's death would go unavenged and, as it had been her and her stupid soft heart that had got him imprisoned in the first place, she couldn't give up after just one failure.

It was true that another attempt on Dante Cardinali's life would be that much harder, considering he'd be on his guard, but what other choice did she have? Failure was not an option, not again.

So she'd regrouped, texted her father that it was taking more time than anticipated but would all proceed as planned and started considering her next move. She'd shifted from place to place to hide her tracks in case Cardinali tried to find her, using nothing but cash in an effort to keep her digital trail to a minimum.

Eventually she'd settled on Rome as a place to lay low for a little while—the apartment she'd found pretty much as low as she could get—to give her time to figure out another way of getting close to him.

But first her cash had run out, then so had her luck, and now he was here because apparently she hadn't been as careful as she'd thought at hiding her tracks.

Yet another failure to add to the list.

The weakness in her legs threatened to move through the rest of her, making her tremble, blackness tingeing the edges of her vision.

Oh, God, please don't let her faint in front of him. She wouldn't be able to bear the humiliation.

'Ah, there you are.' His voice was as deep and as rich as she remembered and his smile was just as beautiful. But there was nothing friendly in it or in his dark eyes. 'You're a difficult woman to find.'

Stella clutched the door handle, blackness creeping further along the edges of her vision like a piece of paper held over a flame and slowly burning. She fought to stay upright, but the nausea she'd been battling the past two days—that wasn't the stomach bug she'd desperately hoped it was—shifted and she had to swallow hard against the urge to be sick.

His gaze sharpened, the smile turning his mouth vanishing. 'What's wrong?'

Damn. He'd noticed.

'Nothing,' she said thickly.

And then her legs gave out.

Dante moved, lightning-fast, and strong arms were suddenly around her, catching her before she hit the floor. Then she was being lifted as the man she was supposed to have killed gathered her tight against his hard, warm chest and kicked shut the door behind him.

Humiliation caught at her and she struggled, but he only murmured, 'Hush.' And, strangely, the will to protest faded, her energy dwindling away to nothing.

As if her body had simply been waiting for him to arrive and take charge.

Shame grabbed her by the throat, but the past few days had been a nightmare of exhaustion, illness and shock, and she just didn't have any strength left with which to fight.

Instead, she found herself relaxing against him and shutting her eyes, conscious of nothing but the warmth of him seeping into her and the iron strength of his body. For some reason there was something reassuring about it which should have concerned her if she'd had the energy for it.

What are you doing? What do you think is going to happen when he finds out?

Ice penetrated the warmth of his hold.

She couldn't handle this right now. It had only been two days since she'd finally forced herself to spend the last of her cash on a pregnancy test, and she hadn't had time to come to terms with the result herself.

She'd been halfway to figuring out a new plan but now that plan was in ruins as the consequences of her failure that night in the hotel room returned to haunt her.

It hadn't been a simple failure. It had been a failure of catastrophic proportions and she still hadn't figured out what she was doing to do.

But now you'll have to.

Yes, she would.

Dante put her down on the ratty couch in one corner of the living area and she found herself almost reaching out to hold onto him as the warmth of his body withdrew. God, she must be even weaker than she'd first thought.

Managing to stop herself at the last minute, Stella gripped her forearms instead as he stepped back, looming over her like a building, his arms folded over his broad chest, his gaze narrowed.

There was a moment's dense, heavy silence.

She steeled herself, ignoring the frantic beating of her heart and the nausea sitting in her gut, lifting her chin and arching a brow at him. She couldn't afford to show him any further weakness. She wouldn't. Her pride wouldn't allow it.

'What just happened?' he asked finally.

'Nothing.' She was pleased her voice was so steady.

'Nothing,' he echoed, disbelief dripping from his tone. 'Darling, you collapsed right in front of me.'

Stella gripped her forearms tighter. 'I'm tired. And I'm not your darling.'

'You look more than tired.' He studied her, his gaze uncomfortably sharp. 'You look exhausted.'

She decided to ignore that. 'So, are the police coming? Isn't that why you're here? To arrest me?'

There was another heavy silence.

'No,' he said slowly. 'I think not. I'll handle you myself.'

And despite her exhaustion and sickness a small, traitorous thrill shot through her, memories tugging at her again of his rock-hard body beneath hers and the length of him inside her, the intense, rhythmic thrust of his hips and how good that had felt…

What would it feel like if he actually had his hands free to 'handle' her properly?

Her mouth dried, her pulse accelerating.

Stop thinking about that. Focus.

Stella gritted her teeth, forcing away the memory, ignoring the throb between her legs that, given how sick she was feeling, shouldn't be there.

'How wonderful for me.' She tried for cool and managed to hit it. Mostly. 'And how did you find me?'

'Money. And a lot of people looking for you.'

He must have paid them a *lot* of money then, because she'd been very careful.

He really wanted to find you.

Of course he had. She'd tried to kill him.

'I see. In that case, congratulations, you've found me.' She gripped her forearms tighter. 'What exactly does the "handling" involve?'

Gold glimmered briefly in his eyes, a glimpse of the heat she remembered the night she'd tried and failed to kill him. 'You know, I hadn't really thought about it. But I'm sure we can work something out.' One corner of his mouth turned up in a smile that held a whole world of sensual promise. 'Can't we, kitten?'

Something inside her glowed hot in response, another helpless surge of desire.

No. She couldn't allow herself to feel this. She'd already made one catastrophic mistake. She wasn't going to make another.

Pressing her nails hard into her skin, she used the slight pain to chase away the heat lingering in her veins. 'I'll leave you my number then. Once you've decided how you want to "work that out" you can contact me. Until then…' she tried an icy smile '…perhaps you might want to leave?'

'Darling,' Dante purred. 'You really think that I'm going to simply leave now I've found you? After you tried to kill me? Who's to say you're not going to try it again?'

Stella swallowed, her mouth dry, the nausea roiling yet

again. She should have eaten something that morning but she hadn't been able to face it. And now hunger was making the nausea worse. Her own stupid fault.

The fainting spell was bad enough, but throwing up in front of him would be ten thousand times worse.

'How about if I promise I won't do it again? Will that do?' She let go the grip she had on her arms, and tried to push herself to her feet, desperate for him to leave. But her legs were still wobbly and she swayed on her feet, dizzy.

Dante's sensual smile vanished and he reached out, putting his hands under her elbows to steady her, looking down into her face, his dark gaze sharp. 'You're not well. Kitten, what's wrong?'

She gritted her teeth against the sick feeling and the strange urge the concern in his voice had prompted, the urge to tell him everything, to let him deal with it. Because now it was his problem too.

But she couldn't. She had her plans and, though they might be in ruins now, there was a chance she could still salvage something from them. And if he knew that she was pregnant he might… Well, she had no idea what he'd do. She only knew that she couldn't risk him finding out.

'It's nothing.'

'It's not nothing. You can barely stand.'

His palms were warm against her skin and there was a part of her that wanted simply to stand there and rest, let him hold her up. A part of her she'd very purposefully excised from her soul years ago.

How ridiculous. What was he doing to her?

Forcing down the urge, she tried to pull away, only to have his fingers tighten, keeping her where she stood. Probably a good thing, now she thought about it, because she had a horrible feeling she wouldn't be able to stand upright if he didn't.

The physical weakness made a hot, sharp anger wind through her. At herself for being so weak, and perversely at him, for being stronger than she was and making her so aware of that fact.

She knew she looked fragile, but she'd worked hard to overcome that by being emotionally strong. And the way he was holding her, with his palms resting under her elbows in support, made that strength feel brittle somehow. As if taking that support away from her would shatter her.

She hated the feeling.

'I'm fine.' She tried to gather enough strength to pull away from him. 'And I don't know why you're so concerned with my health. Don't forget I tried to kill you a month ago.' Might as well name it, as it wasn't likely he'd forgotten that particular aspect of their night together.

If he found that uncomfortable, he didn't show it, his gaze narrowing as he searched her face. Then his hold tightened and he eased her back down so she was sitting once more on the couch. 'Stay there,' he ordered.

Stella wanted to protest, but the sheer relief of not having to hold herself upright took all her energy, so she simply sat there as he turned and strode through the doorway that led to the tiny kitchen area.

Damn him. The last thing she needed was for him to be nice to her.

She leaned back against the couch and let her eyes close, exhaustion overwhelming her for a second. Part of her wanted to curl up and go to sleep, pretend the last couple of days had never happened. Pretend she hadn't slept with the man she was supposed to kill and wasn't now pregnant with his child.

Pretend he hadn't found her and that her plans weren't in ruins.

But that would be futile. All those things had happened—no point trying to convince herself otherwise.

The back of her neck prickled.

Her eyes snapped open.

Dante was standing in the kitchen doorway, staring at her. He was holding a glass of water in one hand and there was a curiously intense expression on his face.

A premonition gripped her.

He knows.

No, that was ridiculous. There was no way he could, not if she hadn't told him.

'What is it now?' She tried to keep her voice level.

Deep in his dark eyes, golden fire leapt, his jaw tight, his beautiful mouth gone hard. 'So were you going to tell me? Or were you simply going to get rid of it?'

All the air vanished from her lungs as shock washed over her.

'And in case you were wondering…' Dante raised his other hand, a piece of paper in it. 'You left this on the counter.'

It was one of the pregnancy pamphlets she'd collected from the pharmacy where she'd bought the test.

Ice collected in her gut, making her feel even sicker, and for the briefest second she debated pretending not to understand what he was talking about. Telling him that those pamphlets weren't hers, but a friend's. Because if he knew the child was his…

It might not be the disaster you're anticipating. This could be the perfect moment to get close to him.

Stella held herself very still, examining the idea. Another attempt on his life was impossible now, because, as much as she hated to admit it to herself, if she hadn't been able to pull the trigger while he'd been lying there bound and helpless she wasn't going to be able to pull it at all.

But there might be another way to salvage her mission. A way to save herself from the failures of the past month and avenge Matteo's death. Redeem herself in her father's eyes, too.

Revenge. Make him hurt somehow, take away something he loved so he could feel the same pain as her family had at the loss of Matteo. It wasn't what her father wanted, but it was still something.

In fact, in many ways, having him remain alive yet broken could be even more satisfying than his death.

However, for that to work she would need to get close to him in order to find out who or what he cared most about.

So…perhaps she shouldn't deny she was pregnant after all.

Perhaps she needed to admit it.

And what about the child?

No, she couldn't think about the child just yet. Not making another mistake was the most important thing for her right now. She would think about the implications of her pregnancy later, when she'd completed her mission.

Stella forced herself to hold his furious gaze. 'I…hadn't decided.' She tried to keep her voice level. 'I only found out a couple of days ago.'

He said nothing for a long moment, but then he didn't have to. There was no trace of the charming smile she remembered. Or the warmth. Or the kindness. There was only anger burning in his eyes.

He's right to be angry with you. It's your fault, after all.

And it was. Her failure. She'd been the one who'd so given herself over to physical pleasure and wanting to prove something to him that she hadn't even thought about a condom. In fact, it hadn't been until she'd realised how late her period was that she'd even remembered she hadn't used one.

Despite her new resolution to finish what she'd started,

heat rose in her cheeks, shame returning under the pressure of his black-velvet gaze.

He didn't say anything, moving over to the couch and stopping in front of her, holding out the water glass. 'Drink it,' he ordered flatly.

His tone made her hackles rise and instantly she wanted to argue. But there was no point risking antagonising him right now. He might actually decide to leave and then she'd have to start all over again with a new plan, the opportunity she had now lost.

In fact, given how angry he was, that might still happen. He was, after all, a notorious playboy and an unexpected child wasn't exactly conducive to the kind of life he led.

No, she needed to be careful here.

Stella took the glass and sipped, the water cool in her dry mouth easing the nagging sickness in her gut.

He watched her, the look in his eyes burning. 'Well?' he demanded, the current of his anger running underneath the rich timbre of his voice like lava. 'Were you going to tell me you're pregnant? Answer me.'

'Yes, of course I was going to tell you,' she said coolly. 'Once the danger period was over.'

'So you're not planning on getting rid of it?'

The question set off a little shock inside her and she answered instinctively before she'd even had a chance to think. 'No. Of course not. Obviously I'm going to have it.'

'Obviously, you are.' The words were flat, the look on his face starkly uncompromising. 'Since that baby is mine.'

That little shock reverberated, stronger this time, reacting to something in his voice. He sounded…possessive, almost. As if he actually wanted the baby.

A hollow feeling opened up inside her, a kind of longing. But it didn't make any sense to her so she ignored it. 'How do you know the baby is yours?' she asked. 'It might not be.'

He snorted. 'Darling, you were a virgin. And, unless you went straight to another man's bed after our little interlude, it's pretty much guaranteed that the child is mine.' Intention blazed suddenly in his eyes. 'But of course, if you require a paternity test, then by all means let's take one.'

The way he looked at her made her tremble, though she didn't understand why, and she had to glance away to cover the momentary weakness.

What on earth was wrong with her? So it seemed as though he wanted the baby. So what? It wasn't going to make any difference. He was still a mistake she had to correct and she would. As soon as she'd figured him out.

'No,' she said. 'That won't be necessary.'

'Of course it won't,' he echoed, something hard and certain in his voice. 'Then again, it'll probably be one of the things I'll have to organise once we get back to my hotel, anyway.'

Stella frowned. 'What? What do you mean "when we get back to my hotel"?'

Dante's dark gaze was steely and utterly sure. 'I mean that I'm leaving in five minutes and I'm taking you and my child with me.'

CHAPTER FOUR

Shock was written all over Stella Montefiore's lovely face, but Dante didn't care. He wasn't staying here longer than five minutes, not given the pallor of her skin or the dark circles under her eyes.

She needed rest and she needed it somewhere safe and that wasn't here.

She was carrying his child.

His child.

The reality of the fact was still echoing inside him like a bell being struck.

He'd seen the pamphlets on the kitchen counter as he'd got her a glass of water. Pamphlets with information on pregnancy.

And he'd felt something yawn wide inside him.

They'd only had sex once that night but... *Dio*. They hadn't used a condom. How was that even possible? He was fanatical about always using protection, but that night... He'd been drugged, had woken to find himself handcuffed to a bed with a gun in his face, only to be blindsided by desire for the very woman who'd threatened him. And she'd been so hot and he'd wanted her so very badly that it hadn't even entered his head to tell her that he had condoms in his wallet.

You fool.

She'd been a virgin. The onus had been on him and he hadn't even thought about it. And now look what had happened.

He hadn't been able to move for long moments, staring at those pamphlets, the realisation that she was pregnant and that the child was his slowly settling down inside him.

After the disaster that was his own childhood, he'd never wanted children for himself. Everything in life was transitory and painful so why not take as much pleasure as you could while you could get it? He couldn't do that with children and a family. In fact, the only family he'd allowed himself was Enzo—mainly because his brother refused to let Dante distance him—but that was it.

He didn't want anything else. He didn't need it.

So where the intense possessiveness came from that wrapped its fingers around his throat, almost choking the life out of him, he had no idea. But it was there, the need to grab Stella and take her away, keep her and his baby safe, impossible to deny.

It made sense in a way, since the woman had tried to kill him, which meant he couldn't trust her, let alone trust her with his child. Taking her somewhere where he could keep an eye on her seemed logical.

He was aware that he was trying to rationalise it, but right now he didn't care. There was an unexpected biological imperative he was responding to and he simply couldn't stop himself.

Except it was clear that Stella had other ideas.

Her stubborn little chin had lifted and, despite her pallor, anger glinted in her silvery blue eyes. 'Go with you?' she asked flatly. 'I think not. But by all means, if you want to—'

'There will be no argument,' Dante interrupted, in no mood for protests. 'You're not staying in this hellhole and risking the life of my child.'

She gave him a look he couldn't interpret. 'Really? And since when does a notorious playboy give a damn about the life of his child?'

A memory shifted inside him, of that ghastly apartment in Naples—very similar to this one in Rome, now he thought about it—and his mother passed out on the couch, the sounds of someone shouting in the hallway outside. And he'd been terrified—*terrified*—that the person who'd been shouting would somehow break down their door and come in. And there would be no one to protect him...

A dull anger that had been sitting inside him for years, that he'd made sure to drown under alcohol and women and too many parties to name, flared to life, bringing with it a latent protectiveness.

His mother hadn't given a damn about *his* life. No matter how many times she'd slurred that she loved him, that she'd take care of him, she hadn't. She'd been drunk when he'd needed her, preferring the oblivion of the bottle to caring for him.

Do you want to end up being like her?

No. No, he did not.

Dante met her guarded blue gaze. 'Strangely enough,' he said, acid edging his tone, 'I find that I do give a damn. Unfortunately for you.'

Her expression turned contemptuous. 'Oh, please, don't tell me that the most infamous man-whore in Europe has had a sudden change of heart. Do the gossip columns know?'

He decided to ignore that, folding his arms and staring at her. 'Kitten, pay attention. Because I'm only going to say this once. You have five minutes to get your things and then we're leaving. And, if I have to pick you up and throw you over my shoulder, then believe me I will do it.'

There was a moment of silence, the tension between

them gathering tight. Her eyes glowed, her beauty in no way dimmed by her obvious exhaustion. Neither, apparently, was her anger.

He didn't care. She wasn't staying here, not when she was pregnant with his child and he didn't trust her one single inch.

Nothing to do with how exhausted and sick she's looking.

Dante dismissed that thought. Yes, she wasn't looking well, but taking her away didn't have anything to do with *her.* He was protecting the baby. Plus, he really needed to deal with the question of her attempt on his life and whether she might have another go.

Stella's expression was still mutinous, and it was obvious to him that she was trying to contain herself, but the silvery glow in her eyes gave her away.

Again, he didn't care. Let her be angry. This wasn't about her and this time it wasn't about him either. This was about their child.

Abruptly, she glanced away. 'Fine. I have nothing I want to take except my handbag on the table.'

Expecting more of a fight, Dante stared at her.

There was a set look on her face and she was holding her forearms tightly. Too tightly. Her nails were digging into her skin. And she'd gone white again, the circles beneath her lovely eyes like bruises. The strands of golden hair hanging around her face looked lank, as if she hadn't washed it in a while, and the jeans and T-shirt she wore were rumpled and stained, as if she hadn't washed those either.

A far cry from the perfect china shepherdess, in her blue satin cocktail dress and her perfect shining hair.

She'd been on the run, from the looks of things, hiding from him. Which meant that finding out she was pregnant must have come as a shock. Certainly enough of a shock that she hadn't been taking care of herself.

Something else shifted in his chest, that protectiveness again. But he didn't want to examine that feeling, so he didn't.

Instead, impatient all of a sudden, and suspecting that the reason she'd made no move to get up was because she couldn't, Dante bent and scooped her up in his arms once again.

'Stop,' she murmured, pushing ineffectually at him, while at the same time her body relaxed, as if his arms were the bed it had been searching for all this time.

That shouldn't have made him as satisfied as it did so he ignored that feeling too.

'Can you walk?' he asked instead, glancing down at her face.

She'd gone pink, which was a damn sight better than the pallor that had been there before. 'Of course I can walk.'

'Then do you really want me to put you down?'

Her mouth firmed and she glanced away again, staying silent.

Satisfied, Dante moved over to the table to allow her to grab her handbag, then turned to the door and carried her out of the apartment.

People stared at them as they passed, but he ignored the stares, just as he tried to ignore the slight, fragile weight of her in his arms. She was all softness and heat, and her scent was warm with a hint of feminine musk, no trace of the overwhelmingly sexual perfume she'd worn in Monte Carlo.

Which was good. Because his body, the traitor, was hardening at her physical proximity and he didn't need that on top of everything else.

In fact, he decided that, given how complicated this particular situation was, it would probably be best if he didn't further complicate it with sex. Denying himself didn't come easy to him, it was true, but there was a time and place for such things, and now was not the time and this was definitely not the place. Even his hotel was not the place.

Because she was not the woman he should be doing any of those things with, and certainly not after he'd already made the catastrophic mistake of having sex with her in the first place.

Ignoring the demands of his body, Dante carried her out of the building, conscious of the dealers and junkies in the hallways and the youths out on the pavement by the front. Giorgio had his wits about him enough to get quickly out of the car and pull open the rear door so Dante could put her inside.

'To the hotel,' Dante ordered shortly once Giorgio was back behind the wheel. And, as they pulled away from the kerb, an odd sense of satisfaction collected inside him. As if for once in his selfish, useless life he'd done something right.

Stella said nothing the entire trip, but he let her have her silence. She looked exhausted and for once he could think of nothing to say.

The hotel wasn't far from the Spanish Steps and the hotel staff, whom Dante all knew by name, were waiting to usher him to his usual penthouse suite.

He had a moment as he helped Stella from the car where he realised that there might be some curiosity about her, given she wasn't exactly dressed like his usual type of woman, and that wouldn't exactly be a good thing.

The Montefiores had fallen a long way since Dante's father had been exiled, but people might be curious enough about Stella to investigate who she was and why she'd suddenly turned up at Dante's side.

It wasn't a comfortable thought. He'd never cared about gossip—usually he openly courted it—but things were different now. He didn't want people drawing conclusions about her and he definitely didn't want anyone finding out about the baby. Not yet, at least. Not until he had some time to decide how best to proceed.

Ignoring half-formed ideas of getting someone to attend Stella, he decided to do it himself, pausing only to give the butler responsible for his suite instructions to bring up some food, while making sure the hotel staff knew to be discreet about Stella's presence, before dismissing everyone and shutting the door firmly.

Then he went into the luxurious living area where he'd left her sitting on the edge of one of the white linen-covered couches, gazing out over the fantastic views of Rome's ancient roof tops.

She wasn't sitting now, though. Clearly exhaustion had overtaken her because she was curled up, fast asleep, her head on one of the white linen cushions, her gilt lashes lying still on her pale cheeks.

Silently he went over to where she lay and looked down at her.

She seemed so small. A tiny, delicate china-doll of a woman with her big blue eyes and her corn-gold hair. A woman who'd first tried to kill him then given him one of the most intense sexual experiences of his life.

A woman who was now carrying his child.

The protectiveness that had washed over him at the apartment washed over him again, a rampant surge of emotion that he hadn't asked for, didn't want and yet couldn't seem to do anything about. It swamped him and he found himself grabbing the pale-grey cashmere throw that had been slung over the arm of the couch and tucking it securely around her so she didn't get cold.

For the baby's sake, naturally. He didn't much care about the woman who'd pointed a gun at his head five weeks ago.

So you do, in fact, care about the baby.

A certain tension settled in his jaw and in his shoulders.

He'd gone through life very happily not caring much about anything, so it came as something of a shock to realise that very much against his will he cared about this.

His child.

Back at that awful apartment where he'd found Stella, he'd thought it was simply about keeping that child safe. But, now Stella and the baby she carried were here in his territory, he was conscious that it went deeper than mere safety.

There was something else inside him, something he was pretty sure was that biological imperative operating again but, whatever it was, the fact remained that the baby mattered to him.

Of course it matters to you. Why else did you insist she have it?

The thought was sharp and deeply uncomfortable.

There had been a time once before when he'd walked away from a problem he hadn't wanted to deal with and he'd had to live with the consequences ever since. Consequences that even now he tried very hard not to think about.

So these days, whenever a situation looked like it might get complicated, he avoided it like the plague. Yet this was the very definition of complicated and for some reason he simply could not bring himself to walk away. Not this time.

The child hadn't asked to be born to a selfish playboy and a potential murderer. The child was innocent. And, if anyone knew what it was to be an innocent caught up in adult problems, it was him.

That baby needed someone to be there for it and, even though Dante knew he was possibly the worst man on earth to be a father, he nevertheless wanted that someone to be him.

Whether Stella Montefiore liked it or not.

STELLA DIDN'T WANT to wake up, but there was something delicious-smelling in the room. And for once she didn't feel sick. In fact, she almost felt hungry.

Except eating would involve having to open her eyes and she didn't want to do that quite yet.

She was lying on something ridiculously soft, and there was something equally as soft tucked around her, and she was warm, and moving felt like an impossibility.

Someone was talking nearby. A man, his voice rich and dark and somehow soothing. He was speaking English and he must be on the phone since she couldn't hear any responses. Something about a child…

Reality hit her like a bucket of ice water dumped straight on top of her head.

The pregnancy test. Dante Cardinali coming to the door. Dante Cardinali finding out that she was carrying his child…

Every muscle in her body stiffened as that deep, beautiful voice rolled over her like a caress.

Him.

She'd been surprised when he'd insisted on her coming back to his hotel suite with him—she hadn't expected him to take responsibility for the baby quite so quickly, not a selfish, dissolute man like him. But it was all going to work very nicely for her plan, so she'd only put up a fight enough that he wouldn't suspect her motives. She'd even let him carry her to the car, nothing at all to do with the fact that she'd been too dizzy to stand.

Without moving, she lifted her lashes slightly so she could see where she was and what was happening.

It looked to be early evening, the pink light making the white walls of the room look as if they were blushing. The large glass doors of the living area were standing open to the terrace outside and there was Dante, standing with his back to her, one hand in his pocket, the other holding his phone to his ear.

She tried to muster some rage at him for the arrogant way he'd brought her here, as if he owned her, but her anger kept slipping out of her grip every time she tried to reach for it.

She was too warm and too sleepy, which was an issue when what she needed to be was cold, on her guard and wide awake.

He turned suddenly and his dark eyes found hers. And, just as it had back in that awful apartment when she'd opened the door to find him standing in the doorway, the impact of his gaze drove all the breath from her lungs.

He was smiling, but it wasn't for her, because as soon as he finished up the call and put his phone in his pocket the smile vanished.

A chill crept over her. It felt as though the sun had gone down even though rays of light were still filling the room.

'You're awake,' Dante said and it wasn't a question.

Since there was no point in pretending she was still asleep she sat up, pushing a lock of hair back behind her ear and drawing the soft wool of the throw around her. 'Yes. So it would seem.'

There was something in his eyes she couldn't read, something that made her uneasy. As if he'd made a decision about something. Had he changed his mind about the baby and called the police after all, perhaps?

No less than what you deserve.

Stella swallowed, fighting not to let any sign of her unease show.

'I had some food delivered.' He nodded towards the small stone table on the terrace, a couple of cushioned stone benches flanking it. The table had been set and there were plates of food on it, tea lights in small glass holders casting a golden glow. 'You should eat.'

It looked warm and inviting, and the smell of the food made her stomach rumble.

She gritted her teeth, instinctively wanting to refuse him yet managing to stop herself at the last minute. Letting him get to her would be a mistake and she couldn't afford any more of those. No, if she was going to figure out a new revenge plan then she had to lull him into a false sense of security, get him to see her as no threat. Which meant not fighting with him.

And you're hungry.

Yes, well, since the nausea had faded it appeared that she was indeed quite hungry.

Stella got up from the couch slowly, pleased to discover that her legs weren't as wobbly as they had been before and that she could at least stand up by herself.

Dante's gaze was completely and utterly focused on her, and she had the impression that if she fainted again he would probably know before she did and would catch her the very second that she fell.

She found the thought intensely irritating.

'I'm fine now,' she said shortly. 'You don't have to stare at me like I'm going to keel over any second.'

His gaze didn't waver. 'You said you were fine before and look what happened.'

'Again, you're very concerned about my health. Why is that?'

'You're carrying my child, kitten.' His expression remained impassive, though there was an acid bite to his tone. 'If you hadn't noticed.'

Stella decided to ignore that for now, taking a couple of tentative steps. No dizziness threatened, so she took a couple more, moving through the doors and stepping out onto the terrace.

Dusk was settling over the city and, even though it wasn't particularly cold, she kept the throw wrapped around her. The air was full of the scents of the food on the table and the ancient city spread out below the terrace, plus the slightest hint of something warm and exotic. Sandalwood. Dante's aftershave.

He hadn't moved, yet somehow she'd got close to him. Which she hadn't meant to do at all. His gaze was very dark in the fading light, the sunset picking up the strange gold lights in his eyes and the odd golden glint in his thick, nearly black hair. That same golden light gilded his skin too, making him look like the angel he'd appeared to be back in that apartment.

A whisper of electricity crackled in the air between them, making her very aware of his height and the powerful body underneath all that cotton and wool.

You remember that body. You remember what it can do.

Oh, yes, she remembered. She remembered acutely. And she wished she didn't. In fact, that had been the one thing she'd wished many times the past five weeks. That she could forget what she'd done and most especially forget what he'd done to her.

You can't forget now. You'll have a reminder for ever.

Her hand had almost crept to her stomach before she stopped herself, though quite why she'd done it she had no idea. She couldn't think of the baby, not yet. Not when she still had a job to do.

Annoyed with herself and her physical awareness of him, she quickly stepped past his tall figure, moving to the table and sitting down on one of the cushioned benches. The food arrayed on small silver platters was simple but looked delicious: cheeses, olives, bowls of salad, hummus and some fresh crusty bread. There were cold meats too, but she couldn't eat that, or at least not according to the pamphlets.

A glass of wine had been poured for Dante, while orange juice in a tall glass stood waiting for her, condensation beading the sides.

She was desperately thirsty all of a sudden.

As she picked up the juice and took a sip, Dante moved to sit opposite, still watching her with that strangely focused look.

'How are you feeling?' he asked, picking up his wine glass and holding it loosely between his fingers.

'Fine. How long was I asleep?'

'A few hours.' His thumb stroked up and down the stem of his glass in an absent movement. 'You should eat. If you've been feeling sick, food will help.'

'I'm well aware of that, thank you.' She knew she should be good and fill her plate, not cause a fuss. But for some reason she felt stubborn and not inclined to do what he said.

Before Monte Carlo, she hadn't thought of him as anything but a target. And then, when she'd finally come face to face with the man, she'd had to think of him as a caricature rather than an actual person in order to do what had to be done.

But since the apartment, when he'd unexpectedly been protective of his child, she had the sense that perhaps he wasn't the caricature of the selfish playboy she'd turned him into. That perhaps there was more to him than she'd thought.

A mistake to think that, though. She could not afford to see him as a person. Once she started identifying with him, revenge would be beyond her, which meant it would be best not to feel anything at all for him. However, if that wasn't possible, then anger was her best bet.

He didn't appear to notice her being stubborn, putting

his wine glass down, reaching for a plate and beginning to heap food on it. 'I know you can't have the ham, but you can eat all the rest.'

'So you're an expert on pregnancy now? Tell me, how many other children have you fathered?'

'Believe it or not, I have none,' he said calmly. 'And, as far as being an expert on pregnancy, my sister-in-law just gave me a quick rundown.' He sent her a quick, burning glance, the corner of his mouth turning up slightly. 'Don't worry, kitten. If I'm not an expert now, I will be by morning.'

She frowned, distracted from her anger for a moment. Dante Cardinali was famous for his determination not to settle down, no matter how many women had tried to make him change his mind over the years. At least that was what her research had indicated.

So why was he suddenly now interested in her pregnancy? And why had he been so quick to take responsibility for the baby back at the apartment?

She'd asked him about it back then, but he hadn't responded and she hadn't pushed, remembering that she wasn't supposed to rock the boat. But now...curiosity grabbed at her and she couldn't help herself.

'What does that mean?' She took another sip of her orange juice, the ice-cold liquid tart and delicious on her tongue. 'You can't tell me you actually want to be involved in being a father, or be desperate to settle down? And especially not with the woman who tried to kill you.'

Something glittered in his eyes and she couldn't tell what it was, though his voice when he spoke was mild. 'I don't know. Are you likely to try and kill me again?'

'I might.' She tried to echo his mild tone. 'I would advise sleeping with one eye open.'

He didn't say anything for a long moment and she found

she was holding her breath, the hand holding her glass on the point of trembling. Then the sharp, glittering thing in his eyes faded, though the wicked glint that replaced it wasn't any better. 'Or I could just sleep with you and keep you thinking of…other things,' he murmured.

Unexpected heat rose in her cheeks, a gentle ache between her thighs, and try as she might she couldn't make either sensation go away.

'You're not going to try again, though,' he went on before she could speak. 'You weren't able to do it five weeks ago and I think it's highly unlikely that you'll manage this time round.'

He was right, but still she hated his arrogant assumption.

'How would you know?' she snapped before she could think better of it. 'You know nothing about me.'

'*Au contraire*, darling.' He put the plate he'd been filling with food down in front of her. 'I know quite a bit about you. In fact, in the five weeks I've spent hunting you down, I compiled quite the dossier.'

Sitting back, he picked up his wine glass again, the movement of his thumb on the stem oddly hypnotising. 'Stella Montefiore, youngest child of Stefano Montefiore. An avid supporter of my father's, even after our family was exiled. But then the Monte Santa Marian government found out about all the money your father tried to send mine, and all the plans they'd made to try and get his throne back. Yet for some reason they couldn't find your father. They could only find his son, Matteo. Who was the one who ended up in jail.' Dante's gaze was unwavering. 'And who died there.'

Old pain twisted in her gut, the guilt she'd thought she'd long put aside welling up and threatening to swallow her whole.

It was still there, that memory. Of the police coming to their house and demanding to know the whereabouts of Stefano and Matteo Montefiore. Her mother had wept incoherently, not able to tell them anything, which had only made them angry. And Stella had been terrified. She'd thought they were going to hurt her fragile, lovely mother, so she'd told the police what they'd wanted to know. That she'd seen her brother and father going down to the old caves by the beach near their house.

She knew that she shouldn't have told them anything, that she should have let her mother get hurt. That she should have let herself get hurt too, because the good of the family mattered more than any one person. Certainly more than herself.

But she'd only been ten and she'd always had a soft heart. She hated to see another creature in pain and it had been more than she could bear to hear her mother crying. So she'd told them.

And, while her father had managed to get away, her brother hadn't been so lucky. He'd been captured and had gone to prison, only to die there five years later.

It was her fault. All her fault.

She tried to hold Dante's gaze, to be hard and cold, the way her father had tried to drum into her to be. 'Yes,' she said steadily. 'He did. Your point?'

'My point, darling, is that I know why you tried to kill me. Your father wants an eye for an eye.' Dante swirled the wine in his glass. 'Or, rather, a son for a son.'

Of course. He wasn't a stupid man by any stretch.

Stella took another measured sip of her orange juice, using the movement to cover the harsh bite of guilt and anger. 'You seem to have all the answers.'

'But I'm right, aren't I?' He glanced at the plate she hadn't touched yet. 'Eat, kitten. Or I might be forced to make you.'

Oh, she would love not to. Or simply to push the plate

away. But she wasn't supposed to be fighting him, and besides, she did need something to eat or else she was only going to feel more sick later.

Picking up an olive, she pointedly held his gaze, then put the olive in her mouth, the sharp, salty taste suddenly making her aware of how ravenous she was. Damn. She swallowed and picked up another. 'My dead brother is no concern of yours,' she said, trying to stay cool, if only to prove to herself she had no issue with talking about it. 'Or, if we're digging up dead family members, perhaps we can talk about yours instead?'

The research she'd done on him had delivered a few truths of its own. Such as the father who'd died in penury in Milan. And the mother who'd abandoned her husband and her other son, taking Dante with her when he'd been only twelve. She'd died too, or so the records suggested, of a head injury in a hospital in Naples.

Dante's gaze flickered at that, which meant she'd scored a point. Good. And then he said, 'You want to talk about my parents? Fine. My father was a power-hungry, selfish man who loved his throne more than his family and who spent the rest of his miserable life trying to get it back. My mother was a drunk who took me away when I was twelve in search of a new life. And we certainly found it in the slums of Naples. She died when I was sixteen, leaving me to find my own way as a gutter rat. Which I did quite well until my brother Enzo found me.' At last, he lifted his glass and took a sip of the wine, watching her from over the rim. 'Any more questions?'

None of that came as a surprise to her—she'd known the facts. But he'd said everything so casually, as if none of it had touched him in any way.

She gazed back at him, curiosity tugging at her again. No, he'd sounded casual, but he wasn't. She could see the faint gleam of gold deep in his dark eyes. Was it anger? Pain? Or something else?

You're not supposed to be curious. He's not supposed to become a person to you.

He wasn't. And asking him questions about his past was a dangerous road to take.

Stella reached for a piece of the bread he'd cut for her, slathering some olive pesto onto it instead. 'No more questions. I have all that information already.' She took a bite of the bread, the sharp taste of the olive exactly what she'd been craving, then chewed and swallowed it. 'You're not the only one with a dossier.'

He lifted one shoulder in an elegant movement. 'In that case, why talk about the past? That's not what's important here. The important thing we have to discuss is what's going to happen with my baby.'

'*Our* baby,' she corrected before she could stop herself, a tiny shock going through her. Since when had she decided that the baby was 'theirs'?

Dante's eyes gleamed. 'Oh, so is that how it's going to be?'

'How is what going to be?' Tension coiled inside her.

'We've already decided that you're going to keep the child. But what happens now? Are you laying claim to it, kitten?'

Her hand had slipped to her stomach, as if she could somehow touch the baby inside her. The baby she'd tried very hard not to think about.

You will be a mother. How can you not think of that?

But how could she think of it? When she still had an important task in front of her?

Taking petty revenge while you have a life growing inside you.

Her throat tightened unexpectedly. It wasn't petty. Matteo had *died*. And he'd died because of her, as her father had never stopped telling her. It was up to her to make up for that death. To make it mean something.

She'd been the one to take on the assassination of Dante Cardinali and she'd failed. Which meant she had to be the one to try and salvage something from that failure. No matter what happened.

She would think about her baby afterwards. When she had the time and the space to concentrate. When Matteo's death had been avenged.

Until then she needed to give Dante what he wanted. Play nice, be meek, mild and biddable. And definitely don't argue with him.

Except that wasn't what happened.

'What if I did lay claim to it?' The words came out despite herself, torn from somewhere deep inside, the tiny part of herself that had remained the soft-hearted ten-year-old she'd once been. 'What if I did want my baby?'

Dante's gaze intensified. 'That, kitten, is a whole other conversation.'

CHAPTER FIVE

She looked so cool and untouchable sitting there staring at him, challenge in her eyes. Completely unruffled by his attempts to disturb her by talking about her family. Coolly telling him she'd probably try and make another attempt on his life. And then challenging his claim on their child.

As if she hadn't been the one to point a gun to his head the month before.

As if she hadn't been the one to take off her clothes and slide down on him, riding them both into the kind of ecstasy he'd only ever dreamt of.

Dio, it turned him on.

And it shouldn't, it really shouldn't. He'd already decided that he wasn't going to sleep with her, that it would make an already complicated situation infinitely worse, and yet...

She was so small and lovely, with the cashmere throw he'd tucked around her while she was asleep now snugly wrapped around her narrow shoulders. She had a bit more colour to her face, the shadows beneath her eyes less like bruises.

But the cool determination in her silver-blue eyes hadn't changed one iota.

Had what he'd said meant nothing to her? Not even the mention of her brother? He thought he'd detected a faint tightening of her mouth when he'd mentioned Matteo, and had experienced a fleeting sense of regret that he'd hurt her. Then again, she'd tried to kill him. And he'd wanted confirmation that she'd targeted him because of the blood debt incurred due to her brother's death.

She hadn't specifically answered that, but her change of subject had told him everything he needed to know.

Yes, he'd been right. Her brother had died, Stefano obviously held Dante's father responsible and he now demanded a price: Dante's life in recompense for the loss of his son's.

It was all very old school, and he might have found it amusing if the predicament he now found himself in hadn't totally been his fault.

But it was.

As much as he mightn't like it, Stella Montefiore was carrying his child. And he needed to make a decision about what to do.

He'd already decided that keeping her near was in his best interests, especially when he couldn't be sure she wouldn't make another attempt on his life, and he'd always been a fan of the 'keep your friends close and your enemies closer' approach.

But it wasn't just his life he was concerned about. It was the life of their baby too. He didn't trust her, which meant she wasn't going anywhere until the danger period of the pregnancy had passed. That would involve keeping her here, as he didn't want the media catching wind of it, plus he could ensure that she had the best medical care and treatment on hand should it be required.

Once the danger period was past, well…that was another discussion they would have to have. He certainly wasn't going to let her go free while she was still a danger to him and he hadn't seen any evidence that she wasn't.

It was either that or he called the police and he didn't want to do that.

They would find out who she was and then the proverbial would really hit the fan.

Since when have you cared what anyone would think?

Well, he didn't. It was his child that he cared about and he didn't like the thought of his son or daughter being born in jail.

Dio, he'd always thought that Enzo had gone slightly mad when he'd discovered he was a father, but now... Now Dante understood his brother in a way he hadn't before.

'And what conversation would that be?' Stella asked coolly. 'Is this the one we're going to have about what happens to our child when he or she is born?'

He stared back at her, just as cool. 'It's the one we're going to have where I tell you that when our child is born he or she will be staying with me.'

Oh, really? Since when did you decide that?

Apparently since right this instant.

Something flared in her eyes, anger probably. Good, let her be angry. She had to know where his line was and this was it right here. He'd lost both his parents—his father to his obsession with the throne, his mother to her obsession with the bottle—and that had been a painful lesson. And, even though he wasn't any better than either of them, he at least had the opportunity to do better, not to cause his own child that pain.

It was a surprise to him that he was considering someone other than himself for a change, but he didn't take the words back. He only met her gaze, letting her see the certainty in his own.

'You?' The word was layered with utter disdain. 'A reckless playboy who cares for nothing but himself? You seriously want your child with you?'

Her tone made his hackles rise, but he knew what she was doing. She was pushing him, just like she'd pushed him the night they'd met, which meant that he'd got under that cool veneer of hers in some way.

He smiled, relaxing against the stone of the terrace parapet at his back. 'You have to admit, it's better than having a murderer for a mother.'

She flushed, the anger in her eyes flaring hotter, and he could feel himself harden.

Dio, why did knowing he got to her affect him that way? Desire had got them into the situation they were in now and giving into it again would only make it worse.

'I know, kitten,' he purred, studying her face. 'You're not actually a murderer yet, but note that you did tell me to sleep with one eye open. And you have pointed a gun in my face and declared that you wanted me to die. The intention was there, no matter that you didn't do it.'

Her jaw had gone tight, her whole body stiff. Which was interesting. What didn't she like? Him pointing out what they both already knew? A sudden distaste about that particular word?

'What do you want me to say?' she asked tightly. 'That I'm not going to make another attempt on your life? Would you even believe me if I said it?'

Dante absently stroked the stem of his wine glass, noting the anger burning in her eyes despite her cool and contained veneer.

You don't believe she'd kill you.

Of course he didn't.

He knew sex. It was as close to a real connection with another person as he'd allow himself. Women showed their true faces to him in bed. When they were under him, transported with ecstasy, they allowed their souls to shine through and Stella had been no different.

He'd seen her soul that night in Monte Carlo and it was

made of passion, joy and a wonder that had extended to include him.

It was not the soul of a killer.

He'd known it when she'd had the chance to pull that trigger and hadn't. And he'd known it the moment he'd watched pleasure overwhelm her.

But maybe she didn't.

'Put it this way,' he said slowly. 'I'd believe you. But I'm not sure you'd believe yourself.'

Shock flared in her eyes, a burst of bright silver as that cool veneer of hers cracked a little. 'What do you mean by that?'

'I mean, I don't think you're a murderer, kitten. I never have.' He studied her, fascinated by the gleam of emotion in her eyes that she couldn't quite hide. 'But you didn't like it when I pointed that out in Monte Carlo and I think you don't like it now. So you tell me. Are you happy to be called a killer, Stella Montefiore?'

An expression he couldn't name rippled briefly over her lovely face before she turned away, draining what was left of her orange juice. Her hand shook as she raised the glass—just a small tremble, but he noted it all the same.

Interesting. Did she really think she was a killer? Perhaps she'd had to tell herself that in order to go through with that first attempt on his life, and perhaps she had to keep telling herself that in order to finish the job.

Curiosity pulled tight inside him in a way he normally didn't allow.

How could this small, lovely woman, who seemed so delicate and vulnerable, who'd been nothing but softness and heat on top of him, think she was capable of taking a life?

Yes, she had a hard shell that she was clinging to for all

she was worth, the veneer of the stone-cold killer. But that was breaking—even he could see that.

Was it he who was making it shatter? Or was it the baby?

An ache he didn't want to acknowledge tightened inside him, which he ignored.

'And I suppose you're fine with being called a selfish playboy?' she said eventually, putting her glass down on the table with a click.

'That's not an answer.'

'Why should I give you one?'

'You don't have to.' He held her gaze. 'But I've seen your soul, kitten. You showed it to me that night you climbed on top of me and rode us both to heaven. And there's nothing dark in it.'

Why should it matter to you what she thinks about herself?

He wasn't quite sure. Maybe self-interest? After all, he didn't want her entertaining any further designs on his life. Then again, if he was so sure she wouldn't go through with it anyway, then what did it matter?

Perhaps this time it's not self-interest. Perhaps you care about her feelings.

Ridiculous. He barely even knew her let alone cared about her feelings.

Stella's cheeks had gone a deep pink, making the blue of her eyes more intense. And this time she didn't look away. 'If you think I'm not going to kill you then why am I still here?'

'You know why. The baby.'

'Strange that a selfish playboy famous for not settling down would suddenly be more than happy with an unexpected baby.'

There was a hot current of anger running through her voice, though she was clearly trying to keep it cool.

Yes, there was passion in her. Anger, stubborn will and fire enough to crack apart the fragile armour she was trying to hide behind.

What would it take to make it shatter entirely? And what would happen if it did?

The unwelcome pulse of desire that hadn't gone away no matter how hard he tried to ignore it beat harder, faster. Along with the tight coil of anticipation.

He shouldn't be thinking such things and he knew it. Temptation was something he'd never been very good at resisting, but he should be resisting it now.

Yet somehow he couldn't stop himself from baiting her.

'And I'm sure a killer such as yourself isn't best pleased to find herself pregnant either,' he commented. 'Surely it doesn't matter to you whether I claim my baby or not? After all, that'll leave you with more time to get on with killing and such.'

Silver flashed in her eyes, her jaw tight, tension in the line of her narrow shoulders.

It's wrong to push her and you know it.

Maybe he did. And maybe baiting her like this was a mistake. Then again, he'd made so many mistakes already, what was one more? Temptation had always been his downfall.

No, hunger for what you know you cannot have has always been your downfall.

The thought didn't make any sense to him so he ignored it.

'I will be a mother regardless of whether I'm happy about it or not,' Stella said fiercely. 'And, since I am, I will not shirk my responsibilities.' Her chin lifted slightly. 'This is my fault, after all.'

She looked so proud and serious and there was a certain

kind of dignity to her. Like a queen nobly taking responsibility for the war she'd just started.

Ridiculous kitten.

This wasn't a war. This was a child.

'Really?' He swirled his wine in his glass, tilting his
head and staring at her. 'So, in between drugging me and
handcuffing me and pointing a gun at my head, then taking off your clothes and seducing me—while a virgin, I
may add—you somehow should also have remembered to
get a condom?'

The flush in her cheeks deepened even further. 'I'm not
a child. I know about birth control.'

'Not, apparently, that night.'

Her eyes glittered. She was fragile and lovely sitting
there wrapped in the soft cashmere throw, yet he could
almost taste the sharpness of her fury. It poured through
the cracks in her veneer like lava through the cracks in a
volcano.

'Why are you pushing me like this?' she demanded.
'What's the point? You say you want our baby, but what
does that mean? That you'll take it away from me the minute it's born?'

Dio, he wanted to see that veneer break apart completely,
watch the fire he could see burning inside her leap high,
the way it had done that night in Monte Carlo.

A mistake. Don't do it.

Except he couldn't seem to stop.

'And shouldn't I?' he shot back, putting his wine glass
back down with a click. 'Don't you think that would be the
best thing for the child?'

'No,' she snapped. 'I don't.'

'Then give me one good reason, Stella Montefiore.' He
put his palms down on the table and half-rose to his feet.
Then, very deliberately, he leaned across the space between

them, getting closer to all that heat, to the fire that burned inside her. 'Give me one good reason why I should trust you with my baby.'

STELLA HAD NO idea why she was letting Dante Cardinali get under her skin so badly. It was only that the way he sat there, all lazy arrogance, secure in the power of his own charisma, needled her.

He seemed so certain of everything about her, firstly with his repeated references to her being a killer, and secondly by mentioning the fact that somehow, because they'd had sex once, he'd seen her soul. And then, to cap it all off, implying that she couldn't be trusted with their child...

She shouldn't let it matter to her, but it did. He might know about her family from what he could find on the web, but he didn't know *her.* And did he seriously believe she couldn't be trusted with a baby? Yes, she might have been prepared to kill him, but she would *never* hurt a child.

Why does his opinion matter to you?

She couldn't answer that question and right now she didn't want to. She was too furious.

And it didn't help that she was *very* aware that he was the most phenomenally attractive man she'd ever seen.

He leaned across the table, the setting sun catching sparks of gold in the dark silk of his hair and outlining the strong lines of his handsome face. Close enough for her to see those very same golden sparks glowing in the darkness of his eyes.

Heat burned there, anger and a kind of demand that made something deep inside her clench tight with anticipation.

'Well?' he demanded, when she didn't say anything immediately. 'Do you have any answer to that at all?'

Of course she had an answer, but she didn't want to give it to him. She shouldn't have to.

Are you sure he hasn't got reason not to trust you?

Stella ignored that thought. The discussion was pointless anyway because, whatever he might say about the fact that she wasn't a killer, she still had a job to do. A mistake to correct. Matteo's death to avenge.

And everything had to wait until that had been accomplished.

So why are you arguing with him? You're not supposed to, remember?

Stella gripped the soft material of the throw draped around her shoulders, staring straight into the hot gaze of the man leaning across the table.

No, she shouldn't be arguing with him. She should be cool, calm and collected, ignoring him as if he didn't matter and nothing he said meant anything.

Because it didn't. He wasn't a person to her. He was barely even a man.

Except that was the problem, wasn't it?

Looking into his hot, dark eyes, feeling the spice of his aftershave and the warmth of his own personal scent wrapping around her, she couldn't think of him as anything but a man.

An overwhelmingly attractive man.

Her mouth dried and she knew she should look away, but she simply couldn't tear her gaze from his.

The atmosphere between them changed. Became electric, volatile.

All it would take was a single spark and the air between them would catch fire.

Stand up. Walk away. He's already got to you once. Are you really going to let him get to you again?

She couldn't. Yet her heartbeat was loud in her ears and

her skin felt tight, prickling all over with the awareness of how close he was.

'Oh, kitten,' Dante said, a rough thread of heat running through his beautiful voice. 'You really need to stop me.'

She should. She wanted to. And yet…his mouth was very close, the shape of his bottom lip the perfect curve. She'd taken a bite out of it in that hotel room in Monte Carlo, testing the softness of it between her teeth. The taste of him had been delicious, a dark, rich flavour that she'd wanted more of. God, she could still remember it even now.

Her own mouth watered. All she'd have to do was lean forward and she could taste him again…

'Kitten.' He sounded even rougher now. 'You're playing with fire—you understand that, don't you?'

It took effort to drag her attention from his mouth, to meet the molten gold gleaming in his eyes, evidence of a desire he didn't bother to hide.

A desire that was just as strong as it had been five weeks ago and just as hot. And against which he was just as helpless as she was.

You could use that.

A hot burst of reaction shuddered down her spine.

And why couldn't she use it? She had no power here, no weapons of her own. She needed something. She hated the feeling of being powerless and weak. It made her feel like she was ten again, after she'd betrayed her brother to the police and she'd had to watch him be dragged away to prison. Powerless to stop it. Knowing she was the one to blame. Her and her soft heart.

She wouldn't be that weak. Not ever again.

Playing with fire? Dante Cardinali didn't know the half of it.

Stella didn't answer. Instead she leaned forward and pressed her mouth to his. She didn't know how to kiss, but that wasn't really the point. This was a power move, a rattle of the sabre. A declaration of war.

Her heartbeat thundered, his lips against hers soft and hot. She could almost taste him and it made her tremble, because there was a hunger inside her and it wasn't enough. She wanted more.

But he didn't move.

Wanting a reaction, she touched her tongue to his bottom lip, tracing the shape of it, exploring gently, hesitantly.

Still, he didn't move.

Frustrated, Stella pulled back. Perhaps she'd been mistaken? Perhaps he didn't want her after all?

But, no, there was fire blazing in his eyes and it nearly burned her to the ground.

'I told you that you shouldn't have done that,' he said.

Then abruptly he pushed himself away from the table top and straightened, moving around the side of the table with all the fluid, athletic grace of one of the great cats.

Excitement gripped her, the thump of her out-of-control heartbeat the only thing she could hear.

This time she was the one who didn't move, watching him come for her, his searing gaze holding hers. And there were no smiles now, no lazy, arrogant charm. The veneer of the playboy had been stripped away to reveal the predator underneath.

Perhaps she should have been scared, because he was very big and very strong, and she was far smaller than he was. But she wasn't scared. No, the opposite. She felt powerful. Because this was her doing. She'd been the one to strip that veneer from him, no one else. Just her. And with only a kiss.

It was intoxicating. She'd never felt so strong.

Dante stood in front of her for a second then, very slowly, he leaned down, putting his hands on the table on either side of her, surrounding her with the power of his muscular body and his heat, the heady spice of his scent.

'What,' he murmured softly, a dark threat in his voice, 'do you think you're doing?'

Stella lifted her chin, wild excitement careening around inside her, every part of her alive and aware of him and how close he was. 'What do you think I'm doing?'

His eyes glittered and for a second she saw the extent of his hunger stark in the inky depths, wide and deep and endless. It stole her breath. 'Don't you dare play with me,' he growled low in warning.

She shouldn't challenge him, not when it was obvious to her that he was close to some kind of edge. But she couldn't help herself. There was a hot tide of exhilaration washing through her and she couldn't shut herself up. 'Why shouldn't I play with you? Or can't you handle it when the boot's on the other foot?'

A muscle flicked in the side of his jaw. 'I can handle it.' The roughness in his voice was pronounced, a velvet caress that made her shiver. 'But you can't.'

She smiled, half-drunk on her own power over him. 'Oh, really?' she challenged, deliberating trying to incite him. 'Try me.'

The look in his eyes seared her. 'Be sure, kitten. Be very sure you know what you're doing.'

'Oh, I know. But I don't think you do…'

But she never got to finish, his lips coming down on hers in a hard kiss that stole the words right out of her mouth and the rest of her breath from her lungs.

It was hot and desperate, his tongue pushing into her mouth, demanding. Taking. But she didn't pull away. She lifted her hands and shoved her fingers into the thick silk of his hair, half-rising from the seat to kiss him back, just as demanding, just as hard.

Then he reached for her, lifting her, and plates were smashing, the sounds of glasses shattering as he shoved the remains of their meal off the table to clear a space. He placed her on the table in front of him, his hips pushing between her thighs, his hands sliding up her back. One hand tangled in her hair, tugging her head back, while the other shoved down the back of her jeans, his hot palm sliding over her bare skin and drawing her right to the edge of the table, pressing the damp heat between her thighs to the hard ridge beneath the wool of his trousers. And then he took control of the kiss and of her, utterly.

It was as if she'd unleashed a hurricane and she was standing right in the middle of the howling wind and driving rain, letting the fury of it buffet her. There was no fear, only an intense excitement and exhilaration, knowing she was the one who'd called this raging storm into being, that it was here because of her.

And she didn't know why that was so damn thrilling, but it was.

She curled her fingers into his hair, trembling as he took what he wanted, and she let him, her mouth opening beneath his, the heat and fire of his kiss igniting her. Turning her to flame so she was burning too, just as bright, just as hot. And she kissed him back, revelling in the rich taste of him, the wine he'd been drinking a subtle flavour that had her desperate for more.

He made a harsh sound, a kind of growl, the hand in her hair pulling harder so her head was drawn back, her throat exposed. Then he tore his mouth from hers, moving down to her jaw, raining kisses over her sensitive skin, nipping at the delicate cords of her neck, licking the pulse at the base of her throat that beat hard and fast for him.

Stella shivered all over, arching back to give him more access, his hot kisses a shower of sparks on her skin. It made her feel tight and hungry all over, desperate and hollow for something to fill her up.

Him.

But he was way ahead of her. He lifted his hands and gripped the thin, cheap material of her T-shirt and, without any effort, ripped the whole thing down the front, exposing her hot skin to the cool air. She gasped, shivering as his palms stroked over her stomach and then up, his fingers gripping the delicate lace of her bra and ripping that apart too.

'Dante.' His name slipped out on a sigh and then, as he shoved the remains of her clothing off her shoulders and his palms found her bare breasts, *'Dante...'*

He said nothing, his mouth at her throat, his hands stroking and cupping her, squeezing gently, his thumbs finding the hard buds of her acutely sensitive nipples and teasing them.

Stella shuddered, her mind going blank as his hot mouth moved further down, finding one nipple and closing around it, sucking hard. Pleasure exploded brightly in her mind, a column of fire lighting her up from the inside, burning away her resistance, burning away all thoughts of power and who had it, who was weak and who wasn't. Of the revenge she had to take and the baby she was carrying.

There was only this fire, this intensity, and the pleasure that was burning them both alive.

It had been so long since she'd touched another person, since she'd been touched herself, and her hands found their way to his suit jacket before she knew what she was doing, shoving it from his shoulders and then scrabbling at the buttons of his business shirt, pulling them apart. Threads ripped, a button or two pinging on the floor of the stone terrace, and then his skin was beneath her fingers, smooth, hot and hard with muscle. His head lifted from her breasts, his mouth on hers again, the hunger in him demanding, and she met it, pushing her tongue into his mouth, exploring him with the same raw demand with which he was exploring her. She shoved at the cotton of his shirt, pushing that off his shoulders too, wanting nothing between her palms and his hot skin. And, *God*, he felt so good. So smooth and hard, with just the right amount of hair prickling against her palms, his muscles tightening as she stroked him.

She felt if she'd been drinking some incredibly delicious champagne that delivered only pleasure, and now she was completely and utterly drunk, and it was wonderful. There were no boundaries, no limitations. There was only this beautiful, *beautiful* man and his hands on her skin, his mouth on hers.

The man you were supposed to kill.

But she couldn't think of that, not now. There was an exquisite pressure building inside her and she was panting, his hands at the fastenings of her jeans, pulling them open. She wanted him to touch her so desperately that she thought she might cry if he didn't. And she never cried. Not since Matteo had been dragged away to prison.

Dante jerked her jeans off, taking her underwear with them, leaving her naked on the stone table, the remains of their meal surrounding them. The harsh sounds of his breathing filled the night and the dark fire in his eyes, the sharp, predatory look on his face, was all she could see.

He stood there shirtless, the setting sun gilding the hard, cut muscles of his chest and abdomen, and she couldn't stop from reaching out to touch him, her hands running lovingly over the width of his powerful shoulders and sculpted chest, his skin a perfect golden bronze.

He wasn't the charming playboy now. No, now he was pure predator, and he was starving for her.

She panted, reaching for the buttons on his trousers,

wanting him, but he growled, knocking her hands away. 'No.' The word was bitten off and rough, and he took her wrists, guiding them behind her back and holding them there with powerful fingers. 'I'm in charge now, kitten. Not you.'

She struggled a little, purely for show's sake, because the feeling of being bound and held by him was like an electric shock straight between her thighs, increasing the already acute pleasure.

And he must have seen it, because he smiled fiercely, hungrily, an unholy light glittering in his eyes. 'You like that, don't you?' he murmured, running his free hand down her shuddering body, his fingers brushing through the slick folds between her thighs.

She groaned, wanting to deny it. Because of course she didn't like it when he was in charge. She wanted to be. Didn't she? And yet she couldn't the deny the electric plea-sure of his touch and how it thrilled her that she couldn't move her hands to touch him back, at how she was at his mercy.

A shiver went through her and she gasped as his fingers stroked her wet flesh, finding the throbbing centre between her legs and gently stroking over and around, making her jerk and shiver in his arms.

'Please,' she gasped, pulling against his hold. 'Oh, please...'

There was a savage glint in his eye, a snarl twisting his mouth as he looked down at her. 'How does it feel to be held down, kitten? How do *you* like the boot being on the other foot?'

A thread of anger wound through the heat in his voice and the gleam of gold in his eyes, and she knew it was about the chemistry burning between them and how help-less he was against it.

But that only thrilled her, made her even more aware of her own power, and she arched up against his hand, pressing herself into his touch. 'Yes,' she moaned softly. 'More. Touch me more.'

He made a rough sound deep in his throat and muttered something vicious under his breath. But she was hardly listening, because then he was pulling open his trousers and pushing them down his hips, taking his underwear with it, and drawing himself out. Then he was urging her to the edge of the table, the furnace of his body pressed right to her bare skin. She groaned at the brush of his skin on hers, at the heat that felt as though it was burning her alive. And she was desperate to touch him, but his grip was too strong. Then he was fitting himself to the entrance of her sex and guiding himself inside, and she could feel the delicious, agonisingly pleasurable stretch of him as he began to push, her body giving way before his, adjusting to accommodate him.

She moaned, the harsh sound of his breathing filling the space between them.

He let her go for a moment, gripping her hips instead, angling her the way he wanted before drawing himself back and thrusting in again. Hard. Deep.

Stella gasped, reaching for his shoulders, her fingernails digging into his skin, revelling in the feel of the tense muscle beneath it.

He made a growling, masculine sound and thrust again, deeper, harder. The pleasure was irresistible, unstoppable, a force of nature she couldn't withstand or hold out against. So she didn't. She wound her legs around his waist and clung on to him, pressing her mouth to his throat, wanting to taste him, to get as much of him as she could any way she could get it. Because she was hungry for something she didn't understand, and the salt and musk of his skin was delicious.

She licked him, kissed him, nipped him, tasted him with every hard, deep thrust. Until his breathing became faster, harsher, and she found herself pushed down onto her back on the table top while he leaned over her, his hands gripping onto the opposite side of the table to give himself more leverage. The rhythm of his hips was hard and sure, his thrusts impossibly deep.

She'd never been to heaven before but she was pretty sure it was like this, on her back on a table, with Dante Cardinali's hard, muscled body inside her, over her, surrounding her in every way possible. His heat overwhelmed her, the subtle spice of his scent cut through with male arousal, and the evidence of his desire for her was in every line of his perfectly handsome face.

He looked like an angel in the process of falling, his features taut and hungry and desperate, a feral light glinting in his eyes.

And she was the one who'd driven him to this point. She was the one who'd made him fall.

She couldn't remember why she was doing this or what point she had to prove any more. There was only him and the sharp intensity of the pleasure slowly ripping her apart.

The orgasm came like a bolt of white lightning, electrifying her, lighting her up from the inside, and she screamed with the pleasure of it. But he didn't stop, he kept on going, forcing her higher, making everything inside her tighten once again before another impossible release.

She called his name, shuddering against him as it detonated inside her a second time, turning her hot face into his neck as the aftershocks rocked through her, feeling him move even faster, a wild rhythm that she couldn't match this time. So she let him go, let him take what he wanted until he groaned, hoarsely muttering something in her ear as his big body shook with the force of the pleasure that was turning them both inside out.

Afterwards there was a long period of silence, the sound of the city below the terrace going about its business as if nothing had changed. As if she hadn't been given a taste of the power that lay in her own femininity. A power she'd never understood even existed until this moment.

Then Dante moved, his hands coming to rest on the table on either side of her head as he pushed himself up a little, staring down at her.

Heat glowed in his eyes, the aftermath of pleasure and something else.

Fury.

'What are you doing to me, Stella Montefiore?' Dante demanded, as though all of this was her fault. 'What *the hell* are you doing to me?'

CHAPTER SIX

Dante's heart was beating so fast it felt as if it was going to come out of his chest, the remains of one of the most intense orgasms he'd ever had making his head ring like a bell. He'd never had a response like this to a woman before and he couldn't work out what the hell was going on.

He'd told himself he wasn't going to make an already complicated situation worse by having sex, that he'd simply ignore the desire he felt for this impossible, lovely woman. But apparently he'd severely underestimated his own need to shatter that cool exterior of hers, get a taste of the passion that flamed beneath it. Slake the sudden, overwhelming hunger that had risen inside him the moment she'd laid her mouth on his.

Dio, he'd lost control, and he never lost control. Not like this.

Beneath him, Stella's gaze was wide, the flush that ran the entire length of her beautiful body making the blue of her eyes seem electric. She was looking at him as though she'd never seen anything like him in her entire life, and despite himself it made satisfaction clench tight inside him.

Because there was no trace of the cool, hard woman who'd sat opposite him just before, ignoring the cracks in the ill-fitting suit of armour she wore. No, there was only this woman instead, soft and passionate and hungry, with wonder glowing in her eyes.

Then the wonder faded, her gaze flickering. 'I'm not doing anything to you,' she said thickly.

Disappointment caught at him, though he had no idea why. Because since when had he wanted a woman to look at him the way Stella had just now? He'd never wanted it. He'd never wanted anything from a woman at all and he shouldn't be wanting anything now.

'Liar.' The word came out in a growl, his anger deepening for no good reason. 'You've been pushing me since the moment you got here.'

'And don't tell me you don't like it,' she shot back, silver-blue glimmering up at him from beneath her silky golden lashes.

Oh, yes, definitely her armour was firmly back in place. Little witch.

He was still inside her and her body was soft underneath his. He could feel her inner muscles clenching around him, and that and the heat of her bare satiny skin along with the scent of sex was making him hard again.

But, despite the challenging look she'd just given him, the shadows beneath her eyes had got more pronounced and there was a certain vulnerability to the curve of her bottom lip.

She was not only inexperienced but also pregnant and physically fragile and he'd just taken her roughly on the table. And, even though they were high up and probably no one would have seen, they were still outside and visible.

What were you thinking?

A certain tightness gathered in his chest. Since his mother's death he'd avoided taking responsibility for anyone else's wellbeing but his own, and it had never bothered him before. But, as it had back in her apartment, the urge to make sure Stella was okay tugged at him in a way he couldn't ignore.

'Did I hurt you?' he asked, searching her face for any signs of discomfort or pain.

She blinked and glanced away. 'No. I'm fine.'

He didn't think she was, though, because there was still a vulnerable look to her mouth and she wouldn't meet his eye. Reaching out, he took her chin in his fingers and turned her face back to his so he could see her expression. 'Kitten, you need to tell me if I hurt you,' he insisted. 'Because, believe it or not, that's the last thing I want to do.'

Her throat moved and he could feel the tension in her jaw, as if she wanted to pull out of his hold but was resisting it. 'I said I'm fine,' she repeated, glaring at him. 'And, no, you didn't hurt me. Okay?'

Which should have relieved him but didn't, because there was an undercurrent of anger in her voice that he didn't quite understand.

But now was not the time to push, so he said nothing, carefully pulling out of her. Then, amid the ruins of their dinner, he followed the instinct that had gripped him since the moment he'd met her, gathering her up in his arms and protectively holding her small, warm body against him.

She didn't protest, merely turned her cheek against his chest and relaxed into his hold as if she trusted him. Which of course she shouldn't. Because he was only taking care of her for his child's sake, naturally, not for any other reason.

And certainly not because he cared in any way about her.

Why would he? When he barely knew her?

Yet still the way she nestled in his arms made something in him want to growl with a possessive, primitive sort of satisfaction, a feeling he'd never had before and didn't particularly like.

Deciding it was probably another biological reaction,

Dante ignored it, heading through the living area and into the bathroom.

Once there, he got rid of the remains of their clothing and turned on the shower, drawing Stella into the huge, white-tiled shower stall. There were about five different shower heads and he turned them all on, holding her as the hot water streamed over them.

She kept her head against his chest, her cheek pressed to his bare skin, her body relaxed against his. Her eyes stayed closed, her lashes spangled with drops of water, and the way she rested against him—as if she was safe—made the possessive feeling inside him deepen still further.

A mistake.

He didn't want to possess her. He didn't want to possess anyone. He didn't want, full-stop. It was safer, less painful and far, far less complicated not to want anything at all.

He'd learned that lesson the day his mother had dragged him away from the brother he'd loved to a lonely, dangerous existence in the gutters of Naples. Where she'd ignored all his childish pleas to stop drinking, seeming to prefer the bottle and the company of the violent boyfriend she'd hooked up with.

Dante had tried to protect her when he'd finally got old enough to give that bastard a taste of his own medicine, only to have his mother scream at him for hurting poor Roberto and then threaten to report him to the police.

Anger that he thought he'd extinguished a long time ago flared into life, glowing sullenly in his gut.

In fact, he'd tried to protect her for years and she'd thrown it back in his face every single time. And then, when she'd got hurt, as she inevitably had, she'd ended up blaming him for it. The way she'd blamed him the night she'd died.

She was right, though. That was *your fault.*

He ignored the thought entirely, getting some shower gel from a bottle on the shelf and stroking it over Stella's skin, washing her gently. She relaxed totally against him, not saying anything, her breathing deep and slow. Almost as if she'd fallen asleep standing up.

No, he didn't want to think about his mother, not here, not now. In fact, what he wanted was to push Stella up against the tiled wall and forget his doubts by exploring her lovely body and making her scream his name again. But he wasn't going to. She was clearly exhausted and needed sleep more than anything else.

Dante finished washing her body then began to wash her hair, as it was clear that hadn't been done in a while. She didn't protest and didn't move, only giving a sensual little sigh as he massaged the shampoo through her scalp. The sound didn't help his aching groin, but he ignored that too, making her hair smooth and shiny with the conditioner before helping her out of the shower and drying her off.

'Why are you being so nice to me?' she murmured as he picked her up again, gathering her close as he carried her out of the bathroom.

'Because you're pregnant and you're tired and you need looking after.' He moved down the hallway and into the massive bedroom with its view out over the rooftops of Rome. Facing the view, pushed up against the opposite wall, was the huge bed piled high with soft bedding and white pillows—he liked to be comfortable.

'No, I don't,' Stella muttered sleepily as he pulled back the duvet and laid her down onto the bed.

'For the sake of the baby you do.' He pulled the covers around her, making sure she was comfortable, ignoring the urge to climb in beside her and hold her soft, naked body against his, protect her while she slept.

She was safe here, and anyway lying beside her would

only make him hard, and he definitely didn't need any more temptation where she was concerned. He'd given in to it out there on the terrace, but he wouldn't again, not with the possessiveness he was already feeling.

Best not to make it any worse.

Dante turned away, only to have her reach out unexpectedly, her slender fingers wrapping around his and holding on.

He stilled and looked down at her. 'What is it?'

Her hair was spread like damp, golden silk all over the pillows, her eyes wide and dark. 'Where will you sleep?'

'The couch probably.' He hadn't thought about it, not that he was tired.

A strange expression crossed her face and then her fingers tightened around his. 'Don't...don't go.'

Surprise caught at him. 'Why?'

'I just...' She stopped, glancing away. But she didn't let go of his hand. 'I'm...cold.'

He didn't think she was and it made something pull tight in his chest, something he didn't want to examine too closely.

He should refuse. Turn around and walk out of the room. Yet he didn't.

Instead he gently tugged his hand free then pulled back the covers and climbed into bed beside her. She settled against him as he arranged her so her spine was to his chest, the soft curve of her bottom fitting against his groin.

He wasn't used to dismissing his body's physical wants, yet he found himself doing so now, ignoring how hard he was and how he ached, biting back a groan as she snuggled back against him, nudging the ridge of his erection.

Then she sighed and relaxed and he found he'd unconsciously spread his palm out on her bare stomach in a protective, possessive movement.

Because of the baby. Of course for the baby.

And yet it wasn't the baby he was thinking of as her breathing deepened and became more regular, her body soft, warm and yielding against him.

It was the feel of her fingers gripping his hand.

As if she was afraid to let him go.

STELLA WOKE TO find sunlight streaming across her face. She was lying tangled in a white sheet in the middle of a massive bed, and she was completely and utterly naked.

She was also alone.

Which was a mercy, given the memories of the night before streaming through her mind in glorious Technicolour. Dante taking her passionately on the table on the terrace. Dante staring down at her with fury in his eyes, demanding to know what she'd done to him. Dante gathering her up in his arms and taking her into the shower, washing her gently before putting her to bed.

Dante looking down at her with surprise as she'd grabbed his hand and begged him to stay...

A wave of humiliation swept through her and she rolled over, burying her face against the cool white cotton of the pillow.

She couldn't think what on earth had possessed her. That she'd let him wash her and put her to bed like a child was bad enough, but then to ask him to stay with her... Why had she done that?

It was true that after the two orgasms he'd given her she'd felt utterly exhausted, what little strength she'd had long gone. And when he'd gathered her up in his arms and held her against his hard, muscular chest she'd felt...safe and cared for.

It had been a strange, intoxicating feeling.

No one had taken care of her when she'd been young.

Not her mother, who had been too busy running around after her brother, and not her father, who hadn't wanted to concern himself with a mere girl. Since her brother, as the heir, had always been more important, she hadn't questioned her parents' priorities. And, if she'd occasionally ached for someone to put their arms around her and tell her she was loved, well, that sensation soon passed if she ignored it.

Except she hadn't ignored it the way she should, had she? Because it had been that need for love that had been her weakness. Her flaw. It had got her brother captured, had broken her mother's heart and had turned her father even colder and harder than he had been already.

She thought she'd overcome that part of herself years ago and she didn't understand what had made her surrender to Dante so completely the night before. What had made her relax against the heat and strength of his muscular body as he'd held her in his arms.

Perhaps it was the chemistry between them that had been the catalyst, blazing so brightly she'd been overwhelmed. Or maybe it was the discovery of her own power over him and the way she'd been able to strip that lazy playboy veneer away from him, exposing all the wild heat and hunger that lay beneath it.

Whatever it was, it couldn't happen again.

Stella closed her eyes, trying not to think about his fingers on her bare skin or how he'd felt inside her, moving hard and hot, holding her hands behind her back as he'd taken what he wanted from her...

No, most certainly it could not happen again.

'You're awake?'

She went still at the deep, rich sound of Dante's voice then rolled over and sat up, clutching the sheet around her, even though she knew it was pointless, considering he'd touched every inch of her when he'd washed her in the shower the night before.

He was leaning against the doorframe watching her, his hands pushed casually into the pockets of his expertly tailored dark-charcoal suit trousers, the look on his beautiful face guarded, leaving her with no idea what he was thinking.

'Yes,' she said coolly, drawing the sheet around her in a more decorous fashion. 'Obviously I'm awake.'

A fleeting ripple of amusement crossed his features. 'You don't fool me with that "ice queen" act, kitten. Not after last night.'

Heat rose in her face. 'Is there anything in particular that you want? I need to get dressed.'

They would not be having any discussions about last night, not if she could help it.

Dante's smile faded as quickly as it had come, the look in his eyes becoming oddly intent, and she was conscious of the tension crawling through her.

Whatever it was he was going to say it was obvious he was deadly serious about it.

'I've been thinking,' he said. 'About what to do.'

The tension began to wind like a clock spring, tighter and tighter. She swallowed. 'What to do about what?'

'I told you not to play games with me.' Gold glinted in his eyes. 'You know what I'm talking about.'

Stella tightened her grip on the sheet. 'The baby, you mean?'

'Yes, the baby.' He shifted against the door frame. Today he wore a dark-blue business shirt, open at the throat, exposing smooth, tanned skin and drawing her gaze to the strong, regular beat of his pulse.

Her mouth dried, her skin prickling all over with heat as she remembered what it had felt like to touch him, and how hot his chest had been when she'd laid her head against it listening to the beat of his heart.

'When our family was exiled from Monte Santa Maria,' he went on, as if he hadn't noticed her staring fixedly at his throat, 'we settled in Milan. However, as you know, my mother wasn't happy with our change in circumstances and, after a year or so, she decided to leave to find something better.' Dante's dark eyes gave nothing away. 'She took me with her, dragging me away from my home, away from what I knew and into a life where there was no stability and no protection. She was more interested in wine and violent men than in looking after me.' His tone was expressionless—too expressionless.

Very much against her will, Stella felt that same stir of curiosity that she'd felt the night before, when he'd related the facts of his life with the same dispassion as he did now. Which was wrong. Facts were fine—she knew them already anyway—but she didn't want to know anything beyond them.

He couldn't afford to become a person to her, not in any way.

'That sounds...appalling.' She wasn't sure what else to say. 'But how does this relate to the baby?'

Dante's gaze darkened, an odd intensity creeping into it. 'I've never done the right thing in my life. I've always avoided responsibility. But I cannot avoid it now. And I will not allow my child to be dragged into the sort of life I had.'

She blinked. 'You think that I would?'

'I don't know. Would you?'

Of course. He didn't trust her. As she already knew.

'No,' she said flatly, forcing away the sudden, hot lick of defensive anger, though why she should care what he thought of her one way or another she had no idea. 'I would not.'

'But I have no guarantee of that.' His voice was hard as iron, his gaze uncompromising. 'You have nowhere to go but that gutter I pulled you from yesterday or back to your parents in Monte Santa Maria. And, make no mistake, you will not be returning to either of those places.'

'I can—' she began hotly.

'Which leaves me with only one option.'

A formless, inexplicable dread began to creep through her. She hadn't thought about where she would go after her task was completed, because she hadn't allowed herself to think about it. And she didn't want to think about it now.

'And no doubt you're going to tell me what that is,' she snapped, angry that he was forcing this on her.

'Our child needs somewhere safe and stable to grow up,' he said steadily. 'And two parents to protect him or her.'

The dread pulled tighter. 'So what does that mean?'

'It means that you, kitten, will be staying here with me.' He paused, his gaze becoming even more intense. 'As my wife.'

Shock punched her hard in the gut and her brain blanked. 'Your wife?' she forced out, her voice hoarse. 'You cannot be serious.'

'I have never been more serious in my life.' There was nothing but darkness in his eyes now, every line of his handsome face set and hard. 'We will need to get married and then I intend to buy a family home where we will live together with our child.'

'But I—'

'It will be a marriage in name only,' he went on, ignoring her. 'I won't require anything from you physically. I'll find another outlet for my own needs.'

Stella fell silent, too shocked to speak, her brain struggling to catch up with what he was saying.

A marriage in name only. With the man she was supposed to revenge herself on. Creating a family with him and their child…

Her heart missed a beat, thundering loudly in her head, and for a second something hungry opened up inside her, a void she hadn't realised was there. Then she shoved the hunger away, before it settled too deeply, as another idea took its place.

This could be the opportunity she was looking for, a way to break him, to take the revenge that she needed for Matteo's sake.

He was famous for caring about nothing, except he cared about the baby. And he cared about giving that baby a home, a family. She couldn't bring herself to use their child to hurt him but…she could use herself, couldn't she?

Last night, on the terrace, she'd got a taste of her own power over him, the feminine power that was all hers. And she'd used it. So why couldn't she use it again? Why couldn't she use that to make him care about her the way he cared about the baby? Obviously, he had the ability to feel something, so there was the potential to make him feel something for her.

Make him fall for her, even.

Why would you think he'd fall for the woman who tried to murder him?

He might not. There were no guarantees. But this passion between them was too potent a weapon to ignore, and besides, what other option was there?

She had to try, at least. For Matteo's sake.

'You don't like that idea?' His voice came unexpectedly, almost making her jump.

Looking up, she found him watching her intently from the doorway.

'Wh-what idea?' she asked, struggling to remember what the conversation was about.

'A marriage in name only.'

'Oh, that.' She was pleased her voice sounded so level. 'That seems…fair.'

His gaze narrowed. 'Fair? I thought you might have more to say about it, quite frankly.'

Of course, he'd be expecting her to argue. And not to do so at least a little would seem suspicious.

You did so well with that last night.

Stella ignored the thought. Last night was last night. She could start by being conciliatory now. And, even though a marriage in name only obviously wasn't going to work, coming on too strong too soon would again arouse his suspicions.

'Is there any point saying anything?' she asked after a moment. 'You've obviously made up your mind. I would think I wouldn't get a say, correct?'

Dante's gaze sharpened. 'Do you want a say?'

'I suppose if a wedding is going to happen then I might want some input, plus I would like to help decide where we're going to live.'

He'd gone very still, watching her.

It made her nervous. Made her want to fuss around with the sheet to cover it.

'You're taking this very well,' he commented at last.

'Did you really expect me to fight?' She made herself meet his gaze, to show him she had nothing to hide. 'I don't have anywhere else to go, it's true, which means that staying here with you makes sense for the baby's sake. The marriage part of it seems extreme, however.' If she was going to put up a fight about anything to allay his suspicions, it needed to be that.

'It makes things easier from a legal standpoint and will also give the child some protection from your family.'

A little shock jolted her. 'My family?'

'They sent you to kill me, kitten,' he reminded her gently. 'Which means I do not want them anywhere near my child.'

She blinked. Of course. What was wrong with her? Her parents would no doubt have a reaction to her pregnancy and she knew already that it wouldn't be good. Her father would be appalled. He'd see it as an example of her weakness, her terrible flaw.

'I see,' she said blankly. She should probably protest that their child had nothing to fear from the Montefiores, but she couldn't say for certain that it didn't. Her father would do anything if he thought it would better their family.

'I'm sure you do.' Dante eyed her a second longer, then pushed himself away from the doorframe and straightened. 'You'll no doubt have some questions at some point. In the meantime, I'll be arranging a doctor's appointment for you.'

A doctor's appointment. A family home. Marriage…

The hungry black void inside her ached, sending a current of longing spiralling through her bloodstream. But she dismissed it.

All those things weren't going to happen. Because she was going to make Dante Cardinali fall for her. Care for her. And maybe let him think that she cared for him too. Then she would take all that away.

Perhaps starting that slowly was a mistake. Perhaps she should start making him fall for her sooner rather than later. Use the chemistry between them while it was still strong. Say…tonight, for example.

Dante's dark eyes scanned her face. 'You have something to say?'

'No.' Stella met his gaze, cold and hard and certain. 'Nothing.'

Yes, tonight. She'd start tonight.

CHAPTER SEVEN

Dante sat back on the big, white linen-covered couch and frowned at the laptop on the coffee table in front of him. He'd called one of his assistants that morning to send through a list of possible family properties, and he'd spent most of the day going through that list, viewing each one online to see whether any were worth visiting. There were a couple of likely looking candidates and he'd already got his assistant to make the arrangements for a viewing time.

He probably should have got Stella's thoughts on them but, now he'd decided what he wanted to do about the situation he'd found himself in, he wanted to move fast. With no half-measures either.

If he was going to claim his child and create the family he'd never had, then he was going to go all the way. He would marry Stella and buy a house where they would all live together as a family.

After all, it had worked for Enzo, so why wouldn't it work for him?

That way he could make sure his child had the best start in life, unlike himself.

He had thought Stella would baulk at the idea but, as he wasn't going to be moved on the decision, he'd decided to make it more palatable and less complicated by making it a marriage in name only. They didn't love each other and, besides, sex wasn't something he needed from her specifically; he could find physical satisfaction elsewhere.

She seemed in agreement, which in retrospect was odd, as challenging him appeared to be what she liked to do best. But he decided not to allow himself to think too deeply about it. Her agreement was all he required and she'd given it to him.

Of course, it had been a bit difficult to think about anything while she'd been sitting there draped in nothing but a sheet, looking all warm, sleepy and sexy.

Dante scowled at the laptop screen as his groin hardened, memories of the night before making him catch his breath.

Marriage in name only? Are you sure?

He forced the desire away. Of course he was sure. He could get sex anywhere. It didn't have to be with her. And certainly not, given how intense the sex had been between them. Because for this arrangement to work the focus had to be on the child, not each other. He didn't want…complications.

And if she wanted to get sex from somewhere else?

Then she could. As long as she was discreet, what did it matter to him?

Yet the thought made his jaw harden and tension coil inside him, the possessiveness he'd felt about her the night before returning and sinking sharp claws into him. And for some reason he couldn't stop thinking about the way she'd reached for his hand, her fingers holding onto him, not wanting him to leave. Almost as if she'd needed him…

His chest constricted, an insistence pulling at him, and he had the horrible suspicion that in fact it would matter to him if she got sex from somewhere else. And that he would *not* like it one little bit.

There came a soft sound from one end of the room and

he lifted his head sharply to find Stella standing in the doorway to the living area.

She had one of the plush, white towelling hotel robes wrapped around her slight figure, her golden hair cascading in a straight, gleaming fall of gold over her shoulders, and there was a strangely hesitant look on her lovely face.

He made a mental note to get one of his assistants to look into getting some clothes for her, as she had nothing but the jeans and ripped T-shirt that she'd been wearing when he'd taken her from the apartment.

Her gaze met his, something he didn't recognise moving in the depths of her blue eyes. A kind of agitation.

He hadn't seen her since that morning, having let her have some space to process what he'd told her while he'd got on with viewing houses and making arrangements. But maybe that had been a mistake. Was she having second thoughts?

'Good evening, kitten.' He pushed the laptop closed and gave her his full attention, studying her face. 'Is there something wrong?'

'No, not at all. I just…wondered what was happening for dinner.' Her gaze flickered away from his before coming back again, as if she didn't want to hold it for long.

How odd.

'I see.' He put his hands on the couch in preparation for rising to his feet and going over to her. 'Then perhaps—'

'Oh no, don't get up,' she interrupted hurriedly, taking a few quick steps toward him. 'Is that the menu I see? I'll come and sit next to you.'

He stared at her in surprise as she closed the distance between them, sidling around the coffee table and sitting down beside him. She looked meaningfully at the menu sitting on top of the coffee table. 'Can I…have a look at that, please?'

She was very close, her thigh brushing his, and he was very aware that the white robe gaped at the neck, giving him a glimpse of bare, pink skin.

Underneath, she appeared to be naked.

Desire welled up inside him, thick and hot and demanding, and he suddenly wanted to pull the tie at her waist and uncover all those silky curves, bare her to his touch. She smelled of the shower gel he'd used the night before, a fresh scent, along with something feminine and musky that made his mouth water.

You really think you can do a marriage in name only?

Dio, he hadn't thought this would be difficult. He'd thought that perhaps, after the night before, the desire would have faded. And it should have. So why had the simple act of her sitting close and wearing nothing but a robe got him so hard?

It shouldn't. He'd made a decision about his child. And that was more important than sex. He didn't need to sleep with her again so he wouldn't.

It was that simple.

Yet her blue gaze was very wide, looking up into his, and her lips were slightly parted in the most gorgeous, sexy little pout. The look on her face reminded him of that night in Monte Carlo, when she'd tried her hardest to seduce him.

Before he'd ended up drugged and handcuffed to the bed.

A premonition gripped him.

Her hand was in the pocket of her robe and he could see the tension in her arm. In fact, now that he looked, there was tension in her whole posture. Her entire body was vibrating with it and in the depths of her silver-blue eyes, behind the glow of desire, was that strange agitation again.

Except he knew what it was now.

Fear.

The tight thing in his chest clenched even tighter, though

it wasn't with anger, not this time. 'Kitten,' he said quietly, staying quite still. 'I already told you. You're not going to kill me. You didn't do it back in Monte Carlo and you're not going to do it now.'

Stella's gaze flared silver with shock. 'What? I don't know—'

He didn't let her finish, instead reaching for the hand she had jammed into her pocket. She resisted, but he was stronger than she was, drawing her hand out despite how she pulled against him.

There was nothing in it. No knife. No gun.

She wasn't here to hurt him.

A sudden and intense relief gripped him, not for himself but for her. For the path that she clearly *hadn't* chosen. Because, while he'd always been certain that she'd never go through with hurting him, he hadn't been sure she wouldn't make another attempt.

There was pain in her eyes and she was breathing fast. 'You thought I was coming to kill you, didn't you?'

'I thought you might try.' He held her gaze so she could see the truth in his eyes. 'But I never thought you'd go through with it. I still don't.'

The narrow wrist he was holding began to tremble, but she didn't look away. 'So what would you have done if I'd actually had a knife?'

'Nothing.' He watched the fierce currents of her emotions shift over her delicate features. 'Because you wouldn't have done anything.'

'You don't know that.' Her voice was husky and threaded through with a very real pain. 'You expected that I would h-hurt you.'

He shouldn't care about this. He shouldn't care about her. Yet for some reason his assumption that she was here to make another attempt on his life had hurt her and he found he cared about that very much indeed.

You know she's not capable of it. But does she?

Dante stared into her eyes, noting the pain she couldn't quite hide and, beneath that, the fear.

It was clear that she'd come to him intending to do something but, as she didn't have a weapon, it wasn't to hurt him.

Except she was still afraid.

Was that because she thought she might? That she was afraid she *would have* gone through with it if she'd had a weapon?

He didn't like that thought. He didn't like that she was afraid, especially when she had no reason to be.

And there was only one way to prove it.

He let go her wrist, got up from the couch and went over to the large sideboard that stood against one wall, pulling open one of the drawers.

'Dante?' Stella sounded bewildered.

He didn't answer. Instead he picked up the long, sharp antique letter opener from the drawer and turned, coming back over to the couch with it.

She watched him, her quickened breathing audible in the quiet of the room, her gaze flaring as she saw what he was carrying. 'What are you doing?' she asked, her voice edged with alarm.

He ignored her. Sitting down next to her, he grabbed her wrist before she could move and slapped the letter opener into her palm. Then he curled her fingers around the handle.

Her gaze darkened as it met his and he could see fear stark in the depths. And his chest tightened, a deep sadness moving through him. Because the fact that she was afraid told its own story.

'Please,' she whispered. 'Don't…'

Without taking his gaze from hers, Dante slowly undid

the buttons of his shirt and drew aside the fabric. Then he took her hand in his, guiding the point of the letter opener to his bare chest. 'My heart is here, kitten.'

Her breathing was fast in the silence of the room, the expression on her face stricken. The light flashed off the sharp blade of the letter opener as her hand shook. 'Why are you doing this?'

Reaching out, he stroked the silky, soft skin of her jaw. 'Because you're afraid. And I want to know why.'

She shuddered as he touched her, glancing down at the letter opener in her shaking hand. 'You shouldn't...trust me with this.'

'Do you want to tell me why not?'

'I might...hurt you.'

'No, you won't.' Gently, he followed the line of her jaw with his fingertips, using his touch to soothe her. 'You didn't back in Monte Carlo and you're not going to now. I wouldn't have given you a weapon if I thought you were even remotely capable.'

'But I was going to. That's what I came here to do now. Hurt you, I mean.'

His thumb touched her full lower lip very gently. 'How, kitten?'

A flush of colour flowed over her skin. 'I was going to seduce you. I was going to make you care for me, fall in love with me. And then I was going to leave.'

Part of him wanted to smile at the sheer naivety of that idea, but that would be unnecessarily cruel, and he wasn't a cruel man. And certainly not to a woman sitting there holding a blade to his heart, her eyes full of tears.

'That isn't possible,' he said. 'You can't make me do anything. And I'm famous for not caring about anyone. But what I am curious about is why you're so very determined to go through with this.'

'My brother—'

'No, I know about your family and why they wanted me dead. What I'm asking is why *you're* so set on taking any kind of revenge you can. Especially when it's obvious you don't actually want to.'

'I have to.' She was looking up at him, her expression full of that strange desperation. As if she was drowning and she was looking to him to save her. 'You don't understand.'

'Try me.'

'It's my fault.' She took a shaken breath. 'It's my fault Matteo died. I betrayed him. And so I owe it to my family and to his memory to go through with this. To be strong for once in my life and not...' She stopped abruptly, her voice cracking.

The tightness in Dante's chest constricted even further. 'Not what?' He cupped her cheek, her skin warm against his palm, encouraging her to go on.

Her throat convulsed as she swallowed. 'Weak.'

'Weak?' he echoed, frowning. 'Why would you think that?'

Her gaze glittered, more pain glowing in the depths. 'I told Papa I was strong enough to do this, that he shouldn't hire someone because it should be one of the family. It should be me, since I got Matteo captured. I promised him I wouldn't let him down again, but...'

The point of the letter opener moved and Dante felt the slightest nick of pain.

A horrified look flickered over Stella's face and she made a soft noise of distress, dropping the letter opener onto the floor as if it had burned her.

He looked down to see blood welling from the tiny cut she'd given him. 'It's just a scratch,' he said easily, ignoring the cut and reaching out to her.

But she jerked away, trembling all over. 'I can't do it,'

she said hoarsely. 'I thought I could. But I can't. I can't do *any* of it.'

Dante caught her slender fingers in his. They were icy cold. 'Hush, kitten. Be still. It's okay.'

But she only looked at him, something naked and terribly vulnerable in her eyes. 'I should have had the strength to go through with it and I didn't. Papa was right. All along he was right. I'm weak, Dante. I'm nothing but flawed.'

STELLA FELT COLD all over, as if she would never be warm again, and she was certain it was only Dante's large, warm hands holding hers that was keeping her from freezing to death right where she sat.

She knew she should pull away, try to recover what she could of yet another failure, but that void in her soul yawned wide and she couldn't seem to move.

It was true. It was all true. She was as weak as she'd always feared. As flawed as her father had always told her she was. She'd tried to be strong, to prove that she was equal to the task she'd taken on, to redeem her brother and assuage her guilt at her part in his capture. But, just as she hadn't been able to pull that trigger, she hadn't been able to cold-bloodedly seduce him either.

Instead she'd ended up telling him everything.

And all because she hadn't been able to stand the fact that he'd thought she was carrying a weapon and intended to hurt him with it.

That he'd been sure she'd never use it hadn't mattered.

He'd really thought she'd come to take his life again and there had been a very deep part of her that had found that terrifying. Because she couldn't blame him for thinking that. After all, she'd been the one to volunteer to kill him, no one else. Who was to say that if the opportunity presented itself she wouldn't do it?

Then he'd given her that opportunity. He'd held that blade to his own chest and invited her to do it, all the while stroking her gently, his dark eyes full of a terrible understanding that had undermined her in a way she'd never expected.

And all she'd been able to think about as she'd looked up into his beautiful face was him taking care of her the night before—washing her body and her hair so gently before tucking her into bed. Staying with her when she'd asked, wrapping her up in his powerful arms and holding her against his chest.

She never should have let him get under her skin the way she had, let the way he touched her and the things he'd said about his life matter to her. But somehow it had happened. And somehow he'd become more than the target he was supposed to be, more than the selfish playboy she'd only read about.

More than the vehicle of her own redemption.

He'd become a man. An actual person.

And she couldn't do it. Just as she hadn't been able to take his life back in that hotel room, she hadn't been able to stand the thought of hurting him at all.

Especially not when all her reasons for doing so were selfish ones.

Dante's hands tightened on hers. 'Not hurting a man doesn't make you weak,' he said forcefully. 'Who told you that nonsense?'

She couldn't tear her gaze away from the blood welling up on his skin where she'd nicked him. It made her feel sick, knowing she'd hurt him, even if it had been accidental.

Yet more evidence of her flaw.

'You're bleeding.' She tried to tug her hands from his, suddenly feeling frantic. 'I need to clean it. You might need stitches.'

His grip on her tightened, the look in his dark eyes intensifying. 'I'm fine. What I want to know is why you think you're weak.'

But there was a sick feeling in her gut, her own heart beating hard in her chest like a bird trying to escape a cage, and she barely heard him. 'Please. The knife was sharp. It could have gone deep and then...'

Dante made an impatient sound. He let her go, shrugged out of his shirt, balled up the cotton in one hand then negligently wiped the blood away with it. The tiny cut began to clot almost instantly.

'There,' he said. 'Satisfied?'

But Stella couldn't stop from reaching out and putting one trembling hand on his hard chest near the cut, wanting to feel for herself that he was still warm. Still breathing. That his heart was still beating the way it should.

And it was. And he wasn't just warm, he was hot. Like a furnace. And there was so much strength beneath all that smooth, bronzed skin. So much power. So much intense, vibrant life.

How had she *ever* thought she could take that from him? Or that she could enact such a stupid, ridiculous substitute plan as making him fall in love with her?

She'd been naïve. So sure that she was as hard and as cold as she'd needed to be. Yet in the end all she'd been was selfish, thinking only of her own need for redemption.

She hadn't even thought about her baby.

Her eyes prickled, full of sudden tears, and she spread her palm out, pressing it hard against him, as if she could absorb that strength, take it for herself. As if the strength in him could heal the flaw in her, make her feel less selfish, less weak, less broken.

'Kitten,' he murmured. 'Talk to me.'

But she didn't want to talk, not right now, so she shook

her head and bent, very gently kissing the cut she'd made instead. His skin burned against her lips, making her shiver, and she pressed her mouth to an unmarked part of his chest, wanting to taste him. Salty and hot and gloriously alive.

He went very still and then she felt his hand in her hair, stroking gently. 'I'm not sure that's a good idea.'

But she didn't want to be soothed or gentled. And she didn't want to be refused. 'Please,' she murmured hoarsely against his skin, desperation coiling inside her. 'I need you.'

His fingers tightened in her hair. 'Kitten…'

She ignored him, making her way up his chest to his throat, kissing him, tasting the powerful beat of his pulse. But it wasn't enough. She wanted more. She wanted his bare skin against hers, his heat melting the cold places inside herself, the places that had frozen the day her brother had been dragged away.

Dante's grip on her hair was too powerful to resist as he gently tugged her head up, the velvet darkness of his gaze meeting hers.

'Please, Dante.' She couldn't hide the desperation and didn't bother. 'I need this. I need *you*.'

And something in his expression shifted, gold glimmering in the inky depths of his eyes.

He didn't speak, yet her breath caught all the same as his grip on her changed and he drew her into his lap, urging her thighs on either side of his lean hips. Then he let go her hair, his hands at the tie of her robe, pulling it open, slipping it from her shoulders and off, baring her.

She reached for him as the fabric fell away, frantic for the touch of his skin on hers, and he responded, gathering her to him, and she gasped at the heat of his body. It was a glory, like the first touch of sun on a land ravaged by winter, and she arched against him, pressing the softness of her breasts to the hardness of his chest.

He made a rough sound, then his hands were on her and he was taking control, bringing them both down on the couch and turning so she was under him, and she moaned at the pleasure that stretched out inside her in response, loving his power and his heat. At how safe and protected she felt.

She lifted her hands and scratched them down his chest, feeling each hard, cut muscle, but then his mouth was on hers and his hips were between her thighs, and he was shoving his trousers down, getting rid of the fabric between them.

She gripped his shoulders, kissing him back feverishly, desperate and aching, need building higher and higher. But his kiss in return was slow and sweet, his hands moving on her gently, stroking, soothing her until she felt unexpected tears pricking the backs of her eyes.

Then his hands were beneath her, lifting her hips, and he was sliding into her, slow and deep, making her moan against his mouth. And he stopped there, deep inside, stroking her, his kisses becoming small nips and gentle licks, easing a part of her she hadn't realised was drawn so tight.

Then he began to move, slowly and carefully, as if she was precious. Her throat closed up and, no matter how hard she blinked, she couldn't make the tears go away. And she couldn't stop them as they slid down her cheeks.

She didn't want to cry, not in front of him. Not while he was deep inside her, the evidence of his strength and power outlined in every muscle, while she was weak and soft and so very broken.

But he didn't say a word, only kissed away the tears and held her tight beneath him, moving in a gentle rhythm that had her gasping his name as the pleasure began to build.

And then she wasn't crying any more, only staring up into his eyes, watching the gold bleed through the darkness until there was no darkness at all, only brilliant light.

Light inside her too, blinding her, a heat so intense it was going to burn her right here on the couch. And she wanted to burn. She wanted to blaze until there was nothing left of her.

She called his name as the fire became too bright to contain, too intense, pleasure flaming out of control. And he held her, kept her safe as she burned to ashes in his arms, before following her into the blaze himself.

Afterwards Stella didn't want to open her eyes. She wanted to lie for ever under Dante's powerful body and never move again. But she could feel him shifting as he drew out of her, the brush of his bare skin on hers making her shiver.

Was he leaving her here? She didn't think she could bear it if he did.

'You should call the police,' she said, trying for bravado. 'Get them to take me into custody. I did try to kill you a month ago, after all.'

'Don't be ridiculous,' Dante said. 'You're not going anywhere.' He sat up then slid his arms around her, gathering her into his lap so she was leaning against his chest, her head on his shoulder.

She didn't have the energy to make a fuss, so she didn't, content to sit there against his warmth, the afterglow of the orgasm, not to mention the aftermath of her own emotional breakdown, making her feel sleepy.

'Now.' Dante's voice was very firm. 'What you are going to do is talk to me. I want to know why you think your brother's death is your fault.'

Stella swallowed. She didn't want to talk about it. Then again, she did owe him some kind of explanation. 'It's a long story.'

Dante settled them both back against the couch. 'I have time and nowhere to be.'

His bare skin under her cheek was warm, his heartbeat strong and steady in her ear. It calmed her.

'My brother died in prison,' she said after a moment. 'He was stabbed in a brawl a few years after he was imprisoned.'

'Yes. I know. It read about it in your file.'

'What you don't know is that it was my fault he was in prison in the first place.'

'Oh? And why is that?'

It was painful to talk about this but she forced the words out. 'Papa and Matteo were plotting to get your father back his throne and the police got wind of it. Somehow Papa knew before they came and he and Matteo managed to get away. Only Mama and I were home and they…interrogated her.'

A shiver moved through her and she concentrated on the sound of Dante's heartbeat rather than the memory of her mother's sobs. 'She was fragile and the police weren't very nice. They made her cry. I was scared for her. Scared that they'd hurt her. Papa told me not to give the police anything, but I…couldn't be quiet. I'd seen Matteo go down to the caves near the beach near our house, so I…told them where he'd gone. So they would leave my mother alone.'

'Of course you did,' Dante said quietly. 'You wanted to protect her.'

He made it sound so reasonable, almost noble, when it was anything but.

'No.' Her voice had gone scratchy. 'It was wrong. Papa told me that I couldn't say a word to the police. He made me promise. He told me that Matteo was the most important person in our family and that he had to be protected. But…they were hurting my mother. And I was scared. And I thought that Matteo would get away—' She stopped abruptly, not wanting to voice it.

'But?' Dante asked after a moment.

The flaw inside her felt suddenly stark and jagged. 'I wanted them to love me. I wanted them to protect me. But they never did. They loved him more. And there was a part of me that wanted him...'

'Gone,' Dante finished with unaccustomed gentleness. 'Part of you wanted him gone.'

She closed her eyes again, unable to bear it, the guilt crushing. 'They took him and Papa was so angry with me. He knew why I'd betrayed my own brother—of course he knew. He told me I was weak, that if I'd truly wanted his love I would have done my duty to my family and not said a word.' Her throat closed and she had to force the rest of it out. 'And then Matteo died and Papa blamed me. He couldn't take it out on me, of course, so when he decided he'd take it out on the Cardinalis I volunteered to do the job.'

Dante reached for her discarded white robe, drawing it around her shoulders. 'Because you wanted to redeem yourself?'

'Yes. And because I wanted to prove to Papa that I was strong.' She tried to blink away the tears, shivering under the robe even though it was warm and Dante's bare chest even warmer. 'That I was worthy of his love.' A tear slid down her cheek. 'It's a flaw in me, Dante. And it caused my brother's death.'

But Dante's fingers were beneath her chin, tilting her head back, and she had no choice but to meet his dark eyes. There was something fierce and utterly sure in them. 'You didn't cause your brother's death, Stella Montefiore. It was his choice to plot against the government, not yours. The police wouldn't even have been after him if he hadn't and you wouldn't have been in that situation.'

'But—'

'And, as for wanting your father's love, that isn't a weakness or a flaw. That's a basic human necessity.' Something in his gaze shifted. 'My mother preferred the bottle to me, no matter how many times I tried to wean her away from it, so I understand what it's like to want something from someone who's never going to give it.'

She took a little breath. 'You didn't try to kill anyone for it, though.'

'No, I simply walked away.' There was a bitter note in his voice. 'And she died anyway.'

Stella stared at him, distracted for a second. 'What happened?'

But he shook his head. 'We're not talking about me. We're talking about you. And you're not flawed, Stella. You're not weak. It takes strength to push through with something you know is wrong, just as it takes strength *not* to do it too.'

'What do you mean?'

'I mean, you were very determined to carry out some kind of revenge.'

'And I couldn't.'

'No, you couldn't. But that's not a weakness. That was your strength. The strength to hold back when everything in you is telling you to do it.'

She wasn't sure he was right about that. But in this moment she couldn't find it in herself to argue. His dark eyes were very certain and there was a deep part of her that craved that certainty.

'You always knew I wouldn't,' she said, staring up him. 'Even back in Monte Carlo. Why?'

'I told you. I saw your soul that night. And it's not the soul of a killer.' His mouth curved very slightly. 'It's the soul of a lover.'

She couldn't stop looking at that mouth. Couldn't stop feeling the heat of the hard-muscled body beneath hers and the ache building between her thighs. An ache that was far more interesting to explore than talking. 'When you said that ours would be a marriage in name only…'

Dante's beautiful mouth curved more. 'Yes? What about it?'

She swallowed. 'Does that start now?'

'Well, seeing as how we're not married yet, no, it doesn't.'

'Good.' Stella reached up and slid her fingers into his thick, dark hair. 'Because you know what I really want?'

Gold flamed bright in his dark eyes. 'Tell me, kitten.'

'You,' she said thickly. 'I want you.'

And she drew his mouth down on hers.

CHAPTER EIGHT

Dante sat in the waiting room of the high-end clinic he'd taken Stella to for her first doctor's appointment. The doctor had wanted a few minutes with Stella alone, which had made Dante want to protest for no good reason that he could see. But he'd held his peace and pretended he was absolutely fine with it.

He was not absolutely fine with it.

Restlessness coiled inside him, a feral sort of feeling that had grown deeper in the past couple of days. Oddly enough, ever since that incident with the letter opener.

He tried to tell himself it had nothing to do with how Stella had told him of her fears then reached for him as if he'd been the air she needed to breathe. Nothing to do with that at all.

Yes, he was continuing to sleep with her, but that was because she wanted it too, and why not? Work out this chemistry now, while they had a chance, because after the wedding that would be it.

Are you sure you want that?

Dante growled under his breath and shoved the thought away. He shouldn't be concentrating on these ridiculous feelings anyway. What he should be concentrating on was the conversation they'd had about where they potentially might want to live.

By mutual unspoken agreement, they'd steered clear of personal subjects, keeping any discussions they did have firmly about the baby.

They'd agreed that since the child would be Italian they would need to live in Italy, but they'd had a minor argument about where. Stella had wanted a house in the countryside, while he'd preferred the city.

He'd shown her the list his assistant had given him and they'd eventually compromised by settling on a couple of places to view—one a *palazzo* uncomfortably near his brother's in Milan and a penthouse in Milan itself.

Dante thought he'd probably end up purchasing both anyway—he was going to need a place to himself, after all, especially to bring any potential lovers he might want to spend the night with—but he didn't want to have that discussion with Stella just yet.

The thought of sleeping with other women left him feeling unenthused and he wasn't sure what to do about it. He'd always planned to stick to his insistence that once they were married they would stop sleeping together, but celibacy wasn't an option for him either.

You could just keep on having sex with your wife.

His whole body tightened at that idea, yet there was something in him that also shied away from it. The sex was good—better than good, truth be told—but there was an intensity to it that made him uneasy.

Maybe because she's starting to matter to you?

Dante shifted in his seat then got up, unable to sit still any more, pacing around the waiting room.

Where the hell was that damn doctor?

His phone vibrated, thankfully distracting him from his thoughts. However, the thankful feelings drained away almost immediately when he saw a text from Enzo pop up on his screen:

Matilda told me you had a conversation with her about pregnancy. What's going on?

Dante sighed. *Dio*, what was he going to tell his brother? Enzo would no doubt find it extremely amusing that his playboy brother's past had finally caught up to him. Except that Enzo had no idea that the woman expecting Dante's baby had tried to kill him and was an enemy of the Cardinalis. And, if his brother ever found out, he'd probably have an aneurysm.

Which meant that until he had Stella safely as his wife Dante was better off not telling him anything at all.

He stared at his phone for a second then quickly typed in a response:

The usual private life drama. You don't want to know.

It's not a problem now, anyway.

That should be enough for Enzo not to enquire further. He usually found Dante's preoccupation with the opposite sex quite dull.

Enzo, however, clearly had other thoughts.

It's not that 'romantic entanglement' is it?

Damn. Why couldn't his brother be uninterested, like he normally was?

Do you really want me to go into laborious detail? Dante texted back. *Or would you rather I work on that PR plan for the new office?*

There was a brief pause and then Enzo finally texted back:

Good point. Carry on.

It should have satisfied Dante that his brother—surprisingly for Enzo—had dropped the subject. But it didn't. It was almost as though Dante actually wanted to talk to Enzo about things child-related, which a couple of weeks ago Dante would have died rather than suffer through.

Things have changed.

Yes. As much as he wanted them not to, they had.

He was going to be a father and he wanted a different life for his child from the one he'd had. A life where his child would be safe, cared for and protected.

And loved.

A hot and painful feeling lanced through him, as though he'd been stabbed.

'You can come in now, Mr Cardinali.'

Dante ignored the sensation, grateful for the doctor's interruption.

Inside the doctor's office, Stella was lying on a special padded bed, dressed in a loose white hospital gown. She looked small and delicate and very pale, her golden hair in a cloud around her head. There was uncertainty in her blue eyes and, when they met his, he thought he saw a small flicker of fear that she quickly masked.

Understandable that she would be afraid. He wasn't exactly feeling calm himself, not when they were going to be getting the first glimpse of the child they'd created together and had no idea what to expect.

But he'd thought, after that night when she'd confessed to him and let him hold her as she'd cried, that she'd trust him at least a little with her fears, not try to hide them. Because she was going to have to trust him at some point, wasn't she?

He wanted her to. They were in this together, after all, and if they were going to be parents they had to trust one another. At least, they were if they were going to give their baby a better childhood than either of them had had.

Crossing the room to where she lay, he reached for her hand, ignoring the sudden surprised look that crossed her face as he did so.

Her fingers were cold so he enfolded them into his palm to warm them up.

Emotions he couldn't read flickered through her eyes and he could feel a degree of tension in her hand, though she didn't pull it away from his.

'You don't need to be scared,' he murmured when she didn't say anything.

'I'm not.' But she wouldn't quite meet his gaze.

'Don't try to hide it from me, kitten. You know I can see that you are.'

Colour stole through her pale cheeks. She kept her gaze averted, watching the doctor bustling around, remaining silent.

But her hand stayed enfolded in his, making the tight feeling in his chest deepen.

'Our baby will be fine,' he went on softly. 'I have you, kitten.'

She stared fixedly at the doctor, doing a good impression of ignoring him entirely. Then her fingers tightened around his, as if she found his presence reassuring, and the protective instinct inside him wound deep into his bones, making him ache.

She thought she was weak, yet she wasn't. She was strong. Yet even so, right now, right here, whether she acknowledged it or not, she needed him.

No one had needed him in a very long time, if anyone had ever needed him at all.

Mama certainly didn't, no matter what she said.

But now was not the time to be thinking of his mother, so he ignored the thought, keeping hold of Stella's hand as the doctor sat down beside the bed and prepared her for the scan.

The doctor talked soothingly about how everything was looking fine and there was no need for concern, and Dante wanted to tell her that he was not concerned at all, but the moment she put the wand on Stella's stomach his throat closed.

Then there was silence as the doctor shifted the wand around, all of them looking at the tiny screen on the ultrasound machine.

'Ah,' the doctor said at last, smiling. 'There is your baby.'

The sound of a heartbeat, fast and regular, filled the small room, and Dante found himself staring into the impossible silvery blue of Stella's eyes. She was looking straight at him this time, everything he'd been thinking himself reflected back in her gaze.

No, they hadn't looked for this. Hadn't wanted it. But it had happened, and now both of them would do anything and everything for the life they'd created between them.

'Give us a moment please, doctor,' Dante ordered, not letting go of Stella's hand or looking away from her.

'Of course.' The doctor rose to her feet. 'Take all the time you need.'

The door closed softly after her and then there was a long moment of silence as he and Stella stared at each other, the baby's heartbeat still echoing in Dante's head, Stella's small hand completely enfolded in his.

'I've decided something,' she said after a moment. 'If our child is a boy, I want him to be called Matteo. For my brother.' There was pain in her eyes, but a proud, strong determination was there too. 'Maybe his death wasn't my fault, yet I'd like to remember him all the same.'

Dante felt something in his chest shift, like sand under his feet, making him feel off-balance in some strange way. He couldn't tear his eyes away from her, feeling the words she'd said inexplicably resonating inside him. 'Yes,' he heard himself say. 'Matteo Cardinali. It has a good ring to it. And, if it's a girl, we can name her for your mother, perhaps?

Her eyes glittered and her grip on his hand tightened.

'What about you? Your family? Don't you have anyone you want to remember?'

His family. His terrible, dysfunctional family.

No, he had no one he wanted to remember, no one female anyway. There was only Sofia, his mother. His lovely, manipulative mother.

Why not her, though? It was a long time ago. You mourned her and then you moved on.

Naturally he'd moved on. But he did not want that tiny life to have her name, to be saddled with the weight of all that history.

Nothing to do with how angry you are at her?

No, he wasn't angry. Not any more. He'd washed his hands of her years ago and when she'd died…well…he'd grieved. But she was the one who'd chosen the path that she'd ended up taking. He'd tried to change her mind, to get her to stop drinking, stop seeing Roberto, but she'd ignored him. And then, on the eve of his sixteenth birthday, she'd told him that if he didn't like it he could leave.

So he had, thinking she'd come after him eventually. That she'd contact him, at least. That she wouldn't just… let him go.

Except that was exactly what she'd done. And the next time he'd seen her she'd been in hospital with a head injury that she'd never woken up from.

She didn't care about you. You've always known that.

The thick, hot anger he'd always tried to deny seemed to come out of nowhere, burning inside him like a flow of lava, but as always he forced it down, pretended that it didn't exist. Because anger meant that he cared, and he didn't. Not in the slightest.

If you truly didn't care, then it doesn't matter what you call your child.

'Dante?' Stella was sitting up now and he was conscious

that she was holding him tightly, as if he was the one who needed reassurance.

Ridiculous. He was fine.

'There's no one in my family I want to remember. In fact, I would rather our child *not* have a name associated with that kind of history.' Gently but firmly he loosened her hold and rose to his feet because he wasn't going to have this discussion, not now. 'Get dressed. Time we went back to the hotel. I have a few properties I want to show you.' Then, without waiting for a response, he strode to the door and went through it.

STELLA GOT OUT of the bath that Dante had run for her, drying herself off before pulling on the soft, blue silk robe he'd bought for her a couple of days ago and belting it tightly at the waist. Then she moved over to the doorway and went out into the living area of the suite.

Dante was sitting at the stone table on the terrace, concentrating fiercely on whatever was on the screen of his laptop. He'd been like that all afternoon since they'd returned from the doctor's office—working, apparently.

She'd found it all a bit overwhelming, the reality of seeing their baby's heartbeat on the ultrasound screen still resonating inside her, along with all the emotions that brought with it. Emotions she'd been trying very hard to deny since she'd first discovered her pregnancy, using her mission as an excuse not to think about it.

But, as she'd well and truly let go of that mission, she had no excuses now.

This was happening. She would be a mother.

It terrified her. She had no idea how she was going to do this, none at all, especially when her own parents hadn't exactly set her a good example. How did a woman who'd been determined to kill a man transform into a good mother?

How could she do the right thing for a child when she'd been so set on doing the wrong thing for so long?

All she knew was that the moment Dante's dark eyes had found hers in the doctor's office she hadn't felt alone. She'd tried to hide how uncertain and scared she was, tried to hold onto the vestiges of her hard armour, but he'd seemed to see her fears anyway. Then he'd taken her hand, wrapping hers in his big, warm palm, and she'd felt that strength of his flow into her and all her fear and uncertainty had simply melted away. Almost as if nothing bad would happen now that he was here.

Stella leaned against the doorframe, studying the man on the terrace. He was in a plain white business shirt and dark-blue suit trousers, the sleeves of his shirt rolled up to expose the strong bones of his wrists and the long line of his muscled forearms. He had his elbows on the table, a line between his straight dark brows as he concentrated.

She was going to have to contemplate all the other bits and pieces of reality that she'd been avoiding, such as the fact that he intended to marry her and buy a house for them to live in together as a family.

An ache collected in her chest.

The past few days he'd been full of plans, showing her potential houses and talking about the kind of life they would build for their child together. She hadn't argued with any of it. Mainly because she had nowhere else to go.

She couldn't go back to Monte Santa Maria, not when her father was still expecting her to return triumphantly, the honour of the Montefiores safely intact.

He'd texted her requesting an update and she'd told him everything was going according to plan. She couldn't tell him the truth, not when she knew he'd only send someone else after Dante to do what she wasn't able to.

He'd discover that she had no intention of following

through with his revenge plans eventually, of course, but she wanted to put that discovery off for as long as possible. To give her time to think about how to handle it.

Her only alternative to Dante's plan would be to insist on going her own way, find her own apartment and get a job, a task made even more difficult by the fact that her only work experience to date was waitressing. And then what would she do when her father found out she hadn't completed the task he'd set for her? And, worse, that she'd had Dante's child? He wouldn't welcome his grandchild with open arms, that was for sure.

No, marrying the billionaire and living in the house he'd bought for them, while he ensured their child got the very best of everything and kept them safe, was obviously going to be the best route forward.

The ache in her chest intensified, though she didn't really understand why, not when this outcome was the best for all of them.

You know why. He'll take care of you, but nothing more.

But she didn't want anything more, did she? Yet she could feel the pieces of that jagged flaw shifting around in her chest, the need for someone to put their arms around her, tell her that she was loved, still raw inside her.

Ah, but it didn't matter what she wanted. She was done with being selfish. The only thing that mattered was that their child would have the best start in life and right now that start was with Dante.

She him watched as he worked for a second longer, wondering at the journey he'd made in her head from being a target, to a media caricature, to a man. A warm, protective man. And yet somehow he'd still remained a mystery.

A mystery she wanted to know more about.

Did he really have no one from his family he wanted to remember? She hadn't asked him about his mother's name for their child, because he'd sounded so angry every time he'd talked about her. But there had to be someone else, surely?

His past was clearly a painful story, but he knew her guilty secret. About her brother's death and her role in it. So shouldn't she know at least a little about his? He would be her husband. They would be living together and bringing up their child. Shouldn't she know something of his family history?

Stella stepped out onto the terrace.

'How was your bath?' Dante asked, not looking up.

'Very nice. Thank you for running it for me.'

'No problem. By the way, I've organised a viewing of the *palazzo* in Milan for tomorrow. I'll get one of the helicopters to take us.'

'Okay.' She came over and leaned against the edge of the table and looked down. His face was set as he stared at the screen, the neck of his shirt open, and he wore no tie.

He was so incredibly attractive, so overwhelmingly beautiful.

Her mouth watered and she very much wanted to bend and kiss his throat, taste his skin.

How are you going to cope with this sexless marriage he's insisting on?

The thought arrowed through her, unexpectedly painful. Another thing she hadn't thought about because she'd assumed it wasn't going to happen. But it was going to happen. Regardless of how many nights she'd spent in his bed, he'd continue to insist that once they were married it would stop. That he wouldn't demand anything further from her physically and that he would find his satisfaction elsewhere.

She did not like that one bit.

But that was a discussion that would lead to uncomfortable places and she didn't want to have that conversation with him. Not now. First she was here to learn more about his family.

Her heartbeat sped up, her palms sweaty. 'I've been thinking about what you said in the doctor's office,' she said hesitantly. 'About not wanting to name our child after anyone in your family.'

His gaze remained on the screen. 'I haven't changed my mind, if that's what you're expecting.'

'I'm not. I just… What happened? With your family, I mean?'

'I told you. I was taken away by my alcoholic mother to live in Naples. She died years ago there.'

'How?'

Dante finally looked up at her, his expression guarded. 'Why do you want to know? It's not a very pleasant story.'

Very clearly, it was not, considering how obvious it was that he didn't want to tell her.

'My brother's story isn't very pleasant either,' she said. 'But I still told you.'

His gaze darkened. 'What is this? A quid pro quo? You tell me a secret and now I have to tell you one of mine?'

Stella didn't flinch. 'I'm going to marry you, Dante. Is it wrong to want to know something about the man who's going to be my husband?'

'It won't be a typical marriage, need I remind you?'

She ignored the slight, fleeting pain that pulled inside her at the words. 'I realise that. But I want to know more about you and your past. About what kind of father you're likely to be.'

A fierce, hot spark leapt to life in Dante's eyes. 'You think I would do anything to hurt our baby?' The question was soft but there was a whole world of threat in his deep, rich voice.

Stella refused to look away. 'No. And that's not what I was implying. Don't be so touchy.'

He made an impatient sound and, strangely, it was he who finally glanced away. 'You want to know what happened to me and my mother? Fine. She never quite recovered from my father losing his throne and so, when we were exiled from Monte Santa Maria to Milan, she started drinking. My father didn't care about anything but being king again, and he certainly didn't care about her. So after a couple of months she decided that she'd had enough. She left and took me with her.'

Bitterness laced his beautiful voice, like arsenic in hot chocolate. 'I didn't want to go. I'd already lost my country, and I didn't want to lose my family, and especially not my brother. But she didn't care what I wanted. All that mattered was that she wasn't alone. We ended up in some dirty tenement in Naples, surviving on nothing because she couldn't hold down a job.' He paused, gold gleaming hot in his eyes. 'You want to hear more or is that enough? It doesn't get any better, I warn you.'

She held his gaze, fascinated by that hot glow, the raw emotion he kept locked inside the darkness of his gaze like a candle flame in a dark room. It reminded her of the way he looked at her in bed sometimes when he thought she was asleep, as if she had something he wanted that he didn't know how to get.

'Yes, more,' she said. 'I can handle it.'

He let out a long breath, then closed the laptop and sat back on the seat. A smile was playing around his mouth, but there was no amusement in it. It looked forced. 'Of course you can. You were going to kill me, after all.'

There was a bite to the words that she was sure was supposed to hurt her, but she ignored it. He was angry because she was pushing him and he didn't want to be pushed. But too bad. Underneath anger there was always pain, as she knew all too well, and she wanted to understand it.

Why? So you can heal him?

The ache in her chest deepened. Well, why not? He'd helped her with the pain of her own guilt. Couldn't she help him in return?

No, she wasn't supposed to care about him. But somehow she did all the same.

'Perhaps I should have,' she said coolly. 'Apparently attempting to kill you is easier than getting you to talk.'

A flicker of emotion crossed his face, the gold in his eyes glowing hotter.

She wasn't surprised. If she'd learned anything about Dante Cardinali, it was that he preferred a fight to honest discussion. Which she had too—at least up until she'd seen her baby's heartbeat on that monitor.

He gave a low, mirthless laugh. 'You're a hard woman, kitten. You don't let me get away with anything do you?'

'Why should I? You didn't let me get away at all.'

His smile this time was more natural, and he got up, moving to where she leaned against the table and standing in front of her. Then he settled his hands on her hips and lifted her onto the table top, pushing himself between her thighs and fitting her against him. He was hard, the heat of him seeping through the fabric of their clothing, and she shivered, loving the delicious press of him against her. But she didn't look away, keeping her gaze on his.

Dante shook his head. 'You're not going to let this go, are you?'

'No.'

'Okay. So, we moved around Naples a lot,' he went on, his tone casual, stripping the words of any emotion. 'Since my mother couldn't stay in any one job too long, it meant she couldn't pay rent. Eventually she took up with a series of men who would help her out sometimes. Her favourite was a bastard called Roberto, who beat her when he was drunk. But for some reason she loved him and when I finally grew big enough to put a stop to him taking out his moods on her—and sometimes on me as well—she blamed me for hurting him. And for us subsequently moving again, because Roberto stopped the money he was giving her.'

Stella's heart squeezed. He sounded as if he'd told this story a hundred times and was bored of it. But she could hear the tension in his voice, an undercurrent of anger and of pain. It made her want to do something for him, but she wasn't sure what, so she put her hands his forearms, her fingers on his bare skin, hoping the contact would give him some comfort.

'I tried to make her stop drinking,' Dante went on, his voice becoming harder and more edged. 'Tried to get her to leave Roberto. I did everything I could think of, telling her that it would kill her if she went on like she was, but she wasn't interested in stopping, or changing what she was doing. So in the end I gave her an ultimatum—told her it was either the bottle or me. I was just sixteen, old enough to look after myself—though, to be frank, I'd been doing that since she dragged me away from Milan—so when she said that she wasn't going to stop, that I should go if I couldn't handle it, that's exactly what I did.'

He smiled, sharp and white. 'I walked out, thinking she'd come after me. That she'd change her mind. But she didn't. For six months I heard nothing and then I got a call from a hospital saying that she was in Intensive Care with a head injury. She'd fallen over after a night drinking with Roberto and had hit her head on the pavement.' A muscle ticked in his jaw. 'I spent a month sitting beside her, watching her slowly die. She never regained consciousness and so she never knew that I'd come back.'

The anger in his gaze gleamed, his fingers gripping her tighter, though she didn't think he was aware of it. 'I never got to ask her why she'd dragged me around Italy with her, since it was obvious she preferred the bottle to me. Or why she wouldn't stop drinking, even when I begged her to. She just died and left me with nothing. Just like she always did.'

Stella swallowed, grief closing her throat. For Dante and the pain that was obviously still raw inside him. 'Dante,' she said thickly, not sure what else to say or what else to offer. Her own parents hadn't left her with anything either.

His mouth twisted in another of those terrible smiles. 'So now you know exactly what kind of man you're marrying, kitten. Stateless. Rootless. A man who'd rather walk away from a problem than have to deal with it, because it's easier to not give a damn.'

Of course. The 'problem' he'd walked away from had been his mother.

'You blame yourself,' she said, before she could think better of it. 'Don't you?'

'What? For the way she died? No, of course not.' Dull anger glittered in his eyes. 'She chose that path herself. I had nothing to do with it.'

'If you truly believe that, then why are you so angry about it?'

'Angry? I'm not angry.' He laughed, but there was no amusement in the sound. 'That would imply that I care. And I don't. Not any more.'

But he was lying, that was obvious. Of course he cared. He cared deeply and she could see the depth of it in the pain that lay underneath all that anger.

'Yes, you do.' She lifted her hand and touched the warmth of his cheek. 'And that's the problem, isn't it? You care too much.'

The smile on his face vanished. 'Is there a point to this?'

His hands firmed on her, his hips flexing slightly, the ridge of his erection nudging against the soft, sensitive place between her thighs. 'Because there are things I'd rather be doing.'

Stella fought back the shiver of pleasure that whispered over her skin. It would be easy to surrender, to let him distract her in the way he was so good at, and part of her wanted to. She wouldn't have this for ever, after all.

But this was important.

'The point is that you're angry,' she said quietly, looking straight up into his eyes. 'And I want to help you the way you helped me.'

His mouth twisted. 'Don't care about me, kitten. That would be a mistake.'

'And is that what you'll say to your child when they tell you that they love you? That it's a mistake? That they shouldn't?'

It was a low blow and she knew it. But, whether he liked it or not, this mattered. For the baby's sake if nothing else.

His gaze went dark, any flickers of gold vanishing from it entirely. 'Don't use our child to manipulate me,' he said, low and hard. 'I won't allow it.'

Stella stared back. 'I'm not. I don't care what you feel for me, but I need to know that you'll care for our child.'

Liar. You care what he feels for you.

She ignored the thought, meeting Dante's black gaze head-on, keeping her fingers pressed to his cheek, letting her know how serious she was.

'Do you really think I wouldn't?' he demanded roughly. 'Why do you think I offered to marry you? Why do you think I'm buying a house for us to live in?'

'You're doing those things to take care of us, Dante. But that is not the same as love and you know it.'

'Love?' The word was a sneer, sharp-edged and painful. 'Since when does love have anything to do with it?'

Her heart gave one hard beat in her chest. She refused to look away. 'Since now.'

STELLA'S FINGERTIPS ON his skin were light, her body against his soft and warm, and he felt as if he was holding a sunbeam in his hands; all he wanted to do was bask in her heat.

He most certainly didn't want to look into the relentless silver-blue of her eyes and talk about the farce that was love. He'd already given her more of himself than he'd wanted, more than he'd given anyone in his entire life, including his brother.

And he wasn't sure why. He'd never felt obligated to be honest with another person simply because they'd been honest with him. In fact, he'd tried never to feel obligated to anyone at all. He didn't want to give any more pieces of his soul away than he had already.

He'd been in a foul mood since they'd got back from the doctor's office and when she'd brought up his family his temper had become even fouler.

Nevertheless, there had been something direct and honest in her gaze that he hadn't been able to refuse. That had made him want to give her something in return for what she'd given him: her secrets and her pain the night he'd made her hold a blade to his chest. The way she'd clutched onto his hand as they'd seen their baby on the monitor. Her pleasure, every time he touched her at night.

Those had all meant something to him, especially when his mother hadn't wanted anything at all from him. She'd ignored what he'd tried to do for her, had thrown all his offers to help her back in his face. And when he'd attempted to help anyway she'd told him that he didn't care. That, if he truly loved her, he'd leave her alone.

Even in dying she'd refused him.

But Stella hadn't. She'd accepted his help, let him take care of her. Let him give her strength and hold her. Stella had never refused him anything. Which meant he hadn't been able to refuse telling her about the life he'd had with his mother. But he'd hoped that, once he'd finished, she'd leave the subject alone.

Apparently not.

'What is it exactly that you're asking?' he demanded, trying to sound like his normal, casual self and knowing he'd failed. 'Because, if you're wanting me to fall on my knees and tell you that I'm madly in love with you, you're going to be disappointed.'

'I know that,' she said without a flicker, full of a quiet dignity that made an inexplicable sense of shame creep through him. 'I'm not talking about me. I'm talking about our child.'

Anger burned sullenly inside him, a dull flame that never seemed to go out no matter how many times he tried to ignore it.

He didn't want to talk about love. He didn't even want to think about it.

Love was his mother throwing a glass at his head when he'd tried to call a doctor for her after a hard night on the tiles. Love was her threatening him with the police after he'd punched Roberto in the face after the bastard had hurt her.

Love was her telling him that she was done with him and he should leave her alone.

Love was her dying in that hospital bed without ever regaining consciousness, denying him his last opportunity to talk to her.

He'd been there, done that and he wanted no part of it ever again.

'Our child will have everything in my power to give,' Dante said, trying to dismiss the subject. 'Call it what you want.'

Yet there was something in Stella's gaze that felt like a hand closing around his heart. 'And if he or she wants to love you?'

The hand squeezed harder. 'I won't stop them.'

'But you won't give them anything back?'

The words twisted inside him like a barb on a fishhook, tearing and painful. 'Do I need to?' He squeezed her gently, flexing his hips, sliding his erection against the softness between her thighs, the delicious ache easing the agony of his memories. 'When they'll get all the love they might want from you?'

Stella's gaze darkened. Gilt curls still damp from her bath stuck to her forehead. She smelled of lavender and musk, and he wanted to bury his face between her breasts, breathe her in. Then maybe lick a long path down between her thighs too, make her scream instead of asking him questions he didn't want to answer, or make him talk about things that should have been left in the past.

Things such as the knowledge that maybe, if he hadn't walked away from his mother, he might have been able to save her.

That she wouldn't have died the way she had.

Because it's your fault. It's always been your fault.

'You don't mean that,' Stella said.

'How would you know? You don't know a thing about me.'

'Wrong.' Her fingertips moved lightly along his cheekbone. 'I know that you care about this baby, whether you like it or not. And I know you want to do the right thing by it.' Her touch moved to his jaw. Why he was letting her touch him like this he didn't have any idea, but he didn't stop her. 'I know you've done nothing but look after me since you brought me here, despite the fact that I wanted to kill you. And I know you're angry. You're very, *very* angry about your mother and, Dante...' She touched his mouth gently, meeting his gaze. 'You have a right to be angry. You needed her and she wasn't there for you, and there is no excuse for that. None at all.'

Tension crawled through him, tugging at his instinct to pull away violently, to turn and leave, no matter how that would hurt her.

But he couldn't do that.

Colour had risen in her skin, making her eyes look bluer. A perfect, pale white-and-gold china shepherdess of a woman. Not a woman he'd ever have picked to hold a gun to his head or end up carrying his child. Not a woman he'd have picked to fight him, challenge him on just about every level there was. Yet she'd done all of those things.

A vulnerable woman too—he couldn't forget that. One who'd been hurt by her past, and whose feelings had been twisted and denied, yet despite that she still had an open heart. She wasn't like him. She would never *not* care.

Which made her the most perfect parent for their child. *Unlike you.*

But he didn't want to think about that, still less talk about it. He was done with anger and guilt. He was done with caring. And he was done with love.

Especially now he had Stella, warm and lush and naked under that thin blue silk robe.

'I think we've done the topic of me to death.' He flexed his hips again, pressing himself against her damp heat. 'I'm more interested in other things.'

Her fingers gripped his forearms tightly, the expression on her face making that fist around his heart squeeze like a vice. 'You can trust me, Dante. I know that sounds strange, coming from the person who held you at gunpoint a month or so ago, but you can. I will never turn you away.'

The tight, painful feeling in his chest grew stronger and he had to grit his teeth against it. 'I don't want your trust,' he growled, knowing he was being a bastard and not caring, because not caring was supposed to be what he did. 'What I want is your body, understand?'

'Yes.' Her gaze was too sharp, too knowing. 'And you can have it. I told you I will never refuse you and I meant it.'

She wasn't supposed to do that. She wasn't supposed just to…give in to him.

His heart rate began to climb, adrenaline pouring through him. 'Bad idea, kitten.' His voice was low and much rougher than he'd intended. 'I'm not in a gentle mood.'

'I don't care. Do your worst. I'm stronger than I look, remember?'

Oh, yes, he remembered.

He lifted her into his arms, because he wasn't going to take her on the stone table like an animal, not again. He could at least be an animal in the comfort of the bedroom where there was something soft to ravage her on.

Bending his head, he took her mouth in a hard kiss, letting her know that he most certainly would take whatever he wanted from her. But she only wrapped her legs around his waist and gripped him tightly, opening her mouth, letting him kiss her harder, deeper. Showing him the truth— that she would never turn him away. Never refuse him. She challenged him and pushed him, gave him the fight that he wanted, and then she opened her arms and took him in, giving him the surrender he craved.

His heartbeat was wild and out of control, the familiar, intense desperation winding around his soul. He didn't know why it was like this with her every time. He couldn't understand it. But he couldn't stop the feeling that was rising inside him, a desperation, a need. To get close to her, have her warmth and softness all over him, under him.

The feeling pushed at him, battered against his heart, and he couldn't wait, not even to get to the bedroom. He stopped in the living area and laid her down on the thick, white carpet that wasn't as soft as he wanted it to be, but her scent and her heat were affecting him so badly that he just couldn't stop.

Pulling open her robe, he exposed her naked body to the late-afternoon sunlight pouring through the window. She was all golden hair and creamy white skin and soft shell-pink nipples. Her gaze was jewel-bright as she looked up at him, full of desire and need. Need for him.

'You want me?' he heard himself growl as he knelt between her thighs and leaned over her, putting his hands on the floor on either side of her head. 'You want me, Stella Montefiore?'

'Yes.' Her chest rose and fell, fast and hard in time with her quickened breathing. 'I do. So much.'

'And only me.' He didn't know why he was demanding this from her, especially when he was still intending their marriage to be a sexless one. But that didn't change the roaring need inside him, the hunger for something he didn't understand. Something only she, with her pride and stubborn determination, with her warmth and her surrender, could give him.

You can't go anywhere else for this. And you don't want her to either.

No. He damn well didn't.

'I've changed my mind,' he said roughly, deciding right there and then. 'Once we're married, you're mine. There will be no one else for you, understand me?'

Her hands came up, her fingers threading through his

hair, her eyes blazing into his. 'Yes, I understand. And there will be no one else for you either.'

He almost laughed, because of course she would demand the same thing from him. Not that he was going to argue.

'I don't need anyone else.' He let her see the truth in his gaze. 'Not when you can give me everything I need.'

A fleeting brightness moved through her face, then she was tugging his head down, her lips meeting his, hungry and wanton.

And he was kissing her, a desperate, hot kiss, the heat of her mouth lighting a fire inside him that he didn't think would ever go out.

That should have been a warning, but he was too far gone to notice. He kissed her, taking what he wanted from her, feverish and desperate, tracking kisses down her neck before lingering in the soft hollow of her throat, tasting her frantic pulse. He wanted to spend more time tasting her, making her even hotter for him, even more desperate, but he couldn't wait. He'd never been able to wait, not with her.

He clawed open his trousers and spread her thighs, pushed himself deep inside her. She gave a soft cry of delight, lifting her hips to meet his thrusts, and he stared down into her face, into those shattered sky eyes, unable to look away. Her body was slick around him, her inner muscles gripping him as tightly as her thighs around his waist. As if she wanted to hold him close and never let him go.

And he shouldn't want her to. He shouldn't like it. It shouldn't feel as if he was somehow home.

But it did. And the feeling didn't go away as the pleasure inside him began to get more intense, more demanding. As he watched the same pleasure rise in her too.

So he eased back on his thrusts, pushing into her in a long, lazy glide then sliding out. Deep and slow. As if there was nothing better to do but this. As if he could do it all day. And he wanted to. He wanted it not to end.

Time slowed down to a pinpoint, to this one eternal moment. To her lying beneath him, her hips moving with his, her fingers twined in his hair, her gaze locked with his. Full of desire, full of need.

For him. Just for him.

'You're amazing,' she whispered, her brilliant gaze on his. 'You're the most amazing man I've ever met.'

It felt like an arrow to the chest, the pain bittersweet and intense.

Because right now, in her arms, for the first time in his life, he felt like he could possibly be that man. The man she thought was amazing instead of the man who'd walked away from a woman he was supposed to be there for. A man who'd let his own mother die, who'd wasted his entire life trying to drown in his own self-loathing, telling himself that he didn't care, not about anything.

But Stella was right, and that was the problem. He did care. He cared about *everything*.

And he thought he probably cared about her most of all.

'Dante,' she murmured, her hands twisting tighter in his hair. 'Take me home.'

So he did, reaching down between them, stroking the sensitive place between her thighs as he thrust, watching her eyes turn pure silver as the climax exploded through her.

Crushing his own cry of release against the softness of her mouth.

Knowing that, one way or another, he was going to end up hurting her.

And trying to tell himself it didn't matter.

CHAPTER NINE

Stella gazed at the magnificent view out of the long, elegant windows of the *palazzo*, over rolling green lawns and terraced gardens surrounding a lavishly tiled pool area, to the small wood that lay beyond all that green.

It was so very beautiful. The perfect family home.

She and Dante were viewing the property he'd chosen near Milan, an old *palazzo* near his brother's, though Enzo and his family spent most of their time on the little island Enzo had bought the year before.

Stella had wanted to know more about Enzo—important, considering the man was going to be uncle to their child—but Dante hadn't been interested in telling her much about him.

In fact, since that evening on the terrace at the hotel in Rome, he hadn't seemed interested in talking to her much at all. It had been at least a week since then and he'd spent the majority of it at his computer or on the phone, organising various things. He was having to deal with a few issues with his business interests—or at least that was what he'd told her—as well as preparations for their wedding.

He'd told her he wanted her input on aspects of it, but she found that sitting down and talking about it made her feel…uneasy. All this talk of love and the importance of vows when both of them knew it wouldn't be a marriage based on anything more than shared parentage. It made her ache. For herself and for their child. For the kind of life that they would have, which sounded so very wonderful on paper, and yet…

Stella stared sightlessly at the lawns that stretched into the distance beyond the windows, trying to ignore the bleakness that gathered inside her.

Dante cared, she knew he did, but he wasn't going to admit it. And she couldn't force him to if he didn't want to. So what would that mean for their baby? What would it mean for their child to grow up with a father who wouldn't admit to the possibility of love?

She'd grown up without that in her life and it was her need for it that had propelled her to pick up the gun and point it at Dante's face. Her weakness, her fatal flaw. She would do everything in her own power to make sure her son or daughter grew up knowing they were loved, but would the love of one parent be enough?

Dante's was a magnetic, charismatic presence. He would have a massive influence on their child, especially given how involved he wanted to be in their life. But how would that child feel to have a father who never told them he loved them?

Pain echoed inside her, a vibration that shuddered through her, reflecting off the empty places in her soul and reverberating like an echo.

She knew how that felt. Never to have someone hold her or tell her that they loved her. That they were proud of her.

It hurt. It hurt so much.

A footstep echoed in the empty room, and then warm arms slid around her waist, drawing her in close to the hot, hard strength of the man behind her.

She should have felt comforted and reassured by those arms, by the power in that body. But right now it didn't feel enough. Like a perfect fantasy that only half came true, the rest of it out of reach for ever.

Her child would feel like that. Wanting something from its father he was never going to give it. Oh, Dante might, at some point, admit to himself what his refusal to deal with his past was doing to him and to their child—because it was definitely his past that was holding him back.

Or he might not. He might never admit it.

You will have to hope that your love alone will be enough for your baby. Because what other option do you have?

She could leave. That was another option. But then where would she go? How would she provide for their child? And would Dante even let her? He wouldn't. Of course he wouldn't.

Can you walk away from him? That's the real question.

The thought sat inside her, a cold, hard reality she'd been trying to ignore for days now.

'What do you think?' Dante murmured, nuzzling against her ear. 'Do you like it?'

He was talking about the *palazzo*, of course, but she liked his arms around her, the feeling of his strength at her back, the warmth of his breath against her skin.

He'd changed his mind about marriage in name only. He'd told her that she was his and that they would find physical satisfaction with each other, and every night he proved it to her over and over.

But her doubts weren't about him and whether a play-boy would ever be faithful—she knew he would be. He was a man of determination and he'd promised her that if she wouldn't get satisfaction elsewhere then neither would he. She believed he meant it.

No, her doubts were about herself. Whether sex would be enough of a stand-in for the hunger that lay in her soul.

Whether a child would fill up that need and whether it was fair to expect a child to do that.

'I do like it,' she said, staring out the windows, conscious of the warmth of the man at her back and the hunger inside her that would go unsatisfied for ever. 'Perhaps it would be good to be close to your brother. Our little one will have a cousin to play with.'

He made a noncommittal sound. 'I'm not sure whether being close to Enzo would be a good thing or not. If you think I'm controlling, you haven't met him.'

'And will I?' She put her hands over his where they rested on her stomach, trying to ignore the doubts. 'Meet him, I mean?'

'You will. At our engagement party.'

Of course. Dante had made sure not a breath of what was happening between them made it into the media. He hadn't wanted anyone to know, or at least not until he was ready. Luckily it had only been a week, so no one had noticed his absence from the entertainment circuit.

She didn't much care about the media—wouldn't a press release do the job? But he'd told her to let him handle it his way. He'd decided on an engagement party as the best way to announce their circumstances, as the media tended to be less intrusive when they thought they were being given the whole story rather than a carefully selected portion of it. He'd made the observation that it would allow news of what was happening between them to reach her family, so she wouldn't have to deal with them.

She appreciated that. She'd told him about her worries concerning her father and what he might do once he'd found out she wasn't going through with his revenge plans. Dante's response had been to send a couple of his representatives to Monte Santa Maria to inform her parents that she was now under his protection, as she would be marrying him. He'd also included a payment of a ridiculous sum of money to keep Santo quiet, plus a warning that if he tried to contact Stella again the police would be called and he would be taken into custody.

Stella was fine with that. She didn't want to hear from her father. She'd made peace with Matteo's memory as much as she could and with her own failure to go through with her father's vendetta.

Except that weakness, that need for love, is still there.

'You are going to invite him, aren't you?' She kept her tone neutral, hiding the doubt that tugged at her.

'Of course I will. He's my brother.' Dante nuzzled her neck, pressing a kiss below her ear and making her shiver deliciously. 'Except we might keep the fact that we met while you were trying to kill me to ourselves for a while, hmm? Enzo's very protective.'

And so was Dante—she knew that for a fact.

'Are you afraid he'll do something to me?' she asked, curious.

Dante gave a low laugh. 'No. He'd be dead before he hit the floor if he tried to hurt you.'

Stella thought he was probably only a little serious. 'So why not just tell him?'

'He'll be angry and we really don't want an angry Enzo. We need to build up to that.'

Her heart ached at the affectionate warmth in Dante's voice. Yet another reminder that, despite what he'd told her, he cared. He cared about his brother, for example, and quite deeply. Why else would he have chosen to look at this *palazzo*—the one near Enzo's?

But he won't ever care about you.

Emotion clogged her throat. She didn't need him to care about her, though, did she? He was going to give her everything else: a place to live, financial support, help in bringing up their child and all the physical pleasure she might want. Did she really need him to care about her too?

You know the answer to that question.

Yes. She did. That was all she'd wanted all her life: someone to care about her. Someone she mattered to. But her parents had only ever wanted Matteo, not her. No one had ever really wanted her.

And now she was going to tie herself for life to a man who didn't really want her either.

Restlessness filled her and suddenly she didn't want to stand there with the warmth of his arms around her like the promise of something she was never going to get. She pushed his hands away and stepped out of his arms, moving over to the window and looking out.

Her heart thumped painfully in her ears and she felt oddly cold.

A silence fell, though she could feel the pressure of Dante's gaze from behind her.

'Kitten?' he asked after a moment. 'Is there something wrong? Something to do with my brother?'

'You care about him.' Stella turned from the view and looked at the man she was supposed to marry. 'Don't you?'

Dante stood there in one of his expensively tailored suits—no jacket today, and no tie either, his black shirt casually open at the neck, his sleeves rolled to his elbows. Her favourite look on him.

He had his hands in the pockets of his trousers and the look on his handsome face was guarded. 'He's my brother,' he said, frowning, as if that was all the explanation required. 'Why do you ask?'

Stella swallowed, not quite sure herself why she was asking. It was just…she couldn't stop thinking about his refusal to acknowledge the fact that he did care. About quite a lot of things. Was it only her he denied that to? Did he ever say that to his brother too?

'So you can care about people, Dante.'

'If you're wanting—'

'Will you ever care about me?' The words slipped from her before she could stop them and she knew she shouldn't have asked as soon as they were out.

But she couldn't take them back even though, as his expression hardened the way it had back on the terrace in Rome, the darkness of his eyes becoming absolute, she desperately wished she could.

It was a door shutting in her face.

No, he wouldn't care about her.

But you want him to.

The realisation opening up inside her was like a sunflower blooming, shining in her heart, bright and beautiful and golden, reflecting glory everywhere.

She'd always wanted someone to care for her, wanted an acknowledgement that she mattered to somebody. But she hadn't known she'd wanted that acknowledgement from Dante. No one else. Just him.

Dante, who wasn't the irresponsible playboy she'd first assumed, but who was warm and caring and protective. Who'd taken care of her, no matter that she'd tried to kill him. Who'd challenged her and pushed her. Who'd held her when she'd been vulnerable and broken, and who'd given her strength when she'd needed it. Not to mention the indescribable pleasure he also gave her every night.

Dante, who didn't want to care, not about anyone.

The sunflower began to wither inside her, its golden brightness fading as cold whispered through her, the icy breath of winter.

'It's okay,' she said suddenly, before he could speak, because she didn't want to hear him say the words out loud. She didn't think she could bear it. 'Forget I said anything.'

But he didn't look away and the set expression on his face didn't fade. His gaze was dark, his beautiful mouth hard, tension gathered in every line of his powerful body. 'Then why did you ask?'

He was angry with her, of course, and why wouldn't he be? They were here to view a house, not have a deep and meaningful discussion about their relationship.

Stella glanced out of the window again, not wanting to meet the anger in his gaze, wishing she'd never said anything. 'It doesn't matter.'

'It's about what I said to you in Rome, isn't it?'

'I don't need you to—'

'Because if you want the truth then here it is. I will care for you, Stella.' His voice was nothing but cold, hard steel. 'But, no. I can never care about you.'

The words felt like stones thrown at her, each one jagged and sharp, leaving a bruise where they landed. And the fact that they were the truth only made the pain worse.

Did you really expect anything different? He told you not to care about him.

He had. Yet she cared anyway.

No, it was more than that, wasn't it? More than simple caring.

She loved him. Because that glory inside her, the warmth, the brightness she felt whenever she looked at him, was love. The pain she experienced herself whenever he hurt, that was love too. The longing to touch him, have his arms around her, have him be the one to fill the void inside her…

What else could it be?

Only love.

Nothing else would hurt as much.

She stared hard out of the window at the cypresses that lined the grand, sweeping driveway, trying to force away the prickle of tears. 'You won't, you mean.'

'Can't, won't. What does it matter?'

'It matters to me.'

'Fine.' His voice was expressionless. 'I won't.'

The trees wavered in her vision as she lost the battle. Two weeks ago she would have blinked the tears back, pretended they weren't there, but now she made no effort to hide them. What was the point when she'd already given her own feelings away?

'I'm not your mother,' she said, though why she was arguing with him she didn't know. Was she hoping to change his mind? 'I'm not an alcoholic battling addiction. I'm just a woman who wants someone to care about her. You do understand that, don't you?'

'Of course I understand that.' Anger threaded through his voice. 'But this isn't about my mother. This isn't about the past. It's about the choice I made for the future years ago and I'm not about to change it.'

The tears ran down her cheek, but she made no attempt to brush them away. She wanted to ask him whether he would change it for their baby's sake, except they'd already had that discussion, and besides she couldn't—wouldn't—use their child that way.

So all she said was, 'Not even for me?'

There was a heavy silence and then footsteps came from behind her. Dante's hands were suddenly on her shoulders, turning her round to face him, his expression tightening as he saw the tears running down her face.

'Stella,' he demanded roughly, something that looked like pain in the depths of his eyes. 'Why does this matter to you so very much?'

She looked up at him, lifting her chin, because even

now, even here, she couldn't resist the challenge. 'Why do you think? Because you matter, Dante. You matter to me.'

His expression tightened, his fingers digging into her shoulders almost painfully. 'I told you not to care, kitten. Remember? I *told* you not to.'

She swallowed, her throat aching, everything aching. 'Too late.'

DANTE COULD HEAR his own heartbeat loud and heavy in his ears, and something was cracking right down the middle of his chest, breaking him in two.

Who knew a woman's tears had the power to do that? His mother had been able to turn hers off and on, depending on what she wanted to get him to do. But there was nothing feigned about Stella's. They rolled slowly down her cheeks, one after the other, pain glowing in her silver-blue eyes.

Silly, *silly* kitten. She cared about him. *Dio*, why on earth would she go and do that? After the warning he'd given her back in Rome? After he'd dismissed all that caring nonsense and showed her that their physical connection could bridge any gap?

It was her own fault, of course. Not his. He'd been very clear about his feelings on the subject. He wasn't going to care about anyone or anything, not again, and he'd told her he wouldn't. She'd known that from the beginning.

So why the sight of her tears and the anguish in her gaze made him feel as if she really had taken that letter opener and plunged it into the centre of his chest, he had no idea.

He tried to dismiss the pain, but it wouldn't go away, and that made him angry. Made him want to crush her to him, cover her lovely, vulnerable mouth with his, make her forget her ridiculous decision to care about him, to give her pleasure instead.

But almost as soon as the impulse occurred to him

and he began to pull her close her hands came up and she pushed them hard against his chest, holding herself away.

'No, Dante,' she said, hoarse and shaken. 'Not this time.'

Tension coiled in him, the sharp, restless need to do something—anything—to stop her from saying the words he so desperately did not want to hear. To take away her pain. 'You said you'd never turn me away.' His own voice sounded as rough as hers. 'That you'd never refuse me.'

'I know.' Bright determination glowed in her eyes despite the tracks of her tears. 'But that was before I knew I was in love with you, Dante Cardinali.'

Love. That damn word again. The word he'd tried to strip down over the years so that it had lost all meaning, become nothing. But he hadn't been successful, had he? Because of course it meant something.

Guilt. Pain.

'I don't want you to be in love with me,' he said viciously. 'I didn't ask for it.'

'I didn't ask for it either.' Her chin lifted higher, a challenge. 'And quite frankly the last thing in the world I want is to be in love with a man who doesn't give a damn. And yet here we are.'

His jaw was tight, his whole body stiff with tension. She was so warm against him, and so soft. All it would take would be the right touch, a kiss, and she'd melt the way she always did. He knew how to do it. He knew how to make her forget.

'So?' He slid his hands down over the delicious curve of her bottom, fitting her more closely against his hardening groin. 'It doesn't change anything.' And it wouldn't. Because he wouldn't let it.

'Dante, no.' Stella pushed harder against his chest, her palms little points of heat on him. 'You don't understand. It changes *everything*.'

A growl escaped him. He didn't want to let her go. He wanted to keep holding her, because he had the awful suspicion that if he let her go he'd never get to hold her again. 'Why?'

Colour had risen in her cheeks, flushing her pale skin a delicate rose. She was so beautiful and yet the pain in her eyes hurt him in ways he didn't understand. 'Let me go.'

'You're going to leave, aren't you?' He couldn't stop himself from asking stupid questions, when what he should have been doing was crushing her mouth under his. 'As soon as I let you go, you're going to walk away.'

She looked vulnerable and yet there was something strong in her too, a determination he'd seen the night she'd tried to take his life. Only this time it wasn't the brittle strength of a woman forcing herself to do something she knew was wrong, it was the enduring strength of a woman knowing she would do the right thing, no matter the cost to herself. No matter her own pain.

'All I wanted was for someone to put their arms around me.' Her voice was very soft, the edges of it frayed and ragged like torn silk. 'To hold me and tell me that I was loved. But no one ever did.' Her gaze remained steady on his, a terrible knowledge glowing there. 'And Dante, if I marry you, no one ever will.'

Such simple words to have such power. It felt as if she'd plunged not just a knife into his heart but a sword sharp enough to cut through stone.

But she was right. If he married her, if he tied her to him, she would never have that. Because he could never give it to her.

Would *never give it to her.*

No. He wouldn't. And it was a choice. He understood that much.

He'd had a choice back when he'd been a teenager and

his mother had told him to go, to leave her alone. And he had. Because he'd been done with her and her constant refusal of everything he tried to do for her. Done with trying to love a woman who'd only dragged him with her because she hadn't wanted to be alone.

Who had never wanted *him*.

Because, if she had, she would have tried, wouldn't she? She would have made some kind of effort to be the kind of mother he'd needed, surely?

Ah, but that was useless to think about. Those questions had no answers and he'd never get them, because she was dead, denying him to the last.

If you hadn't walked away, things might have been different.

And that was the hell of it, wasn't it? Because he *had* walked away. And he would never know if he could have changed things if he'd stayed.

He'd never know if he could have saved her.

Guilt twisted in his heart, but he shoved it away, buried it deep.

This wasn't the same situation and Stella wasn't a fragile, bitter addict, but the choice he had to make was still the same. And he knew he would make the same decision, because he knew exactly how this little story played out.

He would give her everything she wanted, everything that was in his power to give, except that one little piece of himself. And it wouldn't be enough for her. And eventually that would turn to bitterness and anger. It would turn to pain. It would destroy what relationship they did have, and it wouldn't only involve him and her, it would involve their child as well.

The anger inside him, the fire that never went out, flared hot and bitter.

Yes, this was her fault. She was ruining what they had

with her constant need for more. And she was ruining it for their child too.

That's right. Blame her for your own cowardice. Remind you of anyone?

Dante ignored the snide voice in his head. Instead he opened his arms, letting her go and stepping back, the warmth of her body lingering against him in a way that nearly broke him.

'There,' he said, his tone acid. 'If you want to go, go. I won't stop you.'

She looked so small standing there by herself, the silky dress she wore his favourite colour, a pale, silvery blue the exact same shade as her eyes. 'So that's really the way it's going to end?' she asked quietly. 'You walking away again?'

'Does it look like I'm walking away?' His voice echoed with a bitterness and he couldn't hide it. 'No, darling, you're the one who doesn't want what I have to give.'

Her mouth trembled. 'I do want it. I just want *all* of it. I want to be loved, Dante. I want to be loved by you.'

It felt as if she'd swung that sword again, cutting through his chest, through sinew and bone, right into his heart.

'Why?' He ignored the pain, reaching for his anger instead. 'Why can't you be happy with what we have now? I'll give you everything you want. Every damn thing, Stella.'

'I know you will,' she said sadly. 'And maybe that would have been enough for me a week or so ago. But it's not enough for me now.'

'Why not?' He'd taken a step towards her before he realised what he was doing, his hands in fists at his sides. 'Why can't that be enough?'

She was framed by the window, the green of the view behind her, and there was something about it that made her seem very isolated and alone, yet at the same time it highlighted her quiet strength.

He didn't understand how she could ever have thought herself weak.

'Because I'm not the same person I was a week ago. You changed me, Dante. You made me want more. You made me think I deserve more. And I…don't want to live the rest of my life simply being content with whatever you choose to give me.' Her shoulders straightened, her jaw firmed. 'I need to be loved. I *need* it. And I don't want to have to earn it or be forever trying to change your mind to get it. I did that with my father and I don't want to do it again.'

Of course she had. And the fact that he understood her made everything worse somehow.

He felt as though he was trying to hold onto something precious that was slipping through his fingers and it took every atom of will he possessed not to go to her and take her in his arms again, to physically hold onto her so she didn't disappear. 'You'll have the baby,' he forced out through gritted teeth. 'You don't need love from me.'

But she only shook her head slowly. 'No, I won't put that on our baby. It's not fair.' Another tear rolled down her cheek. 'I'm sorry, Dante. I can't do this. I can't spend my life waiting for love from another man who'll never give it to me. I don't want that for our child either.'

Everything was slipping out of his grasp and he had no idea how to get it back. Because to get it back would mean admitting that he cared, and he didn't. He just damn well didn't.

He couldn't afford to.

He had nothing more of his heart left to give anyway.

Not even for your son or daughter?

But anger raged inside him like a bonfire, scorching everything in sight, and he didn't want to think about his child right now. What he wanted was to tell her all this was her fault, that she was the one ruining everything, that he expected better from her than ultimatums.

But he locked the furious words safely away. Smothered the bonfire with indifference. Deprived it of oxygen by slamming the door on every single feeling he had.

And it was easy. Easier than he'd expected.

'Fine.' He tried to sound lazy and casual, the way he always did. 'It's up to you, of course. But this is turning out to be more trouble than it's worth, so you'll forgive me if perhaps we put this marriage situation on hold for the time being.'

Pain flashed across her face; she knew what that tone of his meant as much as he did. And it hurt him. It flayed him alive.

But he ignored that too. Because did she seriously expect him to cave in to her demands simply because she loved him? Ridiculous.

'I understand.' Her voice was level and yet he could hear the hurt laced through it like a crack in a perfect windowpane. 'And the baby?'

'I'll buy this *palazzo*.' He gestured at the empty room, taking care not to look too closely at it as he took a hammer to the fantasies he'd been constructing about it in his head. 'You can live here until the child is born. Then we'll have to work out some other arrangements.'

Her mouth trembled as if her strength was coming to an end. 'I thought you wanted two parents for our child, Dante. I thought you wanted to live with us.'

'So did I.' He held her gaze, let her see the utter indifference in his. Because she was right about one thing: his child was better off without him. 'Seems I was mistaken.'

Sadness filled her eyes. 'So that's your response? You're going to walk away from us? Oh, Dante…'

The disappointment and hurt in her voice made him

want to howl in agony. Instead, he gave a hollow laugh.
'What? You really thought I'd do anything different? Come
now, kitten. You know what kind of man I am. As you've
already pointed out, my child is going to suffer having me
for a father anyway. Might as well live the part.' He forced
himself to turn away, because he wasn't going to stand
there looking at the pain on Stella's face a second longer.
'I'll get a car back to Milan. I think I'll stay there a couple
of days, in fact. You can stay in Rome until the purchase
of this house comes through.' He began to walk towards
the exit, having to force himself to take every step. 'Don't
worry, everything will be taken care of.'

'I *do* know what kind of man you are, Dante Cardinali,'
Stella said from behind him, her voice echoing in the empty
room. 'I only wish you did too.'

Pain reverberated through him, but he didn't turn. 'I'm
sorry, kitten. That man doesn't exist.'

He didn't expect her to call after him as he walked
through the door and, when she didn't, he tried not to tell
himself he was disappointed.

CHAPTER TEN

Dante sat in the rooftop garden of his newly bought penthouse in Milan, where he'd once envisaged putting a luxurious day-bed so he and Stella could spend some 'adult' time in any spare moments they might have while looking after their child.

But as he lolled on one of the white couches under the pergola, yet another glass of wine on the table at his elbow as the sun set over Milan, he decided that perhaps one wasn't enough. He'd get in two. After all, he'd need more than one for all the lovely women he'd be bringing up here, because of course he'd be bringing lots of women up here.

Since he wasn't getting married now, he wouldn't need to be faithful, which meant he could sleep around the way he always had.

It would have been a reassuring thought if it also hadn't filled him with a weary kind of distaste. Perhaps it meant he was getting old.

Or perhaps it means you only want her.

No, that would be ridiculous. Why would he? Stella was gone anyway, back to Rome and the penthouse suite they'd stayed at initially, just as he'd told her to. She was, after all, still pregnant with his child and the *palazzo* wasn't quite ready to accommodate her just yet.

Pain shifted in his chest so he lifted his wine glass and

took another sip. Sometimes alcohol helped and sometimes it didn't.

Looked like it was going to be another day where it didn't.

A footstep made him look up from his contemplation of the view and he frowned as the tall figure of his brother stepped out from the living area and onto the rooftop.

'How did you get in?' Dante demanded.

'The front door was open.' Enzo casually strolled over and sat down on the chair opposite him.

'Nonsense. The front door has a keypad and a lock that automatically engages.'

'Fine. I had someone dismantle the lock.' There was not one ounce of shame in Enzo's expression. 'You weren't answering the door.'

Dante took a sip of his wine and scowled. 'Seems like overkill.'

'It's been five days, Dante. I was worried.'

'Why? I'm fine.' He gestured with his glass at the rooftop around them. 'As you can see.'

Enzo's golden eyes narrowed. 'You are not fine. You look like you haven't slept in days.'

'I haven't.' Dante shrugged. 'A small bout of insomnia. It's nothing.'

But his brother's gaze was sharp and Dante had the uncomfortable sensation that Enzo could read every thought in his head.

'I had a call,' Enzo said after a moment. 'From a woman.'

Dante went very still, something clutching tightly in his chest. 'What woman?'

'I think you know which woman I mean.' His brother looked steadily at him. 'The woman expecting your child. Who's been very worried about you, regardless of the way you walked out on her.'

A spike of pain welled up inside him, leaking through the cracks in the denial he'd laid over the top of it. A denial that had been working very well the whole of the past week until now.

Probably meant he needed to drink some more.

'I don't know what woman you're talking about,' he said flatly, taking another sip.

Enzo's expression darkened. 'I thought you were a man, Dante. Not a coward.'

The denial cracked a little more and this time it was anger leaking out, a hot wave of it. And suddenly Dante lifted his glass and threw it hard against the stone wall of the parapet that bounded the garden.

It shattered, wine dripping onto the stone floor.

There was a silence, broken only by the sound of his breathing, fast and hard, as though he'd been running for days. Which he had been.

Running from the sound of Stella's voice telling him she knew what kind of man he was.

Running from the sound of his own cowardice as he'd told her that man didn't exist.

'Feel better?' Enzo asked mildly.

'No,' Dante said.

'Well.' His brother leaned back in his chair and eyed him. 'This is familiar.'

Oh, yes, he supposed it was. He remembered having a talk with Enzo just like this one when his brother had nearly lost the woman he loved. How ironic that it should be Enzo coming to talk to him now.

'Best to go away, brother mine,' Dante growled. 'I'm not in the mood.'

'Don't be ridiculous,' Enzo said, ignoring him. 'Stella is going to have your child and you're here sulking like Simon does when he's having one of his tantrums. I thought you'd at least behave better than my five-year-old.'

The sound of her name reverberated through him, striking sparks of pain through his entire body. 'Don't,' he said dangerously. 'Don't you dare say her name.'

'Why? Because it hurts you?' Enzo ignored the warning. 'You're a fool, little brother. She told me what went on—and don't worry, she only told me after I demanded she tell me everything. And I can read between the lines. You fell in love with her, and you didn't know how to deal with it, so you pushed her away.'

You fell in love with her...

The words dropped into a quiet space in Dante's head, echoing.

'You're wrong,' he forced out. 'I'm not in love with her. I'm indifferent to her.'

'Is that right? So why did you walk away? Why are you sitting here in an apparently unfurnished apartment, drinking by yourself and refusing to answer the door?' Enzo shook his head. 'You told me once that Mama had her own issues. And I can guess what they might be.' Something in his face flickered. 'I will never forgive myself for the fact that you had to deal with them alone, that I didn't come after you when Mama dragged you away.'

Another crack ran through Dante's denial, jagged and raw. 'You were young. And I coped. I was fine—'

'No,' Enzo said forcefully. 'You didn't cope. And you're not fine. If you were fine, you would be with the woman you loved and readying yourself for the birth of your first child. Instead, you're sitting here drinking, pretending you don't care when any fool can see that you care so deeply you can't deal with it.'

Dante didn't know what to say. He sat there staring at

his brother, feeling the denial start to break apart inside him, and he could do nothing at all to stop it.

'She died, Enzo,' he heard himself say. 'And I couldn't save her. I walked away and let her die.'

Enzo didn't ask who he was talking about. 'Mama chose her own path and you know it. So don't let her choices dictate yours.' He paused, his golden gaze steady and sure. 'You're doing exactly what she used to do, you know that, don't you? Drowning your own pain with alcohol and pushing away the people who love you.'

Dante stared at his brother, conscious of a trickle of ice water dripping down his back. A trickle that became a flood as understanding broke over him.

Because of course Enzo was right. He *was* doing exactly what his mother had done. Drinking away the pain, refusing help. Denying the people who loved him. Hurting them, blaming them...

The way he'd hurt and blamed Stella for the simple crime of loving him and wanting to be loved in return. *Dio*, would he do the same thing to his child too?

Shame swept over him.

'I hurt her,' he said, hoarse and a bit desperate. 'I told her not to care about me and then I...blamed her for wanting more. I blamed her for ruining what we had.' He took a breath. 'It's not her fault. It's mine.'

His brother's gaze softened. 'That's a start. So what are you going to do about it?'

Dante's whole body felt tight. All he could see was the pain in Stella's lovely blue eyes and the tears on her cheeks. Tears *he'd* put there. 'What *can* I do? I walked away from her. I pretended I didn't care and then just left.'

'There's one thing you can do,' Enzo said. 'Accept that

you do care and then spend every second of your life show-ing her exactly how much.'

Dante stared at his brother, into the face of the only other person in his life he'd ever cared about. 'How did you do it with Matilda?' he asked. 'How did you just…put every-thing aside and make that decision?'

Enzo lifted a shoulder. 'It was easy. I finally under-stood that I loved her. That her pain was more important than my own.'

'Easy.' Dante echoed mirthlessly.

But Enzo only shook his head. 'It's about acceptance, brother. Not that river in Egypt.'

It was a lame joke, but then his brother had never been very good at humour.

Just as Dante had never been very good at acceptance.

'All I ever wanted was for someone to put their arms around me and tell me I was loved…'

She'd told him that and it was such a simple thing to give her. Only his heart. And what did his heart matter anyway? Who was he holding onto it for? There was no one else he wanted to give it to but her and, if she took it and ripped it into shreds, what of it? There would be pain and he'd had pain before.

Besides, he owed it to her for the way he'd walked out. He owed her an apology. And if she threw it back in his face it wouldn't be anything he didn't deserve.

And, apart from anything else, he wanted to see her shattered sky eyes just once more.

'I think,' he said. 'That I suddenly need to be in Rome. Urgently.'

Enzo eyed him. 'It's nearly midnight.'

Dante surged up out of his chair. The denial had cracked apart and melted away as if it had never been, leaving nothing but an intense, aching hunger he knew was never going to go away. 'I don't care. I have to go now.'

Enzo snorted. 'Good thing I got the helicopter ready to go, then, isn't it?'

STELLA WAS ASLEEP and dreaming. It was one of the lovely and yet terribly painful dreams that had been plaguing her for the past week, where she would feel strong arms around her and a muscular, powerful body at her back keeping her warm. And a rich, dark voice would whisper in her ear, except she could never hear the words. There were too indistinct.

The dream hurt and always ended the same way, with her waking up alone, a deep, intense yearning in her heart for something she was never going to have.

She hated those dreams.

In fact, as she lay curled up in the bed she'd once shared with Dante, she thought she was having one now, because warm arms slid around her, drawing her against an achingly familiar body. Hot, muscular and smelling of sandalwood, folding around her and keeping her safe.

She gave a little moan of resistance and shivered as she felt lips nuzzle her ear, her whole body falling into longing as that dark voice began to whisper the words she never seemed to hear.

Except right now, alone in her bed, she heard them.

'Stella Montefiore,' the dream said. 'I have something to tell you.' Those arms tightened around her, holding her fast. 'You are wanted. You are loved. And you are loved by me.'

Stella trembled. Was she awake? Or was this still a dream? Because, if it was a dream, she didn't want to wake up.

But the voice was still speaking, that familiar voice that made her want to cry. 'I'm sorry, kitten,' Dante murmured.

'I'm so sorry for the way I left you. For all the terrible things I said to you. I've got no excuse for them other than the one you probably already know. I was afraid. I didn't want to feel anything, I didn't want to care. But I did care. I cared about you.'

She shuddered, not wanting move or speak in case the dream disappeared, a sob collecting in her throat.

'You told me you knew what kind of man I am,' he went on, 'but all I knew was that I was the man who'd walked out on his mother because she wouldn't give me even one single sign that she loved me. And then she died. And maybe if I hadn't walked out, if I hadn't wanted to be loved so badly, I might have been there to save her.'

Stella couldn't keep still any more.

She turned over, heart bursting in her chest, half-terrified of what she would see—that it wouldn't be the man she wanted, just that awful dream again, and she'd be left with nothing.

But it wasn't a dream.

Dante was lying in the bed, his eyes gleaming and black in the dim room, his expression stripped bare. He was in his usual suit trousers and shirt, yet his shirt was creased and had clearly seen better days, and his normally clean-shaven jaw was dark with stubble.

He looked tired and worn and desperate, and still the most beautiful man she'd ever seen.

'You're here,' she croaked, reaching out a shaking hand to touch his beloved face. 'How did you get here?'

Dante didn't smile, only looked into her eyes. 'I had a visit from my brother. He told me that you'd called him because you were worried about me.'

She was still shaking and she couldn't stop. Couldn't stop from running her fingers along his cheekbone either, his skin warm and real beneath her fingertips. 'I did and I was. And I'm not sorry I called him.'

'I'm not sorry either.' Dante's gaze was dark, fathomless. 'Enzo told me I was doing exactly what my mother had done, sitting there blaming everyone else for my pain and pushing away the people I loved. Hurting them...' He stopped. 'You wanted more from me and I hurt you. I was selfish and I blamed you.'

'Dante—'

'No, you were right to want more, Stella. Do you understand? You were right.' He lifted his hand and caught hers where it was pressed to his cheek and held it there. 'I needed to stop pretending I didn't care. To accept that I did. I needed to stop thinking only of myself, stop turning into my own damn mother.' Gently he lowered her hand and kissed the tips of her fingers. 'And, most important of all, I needed to realise that I was in love with you. Because I am, Stella Montefiore. I think I've been in love with you since the moment I woke up to find you pointing a gun at my head.'

Her chest went tight, her heart so full it felt as though it was pressing on the sides of her ribs. 'Is that why you're here?'

'Yes. I wanted to apologise.' The ghost of his charming smile turned his mouth, but there was something desperate in his dark eyes. 'And to tell you that I will love our child too, with the same desperation with which I love you. And also that my heart is yours, if you want it. But, if you don't, I'll leave you in peace. I won't ever bother you with it again.'

A tear leaked out despite her best intentions and, because her voice didn't work, she leaned forward and gave him her answer by brushing her mouth over his instead.

And instantly he moved, his arms going around her,

holding her hard against him and then rolling her beneath him.

'You know that's it, don't you?' he growled, intense gold
flames burning in the depths of his eyes. 'That means I'm
never letting you go.'

Stella got her arms free then raised them and wound
them around his neck, holding onto him as tightly as he
was holding on to her. 'I don't want you to let me go. I want
you to hold me for ever, Dante Cardinali.'

'And if I don't?'

Stella thought about it. 'Then I might be forced to kill
you.'

Dante gave her a sudden fierce, brilliant smile. 'Don't
kill me, kitten. Love me instead.'

So that was what she did.

EPILOGUE

'Where is my cousin?' Simon Cardinali demanded, fixing his uncle with a fierce stare.

Enzo, who was standing outside Stella's hospital door and holding Simon's hand, frowned. 'Simon, where are your manners? You know better than that.'

The little boy pulled a face. 'Sorry, Papa,' he muttered. 'But…where is my cousin, *please*?'

Dante gazed down at his small nephew and grinned. 'She's asleep.'

'But I've got a present,' Simon complained.

'She's still a baby,' Dante explained reasonably. 'And she needs her sleep. She can see your present tomorrow.'

'Tomorrow?' Simon looked aghast. 'But that's *for ever*!'

An exasperated expression crossed Enzo's face. 'I'm going to take you back to your mother.' He gave Dante a glance—he'd already congratulated his brother on the new addition to the Cardinali family. 'How is Stella?'

'She's doing well,' Dante said, and she was. The birth had been tough going, but his kitten had been strong. Stronger than he'd been, at any rate.

'And Sofia?'

Dante thought about his daughter and grinned like a lunatic. 'She's perfect.'

Enzo gave a brisk nod. 'Well, you get some rest too. You look like hell.'

Dante didn't feel like hell. He felt incredible. As if he could do anything.

After his brother and nephew had gone, he went silently back into the private hospital room where Stella and their new daughter were sleeping.

Sofia was awake in her crib, her dark eyes—that he knew would end up being silver-blue, just like her mother's—staring up into his. And he found he could only look at her for a couple of moments at a time because it was either that or his heart would burst out of sheer joy.

He was going to have to learn how to deal with that.

Dante made sure the soft blanket was pulled snugly around his daughter and that she was quiet before moving over to the bed where his wife lay.

Stella blinked sleepily as he sat down beside her and smiled, her hand reaching for his.

He took it, the joy inside him becoming complete.

'You were amazing, my kitten,' he said quietly. 'I never knew how much strength it took to bring a new life into the world.'

Stella's smile deepened. 'You were pretty amazing yourself.'

Dante gave a rueful laugh. 'I did not handle it well.'

'You only swore and shouted twice. And you didn't threaten anyone with death, not once.'

Stella was being kind. Being with his wife while she'd been in pain and he'd been unable to help her had been one of the most difficult things he'd ever had to do.

'You set me a great example,' he said. 'I got my strength from you.'

'Because you were with me.' Her fingers tightened around his. 'We got our strength from each other.'

And she was right, they had. Because they loved each other.

Dante lifted his wife's hand to his mouth and kissed it. 'I love you, Stella Cardinali.'

Her smile was the one she kept for him and him alone. 'I will never get tired of hearing you say that.'

He turned her hand over and kissed her palm, staring into her shattered sky eyes. 'That's good, because I plan to keep saying it every day for the rest of our lives.'

And he did.

Because, as dedicated as he'd once been to being a reckless playboy who didn't feel a thing, he was even more dedicated to being a loving husband and father.

And, as it turned out, he was very good at that.

He was very good indeed.

* * * * *

Crowned At The Desert King's Command

MILLS & BOON

DEDICATION

To Dr. A. R. Coates.
So long, and thanks for all the fish.

CHAPTER ONE

Charlotte Devereaux didn't often think about her death. But when she did, she'd hoped it would be when she was very old and tucked into bed. Or maybe in a comfortable armchair, quietly slipping away over a very good book.

She hadn't imagined it would be of heatstroke and dehydration after getting lost in the desert trying to find her father.

He'd told her he was going to the top of the dune to get a better view of the dig site—nothing major. But then someone had mentioned that they hadn't seen Professor Devereaux for a while, so Charlotte had decided to go and see if she could find him.

She'd gone to the top dune where he had last been seen, only to find it empty. As all the dunes around her had been.

She hadn't been worried initially. Her father did go off on his own so he could think, and he was a very experienced and eminent archaeologist who'd been on many digs in his time. The desert was nothing out of the ordinary for him and the idea of him getting lost was unthinkable.

As her father's assistant, she wasn't entirely inexperienced herself when it came to a dig and finding her way around it, and yet somehow, when she'd turned around to go back to the site, it had vanished. Along with her sense of direction.

Again, she hadn't been worried—her father had talked a lot about how the desert could play tricks on a person's perception—so she'd strode off confidently the same way she'd come, retracing her steps, expecting to come across the site pretty much straight away.

Except she hadn't. And after about ten minutes of striding she'd realised that she'd made a mistake. A very grave one.

Of course she hadn't panicked. Panicking wouldn't help. It never did. The trick, when you got lost, was to stay calm and stay where you were.

So she had. But then the sun had got so hot—as if it were a hammer and she was the anvil. And she'd known that she was going to have to do something other than stand there otherwise she was going to die. So she'd started moving, going in the direction she'd thought the dig site would be, yet still it hadn't materialised, and now she was slowly coming to the conclusion that she was lost.

It was a bad thing to be lost in the desert.

A very bad thing.

Charlotte paused and adjusted the black and white scarf she wore wrapped around her head. She hated the thing. It was too heavy and too hot, and gritty due to the sand. It was also usually damp, because she was constantly bathed in sweat, but she wasn't sweating now and that was also a bad thing. Not sweating was a sign of heatstroke, wasn't it?

She squinted into the distance, trying to see where she was going. The sun was beating her to a pulp. A number of black dots danced in her vision. That was probably another sign of heatstroke too, because she was now starting to feel dizzy.

This was the end, wasn't it?

The rolling golden sands were endless, the violent blue of the sky a furnace she couldn't seem to climb out of.

The harsh, gritty sand under her feet was starting to move around like the deck of a ship and there was a roaring in her ears.

The black dots were getting bigger and bigger, looming large, until she realised that, actually, they weren't dots in her vision. They were people, a whole group of them, dressed in black and riding...horses?

How odd. Shouldn't they be riding camels?

She took a shaky step towards them, hope flooding through her. Were they some of the assistants from the dig? Had they come to find her? Rescue her?

'Hey,' she yelled. Or at least tried to. But the sound escaped as more of a harsh whisper.

The people on horses stopped, and she must be in a bad way because it wasn't until that moment that she remembered that the assistants didn't ride horses and they certainly weren't swathed in black robes, the way these people seemed to be. Neither did they wear... Oh, goodness, they were swords, weren't they?

Her heartbeat began to speed up, and a chill was sweeping through her despite the intense heat.

Her father, who'd been managing the dig, had warned everyone about how close the site was to the borders of Ashkaraz, and how they had to be careful not to stray too far. Ashkaraz had closed its borders nearly two decades ago and the current regime did not take kindly to intruders.

There were stories of men draped in black, who didn't carry guns but swords, and of people who'd accidentally strayed over the border and never been seen again.

Rumours about Ashkaraz abounded—about how it was ruled by a tyrant who kept his people living in fear, banning all international travel both out of and into the country. All aid was refused. All diplomats and journalists turned away.

There had been one journalist reputed to have smuggled himself into Ashkaraz a couple of years back, escaping to publish a hysterical article full of terrible stories of a crushed people living under a dictator's rule. But that was it.

Basically, no one knew what went on inside the country because no one—bar that journalist, and plenty doubted that he'd even been there anyway—had ever been there and come back.

Charlotte hadn't listened much to the stories, or worried about how close to the borders they were. Mainly because she had been enjoying spending time with her father and was more interested in the archaeology they were doing than in rumours about a closed country.

Now, though, she wished she'd paid more attention. Because if the people approaching her weren't assistants from the dig, then they were people from somewhere else.

Somewhere frightening.

She squinted harder at the group on horseback. Oh, goodness, was that a…a person, slung over the back of one of their horses? It seemed to be. A person with distinctive pale hair…

Her heart constricted, recognition slamming into her. She'd recognise that hair anywhere, because her hair was exactly the same colour. It was a family trait. Which meant that the person currently slung over the back of that horse was her father.

Fear wound around her, as cold as the sun was hot. He must have got lost, like she had, and they'd picked him up. And now they'd found her too…

A tall figure in the middle of the group swung down off his horse—and it had to be a he, given that women weren't generally built like Roman gladiators—the sunlight catching the naked blade thrust through the belt that wound around his hips, and the chill that gripped Charlotte intensified.

He came towards her, moving with the fluid, athletic grace of a hunter despite his height and build and the shifting sand under his feet. She couldn't see his face, he was covered from head to foot, but as he came closer she saw his eyes.

They weren't so much brown as a dense, smoky gold. Like a tiger.

And all at once she knew that her doubts had been correct. That this was definitely not a search party come to rescue her. A group of men draped in black with swords at their hips could only mean one thing: they were Ashkaraz border guards and they were not here to rescue her. They were here to take her prisoner because she had almost certainly strayed into the wrong country.

The man came closer, looming over her, his broad figure blocking out the hammer-blow of the sun.

But even the sun wasn't as hot or as brilliant as the gold of his eyes. And they were just as relentless, just as harsh. There was no mercy in those eyes. There was no help at all.

You fool. You should have told someone where you were going. But you didn't, did you?

No, she hadn't. She'd just gone to find her father, thinking she'd only be a couple of minutes. It was true that she hadn't been paying attention to where she'd been going, as she'd so often done as a child, lost in whatever daydream had grabbed her at the time, since that had been better than listening to the screaming arguments of her parents as they'd battled each other over her head.

Even now, as an adult, she found it difficult to concentrate sometimes, when she was stressed or things were chaotic, her mind spinning off into its own fantasies, escaping reality. Though those moments of inattention didn't usually have such terrible repercussions as now, when she was left with the choice of either turning and running away from the terrible man striding towards her across the hot sand, or falling to her knees and begging for her life.

What did these guards do to people who strayed over the borders? No one knew. No one had ever escaped. She and her father were going to be taken prisoner and no one would ever hear from them again.

Running was out of the question. Not only was there nowhere to run, she couldn't leave her father. Wouldn't leave him. He'd had no one else but her since her mother had moved to the States nearly fifteen years ago—and, though he wouldn't exactly win any father-of-the-year awards, his career and all the digs he'd taken her on had instilled in her a love of history and ancient peoples that the dreamer inside her found fascinating.

She had a lot to thank him for, so she'd follow him the way she'd always followed him.

Which meant that she was going to have to throw herself on this man's mercy—if, indeed, he had any.

Fear gripped her tight, and darkness crawled at the edge of her vision. Her lips were cracked, dry as the desert sand drifting around her feet, but she fought to remain upright. She was an idiot for wandering away from the site, it was true, but she wasn't going to compound her mistake by collapsing ignominiously at this man's feet.

She would be polite and reasonable, apologise calmly, and tell him that she hadn't meant to wander into his country by mistake. That her father was a professor and she only a lowly assistant, and they hadn't meant any harm. Also, could he please not kill them, or throw them into a dungeon, or any of the rest of the things her over-active imagination kept providing for her?

A hot wind kicked at the black hem of the man's robes, making them flow around his powerful thighs as he came to a stop in front of her. He stood there so still, as if he was a mountain that had stood for millennia, as enduring and unchanging as the desert itself.

Charlotte held tight to consciousness and something about his merciless golden gaze hardened her spine, making her square her shoulders and straighten up.

She tried to get some moisture into her mouth and failed. 'I'm sorry,' she forced out. 'Do you speak English? Are you able to help me?'

The man was silent a long moment, and then he said something, his voice deep enough that she felt it in her chest, a subtle, sub-sonic vibration. But she didn't understand him. Her Arabic was rough, and the liquid sounds bore no resemblance to the minimal words she knew.

She felt very weak all of a sudden, and quite sick.

The man's golden eyes seemed to fill her entire vision, his stare hard, brutal, crushing utterly her hope of rescue and of mercy.

She would get neither from him and that was obvious.

'I'm so terribly sorry,' Charlotte whispered as the darkness gathered around her. 'But I think the man you have on that horse is my father. We're quite lost. Do you think you could possibly help us?'

Then she fainted dead away at his feet.

TARIQ IBN ISHAK Al Naziri, Sheikh of Ashkaraz, stared impassively at the small body of the Englishwoman collapsed on the sand in front of him.

Her father, she'd said. Well, that cleared up the question of who the man was.

They'd found him unconscious on one of the dunes. After finding him, Tariq and his border guards had then spotted the woman, and had been tracking her for a good twenty minutes. Her zigzag path and the way she'd blundered across the border straight into Ashkaraz made it clear she had no idea where she was going, though what she'd murmured just now clarified things somewhat. She'd obviously been looking for the man currently slung over Jaziri's horse.

Tariq had been hoping she'd turn around and make her way back over the border again, ensuring that she wasn't his problem any more, but she hadn't. She'd spotted them instead and had just stood there, watching him approach her as if he was her own personal saviour.

Given that she was clearly suffering from heatstroke and advanced dehydration, she wasn't far wrong.

He didn't touch her just yet, though, because you could never be too suspicious of lost foreigners wandering over his borders—as the incident with the man who'd been armed and hoping to 'free the people of Ashkaraz from tyranny' had proved only the week before. One of his border guards had been severely injured and Tariq didn't want that to happen again.

It was probably why Faisal—his father's old advisor, who'd now become his—had been unhappy about Tariq approaching this woman himself rather than letting one of his guards do it. But protecting his subjects was his purpose, and he didn't want another injury simply because one guard had been a little careless when dealing with an outsider.

Tariq knew how to deal with them; his guards generally did not.

Especially a woman. They could be the most dangerous of all.

Except this woman didn't look very dangerous right now, crumpled as she was on the sand. She was dressed in a pair of stained, loose blue trousers and a long-sleeved white shirt, with a black and white scarf wrapped around her head, which was paltry protection from the desert sun.

She did actually seem to be unconscious, but since it

could be difficult to tell, and Tariq was naturally suspicious, he nudged her experimentally with the toe of his boot. Her head rolled to the side, her scarf coming loose and revealing a lock of hair pale as moonlight.

Yes, very definitely unconscious.

He frowned, studying her face. Her features were fine and regular and, though he preferred women with stronger looks, she could be said to be pretty. Currently the fine grain of her skin was flushed bright red from the heat and burned from the sun, making the pale arches of her eyebrows stand out.

English, no doubt, given the sunburn. Certainly when she'd spoken he recognised that cut-glass accent, which meant the man they'd picked up was likely English too.

He gave her another assessing look. Neither she nor the man were carrying anything, which meant their camp, or wherever they'd come from, couldn't be far away. Were they part of a tour party, perhaps? Although tour parties generally didn't come this far into the desert—they stuck to the edges, where it was cooler, safer. From where they could easily get back to the air-conditioned luxury of their hotels and away from the sun and the heat and the rumours of a closed country where men patrolled the borders wearing swords.

'Two foreigners in the same stretch of desert,' Faisal said dryly from behind him. 'This cannot be a coincidence.'

'No, it is not. She saw the man on Jaziri's horse. She said something about her father.'

'Ah…' Faisal murmured. 'Then we can safely assume she is not a threat?'

'We assume nothing.' Tariq let his gaze rove over her, scanning for any concealed weapons just to be sure. 'All outsiders are a threat, unconscious or not.'

And it was true—they were. That was why his father

had closed the borders and why Tariq had kept them closed. Outsiders were greedy, wanting what they did not have and uncaring of who they destroyed to get it.

He'd seen the effects of such destruction and he would not let it happen to his country. Not again.

There were always a few, though, who thought it fun to try and get inside Ashkaraz's famous closed borders, to get a glimpse of the kingdom, to take pictures and post them on the internet as proof of having got inside.

There were some who couldn't resist the lure.

They were always caught before they could do any damage. They were rounded up and had the fear of God put into them before being sent on their way with tales of brutality and swords—even though his soldiers never actually touched any of the people they caught. Fear was enough of a deterrent.

Though not enough of a deterrent for this woman, apparently.

'If she is a threat, she is not much of one,' Faisal observed, looking down at her. 'Perhaps she and her father are tourists? Or journalists?'

'It does not matter who they are,' Tariq said. 'We will deal with them as we have dealt with all the rest.'

Which involved a stint in the dungeons, a few threats, and then an ignominious return to the border, where they would be summarily ejected into one of their neighbouring countries and told never to return again.

'This one in particular might be difficult,' Faisal pointed out. His tone was absolutely neutral, which was a good sign that he disapproved of Tariq's decision in some way. 'She is not only a foreigner but a woman. We cannot afford to treat her the way we treat the rest.'

Irritation gathered in Tariq's gut. Unfortunately, Faisal was right. So far he'd managed to avoid any diplomatic incidents following his treatment of outsiders, but there was always a first time for everything—and, given the gender and nationality of the person concerned, Ashkaraz might indeed run into some issues.

England wouldn't be happy if one of its own was roughly treated by the Ashkaraz government—especially not a woman. Especially not a young, helpless woman. The man they might have got away with, but not her. She would draw attention, and attention was the last thing Tariq wanted.

Then there was the issue of his own government, and how certain members of it would no doubt use her as ammunition in their argument on how closed borders didn't help them remain unseen on the global stage, and how the world was moving on and if they didn't have contact with it, it would move on without them.

Tariq didn't care about the rest of the world. He cared only about his country and his subjects. And, since those two things were currently in good health, he saw no need to change his stance on reopening the borders.

His vow as Sheikh was to protect his country and its people and that was what he was going to do.

Especially when you've failed once before.

The whispered thought was insidious, a snake dripping poison, but he ignored it the way he always did.

He would not fail. Not again.

Ignoring Faisal's observation, Tariq crouched down beside the little intruder. The loose clothing she wore made it difficult to ascertain visually whether she carried weapons or not, and since he had to be certain he gave her a very brief, very impersonal pat-down.

She was small, and quite delicate, but there were definite curves beneath those clothes. There were also no weapons to speak of.

'Sire,' Faisal said again, annoyingly present. 'Are you sure that is wise?'

Tariq didn't ask what he meant. He knew. Faisal was the only one who knew about Catherine and about Tariq's response to her.

Given what that led to, he has every right to question you.

The irritation sitting in Tariq's gut tightened into anger. No, he'd excised Catherine from his soul like a surgeon cutting out a cancer, and he'd cut out every emotion associated with her too. Everything soft. Everything merciful.

There was no need for Faisal to question him, because what had happened with Catherine would never happen again. Tariq had made sure of it.

Though perhaps his advisor needed a reminder...

'Do you question me, Faisal?' Tariq asked with deceptive mildness, not looking up from the woman on the sand.

There was a silence. Then, 'No, sire.'

Faisal's voice held a slight hint of apology. Too slight.

Tariq scowled down at the woman. Obviously, given Faisal's clear doubts, he was going to have to deal with this himself.

'I can get a couple of the men to have a look around to see where she and the other foreigner have come from,' Faisal went on, perhaps hoping to assuage him. 'We could perhaps return them both with no one any the wiser?'

It would be the easiest thing to do.

But Tariq couldn't afford 'easy'. He'd instituted the law to keep the borders closed and he had to be seen to uphold it.

A king couldn't afford to be weak.

Hadn't he learned his lesson there?

You should have listened to your father.

Yes, he should. But he hadn't.

'No,' he said flatly. 'We will not be returning either of them.'

He leaned forward, gathering the woman up and rising to his feet. She was so light in his arms. It was like carrying a moonbeam. Her head rolled onto his shoulder, her cheek pressed to the rough black cotton of his robes.

Small. Like Catherine.

Something he'd thought long-dead and buried stirred inside him and he found himself looking down at her once again. Ah, but she wasn't anything like Catherine, And, anyway, that had been years ago.

He felt nothing for her any more.

He felt nothing for anyone any more.

Only his kingdom. Only his people.

Tariq lifted his gaze to Faisal's, met the other man's appraising stare head-on. 'By all means send a couple of men out to see what they can discover about where these two have come from,' he ordered coldly. 'And get in touch with the camp. We will need the chopper to be readied to take them back to Kharan.'

He didn't wait for a response, turning and making his way back to the horses and the group of soldiers waiting for him.

'Perhaps one of the men can deal with her?' Faisal suggested neutrally, trailing along behind him. 'I can—'

'I will deal with her,' Tariq interrupted with cold authority, not turning around. 'There can be no question about her treatment should the British government become involved. Which means the responsibility for her lies with me.'

There were others who remembered the bad times, when Ashkaraz had been fought over and nearly torn apart following Catherine's betrayal, and they wouldn't be so lenient with a foreign woman again.

Not that he would be lenient either. She would soon get a taste of Ashkaraz's hospitality when she was taken to the capital of Kharan. They had a facility there especially for dealing with people who'd strayed into Ashkaraz, and he was sure she wouldn't like it.

That was the whole point, after all. To frighten people so they never came back.

His men watched silently as he carried her over to his horse and put her on it, steadying her as she slumped against the animal's neck. Then he mounted behind her and pulled her back against him, tucking her into the crook of one arm while he grabbed the reins with the other.

'Continue with the patrol,' he instructed Faisal. 'I want to know where this woman comes from—and fast.'

The other man nodded, his gaze flickering again to the woman in Tariq's arms. Tariq had the strangest urge to tuck her closer against him, to hide her from the old advisor's openly speculative look.

Ridiculous. The doubts Faisal had would soon be put to rest. Tariq was a different man from the boy he'd once been. He was harder. Colder. He was a worthy heir to his father, though he knew Faisal had had his objections to Tariq inheriting the throne. Not that Faisal or the rest of the government had had a choice in the matter since his father had only had one son.

Still. He had thought Faisal's scepticism long put to rest. *It is the woman. She is the problem.*

Yes, she was. Luckily, though, she would not be a problem much longer.

'You have objections?' Tariq stared hard at the older man.

Faisal only shook his head. 'None, sire.'

He was lying. Faisal always had objections. It was a good thing the older man knew that now was not the time to voice them.

'As my father's oldest friend, you have a certain amount

of leeway,' Tariq warned him. It would do him good to be reminded. 'But see that you do not overreach yourself.'

Faisal's expression was impassive as he inclined his head. 'Sire.'

Dismissing him, Tariq nodded to Jaziri and a couple of the other guards in unspoken command. Then, tugging on the reins, he turned his horse around and set off back to base camp.

CHAPTER TWO

Charlotte was having a lovely dream about swimming in cool water. It flowed silkily over her skin, making her want to stretch like a cat in the sun. It moved over her body, sliding over her face, pressing softly against her lips…

There was a harsh sound from somewhere and abruptly she opened her eyes, the dream fragmenting and then crashing down around her ears.

She was not swimming in cool water.

She was lying on a narrow, hard bed in a tiny room, empty except for a bucket in the corner. A single naked bulb hung from the ceiling. The floor was cracked concrete, the walls bare stone.

It looked like a…a jail cell.

Her heartbeat began to accelerate, fear coiling inside her. What had happened? Why was she here?

Her father had wandered away from the dig site and she'd gone to find him, only to get lost in the desert. Then those men on horseback had turned up, with her father slung over the back of a horse, and there had been that other man in black robes. That powerful man with the golden eyes, watching her. Tall and broad as a mountain. He'd had a sword at his hip and his gaze had been merciless, brutal…

A shudder moved down her spine.

He must have rescued her after she'd fainted—though

this wasn't exactly what she'd call a rescue. He might have saved her life, but he'd delivered her to a cell.

Slowly she let out a breath, trying to calm her racing heartbeat, and pushed herself up.

This had to be an Ashkaraz jail cell. And that man had to have been one of the feared border guards. And—oh, heavens—did they have her father here too? Had they both joined the ranks of people who'd crossed into Ashkaraz, a closed country?

And you know what happens to those people. They're never heard from again.

Charlotte moistened her suddenly dry mouth, trying to get a grip on her flailing emotions. No, she mustn't panic. Plenty of people had been heard from again—otherwise how would anyone know that the country was a tyranny run by a terrible dictator? That its people lived in poverty and ignorance and were terrorised?

Anyway, that line of thought wasn't helping. What she should be concentrating on was what she should do now.

Pushing aside thoughts of dictators and terror, she swung her legs over the side of the horrible bed and stood up. A wave of dizziness hit her, along with some nausea, but the feeling passed after a couple of moments of stillness. Her face stung, but since there was no mirror she couldn't see what the problem was. Sunburn, probably.

Slowly she moved over to the door and tried to open it, but it remained shut. Locked, obviously. Frowning, she took another look around the room. Up high near the ceiling was a small window, bright sunlight shining through it.

Maybe she could have a look and see what was out there? Get a feel for where she was? Certainly that was better than sitting around feeling afraid.

Charlotte stood there for a moment, biting her lip and thinking, then she shoved the bed underneath the window and climbed on top of it. Her fingers just scraped the ledge, not giving her nearly enough leverage to pull herself up. Annoyed, she took another look around before her gaze settled on the bucket in the corner.

Ah, that might work.

Jumping down off the bed, she went over to the bucket, picked it up and took it back to the bed. She upended it, set it down on the mattress, then climbed back onto the bed and onto the bucket. Given more height, she was able to pull herself up enough to look out of the window.

The glass was dusty and cracked, but she could see through it. However, the view was nothing but the stone wall of another building. She frowned again, trying to peer around to see if she could see anything, but couldn't.

Perhaps she could break the glass?

Yes, she could do that, and then…

A sudden thought gripped her. Carefully, she examined the window again. She was a small woman, which had proved useful on many occasions, such as in hiding from her parents when the shouting had got too bad, and maybe it could be useful now?

Or maybe you should just sit and wait to see what happens?

She could—but this wasn't just about her, was it? She had her father to consider. He might be in another jail cell somewhere or he could even be dead. Dead and she would never know.

You really will be alone then.

Cold crept through her, despite the sun outside.

No, she couldn't sit there, helpless and not knowing. She had to do something.

Decisive now, she stripped off the white shirt she was wearing—her scarf seemed to have disappeared somewhere along the line—and wrapped it around her hand. Then she hammered with her fist on the glass. After a couple of strikes against the crack already running through it, the pane shattered beautifully.

Pleased with herself, she made sure that there were no sharp shards there, waiting to cut her, and then before she could think better of it she wriggled through the window.

A large man wouldn't have made it. Even a medium-sized man would have had difficulty.

But a small woman? Easy.

She fell rather ignominiously to the ground, winding herself, and had to lie there for a couple of moments to get her breath back. The sun was incredibly hot, the air like a furnace. Definitely she was somewhere in Ashkaraz, that was for sure.

But then she was conscious of a sound. A familiar sound. Traffic. Cars and trucks on a road…horns sounding. People talking…the first few bars of a very popular pop song currently hitting the charts rising.

Puzzled, she pushed herself to her feet and found herself standing in a narrow alley between two tall stone buildings. At the mouth of the alley there appeared to be a street, with people walking past.

Despite her fear and uncertainty, an unexpected thrill of excitement caught at her.

She was in a closed country. A country no foreigner had seen for over twenty years. No one except her.

As her father's assistant she'd become interested in archaeology and history, but it had always been society and people that had fascinated her the most. Ashkaraz was reportedly a throwback to medieval times, a society where time had stood still.

And you might be the first person to see the truth of it.

Nothing was going to stop her from seeing that truth, and she eagerly started towards the mouth of the alleyway.

Nothing could have prepared her for the shock of seeing an Ashkaraz street.

Part of her had been expecting horses and carts, a medieval fantasy of a middle eastern city, with ancient souks and camels and snake charmers. But that was not what she saw.

Bright, shiny and very new cars moved in the street, beneath tall, architecturally designed buildings made of glass and steel. People bustled along on the footpaths, some robed, some in the kind of clothes she would have seen on the streets in London. In amongst the glass and steel were historic buildings, beautifully preserved, and shops and cafés lined the streets. People were sitting at tables outside, talking, laughing, working, looking at their smartphones.

There was an energy to the place, which was clearly a bustling, successful, prosperous city.

Definitely not the poverty-stricken nation with a beaten-down populace crushed under the thumb of a dictator that the rest of the world thought it to be.

What on earth was going on?

Amazed, Charlotte stepped out onto the footpath, joining the stream of people walking along it, oblivious to the glances she was receiving.

There was a beautiful park up ahead, with a fountain and lush gardens, lots of benches to sit on and a playground for children. Already there seemed to be a number of kids there, screaming and laughing while their indulgent parents looked on.

This was…incredible. Amazing. How was this even possible? Was this the truth that Ashkaraz had been hiding all along?

She was so busy staring that she didn't notice the uniformed man coming up behind her until his fingers wrapped around her arm. And then a long black car pulled up to the kerb and Charlotte found herself bundled into the back of it.

She opened her mouth to protest, but there wasn't even time for her to scream. Something black and suffocating was put over her head and the car started moving.

The fingers around her arm were firm—not hurting, but definitely ensuring that she couldn't get away. Fear, coming a little late to the party, suddenly rose up inside her, choking.

Did you really think you could escape from that jail cell and start wandering around like nothing was wrong?

She hadn't been thinking—that was the problem. She'd got out of that cell and then been caught up in the wonder of the city outside it.

Charlotte slumped back in the seat, trying not to panic. Now, not only was her chance to escape gone but so was her father's.

And it was all her fault.

The car drove for what seemed like ages and then slowed to a stop. She was pulled out of it and then taken up some steps. Sun and heat surrounded her for a second, and then she must have been taken inside because the sun had disappeared, to be replaced by blessedly cool air. Her footsteps echoed on a tiled floor, and there was the scent of water and flowers in the air.

She couldn't see a thing through the black fabric around her head, and her sense of direction was soon gone as she was pulled down more corridors, around corners, and up yet more stairs.

Were they taking her back to that cell? Or were there worse things in store for her? Would they perhaps murder her? Make her disappear? Hold her prisoner for ever?

She was just starting to be very, very afraid when she

was pulled to a stop and the fabric covering her head was abruptly tugged off.

Charlotte blinked in the bright light.

She appeared to be standing in a large room lined with shelves, containing lots of books and folders and filing boxes. The exquisite tiled floor was covered in thick, brightly coloured silk rugs, the walls also tiled, in silvery, slightly iridescent tiles. There was a window in front of her that gave a view onto a beautiful garden, where a fountain played amongst palms and other shrubs, as well as many different kinds of flowers.

A huge, heavy desk made of time-blackened wood stood before the window. The polished surface was clean of everything except a sleek-looking computer monitor and keyboard, and a small, elegant silver vase with a spray of fresh jasmine in it.

This was certainly *not* a jail cell. In fact, it looked like someone's office…

She blinked again and turned around to see two men stationed on either side of the double doors. They were dressed in black robes with swords on their hips, their faces absolutely impassive.

She would have thought the robes and swords only ceremonial, except they didn't have the clean and pressed look she would have expected. The fabric of their robes was dusty and stained around the hems, as were the boots the men wore. And although the edges of the swords were bright, was that…blood she could see on the steel? Surely it couldn't be.

Charlotte stared, her heartbeat getting faster and faster, and then suddenly from behind her came the sound of a door opening and closing.

She turned back sharply to see that a man had come

into the room from a door off to her left, and he was now standing beside the desk, staring at her.

He was very, very tall and very, very broad, built more like an ancient warrior than a businessman. The muscles of his chest and arms were straining the white cotton of his business shirt, and the dark wool of his suit trousers pulled tight around his powerful thighs.

His face was a harsh composition of planes and angles that nevertheless managed to be utterly compelling, with high cheekbones and an aquiline nose, straight black brows and a beautifully carved mouth.

'Handsome' was far too bland a word for him…especially as he radiated the kind of arrogant charisma reserved only for the very powerful and very important.

But that wasn't what held Charlotte absolutely rooted to the spot.

It was his eyes. Burning gold, with the same relentless, brutal heat as the desert sun.

It was the man who'd approached her in the desert. She was sure of it. She'd never forget those eyes.

He said nothing for a long moment and neither did Charlotte, since she couldn't seem to find her voice. Then his gaze shifted to the men behind her and he gave a slight tilt of his head. A couple of seconds later she heard the door shut behind her, the men clearly having obeyed some unspoken order and left.

The room abruptly felt tiny and cramped, the space too small to accommodate both her and the man in front of her. Or maybe he seemed to get larger and more intimidating, taking up all the air and leaving none for her.

She lifted her chin, trying to get her heartbeat under control at the same time as trying to hold his relentless gaze, but she couldn't seem to manage both—especially not when he moved suddenly, coming over to the desk and standing in front of it, folding his arms across his massive chest.

Bringing him quite a bit closer.

She resisted the urge to take a step back, hating how small and insignificant his sheer size made her feel. It was exactly the same feeling that had filled her when her parents had argued and she'd hidden under the dining room table. They'd never noticed that she'd left her seat—which was ironic, since more often than not they had been shouting about her.

Clasping her hands in front of her to prevent them from shaking, Charlotte took a small, silent breath. 'Um…do you speak English?' Her voice sounded thin and reedy in the silence of the room.

The man said nothing, continuing to stare at her.

It was extremely unnerving.

Her mouth had dried and she wished her Arabic was better. Because maybe he didn't understand English. She wanted to ask him where her father was and also to thank him for saving her.

He put you in a cell, remember?

Sure, but maybe that hadn't been him. He might look like a medieval warrior, but the suit he was wearing was thoroughly modern. Perhaps he was an accountant? Or the chief of the jail she'd been put in? Or a government functionary?

Yet none of those things seemed to fit. He was too magnetic, too charismatic to be anyone's mere functionary. No, this man had an aura about him that spoke of command, as if he expected everyone to fall to their knees around him.

Sadly for him, she wouldn't be falling anywhere in front of him.

Except you already have. In the desert.

That, alas, was true.

'I'm s-sorry,' she stuttered, casting around for something

to say. 'I should have thanked you for saving my life. But can you tell me where my father is? We got lost, you see. And I... I...' She faltered, all her words crushed by the weight of his stare.

This was silly. Her father could be dead or in a jail cell and she was letting this man get to her. She couldn't get pathetic now.

Perhaps introducing herself would help. After all, she'd had no identification on her when she'd collapsed, so maybe they had no idea who she or her father were. Maybe that was why she had been put in the cell? Maybe they thought she was some kind of insurgent, hoping to...?

But, no. Best not get carried away. Keep thinking in the here and now.

'So,' Charlotte said, pulling herself together. 'My name is—'

'Charlotte Devereaux,' the man interrupted in a deep, slightly rough voice. 'You are an assistant attached to an archaeological dig that your father, Professor Martin Devereaux is managing in conjunction with the University of Siddq.'

His English was perfect, his accent almost imperceptible.

'You both come from Cornwall, but you live in London and at present are employed by your father's university as his assistant. You are twenty-three years old, have no dependents, and live in a flat with a couple of friends in Clapham.'

Charlotte could feel her mouth hanging open in shock. How did he know all this stuff? How had he found out?

'I...' she began.

But he hadn't finished, because he was going on, ignoring her entirely, 'Can you tell me, please, what you were doing out there in the desert? Neither you nor your father were anywhere near your dig site. In fact, that is the whole reason you are here. You crossed the border into Ashkaraz—you do understand that, do you not?'

She flushed at the note of condescension in his voice, but took heart from the fact that he was talking of her father in the present tense.

'Are you saying that my father is alive?' she asked, needing to be sure.

'Yes,' the man said flatly. 'He is alive.'

Relief filled her, making her breath catch. 'Oh, I'm so glad. He wandered away from the site, the way he sometimes does, and I went to try and find him. I walked up a dune and somehow—'

'I am not interested in how you got lost, Miss Devereaux,' the man interrupted, his voice like iron, his golden stare pitiless. 'What I am interested in is how you somehow got out of a secure facility.'

Charlotte swallowed. Briefly she debated lying, but since she was in a lot of trouble already there was no point in making it any worse.

'I...smashed the glass and crawled out of the window.' She lifted her chin a little to show him that she wouldn't be cowed. 'It really wasn't that difficult.'

'You crawled out of the window?' he repeated, his voice flat, the lines of his brutally handsome face set and hard. 'And what made you think that was a good idea?'

'I've heard the rumours,' she said defensively. 'About how people who stray over your borders disappear for ever, never to be seen again. How they're beaten and terrorised. And I didn't know what had happened to my father.' She steeled herself. 'I saw an opportunity to escape, to see if I could find him, and so I took it.'

The man said nothing, but that stare of his felt like a weight pressing her down and crushing her into dust.

You're really for it now.

Charlotte gripped her hands together, lifted her chin another inch and stared back. 'We're British citizens, you know. You can't just make us disappear like all the rest. My dad is a very well-respected academic. Once people realise we're missing they'll send others to find us. So you'd better tell whoever is in charge here that—'

'No need. All the interested parties already know.'

'Which interested parties?'

His face was impassive. 'Me.'

'You?' Charlotte tried to look sceptical and failed. 'And who exactly are you?'

'I am the one in charge,' he said, without any emphasis at all.

'Oh? Are you the head of the police or something?'

It would explain his aura of command, after all.

'No. I am not the head of the police.'

His eyes gleamed with something that made her breath catch.

'I am the head of the country. I am the Sheikh of Ashkaraz.'

CHARLOTTE DEVEREAUX, ALL five foot nothing of her, blinked her large silver-blue eyes. Shock was written across her pretty, pink features.

She should be shocked.

She should be quaking in those little boots of hers.

He'd only just been notified of her escape and her jaunt down Kharan's main street, and to say that he was angry was massively to understate the case.

He was furious. Absolutely, volcanically furious.

The fury boiled away inside him like lava, and only long years of iron control kept it locked down and not spilling everywhere, destroying everything in its path.

Because he had no one to blame for this incident but himself. He was the one who'd elected to bring her back to Kharan and not to follow Faisal's advice to return her and her father to the dig site from which they'd come.

No, he'd decided to handle her himself, to make sure she was taken back to Kharan and had the medical treatment she required. Her father had needed more, and was still unconscious in a secure hospital ward. She had been transferred to the facility where they kept all illegal visitors to Ashkaraz.

Normally those visitors tended to be men. They were not usually little women who could wriggle through small windows. He hadn't even known the cell she'd been put in *had* a window.

Not that it mattered now. What mattered was that this woman had escaped and had somehow stumbled unchecked into Kharan, and she had seen through the lies he and his people told the world.

Far from being a nation stuck in time, mired in poverty and war, it was prosperous and healthy, its population well-cared-for and happy.

And it was a wealthy nation. A *very* wealthy nation.

A nation that had to hide its wealth from the rest of the world or else be torn apart by those desperate to get their hands on it—as had occurred nearly twenty years earlier.

He couldn't allow that to happen again.

He wouldn't.

Catherine had been at the centre of it twenty years ago and now here was Charlotte Devereaux, another foreign woman causing another diplomatic incident.

This time, though, he would not be a party to it, the way he had been with Catherine. He'd learned his lesson and he'd learned it well, and he would not be giving this woman the benefit of the doubt.

'Oh,' she said faintly. 'Oh. I... I see.'

Her voice had a pleasant husk to it. Somewhere along the line she'd lost her scarf, so her silvery blonde hair hung in a loose ponytail down her back, wisps of it stuck to her forehead. The angry red of the sunburn she'd got out in the desert had faded slightly, leaving her pale skin pink. It made the colour of her eyes stand out, glittering like stars. She wore the same pair of loose blue trousers she'd had on in the desert, though the white shirt had gone, leaving in its place a tight-fitting white tank top.

It did not escape his notice that, though she was small, she had a surprisingly lush figure.

'I am sure that you do not see,' he said, forcing those particular observations to one side. 'Because your little excursion has put me in a very difficult position.'

She gave him a cool look that pricked against something inside him like a thorn, needling him. 'Indeed? How so?'

It was not the response he'd hoped for. In fact, nothing of her behaviour was the response he'd hoped for. She should be afraid. As any woman—or any person, for that matter—who'd woken up to find herself in a jail cell would be. Especially given the rumours she must have heard about Ashkaraz.

She should be terrified for her life, not standing there giving him cool looks as if he was nothing more than a mere functionary and not the king of his own country.

'Miss Devereaux,' he said, his anger still raw. 'You are not at all showing proper deference.'

She blinked those glittering silvery eyes again. 'Oh, I'm not? I'm sorry. I don't know the customs—'

'You would curtsey before your queen, would you not?' He cut her off coldly. 'I am king here. My word is law.'

'Oh,' she repeated, lowering her gaze. 'I didn't mean

to offend.' Then she made an awkward curtsey, her hands fluttering at her sides.

He narrowed his gaze at her. Was she making fun of him? He didn't think so, but you could never tell with foreigners.

It didn't improve his temper.

Then again, he shouldn't be taking his temper out on her, full stop. A king should be above such things, as his father had always told him. A ruler needed to be hard, cold. Detached from his emotions.

Except he could feel his anger straining at the leash he'd put on it. He wanted her on her knees, begging his forgiveness.

Are you sure that's the only reason you want her on her knees?

Something shifted inside him—a strange pull.

She was…pretty. And, yes, there was a physical attraction there. Perhaps that accounted for the reason this particular woman tried his temper so badly. Not that an attraction would make the slightest difference. As he'd told Faisal out in the desert, he'd treat her exactly the same way he treated every other intruder.

'It is too late for that,' he said implacably. 'You have offended already. You escaped your cell and found your way into the city.'

She was standing with her small hands clasped, but this time the expression on her face wasn't so much cool as uncertain.

'Yes, well…as I was going to explain, I didn't mean to. I just wasn't sure what you were going to do with me or my father.'

'We would have done what we do with all illegal visitors to Ashkaraz. You would have both been sent back to your home country.' He paused. 'But we cannot do that now.'

Her pale brows drew together. 'Why not?'

'Because you have walked down the main street of Kharan and seen the truth.'

'What? You mean all the nice buildings? The new cars and smartphones and things?' Her mouth, full and prettily pink, curved. 'It's such a beautiful city. How is me seeing that a problem?'

'Because you will tell other people, Miss Devereaux.'

What he had to tell her now wouldn't be welcome, yet she had to understand the gravity of the situation.

'And they will tell others, and so it will go on until the whole world learns the truth. And I cannot let that happen.'

She was still frowning. 'I don't understand...'

'Of course you do not. But you will have plenty of time to work it out.'

Another ripple of uncertainty crossed her face. 'That sounds ominous. What do you mean by that?'

'I mean that we cannot send you back to England. We cannot send either of you back to England. You will have to remain in Ashkaraz.' He paused again, for emphasis. 'Indefinitely.'

CHAPTER THREE

Charlotte's mouth had gone bone-dry. 'E-Excuse me?' she stuttered. 'I'm sorry, but I thought you said "indefinitely".'

The man—no, the Sheikh—looked at her with the same unyielding merciless stare he'd been giving her ever since he'd walked in here. As if he was furiously angry and trying to hide it. He was doing a very good job of it, but she recognised his expression. It was the same expression her father had used to have when he was furious with her mother and trying very hard not to show it.

Ever since her parents' relationship had broken down she'd become particularly sensitive to suppressed emotion, because even though the shouting had been bad, her parents' silent fury had been worse. It had filled the whole house, making her feel as if she was being crushed slowly in a vice. She'd had to run away when it got like that—except right now there was nowhere to run.

Then again, she wasn't the frightened girl she'd been back then. She'd learned to shield herself from people's inconvenient emotions by being cool and polite. Though that boat had long since sailed in this case.

The Sheikh's relentless golden stare was inescapable. 'I did,' he said succinctly.

'But you can't mean that.' She swallowed. 'You can't just keep us here for...for ever.'

'My word is law, Miss Devereaux,' he said in that implacable way. 'I can do whatever I please.'

A laugh escaped her, even though she hadn't meant it to, and it sounded shrill in the quiet of the office with the fountain playing outside. 'I'm not going to tell anyone what I saw. I promise I won't. Not that I saw anything anyway— a few buildings, nothing much—'

'Your promises are not sufficient.'

There was no answering amusement in his eyes. None in his face either.

Her chest constricted, and there was a kernel of ice sitting in the pit of her stomach. 'That's ridiculous. No one will even believe me anyway.'

'Some people will. And they will tell others. And soon there will be more like you, coming across our borders, wanting to see the truth for themselves. It is attention this country cannot afford.'

Abruptly, he turned away, striding around the side of the desk, moving with the lean grace of a panther.

'No, you cannot leave. You will have to remain here.'

'People will come and find us,' she insisted. 'An eminent professor and his daughter can't just go missing in the desert without someone doing something.'

'Plenty of people go missing in the desert.'

He stood behind his desk, a massive, powerful figure, and the sunlight fell on his glossy black hair. Putting his hands on the desktop, he leaned on them, never breaking eye contact with her.

'They will think you got lost and perished.'

'But not without searching for us,' she argued, because this was insane. Preposterous, even. 'You'll have search parties all along your borders, looking for Dad and me. And everyone has heard all the rumours about Ashkaraz. Don't think people won't be looking your way.'

He said nothing for a long moment and she had the sense that she'd scored a hit. Good. Because right now that kernel of ice in her gut wasn't going away. It was getting bigger, freezing her.

If you'd only waited in the cell...

Charlotte ignored the thought. Instead she took a surreptitious breath and stared back at the Sheikh, completely forgetting the fact that he was actually a sheikh and maybe that was rude. Then again, he'd threatened to keep her prisoner here indefinitely, and that certainly wasn't polite.

'Are you threatening me, Miss Devereaux?' he enquired at last, his voice silky and dark and full of danger.

Charlotte was suddenly keenly aware of how thin was the ice upon which she was standing. She had no power here. None at all. And yet here she was, arguing with the king himself.

'No, I'm not threatening you. I assure you, I wouldn't dare.'

And yet she had to do something. On the one hand she couldn't afford to anger him—not when he was already angry—but on the other she couldn't allow both herself and her father to be buried in a prison cell for the rest of their lives.

Perhaps she should try and appeal to his humanity?

Before she could think better of it, she moved around the side of the desk and put a tentative hand on his arm. 'Please,' she said, looking up at him, trying not to sound as if she was pleading. 'You don't have to do this. You can just let us go and it'll be fine.'

His gaze dropped to her hand on his arm and then moved back up again, and she was suddenly aware that his skin was very warm beneath her hand, that the feel of his muscles was like iron. And she was aware, too, of his scent—warm and spicy and masculine. He was very large, very powerful, and he was watching her like a predator, intense and focused. His gaze was all gold, like a tiger's, and just as hungry.

Something unfamiliar shifted down low inside her...a kind of heat and a very feminine awareness she hadn't experienced before.

She had never bothered with men. While her friends had been out clubbing and on dating apps she'd preferred staying at home with a book. Because after the front row seat she'd had watching her parents' toxic relationship she'd decided she wanted no part of that. It was easier to retreat between the pages of her book, where there were no arguments, no screaming, no suffocating silences or the kind of seething quiet that presaged a major emotional hurricane—where princes remained fantasies and fantasies ended with a kiss.

She'd never missed having a man in her life. Never wanted one. The only kisses she'd had had been in her imagination, and she'd never met anyone who had made her want to think about more than kisses.

But now, feeling the solidity and strength of the Sheikh's arm beneath her hand, being close to his powerful body, aware of his warmth and rich, spicy scent... She couldn't seem to catch her breath.

'Are you aware,' he murmured, and the soft, silky darkness of his voice was totally at odds with the blazing gold of his eyes, 'that touching the Sheikh without permission means death?'

Oh, dear.

Instinctively she tried to jerk away, but he was too quick, his other hand coming down on hers in a blur of motion, pressing her palm to his forearm.

The heat of his hand against her bare skin was scorching, making her pulse accelerate, and all thought was fragmenting under the pressure of his brilliant gaze.

Was this a distraction?

Was he trying to use his male wiles on her to make her forget what she was saying?

That's ridiculous. He's a sheikh. He can do whatever he likes. And why would he use his wiles on you anyway?

That was a very good point. But, regardless, she couldn't let him get to her. He might very well be the king, but she was a British citizen and she had rights. And surely what he was doing was against the Geneva Convention?

'We're nothing to you,' she said, trying not to sound breathless, hoping to appeal to him in terms he might understand. 'We're insignificant English people. If Dad is unconscious, then he hasn't seen anything, and I don't have a lot of friends so I don't have any people to tell anyway. Your secret is safe with me. And if I accidentally do let something slip, then you…you can come to England and arrest me. Your Majesty,' she added, for good measure.

There was a long and suffocating silence and the pressure of his hand over hers was relentless, burning.

He's not going to let you go.

A small burst of unexpected anger broke through her determined calm. No, he couldn't do this. He couldn't insist she stay here indefinitely, couldn't touch her the way he was doing, and he certainly couldn't keep her prisoner. She wasn't going to allow it.

Determined, Charlotte met his gaze head-on. 'If you let us go now, and without a fuss, I won't tell the media I was held here against my will.'

There was another suffocating silence.

'You,' the Sheikh said softly, 'are either very brave or very stupid, and I cannot tell which it is.'

Charlotte's cheeks burned, but she didn't look away.

She was probably being the latter rather than the former, in issuing him such a threat, but what choice did she have?

She didn't want her father to suffer for the mistake she'd made. He'd been awarded custody of her after his bitter divorce from her mother, and she'd never wanted him to regret that, even though she knew he did.

Perhaps if she hadn't run away that last time, forcing her parents to call the police and causing all kinds of fuss, then she wouldn't have felt so bad about it. But she had run away. And the next day her mother had called it quits and her father had ended up with her.

She'd always tried to be good after that. Never running away again, never causing a fuss. Trying to be interested in all the things he was interested in and later, when she was an adult, becoming his assistant and general dogsbody, doing whatever was required.

Including getting him imprisoned for life by a dictator.

Her breath came shorter, faster, though she tried to remain calm.

'Well?' She lifted a brow, trying to sound as if she was merely waiting to hear whether he'd like a cup of tea or not, rather than asking what he was going to do about her threat of a diplomatic incident.

He said nothing, just watched her as he spread his fingers out, his hand completely covering her own. His skin was hot, like a brand, with the same heat that burned in the merciless gold of his eyes.

She had angered him, that was clear, and she should be terrified by that. But for some reason she wasn't. He was standing very close, huge and strong and so very powerful, and yet there was something in the heat of his gaze that made her breath catch.

She didn't know quite what it was, but an instinct she hadn't known she possessed told her that she wasn't without power here. That she had the ability to get under this Sheikh's skin.

It made adrenaline rush in her veins, made her want to push, see how far she could go—which was *not* like her at all. She normally ran from anger, not towards it.

His fingers curled around her hand, holding it for a brief, intense moment. Then he pulled it from his arm and let her go, rising to his full height, towering over her.

She could still feel the heat of his fingers as if they'd been imprinted on her skin, and she wanted to put her hand behind her back or in her pocket to hide it, as if it were visible. But there was no hiding from him.

His eyes gleamed briefly, as if he understood something she didn't, making her blush. But all he said was, 'That, Miss Devereaux, is what is commonly known as a threat. And, as I have told you once already, I do not respond well to threats.'

Charlotte opened her mouth to protest, her heart hammering in her chest. But he must have done something—pressed some button on his desk—because the doors had opened and the guards were coming in.

He said something to them—a sharp order she didn't understand—and suddenly they were on either side of her, hemming her in.

She swallowed hard. 'So is this how you treat guests in your country? You get your guards to drag them back to the cells?'

'We do not have "guests" in this country, Miss Devereaux, and you will not be going back to a cell.'

His fierce gaze shifted to the guards and he nodded to them once.

And then there was no time to say anything more as she was ushered firmly out of the room.

TARIQ PACED BACK and forth in front of the window in his office, coldly furious.

It had been a long time since he was quite *this* angry. Then again, it had been a long time since anyone had issued the kind of threat the little Englishwoman had—all cool and polite and straight to his face.

What made her think that she—a mere nobody—could threaten the king of an entire nation? Looking up at him with her big blue eyes, all beseeching, appealing to him as if he had mercy in his heart instead of cold stone.

And then—then!—to put her hand on his arm as if he was an ordinary man...

You are *an ordinary man. You're just angry that you're responding to her as you did to Catherine.*

That the thought was true didn't make it any more welcome. Because he couldn't deny it. He'd ignored the initial pull of attraction, had dismissed it entirely, and yet as soon as she'd touched him he'd felt his body respond as if it had a will of its own.

The light pressure of her fingers on his arm had caused a sudden rush of awareness of her feminine warmth and her small, lush figure next to his. She'd smelled of something sweet and subtle that reminded him of the flowers in the gardens outside—roses, perhaps. And then those eyes looking up into his had got even bigger, her cheeks even pinker, and he'd known she felt the same pull between them that he did: physical chemistry.

He was an experienced man, and he knew well enough when he was attracted to a woman, and he was attracted to this one. Strongly so. Which did not help his temper in the slightest, considering he was supposed to be treating her the way he treated all intruders.

Physical desire, however, was something easily dealt with. Her threat to him just now and the challenging look in her blue eyes was not. She had him over a barrel and she knew it.

Because if he kept her and her father the British government would certainly have something to say about it, surely?

Yes, their disappearance could be easily explained by some story of their having got lost and perishing in the desert, but search parties would be sent out. Other governments would know the border of his country wasn't far away from the archaeological site, and those rumours that kept people out would also make people suspicious. Enquiries would be made. Questions would be asked. Ashkaraz would receive attention.

And he did *not* want attention—not from the outside world.

The only reason Ashkaraz remained autonomous and free was because its borders were closed and no one knew anything about it. They didn't know about the massive oil wealth upon which the country sat. Or about how that oil was channelled through various private companies so no one would know where it came from. Or about how that wealth came back into the country and was used to pay for hospitals and schools and other social services.

Ashkaraz was wealthy and prosperous but it came at a price—and that price was isolation from a world that would try and take that wealth from them. Because people were greedy. As he knew to his cost.

Tariq came to a stop in front of his desk, his jaw tight, and had to take a moment to uncurl his fingers, relax the tension in his shoulders, dismiss the anger that burned in his gut. He needed to spend some time in the palace gym— that was what he needed. Some boxing or sword practice with an opponent. Or perhaps he needed to call one of the women he sometimes spent the night with, work out his tension that way.

First, though, he needed to decide exactly what to do about his pretty English captive.

He couldn't risk letting her go, so her father would have to stay too—because he couldn't have the man out and about in the world, demanding his daughter's return.

Yes, she might very well promise not to tell anyone about Ashkaraz, but all it would take was one slip, one accidental confession to the wrong person, and curiosity would start. One person would tell another, and then they would tell a couple more, and on it would go. And then, like a rock-slide, it would get bigger and bigger. The border incursions they already had would get worse. Until one day Ashkaraz would no longer remain hidden.

He couldn't risk that. The balance was already fragile; he couldn't allow it to tip.

But keeping them both here would garner unwelcome attention too.

Unless she stays here willingly.

That was a possibility. That way she could contact the British authorities, tell them that she was alive and well and not to look for her, because she had chosen to stay here.

It would be the perfect answer to all his problems but for the tiny fact that she was *not* willing.

So how to make her?

The answer to that was obvious: her father.

He could let Professor Devereaux go—he, after all, had seen nothing—on the understanding that his daughter would tell the British government that she was alive and well and perfectly happy to stay in Ashkaraz.

The idea solved his little diplomatic problem quite nicely, and he was feeling pleased with himself—until thirty minutes into a meeting with Faisal, when his advisor said, 'You won't like what I'm going to say, Your Majesty, but Almasi wants a decision made about his daughter.'

Tariq, who had been standing with one hip propped against the edge of his desk, his arms folded, was instantly irritated. Almasi was a high-ranking member of his government who'd been angling to have his daughter considered as potential sheikha for the past couple of months. His government in general had been putting pressure on him for a couple of years to marry and secure the succession, but Almasi had been particularly vocal. Mainly because he had an of-age daughter whom he thought would be perfect as Tariq's wife.

Tariq disagreed. Almasi's daughter was a nice woman, but he didn't want anything to do with Almasi himself, or his grasping family. That was the problem with the majority of eligible women in Kharan, and in Ashkaraz in general—they were attached to families who wanted to have a stake in determining the way the wealth of their little nation was distributed. Which would have been fine if it was for the good of the country. But Tariq knew it wouldn't be. It would be for the good of only particular families, and that he wouldn't stand for.

Greed wasn't confined only to outsiders.

Catherine's family had certainly been grasping, so he preferred any woman he might consider marrying not to have such connections.

'I am not going to marry his daughter, no matter what he or the government thinks,' Tariq said, his tone absolute.

Faisal was quiet a moment. Then, 'There is the issue of succession,' he said delicately. 'It must be dealt with, as you know.'

Of course he knew. It was a perennial theme.

'The succession does not have to be dealt with now.'

But the other man's dark gaze was far too perceptive. 'I

understand why you have been reluctant, sire. After Catherine, who would not be? But, forgive me, you are not getting any younger. And Ashkaraz needs an heir.'

Something dark coiled tightly in Tariq's gut. He didn't want to think about this now. In fact, he never wanted to think about it. And it didn't help that the old man was right. Ashkaraz *did* need an heir. He just didn't want to be forced into providing one. The fact that it was all to do with Catherine and what had happened between them he knew already, but it didn't make him any less reluctant.

A ruler had to separate himself, keep himself apart, and that had always seemed to him the very antithesis of marriage. But then, a royal marriage didn't require much involvement beyond the getting of an heir. Or at least, that was what his father had told him. And since Tariq's mother had died when Tariq was young, and he'd never had an opportunity to observe a marriage for himself, he had no reason to disbelieve him.

Certainly, though, if he wanted to secure the future of his country an heir would need to be provided whether he liked it or not—or, indeed, whether any of the candidates presented for the begetting of said heir were suitable or not.

And they weren't. None of them were.

'If you want an heir, then you must bring me better candidates for a bride,' he said impatiently.

'There are no more suitable candidates.' Faisal seemed unmoved by his impatience. 'As our borders are closed we have removed ourselves from the world stage, so you cannot get a bride from elsewhere.'

Again, his advisor wasn't wrong. About any of it.

Tariq bared his teeth. 'Then where do you suggest I get a bride from? The moon?'

As soon as he said the last word a memory caught at him...of a lock of hair the colour of starlight showing from underneath a black and white scarf. Hair that had caught on his black robes as he'd lifted her onto his horse.

There is your answer.

It was a preposterous idea. Marry the little English-woman he'd found in the desert? An archaeological assistant. A woman who wasn't rich or titled? Who wasn't anyone important in any way? A nobody?

She is perfect.

The thought stuck inside him like a splinter.

Catherine hadn't been a nobody. She'd been a rich American from a wealthy family, beautiful and privileged. She'd certainly thought herself entitled to the love of his father the Sheikh, and when that Sheikh hadn't given her what she wanted she'd set her sights on the Sheikh's teenage son...

She'd been greedy, and his father, fully aware of that greed, had kept the secrets of his country's wealth from her. But Tariq hadn't.

She'd promised to stay with him for ever if only he'd tell her how Ashkaraz had got so rich.

And so he'd told her.

A week hadn't even passed before her family and the companies they'd owned had begun to put pressure on Ashkaraz and its parliament, demanding oil rights for themselves by bribing a few of the right people.

It had nearly ripped his country apart.

But Charlotte Devereaux had only her father, and a mother who'd moved away long ago. There were no brothers or sisters. No elderly relatives. There'd be no one to come after her and try to grasp a piece of Ashkaraz's wealth. And, because she wasn't associated with any of the families here either, there'd be no family members in Ashkaraz trying to get rich.

Yes. She was perfect.

You would like her in your bed too.

The memory of her heat next to him coiled itself tightly inside him. That would not be…unwelcome. It would be a good outlet for his physical desire and, because she was an outsider, he would never be in danger of wanting more than that. She would remain a constant reminder of his failure with Catherine. A constant reminder of the dangers of emotion.

The government wouldn't be happy, and the old families whose influence he was trying to negate would be even less so. But he wasn't here for their happiness. He wasn't here for divisiveness or self-importance. For one family putting itself above another.

He was here to protect his people, and the government would have to accept his choice of wife whether they liked it or not.

The only issue remaining was how to get her to accept it. Because if she hadn't liked the thought of being *held* here indefinitely, she would like the thought of being *married* to him indefinitely even less.

Then again, he wasn't just anyone.

He was the king.

And he had her father. If he made letting the old man go conditional upon her agreeing to marry him she'd naturally have to accept.

He'd have a suite of rooms set aside for her here in the palace, as befitted her future station, and she'd have access to his considerable wealth and power.

Her life here would be very comfortable indeed.

Certainly better than a shared flat in Clapham.

In fact, the more he thought about it, the better the idea became. Marrying Charlotte Devereaux would solve a great many of his existing problems.

'Not the moon, sire,' Faisal said, oblivious to Tariq's stillness and silence. 'We shall simply have to—'

'No need,' Tariq interrupted, pushing himself away from his desk. 'I have a suitable candidate in mind already.'

Faisal didn't often appear shocked, but he certainly seemed so now. 'I thought you said you had none?'

'One has suddenly occurred to me.' Moving around the side of his desk, Tariq sat down. 'Call a meeting of the council,' he ordered, and then smiled. 'I have an announcement to make.'

CHAPTER FOUR

Charlotte was taken to what was quite obviously a library—and, given that it was a very beautiful library, she wasn't quite as scared as she otherwise might have been.

Ornate carved wooden bookshelves lined the walls, stretching from the floor to the ceiling, and there were low couches and divans scattered here and there, strewn with brightly coloured silk cushions. Small tables stood near each couch, the perfect height for cups of tea, and if reading palled there was always the view. Because, like the office she'd been in, the library faced the beautiful walled garden and through the open windows the liquid sound of the fountains played.

It was an extremely pleasant place to sit, even with the two armed guards on either side of the door, though it was an odd choice for a place where the Sheikh might keep a prisoner. Not that she was complaining, since it was a million times better than the jail cell she'd expected to be dragged back to.

She wasn't sure how long she'd been there, but it was enough time for her to have inspected the bookshelves and found quite a few English language books in various genres. She would have been happy to curl up with one on one of the divans.

She'd had enough time to wonder, too, what was going on and what the Sheikh was going to do with her.

She should never have threatened him—that had been a mistake. She couldn't think why she had done so, or even where her bravery had come from. She'd only been conscious that for some reason she affected him, and she'd let that little taste of power go to her head.

And now both she and her father would pay for it.

The fear she'd been ignoring collected inside her once more, and it was still there when hours or minutes later— she wasn't sure which—the guards took her out of the library and down some more of the echoing, beautifully tiled and arched hallways. They passed glittering rooms and ornate alcoves, went down some elegant staircases and past yet more colonnaded gardens and fountains.

The Sheikh's palace was beautiful, and if she hadn't been afraid for her life she would have loved looking around it. But she *was* afraid, and all the beauty around her only made her more so.

She had very much hoped she wouldn't be taken back to that jail cell, and she wasn't. Instead she was shown into a series of interconnected rooms like a hotel suite, with big French doors that opened out into yet another walled garden, though this one was smaller. It had a fountain, too, and delightful beds of roses and fruit trees. The rooms were tiled in subtle, glossy variations of white, giving the walls a lovely textured feel. And there were more beautiful silk rugs on the floors dyed in deep, jewel colours, and low couches to sit on strewn with silken cushions.

Charlotte tried to ask the guards what was going on, why she was there and not in a cell, but either they didn't speak English or they'd been instructed not to speak to her, because they ignored her questions, leaving her alone in the rooms before going out and locking the door behind them.

So, still a prisoner, then, but now her cage was a gilded one.

After they'd gone she explored a little, finding that one of the rooms had a huge bed mounded with pillows standing against one wall, while another contained a beautiful tiled bath and a large shower.

She couldn't understand why the Sheikh was holding her here, in rooms that seemed more appropriate for a visiting head of state than for some illegal alien he'd picked up unconscious in the desert.

None of it made sense.

Left with nothing else to do, Charlotte paced around the main living area of the suite, her brain ticking over. She didn't know why she was here and not in a cell, and she didn't know what was going to happen to her or her father other than that the Sheikh wasn't letting either of them go.

That made her feel cold inside—not for herself, but for her father. He was an eminent professor with a career back in London, and lots of friends and colleagues, and he would hate to be separated from any of it.

Especially when he finds out that all of this is your fault.

The cold inside her deepened.

She'd been the one to break the window and go looking around outside. If she had simply stayed put, then her father would be safe and so would she. Maybe they'd even be on their way back to the border and none the wiser about Ashkaraz.

But that wasn't what had happened.

And if it's your fault, then it's up to you to fix it.

That was true. But how?

She came to a stop in front of the windows, looking at the pretty rose garden outside, thinking.

There really was only one way to fix it. She was the one who'd blundered out onto the street and seen what she shouldn't have, not her father. He was blameless. Maybe she could convince the Sheikh to let him go if she agreed to remain here? She didn't have a career, like her father did, or friends. No one would miss her.

Your father wouldn't miss you either.

Charlotte pushed that thought aside, hurrying on with her idea. The professor surely wouldn't argue with her, and she could reassure him that everything was fine so he wouldn't think she was being held against her will. She could reassure the British authorities too—keep them away from Ashkaraz's borders, appease the Sheikh.

An unexpected shiver went through her as she thought of him again. Of his intensely masculine, powerful physical presence. His large hand over hers, his palm burning against her skin. The hard muscles of his forearm and his fierce golden stare. The anger she had sensed burning inside him no matter how cold his expression.

Could she appease a man like him? Did she have the power? But she'd got to him in some way earlier, she knew it, so maybe she could do it again.

If she wanted to save her father she would have to.

And what about you? Staying in a strange country all alone for the rest of your life?

Charlotte ignored that. She'd deal with it later. Right now, making sure her father was safe was more important.

The time ticked past and she spent it exploring the small suite of rooms and admiring them in between wondering what on earth was going on and trying to keep her feelings of panic at bay.

At last the doors opened, admitting two exquisitely robed women. One carried a tray of food, the other an armful of silvery blue fabric. The woman with the tray put it down on a small table near the window, while the other laid the fabric across a low divan nearby.

'Tonight you will dine with His Majesty, Sheikh Tariq Ishak Al Naziri,' said the woman near the tray in lightly accented English. She gestured at the fabric spread out on the divan. 'His Majesty has provided suitable attire for you and some refreshment in the meantime. I will come and collect you at the designated hour.'

Charlotte stared at the woman in astonishment. Attire? Refreshment? *Dining?*

What on earth was going on?

'But why?' she burst out. 'And what about my father? Why am I being kept here? What does the Sheikh want with me?'

But the woman only smiled and shook her head, and then she and the other woman turned around and went out, leaving Charlotte alone again.

Okay, so clearly no one was going to answer her questions. Which meant she would have to get answers from His Majesty Sheikh Tariq himself. And she was not going to be put off again by his golden stare and his gentlemanly wiles. She would insist he answered her and then she'd request that he send her father home.

The thought made her feel a little better, so she helped herself from the small tray of food—flatbread still warm from the oven and spicy dips, along with some fresh fruit. Once she'd eaten, she wandered into the bathroom to examine it in greater detail—and then decided that if the Sheikh was housing her in such luxurious accommodation she was going to take advantage of that fully.

So she stripped off her dirty clothing and had a long, hot shower, using delicious rose-scented body wash and shampoo. After her shower, wrapped in a big fluffy white towel, she went back into the living area where the 'suitable attire' had been spread over the divan near the window.

The 'attire' proved to be very pretty robes in silvery blue silk, with roses embroidered around the edge in heavy silver thread. Charlotte put out a hand and gently touched the fabric. It was cool and soft beneath her fingertips. But he'd provided this for her, and part of her didn't want to wear it purely because he'd told her to. Part of her wanted to turn up to this dinner in her own filthy clothes and to hell with him.

But she didn't allow herself such petty rebellions these days—plus, there was no point in angering him needlessly. Not when she had her father's safety to consider as well as her own. Also, she didn't know his country's customs, and causing offence purely because she was angry would be stupid.

Better to wear the robes…be polite, courteous. And then tell him what was what.

Besides… She stroked the fabric again, enjoying the feel of it. The robes were beautiful and she'd never worn anything like them before. Princesses in fairy tales always wore beautiful dresses, and as a child she'd often wished she could have a beautiful dress too. But her mother had never been particularly interested in what Charlotte had wanted. She'd never been interested in Charlotte at all.

You're a prisoner in a strange country, with no idea of what the future will hold for you, and yet you're thinking about how nice it will be to wear a pretty dress?

Well, why not? Her own clothes were filthy, and who knew what was going to happen to her afterwards? She might never get the opportunity to wear a pretty dress ever again.

Dropping the towel, Charlotte dressed herself in the robes, feeling the fabric deliciously cool and smooth against her skin. Then she went to stand in front of the full-length mirror in the bedroom and adjusted the material. She looked…nice, she had to admit. And she felt a little more in control now she was clean and dressed—even in 'suitable attire'.

If she was going to beg a favour from a king, she'd better look the part.

The robed women didn't come back for a long while, and Charlotte tried to fill in the time by examining every inch of her suite and then by having a small nap.

At last the light began to fade, and then a knock came at the door. It opened to reveal one of the robed women.

Charlotte pushed herself up from the divan she'd been sitting on, her heart thumping hard in her chest. The woman gave her a brief survey and there was a satisfied look in her eyes that made Charlotte feel a tiny bit better. Obviously her choice to wear the robes had been a good one.

'His Majesty will see you now,' the woman said. 'Please follow me.'

Nervously clasping her hands in front of her, Charlotte did so, noting the two guards that fell into step behind her as she left the suite.

The corridors were silent but for the sound of the guards' boots on the tiled floor. Her own steps were muffled by the pair of silver slippers she'd put on, which had come with the robes.

She tried to take note of where they were going, but after a few twists and turns, more stairs and more long corridors, she gave up, looking at the high arched ceilings instead, and the glittering tiles on them that caused the light to refract and bounce. They were beautiful, and she got so lost in them that for a couple of minutes at least she forgot that she was going to meet the terrifying man who was king.

Eventually the hallway opened up, and to her delight

Charlotte found herself stepping out into the colonnaded garden she'd seen through the windows of the Sheikh's office. The air was as cool and soft as the silk she wore, and laden with the scent of flowers and the gentle sound of the fountains splashing.

The woman led her along a path to the central fountain itself, and then stopped and gestured.

Charlotte's breath caught.

In the dim twilight, tea lights in exquisite glass holders leapt and danced. They'd been set on a low table, their flames illuminating the multitude of cushions set on the ground around it and glittering off glasses and cutlery. Bowls full of food sat on the table—sliced meats and dips and more of the flatbread.

It was like something straight out of one of her favourite books, *The Arabian Nights*, and for a second she could only stand there and stare.

Then she became aware of the man sprawled on one of the cushions at the table, watching her. He rose as she approached, fluidly and with grace, until he towered over the table and her, the candle flames making his golden eyes glow.

He wasn't wearing the suit trousers and shirt she'd seen him in earlier that day but black robes, their edges heavily embroidered in gold thread. They suited him, highlighting his height and the broad width of his shoulders, and the sense of power that rolled off him in waves.

The flickering light illuminated his face, and his features were set in a fierce sort of expression that made her heart race. He wasn't angry now, it seemed, but he'd definitely decided something—though what it could be she had no idea.

What jailer set out a beautiful dinner like this if a prison cell was all that awaited her? It didn't make any sense.

'Welcome, Miss Devereaux.'

His deep voice prowled over her skin, soft and dark as a panther.

'Thank you for joining me.'

Charlotte resisted the urge to shift on her feet, uncomfortable as his intense gaze roved over her. She didn't know how she knew, but she had the sense that he liked what he saw. Which made it difficult to think.

'Well,' she said stoutly, pulling herself together. 'It wasn't like I had a choice.'

The corner of his hard mouth curved and for a second Charlotte couldn't do anything but stare at him, her breath catching at the beauty of his smile.

'That is true,' he acknowledged. 'But I am glad you came without the necessity of guards dragging you.'

It was very clear that if she had refused then, yes, the guards would have dragged her to meet him.

Fear flickered through her, and the old urge to run away and hide gripped her. But she ignored it, steeling herself. Best to get this out of the way first.

'Your Majesty,' she began formally. 'I've been thinking and I want to—'

'Please,' the Sheikh interrupted, gesturing to the table. 'Sit.'

'No, thank you.' Charlotte's palms were sweaty, her heart showing no sign of slowing down. She needed to say this and fast—before she changed her mind. 'I know that you've decided not to let my father and me leave, but I have a request to make.'

His expression was impassive. 'Do you, indeed?'

'Yes, I think—'

'Sit, Miss Devereaux. We shall have this discussion as we eat.'

'No. I need to say this now.' She took an unsteady breath,

meeting his fierce golden stare. 'If you let my father go, I'll stay here. And I'll do so willingly.'

TARIQ SAID NOTHING, watching Charlotte Devereaux's pale face in the flickering candlelight. It was obvious she'd been thinking hard in the time she'd been cooling her heels in the sheikha's suite. And he had to admire her courage; it couldn't be easy, facing a lifetime in a strange land, even if it meant her father went free.

But that was good. She would need that courage and she would need strength too, for the role he would give her. The sheikha would need both.

She certainly made a pretty picture, standing there in the robes he'd chosen for her. The silver-blue suited her pale skin and deepened the colour of her eyes. She'd clearly washed her hair, and it lay soft and loose over her shoulders and down her back, the pale mass curling slightly.

He was pleased she'd worn the robes, and pleased that she'd decided to make an effort. Because that was all part of his plan.

The council had been in an uproar at his abrupt choice of wife, as he'd expected, so he'd deliberately had the robes sent to her, and then had her walked through the palace so everyone could observe the picture of quiet elegance and strength that she presented.

He hadn't been certain she would wear the robes, or that she wouldn't make a fuss about attending his dinner, but he'd counted on her English manners preventing her from making a scene and so far he'd been proved right.

He was pleased with that too.

And now she'd just volunteered to stay willingly if he let her father go, which made things even easier.

Don't feel too pleased with yourself. You haven't told her about the marriage yet.

No, he hadn't. He'd hoped to take his time with his proposal, feeding her the excellent food his chefs had provided and pouring her wine from his extensive cellars. And then perhaps some civilised conversation to set her at ease.

But, judging from the fear in her pretty blue eyes and the way she had her hands clasped together, spinning it out might not be such a good idea. Her finely featured face was set in lines of determination and she was standing very straight, as if bracing herself for a blow, so maybe he should deliver it. A quick, clean strike.

The candlelight glittered off the silver in her robes and glimmered in her lovely hair, making her look like a fall of moonlight in the darkness of the garden. And it prompted something to shift uncomfortably inside his chest—something that felt a lot like sympathy.

Which was wrong. He couldn't afford to be sympathetic. He had been sympathetic with Catherine the night he'd found her weeping beside this very fountain, and his heart—the traitor—had twisted inside his chest at the sight of her tears.

Sympathy was not the only thing you felt that night, remember?

Of course he remembered. How could he forget? He'd also been angry, burning with a frustrated rage that he hadn't been able to control. A volatile cocktail of emotion that had turned dangerous in the end.

He wouldn't do that again.

He had to be hard, cold. Ruthless. He couldn't risk being anything else.

'That is certainly a brave request,' he said, ignoring the tightness in his chest. 'You might change your mind when you hear mine.'

She blinked in surprise. 'Y-Yours?'

Tariq dropped his gaze to the cushions opposite. 'Sit down, Miss Devereaux.'

He didn't make it sound like anything less than the command it was, and after a brief hesitation she took a couple of faltering steps towards the table, then sat down awkwardly on the cushions.

Satisfied, he sat down himself, studying her pale face. And, even though he thought he'd shoved aside that brief burst of sympathy he'd experienced, he found himself pouring her a glass of the cool white wine and then putting a few tasty items of food on a plate for her.

It was the custom in Ashkaraz for a prospective groom to woo his potential wife by feeding her, so the dinner had been organised very deliberately, to make sure everyone knew exactly what his intentions were. But right now all he was conscious of was that she was quite pale, and that possibly the food he'd had sent to her room hadn't been enough. She really needed to have something more substantial—especially given what he was going to tell her.

He pushed the wine glass in her direction, and then the plate of food. 'You should eat.'

Her pretty mouth tightened, full and lush and pink. 'No, thank you. I'm not hungry.'

Her chin had lifted and there was a slight but unmistakable glow of defiance in her blue eyes.

Faintly amused by her show of spirit, despite himself, he nearly smiled. 'If you want to spite me, there are other, better ways of doing so.'

Colour tinged her cheeks. 'Oh, yes? And what are those?'

'Any number of things—but if you think I am going to tell you what they are, you are mistaken.'

She narrowed her gaze, ignoring the food and the wine. 'Excuse me, Your Majesty, but what is all this for? This dinner? The rooms I was locked in? These…clothes?'

One small hand went to the embroidered edge of her robe, the tips of her fingers running over it. She liked it, he could tell, even though she probably didn't want to.

'I thought I was your prisoner.'

'If you were truly my prisoner you would be back in that jail cell.'

'But you said I was to be here indefinitely. That I was—'

'That is part of the request I have to make,' he interrupted calmly. 'Though perhaps you should have a sip of wine and something to eat before we discuss it.'

Little sparks glittered in her eyes. 'Like I said, I'm not hungry.'

Well, if she didn't want to eat he certainly wasn't going to force her, and nor should he draw this out any longer than he had to.

What happened to a quick, clean strike?

She and her white face had happened.

She and the sympathy that seemed to sit in the centre of his chest whether he wanted it to or not.

'Do not eat, then.' He shoved that sympathy aside once again. 'It makes no difference to what I have to say to you.'

Her gaze narrowed even further, but she didn't speak, merely sat on the cushions, as straight-backed and dignified as the sheikha she would soon be.

'The safety of my country is of paramount importance to me, Miss Devereaux,' he began, holding her gaze so he could see that she understood. 'And protecting it is my purpose as king—a purpose I take very seriously indeed. So when the safety of my country is compromised I must take certain steps.'

'I see. Such as keeping me here, despite the fact that I'm not a threat?'

She was still angry, and he supposed he couldn't blame

her. Not when she didn't know the history of the country she was dealing with.

Or your role in it.

But she didn't need to know that. No one did. It was enough that he was working to fix the mistake he'd made, and fix it he would.

'It is not you who gets to decide what is a threat to Ashkaraz and what is not.' He didn't bother to hide the chill in his voice. 'That is my decision.'

Again, colour crept through her cheeks, but she didn't look away. 'You were talking about certain steps. What are they?'

'Keeping you here is definitely one of them. But there are other threats to my kingdom that have nothing to do with you.'

'Okay—fine. I get that. But I still don't understand what this has to do with giving me dinner.'

'A kingdom can be threatened from within as well as without. And there are certain families who put themselves first, over the people of this country.'

He could feel the anger gathering in him again. Cold and terrible anger at the web of alliances that had been forged purely for personal gain and how those very same people who had taken advantage of his father's generosity now looked to take advantage of his.

'I will not have it,' he went on, his voice on the edge of a growl. 'I will not have my council or my government divided, and I will not have one family being awarded more importance than another.'

Her defiance had melted away, and he saw a bright curiosity burning in her eyes. 'No. I can imagine not. But I'm not sure what this has to do with me.'

He bared his teeth. 'If you let me finish, I will tell you.'

She gave a little sniff. 'I wasn't interrupting. Please, go on.'

Her hand moved to the wine glass and she picked it up, taking a sip. Then she looked down at the plate he'd set in front of her and idly picked up an olive, popping it into her mouth.

Clearly she was hungrier than she'd said. Satisfaction moved through him that she was finally eating the food he'd presented to her, allaying his anger somewhat.

'I need a wife, Miss Devereaux,' he said, watching her. 'The royal succession must be ensured and my council wish this to happen soon. But I will not give in to factions—which means I cannot choose a bride from within my own country. There is no shortage of candidates, but none are suitable.'

Her brow wrinkled as she put the olive pit on her plate, then picked up another olive, chewing thoughtfully. 'That's unfortunate. Can't you choose a bride from outside the country?'

'Our borders are closed—so, no, I cannot.'

'That's *very* unfortunate, in that case.' Once she'd finished the olive she picked up some flatbread, dipping it in the hummus he'd spread on her plate. 'Isn't there anyone you can choose?'

'Not from among the candidates that have been put before me. They all have families who are greedy, grasping. Who want political influence.'

'You can't just tell them no?'

There was no anger at all in her expression now. Her attention was focused on the puzzle of finding him a wife. And if she found it strange that he was discussing it with her, she didn't show it.

Why are you explaining yourself to her? You are the

king. Your word is law. Simply tell her she will be marrying you and be done with it.

The thought needled at him. Because explaining was exactly what he was doing and he wasn't sure why.

Perhaps it had something to do with her initial fear and then that little spark of defiance. And the way she'd absently started eating, no matter that she'd made a point of telling him she wasn't hungry.

There was something artless and innocent to her that he found attractive, and it was very much the opposite of what he was used to from the people around him. They were all greedy, all wanted something from him, and they were never honest about it. They lied and manipulated, as Catherine had done, to get what they wanted.

No wonder his father had taught him that isolation was the best lesson for any ruler. To rely on his own judgement and not be swayed by anyone or anything, still less the promptings of his own heart.

Once he'd thought his father had been wrong—but that had been before Catherine, before he'd learned otherwise, and now he filled his heart with marble and his will with steel. Nothing got through. Nothing made him bend.

How does that explain the sympathy in your heart for this woman?

He didn't know. And he didn't like it.

'I cannot "tell them no",' he said flatly. 'Not outright. That would cause more division and dissension, so I must be cautious.'

She frowned. 'Then how are you supposed to find a wife?'

Did she really have no idea what he was leading up to? Did she really not understand?

Tariq searched her face, seeing only puzzlement. 'I have found one.'

Only then did something flicker in her eyes—a flash of apprehension. 'Oh?'

He stared at her, looking for what he didn't know. 'You are not going to ask me who it is?'

Her mouth opened and then closed, and then she tore her gaze from his, looking down at her plate. Her hands dropped to her lap. The candlelight glittered off her pale lashes and her hair, giving her an ethereal, fragile air.

And that strange feeling in his chest, that sympathy that wouldn't go away, deepened. He fought it, because it couldn't gain ground in him. He wouldn't let anything like it take root inside him again.

There was silence and he waited.

Because she'd guessed—he was sure of it—and he wanted her to say it.

'You can't…' she murmured, not looking up. 'You can't mean…me.'

'Can I not?'

Her lashes quivered against the smooth, pale skin of her cheeks and she went very still, tension radiating from her. 'I don't understand,' she said eventually.

'What is there to understand? I need a wife, Miss Devereaux. I need the succession secured and I need my council happy. And I need to put those aristocratic families seeking to use their position to their advantage back in their place.' He paused, making sure that soft, weak feeling inside him was gone. 'I had no suitable candidates, no prospect of any, and then you turned up. You are perfect for the role.'

There was more silence, broken only by the splashing of the fountain. She didn't move, kept her gaze on the table, but he could almost feel her shock.

'You have no family except your father,' he went on. 'And, more importantly, you have no family here. Which means there will be no one using you to better themselves or their position. You are an outsider with no connections, and that makes you ideal.'

Her long, pale throat moved. 'But…but I'm just a woman you picked up in the desert. A nobody.'

'Which is precisely why you are perfect.'

She looked up suddenly and he thought he saw a flicker of hurt in her eyes. But then it was gone and the anger was back.

'You can't marry me,' she said. 'I'm sorry, but you just can't.'

'Give me one good reason.'

'I don't even know you, for God's sake.' Her face had become quite pink. 'We only just met this morning.'

He shouldn't, but he couldn't deny that he liked her sudden display of temper. He preferred a woman with spirit, and outrage was better than fear.

'Knowing someone is not any prerequisite for a royal marriage that I am aware of,' he said calmly. It would no doubt aggravate her, but she could do with a little more aggravation. It would give her something to fight against. 'And we will have plenty of time to get to know one another.'

'You're assuming I'm going to go through with it,' she shot back. 'Well, just a heads-up for you: I'm not. And you can't make me.'

He wished he didn't have to. But he was going to.

'*Au contraire*, Miss Devereaux. I can certainly make you. For example, if you do not agree, then your father will remain here as my guest. Along with yourself.'

The pink in her cheeks deepened, creeping down her neck. 'So you're going to use Dad to force me to marry you? Is that what you're saying?'

For a second he allowed himself a shred of regret that

he had to do this to her, that he couldn't simply let her go back to her life in England along with her father.

Then he excised that regret from his soul. He couldn't let her return to her life. He had a duty to his country to fix the mistake he'd made all those years ago, when he'd put his own feelings ahead of what was best for his nation.

It was a mistake he would not make again.

'Yes,' he said, making his voice hard. 'That is exactly what I am saying.'

Temper glittered in her eyes, stronger this time. 'What about me? What about my wishes? What if I don't want to marry you?'

He met her furious blue gaze. 'I am afraid that you do not get a say. If you do not agree, I will keep your father here.'

She took a little breath, her jaw tight. 'Then maybe he'll have to stay here. He might even like it. It might be just the kind of thing he'd enjoy.'

It was a bluff and they both knew it.

'Are you saying that your father would enjoy being cut off from his colleagues?' Tariq asked. 'From his position as professor? He is an eminent man. He is used to having respect—used to having intellectual discourse with his peers. How will he cope being cut off from all of that? And what will he think of your choice? Because as much as I am choosing for you, you are choosing for him.'

That lovely lush mouth of hers tightened again, and the glow of anger in her eyes was even more intense. She wasn't so much a fall of moonlight now but an angry storm, full of lightning and thunder. A passionate woman.

You will enjoy exploring just how passionate.

Oh, yes, he would. Very much so.

Oblivious to the tenor of his thoughts, she said angrily, 'You have an answer for everything, don't you?'

'Of course. I am the king.' He softened his voice to mollify her. 'It will not be so bad, *ya amar*. As my wife, you will be sheikha. You will have access to my wealth and power. You may live whatever life you choose as long as it does not threaten this country or its people.'

She remained determinedly unmollified. 'Essentially, though, I will still be your prisoner.'

'You will be my prisoner whether you marry me or not.'

His patience was beginning to fray now, because people generally did whatever he wanted them to do, and if he told them to jump they asked *How high?* They did not sit there arguing with every word he said.

'The only thing you have to do, Miss Devereaux, is determine your choice of cage.'

CHAPTER FIVE

Charlotte sat across from the Sheikh, conscious of only one prevailing emotion: anger.

She simply could not believe what he'd said.

Marry him? Marry the *king*?

Her heart was fluttering like a furious bird in her chest, her pulse wild beneath her skin, and she had a horrible feeling it wasn't only anger that she was feeling. But, since anger was preferable to anything else, she clung on tightly to it.

He'd explained why he'd chosen her and yet it still didn't make any sense.

Yes, she was a nobody, with no connections—a foreigner, an outsider. But did he really need to keep emphasising how alone and common she was? Or was that in order to make her feel isolated? So that she felt she wouldn't have any choice but to marry him?

Not that his motives were the most important thing right now.

Not when all she could think about was the word 'marriage'.

It made her feel cold all over. Because all she could think about was her parents, screaming at each other. And when they hadn't been screaming, there had been dreadful silences full of resentment and bitterness.

Not all marriages were like that, she knew, but her parents' marriage had put her off for life, and nothing she'd seen so far had made her want to change her mind—still less the thought of being married to this…complete stranger.

She didn't want to marry him.

She didn't want to marry anyone.

You might not have a choice.

It certainly seemed that way, since it was obvious he felt very strongly about protecting his country. In fact, the way he'd spoken about his purpose had fascinated her, and she'd been intrigued by the conviction glowing in his eyes.

Until he'd spoiled it by telling her that she was going to be his wife.

He was staring at her now, apparently impervious to the anger rising inside her. The planes and angles of his face were impassive, his golden stare cold. He looked like a god of ancient times, weighing the contents of her soul, determining whether she would go to heaven or hell.

Except that it was she who had to make the decision. Or at least he'd given her the illusion that she did. And illusion it was, since either she married him or he kept her father in Ashkaraz.

How is this any different from you staying here in return for your father's freedom?

It was *very* different. Before, she'd imagined she'd simply be allowed to have a life here—and, though she hadn't thought about that life in any detail, it hadn't seemed as depressingly final as marriage.

She had a brief vision of herself doing something completely and uncharacteristically violent, such as hurling the contents of her wine glass in his face or upending the table, but that felt far too close to something her mother or her father might have done, so she ignored it.

Instead, she forced herself to sit very still, her jaw tight, her back rigid. 'And if I decide to be a prisoner and not marry you?'

The food she'd eaten sat uncomfortably in her stomach. His straight dark brows drew together and the effect made her breath catch. He was forbidding in his black robes and that slight frown only made him more so.

'Then you are quite welcome to return to the cell you escaped from.' His voice was as dark and deep as the ocean. 'And your father with you.'

A quiver went through her. Return to that small, cramped, bare room? With the bucket in the corner? And the hard bed? And her father too… He would hate it and she knew he would. The horrible Sheikh was right. He would hate being cut off from his colleagues, from his work, from his life back in England.

Another thing to blame you for.

Charlotte swallowed. She'd tried so hard to be good for him, but sometimes she wondered if it would ever be enough. Perhaps this sacrifice finally would be? After all, it *was* her mistake that had got them into this mess.

You're seriously contemplating marriage to this man?

Maybe. Maybe it wouldn't be as bad as she thought. Her parents had once thought themselves in love, and that was why it had gone so wrong—or at least that was what her father had told her. Love turned toxic, was a recipe for disaster.

This would be a different kind of marriage from the one her parents had had right from the start, since she barely knew this man, let alone loved him. There would be no toxic emotion since she had no emotion about him to begin with.

That's a lie.

Charlotte chose to ignore that particular thought.

Her hand shook as she reached for her wine glass, taking a sip of the cool liquid. It was pleasantly dry, as she preferred her wine to be, and soothed her aching throat.

The Sheikh merely watched her with those predatory tiger's eyes.

'Why are you bothering with this?' she snapped in sudden temper, uncomfortable and not knowing what to do with herself. 'The dinner? The robes? Why are you even bothering to ask me? When you could simply drag me down the aisle and make me say "I do" right now?'

'Because I am not a monster—even though I might appear to be one. And I thought you would appreciate at least the illusion of choice.'

'Yes, well…' She put the glass down with a click, splashing the wine slightly. 'I don't appreciate it.'

He tilted his head, watching her. 'You are angry.'

'Of course I'm bloody—'

'Angry rather than scared. Why is that?'

She didn't want to answer. Because she had a horrible feeling that she was, in fact, scared, and that if she thought too much about it she'd end up scurrying away like a frightened mouse. And she couldn't do that. Not in front of a predator like him.

Instead, she clutched her courage and lifted her chin higher. 'There's not much point in being scared, is there? That's not going to get me very far.'

'Anger will not either,' he pointed out. 'Though anger is a far more useful emotion.'

'It's not very useful right now. Especially since I'm assuming that emptying my wine glass in your face will result in my death?'

Unexpectedly a flicker of something crossed his features. It was gone too fast for her to tell what it was, but she caught the gleam of it in his eyes, fierce and hot and completely at odds with the cold expression that had been there before.

It was almost as if he liked her anger, even approved of it, which was a strange thing to think. Yet she couldn't shake the thought, and for reasons she couldn't have explained knowing that somehow eased her fear and bolstered her courage.

'I would not recommend doing it.'

A thread of something she didn't recognise wound through this dark voice.

'So, I take it you accept my proposal?'

She glared at him. 'Do you need my acceptance?'

'No.' There was no sympathy in the word, and yet no triumph either. It was simply a statement of fact.

'So why the need for all…' she waved a hand to encompass the table and the robes she wore '…all of this?'

The fierce glow in his eyes was still there, and the way he sat back on the cushions, large and muscular and dangerous, sent an inexplicable thrill arrowing down her spine.

This man was going to be her husband.

And you know what that means, don't you?

It should have occurred to her before, and yet it hadn't—the realisation that marriage didn't just mean standing up and vowing to love one another till death do you part. There was another part of a relationship that marriage brought, wasn't there? A part she'd had no experience with whatsoever.

Sex.

An unfamiliar feeling twisted, right down deep inside her, and though fear was a part of it, it wasn't the only part. There was something else too—something to do with that thrill at the warmth of his body she'd experienced earlier that day and the feel of his arm beneath her hand. The awareness of him, of the amount of space he took up, an entirely physical awareness...

Her mouth went dry and she wanted to look away, suddenly sure that he could see exactly what she was thinking, exactly what realisation she was only just now coming to. Because those golden eyes would see everything.

She reached for the wine again, picking it up and taking another desperate sip to moisten her throat, her heartbeat thudding in her ears.

He couldn't want her to have sex with him, surely? She wasn't beautiful. She wasn't experienced. He would have his pick of lovely women as king, and he definitely wouldn't ever have picked her—not if she hadn't turned up so conveniently out in the desert.

He's mentioned securing the succession.

Yes, he had, but still...

'You have a question?'

His voice wrapped around her, velvety and soft in the darkness, as if he knew exactly what she was thinking.

'Ask me.'

She should, she knew that, but she couldn't bear the thought. She didn't know what she would do if he told her that, no, sex with him would not be required. Or what she would do if he said that, yes, it would.

Probably burst into flames with embarrassment either way.

'N-No,' she stuttered. 'I don't have a question.'

She steeled herself to meet his gaze. And she didn't understand the glitter in his eyes, because it looked like anger, and yet she didn't think it was. It was far too intent, far too focused.

'Open your mouth, *ya amar*,' he ordered quietly.

It was not what she'd expected him to say and it took

her by surprise—so much so that she'd already opened her mouth to obey him before she realised what she'd done.

Snapping it shut almost immediately, she gave him a suspicious look. 'Why?'

He leaned forward and picked up one of the strawberries sitting in a silver bowl. 'It is the custom in Ashkaraz for a prospective groom to feed his chosen bride. So open your mouth, Miss Devereaux, and signify your acceptance.'

This time there was no doubt about the sharp-edged glitter in his eyes. It was all challenge. And even though she didn't want to obey him, she felt something rise up inside her in response.

It was just a stupid strawberry. And maybe it was a custom here, but it didn't mean anything to her.

It means you accept that you will marry him.

Well, she had no choice about that. And if she had to stay here indefinitely surely it would be better to stay here as the sheikha—whatever that meant—than it would be as a prisoner in a cell.

And who knew? If she was queen maybe she could even change things for herself. Influence him to open up the borders so she could go home eventually. It was an idea. She didn't have to simply bow to his wishes for ever.

The decision hardened inside her and she caught his gaze with hers, letting him know that she wasn't going to lie down and be his doormat no matter what he thought. Then she leaned forward slightly and opened her mouth.

A flame leapt in his eyes, and though she didn't know what it meant, something deep inside her did, and it was making her heartbeat race, all her awareness focus abruptly on him.

He held out the strawberry, brushing the fruit along her mouth at first, tracing her lower lip in an almost-caress that made her mouth feel full and oddly sensitive, made another little shiver snake down her spine.

She went still as he did it again, this time tracing her upper lip with the strawberry before placing it gently in her mouth and holding onto the stem.

'Bite down, *ya amar*,' he ordered, and she did, sweetness bursting onto her tongue. Then he withdrew his hand, taking the stem with it, his fingers brushing her lower lip and leaving a trail of hot sparks in its wake.

Charlotte swallowed the strawberry, but she wasn't concentrating on the taste. All she could feel was the brush of his fingers on her mouth, and she nearly raised a hand and touched her lips herself.

He was watching her, and she didn't know what he'd seen in her face but something had satisfied him, she was sure. That hot, golden glow was burning in his eyes again and she still didn't know what it meant.

You do. Come on.

Maybe. But she didn't want to think about that. Didn't want to think about why her mouth felt so sensitive and why her heart was beating so hard. Why there was an unfamiliar ache down low inside her.

'Well?' she said thickly, trying to pretend that ache wasn't there. 'Is that all I need to do, then?'

He dropped the stem back in the bowl 'That is all.'

'Good.'

Her hands were shaking and she didn't like it. Suddenly all she wanted was to be alone, away from here. Away from *him*.

'I—I'm tired, Your Majesty. If you don't mind, I'd like to go back to...' She gestured at the doorway into the palace, then pulled at her robes, getting awkwardly to her feet without waiting for his agreement.

He rose far more fluidly than she and her heartbeat became a roar as he moved around the table towards her, all tall, dark muscularity, the hem of his robes flaring out around his booted feet.

'Oh, no…it's okay.'

She took an unconscious step back, as if putting some physical distance between herself and him would separate her from the strange feeling careering around in her chest. A feeling that she suspected might be excitement even though it also felt like fear. A feeling she didn't want, whatever it was.

'I can find my way back myself.'

The Sheikh stopped, candlelight flickering off the gold embroidery of his robes, and she thought she caught amusement in his eyes. But then it was gone.

'Very well.' He raised a hand and instantly the robed woman stepped out of the shadows of the doorway, as if she'd been standing there waiting for his command all this time. 'Amirah, please escort Miss Devereaux back to her suite.' In the darkness his eyes gleamed, a tiger on the prowl. 'Sleep well, *ya amar*. Tomorrow you will be busy.'

Heartbeat thumping, Charlotte let herself be led away.

'Excuse me, Amirah,' she said hesitantly as they went down the echoing, dimly lit corridors. 'What does *ya amar* mean?' It had been bothering her.

'It means "my moon",' Amirah murmured. 'Or "my most beautiful". It is an endearment.'

Charlotte felt her cheeks get hot. His "most beautiful"? Well, that was a lie. She wasn't beautiful and she certainly wasn't his.

But soon you will be.

Charlotte ignored the shiver that went down her spine at the thought.

It wasn't excitement. It just wasn't.

She didn't see the Sheikh over the next couple of days, which was a good thing. And she might have spent those days pacing around in her suite, reflecting over and over on the wisdom of her decision, had not Amirah turned up at her door the next day, informing her that she was now to be Charlotte's assistant and had been asked to help her with the list of tasks His Majesty had assigned to her. Then she'd brandished said list and Charlotte, craving distraction, had grabbed it with some relief.

The Sheikh had asked her to familiarise herself with the history, customs, people and language of Ashkaraz, which made sense since she was going to be queen. And since she'd always found learning interesting she'd thrown herself into study with abandon, especially as it involved spending a lot of time in the beautiful library she'd been taken to when she'd first got to the palace.

There were also culture and protocol lessons—which she found very interesting too—not to mention a lot of scrubbing and oiling of her body—which she found less interesting—including plucking and face masks and hair wraps. The beautification process for an Ashkarazi bride, apparently.

In between all of this the Sheikh sent updates on her father's condition and then, on the third day, a note to say that the professor had been taken to the border and would be released within hours. She was to send him an email, confirming her decision to stay in Ashkaraz, as well as an announcement that she would be marrying His Majesty, Tariq ibn Ishak Al Naziri.

Typing it felt unreal, as if it was happening to someone else, and a burst of homesickness made her wish for a phone call and the sound of her father's voice to steady her. But when she asked Amirah if a phone call was possible she was advised that it was forbidden.

At first she was merely annoyed, but as the day went on, with yet more beauty treatments that included being poked and prodded and then a fitting session for a wedding gown that involved being swathed in yards of white silk, Charlotte's annoyance soon turned to anger.

Everything was new and strange, and it was going to take her a while to get used to her new position in life. All she wanted was the sound of a familiar voice. Some reassurance that she was doing the right thing. That wasn't too much to ask, was it?

She'd already asked Amirah to beg the Sheikh for special dispensation for a call, especially since she had no idea when or even if she'd see her father again, but apparently 'forbidden' really meant forbidden.

There would be no phone calls for her.

Charlotte tried very hard to force her anger away, but for some reason she couldn't ignore it. Nor was it helped by her homesickness. And by the time the afternoon rolled around her emotions had begun to bubble away inside her like a saucepan full of water boiling on a stove.

She'd been preparing for a visit to the historic and apparently very beautiful palace baths, but as her anger had risen she'd decided to find the Sheikh first and tell him exactly what she thought of his phone call ban.

Over the past few days a steady stream of clothing had arrived in the suite—not only traditional robes, but expensive designer dresses, tailored trousers and shirts, blouses, as well several pairs of jeans and T-shirts. There was also underwear, silk and lace, in various pretty colours, which she'd tried to ignore because she felt strange about it. It was even stranger to wear the clothing and find that it was all the right size and fitted her perfectly.

In amongst the items she'd unearthed a very lovely bikini that had jewels sewn all over it. She had no idea if the jewels were real—if so, then the bikini wasn't very practical for swimming in, although it wasn't practical even if they weren't real—but still, it was the only bathing suit she had, and if she wanted to go to the baths, then that was what she'd have to wear.

Amirah had laughed and told her not to be so silly. Bathing naked was the done thing, and no one would bother her once it was known that the sheikha-to-be was bathing there. But there was no way she was bathing naked in public, so she pulled on the bikini, then a gauzy silver robe over the top of it, and, belting the robe around her waist, she went in search of the Sheikh.

However, he was nowhere to be found, and people seemed reluctant to tell her where he was. After half an hour's fruitless search, even more furious than she'd been initially, Charlotte decided to visit the baths anyway and look for him later. Certainly that would give her some time to cool off, and that was a good thing when it came to asking for a favour.

Except as she approached the arched entrance to the baths she saw two black-robed guards standing on either side of the door. She knew who they were now: the sheikh's personal guards. Which, of course, meant that he was inside.

Her temper was not improved by the news, since she'd been hoping to calm down in some peace and quiet. And a part of her was very tempted to simply turn around and go back to her rooms. But running away wouldn't get her a phone call, so she steeled herself, opening her mouth to demand entrance.

Yet before she'd even managed to get a word out, the guards stood aside for her, their faces impassive.

Charlotte shut her mouth with a snap, lifted her chin, and swept on past them, entering an echoing, humid space with high arches and columns set around a huge tiled pool. The walls had the same beautiful tiles as the rest of the palace, though these were in gorgeous shades of blue, and steam wreathed the huge columns that lined the edges of the pool. Light drifted down from the ceiling through hidden windows, illuminating the baths with a diffuse light.

A man was swimming in the pool, his stroke clean and powerful, his large muscular body moving through the water with all the deadly grace of a shark.

It was him. The Sheikh.

An unexpected shiver rippled through her, and the anger sitting in the pit of her stomach twisted strangely. There was something about him she couldn't take her eyes off, and instead of calling to interrupt him she found herself standing at the edge of the pool and watching him swim instead.

But he must have noticed her anyway, because his stroke slowed and gradually he came to a stop, standing up in the water and raising a hand to push his wet black hair back from his face.

And Charlotte realised she'd made a grievous error.

She very carefully hadn't thought of that night beside the fountain, losing herself instead in the tasks he'd set her over the past couple of days. Hadn't thought about the feelings he'd evoked, the anger and the strange sense of excitement as he'd brushed that strawberry over her lips, the fierce rush of adrenaline as he'd stared at her, challenge burning in his golden eyes.

And if he had accidentally found his way into her thoughts she'd distanced herself from him, turning him into the tall, dark and intimidating Sheikh instead, swathed in his robes of state. Safely removed from her by his position.

Yet it wasn't the robed Sheikh who stood in front of her now, but a man.

A magnificent, completely beautiful man.

Water streamed down his powerful body, outlining every perfect muscle from his wide shoulders to his broad chest, to the chiselled lines of his abs. His bronzed skin was marked here and there by scars, but nothing could detract from the fact that he was a work of art. There was not an ounce of fat on him and he was muscled like a Greek god, radiating the same sense of arrogant power.

And yet although he might look very much a man in the pool right now, every soaking wet inch of him was a king.

The distance she'd put between herself and her feelings felt abruptly tenuous, fraying as the diffuse light ran over his magnificent body. Her skin prickled with an undeniable heat. Her hands itched, as if she wanted to touch him, to see if he felt as hard and as smooth and as hot as he looked, forcing her to fold her arms and tuck her hands firmly into her armpits to stop herself from reaching for him.

'Good morning, Miss Devereaux.'

His deep, dark voice echoed in the tiled space and his golden stare caught hers, a knowing look in it.

'Have you come to join me for a swim?'

The prickling heat crept up her neck, warmed her cheeks, and she was very conscious that the humid air of the pool was making the gauzy fabric of her robes stick to her skin, and that all she had on beneath it was the silly, impractical little jewelled bikini.

'No,' she said stoutly, folding her arms tighter across her chest, determined not to let him get to her. 'I'm here to discuss the fact that you won't allow me a phone call with my father before he leaves.'

'Really?'

His gaze dropped down her body in a way that made her face feel even hotter.

'And yet you seem to be wearing the bikini I had sent to you.'

Damn him for noticing.

Charlotte shifted uncomfortably, felt the tiles warm and slick beneath her feet. 'Yes, well…you're already in here and I prefer to swim by myself. Now, about that phone—'

'Do not let me stop you,' he murmured. 'I would hate for you not to enjoy the water because of me.'

Another tiny shiver swept over her at the silky note in his voice and she couldn't seem to drag her gaze from the way the light fell on his wet skin.

Heavens, what was wrong with her? This man was a stranger to her, she'd barely even spoken to him, and yet all she could think about was what he would feel like beneath her fingers.

You're attracted to him. A good thing, considering he's going to be your husband.

She felt breathless at the thought, which irritated her, because she didn't want to feel anything at all about the man who'd essentially kidnapped her and was now holding her prisoner in his country.

'I don't want to swim right now,' she said primly. 'I want to talk about this phone call.'

Something gleamed in his eyes. 'Come into the pool, *ya amar*, and we will discuss it.'

Oh, she recognised that look. She'd seen it before, that night beside the fountain, when he'd told her she was to marry him. Fierce challenge. A dare.

And, much to her annoyance, she could feel a part of herself wanting to answer that challenge, to surprise him, make him see that she wasn't just his prisoner but a force to be reckoned with.

A stupid thing to want when she didn't care what he thought of her.

She didn't want to swim. She didn't want to get anywhere near him. And she wasn't his 'most beautiful', so he could stop calling her that too.

All she wanted was to talk to her father on the phone—that was it.

'I have already told you I don't want to swim,' she said, knowing she sounded sulky and yet unable to help it. 'Why do you keep insisting?'

'Because I have been neglecting you for the past couple of days.' The water rippled around his narrow hips as he moved closer. 'And I would like to catch up with what you have been doing.'

'I've been doing everything you asked me to do.' It seemed to take immense effort to keep her gaze on his face, not to look down and follow the muscled lines of his body. 'That's all.'

'Amirah tells me you have been diligent in your reading and an apt pupil in your language and protocol lessons.'

Charlotte shrugged, trying to ignore the way the light was moving over his chest as he breathed, his skin glistening. 'I like to study.'

He moved closer still and she couldn't help herself. Her attention dropping down over him again and... Was he wearing swimming trunks?

She blinked and looked away, her face suddenly flaming. No, he was not.

He's naked. He's standing in the water, naked.

Her pulse sounded loud in her ears—so loud it was a wonder he didn't hear it himself—and her mouth was bone-dry. Amirah had told her the custom was to swim naked, but Charlotte had never expected that to apply to the Sheikh himself. That she'd find him swimming naked and completely unashamed of the fact.

Not that he had anything to be ashamed about, from the looks of things.

Don't look at him, idiot.

That was a very good plan. Because the more she looked at him, the more breathless and unsteady she felt, and she didn't like it. Not one bit. She preferred to be in control of both herself and her feelings, not at their mercy.

Perhaps she'd simply pretend he was standing in front of her fully dressed and not…not…

'Is there something wrong?'

His voice was laced through with a fine thread of amusement that scratched at her thin veneer of calm, threatening to crack it.

'No, of course not.' She steeled herself to meet his gaze again, determined not to let him see how he affected her. 'What makes you say that?'

'You are blushing very hard, Miss Devereaux.'

Oh, yes, he was very definitely amused, damn him.

'Why is that?'

Curse her pale skin. And curse him into the bargain.

Well, there was no point pretending now. Might as well give him the truth. 'Because you're naked, that's why. And, no, I'm very much *not* swimming with you. Not like that.'

'Why not?' One dark brow arched. 'Are you afraid?'

The question echoed off the tiled walls, and the deep vibration of his voice set something vibrating inside her too.

Was he making fun of her? Or was this about something more?

Oh, but she knew the answer to that. He was challenging her, pure and simple, and the part of her that wanted very much to answer that challenge was getting stronger. Because wouldn't it be satisfying to set his arrogance back on its heels?

Using your fear, though. That's a clichéd move.

Yes, it was—which meant that the only real response was to stay cool and calm, turn around and walk out.

Yet she didn't. She stayed where she was, rooted to the spot, angry and getting angrier. At herself for her conflicting emotions and at him for making her feel this way. Because it was definitely his fault. She'd never had any trouble controlling her anger before—never had anyone get under her skin the way he was doing right now.

And the real problem was that the longer she stood there, the more she revealed—and he knew it. In fact, he was looking at her now as if he could see her every thought, knew her every feeling, knew that she was afraid and that he was the cause. And he liked it.

'I will not touch you,' he said softly. 'If that is what you are afraid of.'

Oh, yes, he could see her fear. Bloody man.

Her jaw felt tight, aching. 'I am *not* afraid.'

'Get in, then. And we will discuss your phone call.'

She didn't want to. But she couldn't stand there doing nothing any longer.

Before she could think better of it Charlotte moved to the edge of the pool.

Then dived straight in.

CHAPTER SIX

Tariq had not expected that. He'd been baiting her, admittedly, and it was probably unfair of him, but she'd turned up during his private swimming time, her silver-blue eyes glowing with anger, wearing a gauzy piece of nothing he could see straight through and the tiny jewelled bikini he'd provided for her on a whim, and… Well, he was a man. And she was very much a woman.

If he thought about it, he'd no doubt find it a little disturbing, how affected he was by her.

But he'd decided not to think about it.

Her vulnerability was the issue, not her anger, and with her standing there arguing with him, the transparent robe clinging to her small curvaceous figure and all that silvery hair curling in the humidity of the baths, it hadn't seemed a bad thing to indulge his urge to push her, bait her just a little. Stoke her anger to see how hot it flared and whether she would burn along with it.

And indeed she had—beautifully, as it turned out.

Her response to him was all he could have hoped for, and he very much liked how uncomfortable his nakedness had made her. Because it was obvious why she was uncomfortable, and it wasn't due to her not liking his body. He knew when a woman wanted him, and his pretty little fiancée very much did, whether she was aware of it or not.

Still, he'd expected to have to drag out some more ultimatums before she finally got in the pool with him. And
even then he'd thought she might slip in quietly, perhaps
a little hesitantly.

He hadn't thought she'd dive right in, barely making a
splash.

She came to the surface, water coursing down her body,
the gauzy robe now completely transparent and sticking
like a second skin to her lush curves. With her hair lying
silky and wet over her shoulders, and water drops caught
on her lashes, she looked like a mermaid.

His body tightened, hardening as she lifted her arms to
push her hair back. Her breasts rose with the movement,
and the jewels on her bikini top glittered only slightly less
brightly than her sapphire eyes as she met his gaze.

She was all challenge now, no longer calm and prim,
the way she had been on the edge of the pool, and he felt
something in him wanting to push her even harder, to see
exactly what she was made of.

Because he had a feeling it was of stronger stuff than
he'd initially anticipated. She'd been shocked at the ultimatum he'd presented her with the night he'd given her dinner,
but then she'd got angry, giving him a glimpse of steel, and
he'd very much liked that.

'So,' she said, holding out her hands. 'As you can see,
I am now in the water. Can we have a conversation about
my phone call now?'

Perhaps she didn't know the effect she presented in this
moment—all pale, gleaming skin, her every curve highlighted by the gems on her swimsuit. Because if she had
she might have requested more from him than a mere phone
call. But plainly she didn't, and that was just as well since
he might have given it to her.

She was a such a pretty, pretty thing.

And in addition to her steel he'd also had a glimpse of her passion that night beside the fountain, and he wanted to test it. Wanted to see if that passion truly did extend to him. Because her desire was going to be fairly crucial when it came to the provision of an heir; he would never force himself on an unwilling bride.

He'd held that strawberry out towards her, a challenge for her to accept, and accept it she had. He'd taken advantage, brushing the strawberry over her luscious mouth, watching her eyes grow round and then glow bright. Watching as her small white teeth had sunk into the flesh of the berry, taking a bite. When he'd withdrawn his hand he'd allowed his fingers to brush her lower lip, and it had been just as soft and silky as it had looked.

The memory of that mouth had taunted him for the past two days, no matter how many meetings and other duties he'd immersed himself in, and he couldn't seem to stop looking at it now. It was just as full as it had been that night, just as pink, and now sheened lightly with water.

Perhaps he needed to test her again, push her further. See how receptive she was so he knew what he'd be dealing with come their wedding night.

Slowly, he moved over to where she stood, then stopped in front of her. She tipped her head back to look at him, folding her arms again, but he saw the movement of her throat as she swallowed and noted the flicker of apprehension in her eyes as he came close.

He'd seen that same apprehension that night beside the fountain, but he'd put it down to shock. He had, after all, delivered an ultimatum with which she hadn't been at all happy. However, it surely wasn't shock now, so what could it be? She liked his body—that wasn't the issue—so it had to be something else. But what?

'I thought you said you were not afraid of me,' he murmured.

She blinked. Clearly she hadn't expected him to notice. 'I'm not.'

'But you are afraid?'

'N-no.'

The stutter was slight, but he caught it, narrowing his gaze and studying her more intently. 'Do not lie to me, Charlotte.'

She shifted in the water as he said her name, as if the sound of it affected her in some way.

'Well, okay. I suppose I am a little…apprehensive. But that's only because you're not wearing anything.'

'I will be your husband,' he pointed out. 'My not wearing anything is something you will have to get used to.'

Her blush deepened. The line of her shoulders was tense, and he had the odd urge to put his hands on her and stroke that tension away, ease her fear. But that would set a dangerous precedent, and not one he could afford.

And besides, he had the sense that it wasn't actually his nakedness that was the problem.

He took another experimental step towards her, watching as her eyes widened and her mouth opened slightly. And then something else flickered to life in the deep blue of her gaze.

Oh, she was bothered by him—of that he had no doubt. But it wasn't because she was afraid of him.

'So,' she said, quickly and sharply, as if she were using the words to stop him in his tracks. 'What do you want for a phone call?'

Momentarily distracted, he did stop. 'What do you mean?'

'You're very fond of ultimatums. *"Marry me or your*

father stays here. Get in the pool if you want to discuss a phone call.'" Her chin lifted even higher. 'So now I'm in the pool, what do you want in return for giving me that call? Because I can sense an ultimatum coming already, believe me.'

He might have found fault with the accusing note in her voice had he not already decided that she was using the phone call issue as a distraction. He also knew what she was trying to distract him from. But, unfortunately for her, it wasn't going to work. Since he'd decided on marriage securing the succession was going to be important, and he couldn't leave anything to chance.

Such as her being bothered by her own response to him.

'What is disturbing you, *ya amar*?' He took another step closer. 'Tell me the truth so we can discuss it.'

'The phone call—'

'It is not the phone call,' he interrupted flatly, taking yet another step, until mere inches separated them. 'You are afraid, and I do not think it is me you are afraid of, but yourself.'

She hadn't moved, yet her tension was obvious as her head tipped back so she could look up at him. The colour of her eyes had darkened and her mouth was slightly open, the pulse at the base of her throat racing.

'I...' she said hoarsely. 'I don't know what you're talking about.'

'I think you do.' He reached out and slid a careful hand behind her head, pushing his fingers through her wet hair and cradling the back of her skull in his palm.

She stiffened, and he could feel the tension in her neck, see it in the awkward way she was trying to hold herself away from him.

'Your Majesty...'.

'"Your Majesty" is unnecessary. You may call me Tariq.'

Her throat moved as she swallowed, her gaze pinned to his. 'I'm happy with Your Majesty.'

Stubborn girl.

'You cannot call your husband *Your Majesty*,' he said, amused. 'Say my name, Charlotte.'

He stroked his thumb over the tight muscles at her nape, watching as her eyes darkened even further, her pupils dilating into black. Oh, yes, she was certainly responsive to him, and it was exactly the kind of response he'd been hoping for.

'T-Tariq.'

His name was soft and smoky sounding, the slight stutter of it somehow erotic.

Ah, perfect.

He could feel himself harden, his own pulse beginning to ramp up. The slow melt of her resistance was unexpectedly seductive. Going slowly and carefully had never appealed to him much before, but he could certainly see the allure now.

'That's better.' He drew her close, so they were almost touching, continuing to stroke the back of her neck, soothing her. 'You know, do you not, that wanting one's husband is perfectly acceptable?'

She was breathing very fast, her gaze dropping to his mouth and staying there. 'I... I don't want you.'

He nearly smiled at the obviousness of the lie. 'Of course you do not. That is why you have not told me to stop.'

Charlotte drew in another shaky little breath, yet her gaze didn't move from his mouth and her head lay heavy in the palm of his hand, the tension bleeding out of her muscles completely.

'I should.'

'Why?' He searched her flushed face. 'Physical desire is nothing to be afraid of.'

She gave him a brief, fleeting look before she looked away again. 'I wouldn't know. I've…never felt it before.'

So… All of this was new to her. Perhaps she was even a virgin…

A deep possessiveness he hadn't known was inside him stirred, along with a satisfaction that would have disturbed him if he'd thought about it in any depth.

But he didn't want to think about it in any depth, so he didn't.

'You feel it now.' He didn't make it a question.

Her lashes fell, her gaze once more going to his mouth, as if she couldn't help herself. She didn't speak. But then she didn't need to. He knew the answer already.

Of course she felt it.

'Say it again,' he murmured. 'My name.'

'Tariq…'

The word had barely left her lips before he'd bent and covered them with his in a feather-light kiss. A mere brush across her mouth. To taste her and tempt her. To test their undeniable physical chemistry.

She went very still, her body trembling.

He'd intended to end the kiss almost as soon as it had started, thinking that would be sufficient, and yet he found he couldn't pull away, that something inside him was catching fire.

He touched his tongue to her bottom lip instead, tracing the line of it the way he'd traced it with that strawberry, and she trembled even harder. Then her lips were softening, opening for him, and he couldn't stop himself from deepening the kiss, allowing his tongue to sweep in and taste her.

Oh, so sweet… Like that strawberry. Like honey. Like the late-summer wine that came from the vineyards in the valley to the south.

He spread his hand out on the back of her head, his fingers pushing into her hair, holding her still as he kissed her more deeply, chasing that sweetness.

She gave a little throaty moan. The sound made all the blood in his body rush to a certain part of his anatomy, and all of a sudden the kiss turned hot—far hotter than he'd intended.

This was supposed to be a test. For her, not for him. And yet he found that he was the one on the edge of control.

He wanted her robe gone. Her bikini gone. He wanted her naked and up against the wall of the pool. He wanted to be inside her.

Her hands touched his chest, her fingers pure electricity on his skin.

If you do not stop now, that is exactly what will happen.

And it must not. He knew what happened when he didn't control himself…when he let passion get the better of him. Distance—that was what his father had taught him. Distance and detachment. And that was not what was happening now.

It took every ounce of will he had, but he managed it, tearing his mouth from hers and letting her go.

She was staring at him in shock, her mouth full and red from the kiss, her eyes round as saucers and dark as midnight.

'I will arrange your phone call,' he said brusquely.

Then he turned around and left the pool before she could say a word.

'I DON'T LIKE IT, Charlotte.'

Her father's voice sounded cracked and tinny down the phone.

'I don't like it at all.'

Charlotte gripped the phone Tariq had handed to her

hard and tried to ignore her future husband, standing on the other side of the desk, his face impassive.

He'd been as good as his word in arranging the call, though he'd offered no explanation for his sudden change of heart. She thought it might have something to do with what had happened between them in the baths the day before, but she wasn't sure.

She was trying *very* hard not to think about that herself. Though it was difficult when he'd insisted on remaining in the room while she spoke to her father, watching her with his intent golden stare.

'It's okay, Dad,' she said, trying to be reassuring. 'Like I was saying, we met and…f-fell in love, and he asked me to marry him. And I said yes.'

'But it's only been three days,' her father pointed out, sounding cross.

'Isn't that how long it took you to decide to marry Mum?'

Her parents had had a mad, passionate, whirlwind romance—at least that was what her father had said, always bitterly—followed by a quick wedding. And then, years later, an acrimonious divorce.

With her in the middle.

She was suddenly even more conscious of Tariq, just on the other side of the desk, staring at her intensely. His presence was intimidating, pressing in on her, making her skin prickle with heat at the memory of his mouth on hers, the feeling of his hand cradling the back of her head, his body tall and powerful and so achingly close.

Speaking of mad and passionate…

That had been her yesterday, at the baths. Her heartbeat had been frantic, her skin too tight and too hot. She'd been overwhelmed by him, by the taste of him—something indescribable that reminded her of dense, rich, hot chocolate. Sweet and decadent and dark.

She should have stopped him, but when he'd touched her she hadn't even been able to remember why it was wrong to want him anyway. He'd told her that physical desire wasn't anything to be afraid of and in that moment, with the way he'd held her and the gentleness with which he'd explored her, fear had been the last thing she'd felt. All she'd been conscious of was her hunger. For him.

Her pulse was beating hard now, almost drowning out her father's voice.

'Yes, that's true,' he was saying. 'But look what happened there. That woman ruined my life and nearly destroyed my career, while she got to swan off with her divorce settlement, footloose and fancy-free.'

Meaning without the millstone of her daughter hanging around her neck, presumably, though Charlotte didn't ask him that. She knew his thoughts on the matter. If she hadn't got so afraid and run off during one of their more bitter arguments, staying out the whole night while her parents called the police, trying to find her, her mother might have continued to fight the custody battle and would probably have won.

But her mother hadn't continued to fight. She'd deemed Charlotte too much of a problem and left her with her father.

'Well,' her father went on crossly, not waiting for her to speak, 'I suppose if that's what you want to do, then that's what you want to do. But now I'll have to find myself a new bloody assistant.'

So he might never see his daughter again and all he could think about was hiring a new assistant?

Did you expect it to be different? For him to care?

No—and that was the sad thing. She didn't. He'd never made a secret of how unhappy he'd been when he was granted full custody of her, how she'd limited him in terms of his career, and how if she hadn't gone running off that night things would have been different.

The fact that she'd tried very hard *not* to be an impediment to his career as a kid, and then as an adult—had actively tried to help him with it, in fact—didn't seem to register.

'Sorry, Dad,' she said, not knowing what else to say. The pressure of Tariq's gaze was like a weight, pressing down on her.

'Can't be helped, I suppose,' her father muttered. 'Look, I'd better go. These soldiers look like they're ready to get rid of me. Speak soon.'

The call disconnected.

He doesn't care and you know it.

Her eyes prickled, which made her angry. Because, yes, she did know it. She always had. The professor resented her, so why she kept trying to change his mind about her she had no idea.

He's all you have—that's why.

But that didn't bear thinking about—especially not with Tariq still staring at her so intently. She didn't want him knowing how little she was valued by the only important person in her life, and she especially didn't want him seeing her tears.

So she swallowed down the lump in her throat, blinked the moisture from her eyes and handed him back the phone. 'Thank you,' she said, pleased that her voice at least sounded level. 'I don't think there will be any repercussions for you.'

He took the phone and slid it back into his pocket, but his gaze didn't leave her face. 'What did he say to you?'

So he'd picked up on her upset. Wonderful.

'I don't think that's any of your business.'

'You will be my wife soon,' he said flatly. 'Everything you do is my business.'

There was a stillness to him, an intensity that unnerved her. Though that wasn't the only unnerving thing about him. In suit trousers and a black business shirt open at the neck, displaying bronze skin and the beat of a strong pulse, he had a charisma that was undeniable.

She found herself staring at that pulse and thinking about what it would be like if she brushed her mouth over it. What his skin would taste like. What he would do if she did that…

'Charlotte,' he said softly. 'Up here.'

She jerked her gaze up to his, her cheeks hot with embarrassment. Because of course he'd know exactly what she was thinking—like he had in the baths yesterday. She'd tried to hide it, tried to distract him with her request for a phone call, but he hadn't been deflected. He'd been relentless, getting the truth out of her whether she wanted to give it to him or not.

You liked giving it to him.

The taste of him was suddenly in her mouth, the memory of his lips on hers scorching.

'He said nothing,' she murmured thickly, trying to shove the memories from her head. 'Just that he'd have to get a new assistant.'

The gold of Tariq's eyes was molten, the heat in them like the desert sun. As if he was angry. But she couldn't imagine why he would be.

'That is all?'

'Yes.'

'It upset you?'

'Of course it upset me.' She tried to keep her voice level. 'He's my father and now I'll never see him again.'

Tariq's gaze narrowed. 'I do not think that is why you are upset.'

But she didn't want to have this particular conversation. She felt too raw, too uncertain. There was the pain of her father's dismissal and her own anger, as well as the press of that unfamiliar hunger every time she looked at the Sheikh, standing behind his desk. The memory of his kiss still burned in her mind and she didn't want it there.

She looked away. 'Perhaps we could talk about this at a different time? I have to—'

She didn't hear him move, but he must have done because suddenly one large hand was cupping her cheek, his thumb brushing over her skin. 'You hoped for more from him?'

Her heart was beating loudly in her ears again and his body was inches away. His palm against her skin was hot, and part of her wanted to jerk away while another part wanted to lean into his touch. It had been such a long time since anyone had touched her quite like this. A long time since anyone had been interested in her feelings.

'Yes, I did,' she said, not sure why she was telling him this when she'd been so determined not to. 'I hoped he might be upset that he wouldn't see me again rather than because he'd have to get a new assistant.'

His thumb brushed her cheek again and she didn't want to look at him. Because he was too close and that raw feeling in her chest wouldn't go away. Those golden eyes of his would see her vulnerability all too easily, and he'd know how badly her father's easy dismissal had hurt.

And then he'll want to know why.

Yes, he would. And she didn't want to tell him.

'He knows that he will not see you again?' Tariq asked.

'I told him.' She swallowed, gathering herself, then pulled away from his touch and forced a smile on her face. 'He's absent-minded a lot of the time, so I'm not sure he listened. Anyway, that's that, I suppose. What made you change your mind about giving me the call?'

Tariq's hand dropped and he remained where he was, making no move towards her. But he continued to study her, his gaze unsettling in its intensity. 'Maybe it was your kiss,' he murmured.

And any relief she felt that he'd dropped the subject of her father vanished as heat filled her at the reminder of what had happened the day before. She was conscious once again of the throb of hunger down low inside her.

The space between them suddenly felt electric, crackling with a strange static charge that had her breath catching.

'If you are thinking that our marriage will be in name only, you are wrong, Charlotte,' he went on, his voice even lower and deeper. 'You do understand that, do you not?'

Don't pretend you don't know what he's talking about.

Her mouth was dry and she couldn't seem to find any air. Because of course she knew what he was talking about— and it was something she'd conveniently not been thinking about. At least not until he'd kissed her.

He meant sex.

And he meant that he intended to have sex with her.

Heat swept through her, burning everything in its path, and she had to turn away so he wouldn't see the way her face flamed.

'Of course I understand,' she said automatically. 'Goodness, look at the time. I have to—'

'I would not want there to be any misunderstanding.' There was no mistaking the intent in his words, or the dark hint of sensuality that threaded through his tone. 'We have a certain…chemistry, *ya amar*. And I fully intend to explore that as thoroughly as possible.'

A certain chemistry…

He wants you.

The thought blazed in her brain for a second, bright as neon. She hadn't thought about how she might affect him— mainly because she'd been too busy thinking about how he affected her. But he'd kissed her for a long time yesterday, and the kiss had soon turned hotter, deeper. He'd become demanding, and his grip on her had tightened, his body responding. And then he'd let her go abruptly, with something blazing in his eyes that had looked like anger.

She hadn't thought about why he might have been angry—hadn't thought at all about why he'd let her go either. She'd tried to put it out of her mind entirely.

But maybe she should think about it. Maybe she had was some power she'd never expected to find.

'I see,' she said slowly, turning over the discovery in her head.

'Do you? Look at me, Charlotte.'

There was no resisting the command and she didn't, turning back to him, her gaze clashing with his. And for a moment she was back in the desert, with the sun a hammer-blow of heat, crushing her with its force.

'Tell me you understand,' he said.

She met the ferocity in his eyes, for some reason feeling less vulnerable than she had a moment ago. The knowledge that she wasn't without power here was giving her a courage she hadn't expected to feel.

'I understand.'

He stared back at her for a long, uncounted moment. Then he turned around and went back to the desk.

'I suggest you do some research on the marriage customs of Ashkaraz,' he said, sitting down. 'Amirah will show you which books to read in the library. Some of them you should find quite interesting.'

His attention was on his computer screen now, which obviously meant that she was dismissed.

But that was good.

She had a lot to think about.

CHAPTER SEVEN

Tariq had never been one for weddings, and he hadn't been particularly interested in the preparations for his own. Not when it was the wedding night he couldn't stop thinking about. To a disturbing degree.

Then again, focusing on physical pleasure had been better than going over his behaviour in his office the day she'd spoken to her father, and how he'd given in to the disturbing urge to comfort her.

He still didn't understand why he had, or why the need to do so had hit him so strongly. All he'd seen in her blue eyes was a flash of pain. And then she wouldn't tell him what the problem was, so he'd gone around the desk, reaching for her and cupping her cheek before he'd been able to think better of it.

A mistake.

He couldn't afford slips like that and he knew it.

So for the past week he'd distanced himself from her, busying himself with his duties as well as with preparations for the wedding. And there had been a lot to prepare, since he wanted the whole business over and done with as quickly as possible.

As per royal custom, the ceremony itself was being held on the palace steps, in full view of his people.

Charlotte was robed in gauzy white silk, embroidered

all over with silver and belted at the waist with a silver sash that had long sparkling tassels falling almost to her ankles. Her hair was loose, as was also the custom, and gleaming in the sun, and she wore a simple platinum circlet around her brow, with one of Ashkaraz's rare blue diamonds in the centre.

Her face was very pale as she appeared, and it went even paler as she saw the assembled crowds. But she didn't hesitate as she was led to where he stood, alongside the officiant who would conduct the ceremony.

His people hadn't been given much time to come to terms with their Sheikh marrying a foreigner, but as soon as Charlotte appeared they gave her a hearty cheer. Apparently they were as susceptible to a white wedding gown as he was.

And he was.

He couldn't take his eyes off her as she joined him on the steps, all silvery and white and bright as the moon. Beautiful, too, and delicate. He hadn't thought that would affect him, but it did.

And as she recited the complicated vows without a single hesitation he was conscious of that dark satisfaction sweeping through him again—the same feeling he'd had in the baths that day. A feeling he'd not experienced about a person before. Not when his life had been all about feeling nothing for individual people at all.

It was the whole that was important—at least that was what his father had taught him. His country and his people were what he ought to have uppermost in his mind. He did not need to concern himself with specifics.

Yet he was aware, as her vows were being said, that he was feeling something very specific now—and that feeling was centred entirely on a person.

Mine, the feeling told him. *She is mine.*

He hadn't had anything that was his before—not one single thing. All of it had been for 'the Sheikh' rather than the man. All except Catherine. And even she had been his father's first. Never his.

But Charlotte was. Charlotte was his completely.

He felt almost savage as the vows were completed and their hands were joined. Her delicate fingers were cool in his, and he was already thankful for the traditions of Ash-karazi royal marriage that required the bride and groom to retire immediately after the wedding to an oasis in the south, sacred to the royal family, for three days, to ensure the getting of an heir.

It should have been disturbing to feel this intensely about a woman, but it had been some time since he'd taken his pleasure, so it was no wonder that was all he could think about.

After the vows and rings were exchanged, and the people had cheered their new sheikha, Tariq wasted no time in taking Charlotte's elbow and whisking her from the palace to the helipad, where his helicopter stood ready to take them to the oasis.

She gave him a startled look as his guards fell into step around them and he urged her along the path to the helipad. 'Where are we going? Isn't there a reception or a party? I read that—'

'You read, presumably, about what happens directly after a royal wedding here?'

She flushed, the colour standing out beautifully on her pale skin. 'Oh, the sacred oasis. Of course.'

The shy way she said it only made the savage feeling inside him grow more intense, and it was a good thing that there was no more opportunity for talk as they came to the helicopter.

He helped her into it, bundling the long white skirts

of her wedding robes around her, and a few minutes later they were in the air, soaring high over the city of Kharan and then following the long valley down to where the oasis was situated.

It was about an hour from the palace, in isolated, rocky desert, and surrounding the bright green and blue jewel of the oasis were palm trees and grasses.

The chopper took them down, and when it had landed Tariq helped Charlotte out. Palace staff had spent the last day or so setting up the tents that contained all the facilities both of them would need for three days alone, and a couple were still there to help unload their luggage from the helicopter.

Charlotte was silent as Tariq led her over to a low divan set under some shady palms, then went back to help with the unloading of the helicopter. He didn't have to do it, but he couldn't sit still waiting for everyone to leave. He wanted them gone, and quickly.

Another couple of minutes later and the chopper was rising into the air and heading back up the valley to Kharan, leaving Tariq finally alone with his bride.

She'd remained sitting on the divan under the palms in a pool of white and silver silk, her hands clasped in her lap, her silvery hair loose down her back. A smile curved her mouth as he stalked over to her, though he could see it was forced.

'So,' she said breathlessly, 'I guess this is where we are. In the oasis.'

He stopped in front of her, studying her face. A fine sheen of sweat gleamed on her brow, because it was only late afternoon and still suffocatingly hot, despite their proximity to the water. It wouldn't cool down till well after dark.

But he didn't think it was entirely the heat that was making her sweat.

She was nervous.

His own need was beating inside him like a drum, and the urge to pick her up and take her to the bedroom tent was almost overpowering.

Why the impatience? You have plenty of time.

That was true. They did have three days, after all. And maybe it would even do him good to practise some restraint—especially after the incident in the baths when he'd almost forgotten himself. He was supposed to remain detached, after all.

Yet he didn't feel detached now. He wanted her skin damp and slippery from something other than the heat and her silver-blue eyes full of fire. He wanted more of the kisses he'd taken from her, and the taste of her latent passion on his tongue. He wanted to rouse it, stoke it. Make it burn for him and only for him.

And why not? She was his wife now. And he'd told her that their marriage would not be in name only. She had always known what would be expected.

But it was not her choice to marry you—remember that. You railroaded her into it.

He didn't know why he was thinking about that now. Not when his body was hardening, desire and possessiveness coursing through him. And it wouldn't change the fact that although she might not have had a choice about the marriage, she still wanted him. He hadn't forgotten the throaty moan she'd made when he'd kissed her in the baths, or how her mouth had opened beneath his, wanting more.

Her attention was on him, she was watching him, and she must know what he was thinking because he could see that familiar flicker of apprehension in her eyes. But the heat he remembered from the baths was burning there too.

Oh, yes, she wanted him. But she was afraid of it.

'Do not look so frightened, *ya amar*,' he said, a rough

edge creeping into his voice. 'I have already told you that I will not hurt you.'

'I'm not frightened.' Her hands twisted in her lap, her gaze darting around, looking everywhere but at him. 'Could we perhaps go for a swim first? I'm rather hot.'

His patience thinned, irritation coiling with the desire twisting inside him. 'You are lying, Charlotte. And I have told you already that will not work. Not with me. And definitely not now we are about to consummate our marriage.'

Her lashes fell. 'I'm not lying.'

'Then why are your hands twisting in your lap? And why will you not look directly at me?'

She was already flushed with heat and now her cheeks went even pinker. With a deliberate movement, she unclenched her hands, laying them flat on the white silk of her skirts. Then her lashes rose and she looked at him.

'There. Is that better?'

'No,' he said impatiently. 'Do not play with me.'

'I'm not playing with you,' she shot back, and there was the slight edge of temper rising in her voice. 'I'm only trying to—'

'And do not try to placate me either.'

He didn't want to stand there arguing with her. He wanted to take her to bed. But her nervousness and vulnerability were making his chest tight and he didn't like it.

Detachment—that was what he had to strive for. Detachment and isolation. Not being concerned with another person's feelings.

'I'm *not* trying to placate you.' Charlotte pushed herself to her feet, her cheeks red, her blue eyes full of anger. 'I'm nervous, if you must know. I told you the truth in the baths when I said I hadn't felt anything physically for a man before. I haven't. But I feel something for you and I... I don't know what do.' She stopped, took a breath, and glanced away. 'I'm a virgin. And I… I don't want to disappoint you.'

He went very still.

She is yours completely.

He'd suspected she was innocent already, and yet the possessiveness that deepened and broadened in response to her confession was almost shocking.

Yes, she was his. Completely. And why she would think he might find that disappointing was anyone's guess.

'You should have told me,' he growled. 'That is something I need to know. And as for disappointing me…' He stared hard into her flushed face. 'Why would you think that?'

Her jaw tightened, her discomfort obvious, but she didn't look away this time. 'You didn't choose me because you wanted me, Tariq. You chose me because I was convenient.'

'But you must know that I want you. Surely that kiss in the baths told you that?'

'That doesn't change the fact that you wouldn't have married me if I hadn't accidentally wandered into your kingdom.'

'No, I would not.' He couldn't lie; it was the truth. 'But what does that have to do with anything? Do you want me to feel something for you? Is that what you are asking?'

Emotions flickered over her face, but they were gone so fast he couldn't tell what they were.

Then her gaze dropped again, her shoulders drooping. 'No,' she said. 'That's not what I'm asking. Forget I said anything.'

It was not what he'd planned. And it wasn't what he wanted. That tightness in his chest was back, and he didn't know why the sight of her looking so defeated affected him the way it did. It reminded him of the expression on her face that day in his office, during her father's phone call, the bright flash of hurt.

Which shouldn't matter to him. Her self-doubt had nothing to do with him. And yet he couldn't let it go.

He reached out, took her chin in his hand and tilted her head up so her gaze met his. 'Do not change the subject. Answer me, Charlotte. Why do you think you would be a disappointment?'

'You…are stuck with me.' There was a catch in her voice. 'And let's just say that hasn't worked out well for me before.'

Her skin was so soft, so silky. He rubbed his thumb gently along her lower lip, unable to stop himself from touching her, the need inside him becoming even fiercer.

But this was too important to interrupt. 'Tell me,' he ordered quietly.

She let out a soft breath, her lashes falling again, the sunlight turning them to pure silver. 'My parents had a very bitter divorce. My mother decided not to contest custody so Dad ended up with me. He was not…happy about it. Said it would affect his career.'

Tariq frowned, staring down at her lovely face, conscious of yet another unwanted emotion threading through him: anger. On her behalf. Because what kind of father would say that to his child? What kind of father would make sure his child knew she wasn't wanted?

His own father had been strict, and Tariq had been so angry with him—yet Ishak had done what he had because he'd wanted Tariq to be the best king possible. Of course Tariq had ended up disappointing him in the end, but that hadn't been his father's fault. And he was making good now.

And so was she. Sacrificing her freedom in return for her father's. Making the best of marrying a complete stranger.

Throwing herself into all the tasks he'd set her, learning his language and his customs without complaint.

She is trying. Like you are trying.

The need inside him twisted, deepened, ached. Became something more.

'Well, you are not a disappointment to me,' he said before he could stop himself. 'You are the opposite. You are beautiful and loyal and you have done what you could in a situation you did not choose and did not want. You are everything I want in a wife.'

There was something fearfully hopeful in her gaze as it searched his, as if she couldn't quite bring herself to believe him yet wanted to.

'But I'm not experienced. I don't know—'

Tariq put his thumb gently over her mouth, stopping the words. 'I do not need you to be experienced. I have enough experience for both of us. Now...' He paused, letting her see what burned inside him: the desire for her. 'I am tired of waiting, Charlotte. And I do not want to talk. What I want is to take you to bed.'

Her lips were soft and full beneath his thumb, the blue of her eyes darkening. There was already a sheen of perspiration on her skin and wisps of hair were sticking to her forehead—not a good thing when what he was planning to do to her would make her even hotter.

He frowned. 'Perhaps you do need cooling down first, though.'

'Oh, but I'm not—'

Decision made, he didn't wait for her to finish, dropping his hand and giving in to the need to get close to her by gathering her small, curvy figure in his arms.

She gave a soft gasp, but didn't protest, tipping her head back against his shoulder as his grip tightened, her eyes very blue in her flushed face.

'I thought you were tired of waiting?'

'Who says I will wait?' He began to stride through the palms, anticipation coiling inside him. 'A swim can involve all kinds of things.'

She blinked, obviously thinking about this. 'Oh. So you might…um…?'

'Consummate our marriage in the water?' he finished. 'I might.'

Judging by how hard he was right now, it might even be inevitable.

He didn't want to pause to undress her, so he walked straight into the oasis, wading out into the middle, still carrying her. The water was deliciously cool against his own hot skin, making his wedding robes stick to him, and as it flooded over her she gave a little gasp, wriggling against him.

'But I'm still dressed!'

'I realise that.' He moved deeper, until the water was at his chest and she was clutching at him, white silk floating all around her, her breathing fast at the shock of the water.

'But what about a swimsuit?'

'You do not need a swimsuit.'

Her weight in his arms was slight, her body warm, her hands gripping his robes tightly.

He glanced down at her, noting how her flush had receded. 'You are feeling cooler now?'

'Yes, much better, thank you.'

A crease appeared between her fair brows as she met his gaze. The water was lapping at her hair, making it float around her like fine silver thread.

'You're really quite kind, aren't you?'

He wasn't sure what went through him in that moment. It was a wave of something he wasn't familiar with. Almost as if he…liked what she'd said. Which was strange.

Because he wasn't kind, and nor did he want to be. Kindness reminded him of mercy, of sympathy, of the soft feelings he associated with Catherine. Of his weakness when it came to his own emotions. Anger. Desire. Need.

But he wasn't going to think about those things.

Instead, he shoved away the warmth that threatened, concentrated instead on the desire burning like fire in his blood.

'No,' he said, adjusting his hold on her to reach for the silver belt at her waist. 'Kind is one thing I am not.'

And then he pulled hard, systematically beginning to strip her robes from her body.

CHAPTER EIGHT

Tariq's fingers on her were firm as he stripped away her heavy, water-soaked robes, but it was the look on his face that made her breath catch.

His jaw was tight, tension radiated from him, and his features looked as if they'd been carved from granite. The only thing that wasn't hard and cold was his gaze, and a kind of molten intensity was burning in his eyes.

Burning in her too.

What had she said? That he was kind? He'd been kind to her that day she'd spoken to her father, and he'd been kind to her just before, underneath the palm trees, as nervousness and the strangeness of the whole day had got to her. As she'd been overwhelmed by the fact that she was now married to a king and that he was going to take her virginity, probably right where she stood.

He'd looked so stern, so forbidding as the helicopter had left. And the courage that had carried her through the wedding ceremony in front of seemingly the entire city had deserted her.

She'd tried to pretend she was fine, but suddenly, under his intimidating stare, all she'd felt was doubt. In herself, and in what was going to happen, and in the intensity of her own desire too.

It had only occurred to her then that, as much as she

hadn't had a choice in their marriage, perhaps neither had he. He needed an heir, and he hadn't been able to choose a wife from his own people because he had an entire country he had to protect. And she'd been convenient.

Really, when she thought about it, it seemed he'd been stuck with her the same way her father had been stuck with her.

It shouldn't matter, but somehow it did. She didn't want him to be stuck with someone he was only going to be disappointed in—and she *would* end up disappointing him. She wasn't one of his people and she didn't speak his language. She didn't know his customs or what was expected of her.

She was a virgin with no experience whatsoever.

How could that not be disappointing to a man like him?

And yet he'd cupped her cheek in his hand, his gaze fierce with conviction. And he'd told her that she was beautiful. That she was loyal. That she was everything he'd hoped for.

He *was* kind, no matter what he said, and she didn't know why that made him so angry.

Maybe you should ask him?

She probably should—except now was not the right time, given the way he was looking at her, as if he wanted to eat her alive.

A shiver coursed through her and it had nothing to do with the water lapping around her. Even forbidding and hard, the impact of him was like a gut-punch. She'd felt it the moment she'd met him on the steps of the palace, just before the ceremony. He'd been dressed in white, as had she, but his robes had been embroidered with gold. The white had set off his inky black hair and his bronze skin, and the gold thread had struck sparks from the deep gold of his eyes as he'd looked at her.

And for a second she hadn't been able to breathe. Because he had been so…overwhelming. Beautiful, and strong, and powerful. So achingly charismatic. He had drawn every eye, commanded all the attention.

She found it difficult to breathe now, as he stripped the long-sleeved over-robe off her, let the water move silkily over her bare arms, then began to pull at the ties of the long sleeveless tunic she wore.

'What's wrong with being kind?' she asked, not knowing she was going to say it until it was out and then, given how his features hardened still further, regretting it.

'There is nothing wrong with being kind.'

He pulled off the tunic, then tugged down the long, loose trousers that she wore underneath.

'But you're angry.'

She stared up into his face, trying to figure out why a simple compliment should bother him quite so much, but his expression remained impassive. Again, except for his eyes. They burned brilliant gold.

'Now is not the time for conversation, *ya amar.*'

His voice was rough and full of authority, and she couldn't help shivering as his hands stroked up her bare legs, his palms hot against her skin in stark contrast to the cool water.

'I know, but—'

She stopped abruptly as his hand slid around her, deftly undoing the clasp of her white lace bra and stripping it from her. The water licked over her skin, making her nipples harden, and everything she'd been going to say vanished from her brain.

'But what?' His gaze dropped to her bare breasts, his eyes glittering, heat flaring higher in them.

And she couldn't think.

Couldn't even form one rational thought.

Because he was tugging down the scrap of white lace that was her knickers, and then they were gone too, and there was nothing at all between her and his merciless golden stare.

She was naked now. Naked in front of her husband.

He adjusted his hold on her again so she was lying back in his arms, her body stretched out, completely bare to his gaze. And she trembled slightly, waiting for the urge to run and hide, to cringe away.

But it didn't come. Instead she wanted to stretch out under his hot stare, to watch the flames in his eyes burn higher. Wanted to see how she affected him. Because she did, and it was obvious. The beautiful lines of his face were sharpening with hunger.

How strange… Though she was in the water, and completely naked, she felt more powerful than she had standing before him fully dressed. Like that day in his office, when she'd got an inkling of how much she affected him. Though that had only been a ghost of what she felt now.

Now her power was fully realised.

Brave in a way she hadn't been before, she lifted her hand and touched one carved cheekbone, running her fingers along his smooth, warm skin.

Something ignited in his eyes and he made a growling sound deep in his throat. Then abruptly he turned, carrying her out of the water and towards the little cluster of tents pitched in the shadow of the trees.

He ducked inside the biggest one, and Charlotte had an impression of a floor covered in silken rugs, with low couches and cushions set up in one corner, before Tariq threw her, still dripping wet, onto a huge bed with a carved wooden base. It was made up with fresh white cotton sheets and piled high with pillows, and it was incredibly comfortable. Not that she was particularly concerned with comfort right now.

He didn't follow her right away, his hands going to his own soaking wet wedding robes and stripping them off carelessly, leaving them in a heap on the floor. She found herself watching him, unable to look away.

She knew what he looked like naked because of the baths, and he was every bit as magnificent as she remembered. Yet this time, as he shoved down the loose trousers he'd been wearing, and with them his underwear, she was able to see what the water of the baths had been concealing.

Heat leapt inside her. Her face was burning...everything was burning.

He made no attempt to hide the long, hard length that curved up between his thighs, stepping naked and arrogant from his wet clothes. She couldn't stop looking at him.

He'd told her that it wasn't wrong to want him, that physical passion wasn't anything to be afraid of, but she couldn't help the apprehension that coiled inside her now. And it wasn't because she was afraid of him. She was afraid of herself, and of the hunger inside her getting deeper. Stronger.

After her parents' divorce intensity had always scared her, so this was frightening. She wanted him so much. Part of her wished he'd push her back on the bed and take her the way she imagined kings took their brides. Hard and fast, with no mercy. Then she would have no choice but to give everything to him. No choice but to surrender to that hunger and not think about how to ignore it or force it away.

Not think about where that hunger might lead.

Except Tariq didn't make a move towards her. He stood there, staring at her, his demanding gaze hot on hers.

'Come to me,' he commanded.

Heat pulsed down her spine before spiralling into a tight knot down low between her thighs. She found herself obeying almost helplessly, pushing herself off the bed and walking the few steps that separated them. Her pulse was hammering in her ears as she came close, deafening her, and her mouth was bone-dry. She felt dizzy, but she didn't think it was the heat of the sun this time.

No, it was him.

Her husband.

He was so tall, towering over her, a wall of heat, hard muscle and bronzed skin. And the expression on his face was ferocious.

'You want me,' he said.

It wasn't a question, but she answered all the same. 'Yes…' Her voice sounded hoarse and thick, the word unsteady.

'Say it,' he ordered, relentless.

Her heartbeat was racing, the strength of her own need building like a storm. He was going to demand an acknowledgement from her, that was obvious, which meant the time for pretending was over and she knew it. It would be pointless anyway—especially when he saw straight through her.

'I…want you,' she whispered.

His eyes gleamed, and his obvious pleasure made something hot glow inside her chest.

'Then go down on your knees, *ya amar*, and show me how much.'

TARIQ KNEW HE was indulging himself. That he didn't have to make his virgin wife go on her knees before him. But what she'd said to him out in the oasis had stuck in his head.

'Kind', she'd called him.

And so he'd stripped her bare, trying to prove—to her, to himself—that he was nothing of the sort. Yet even then, naked and wet in his arms, she'd looked up at him as if she knew something about him that he didn't, lifting her hand to touch his cheek.

And perhaps she did know something he didn't. Because the second her cool fingers had touched him something had opened up inside him—a hunger he hadn't realised he felt. A hunger that had nothing to do with sexual desire. And he had known all at once that she was more dangerous than he could possibly have imagined.

No one had touched him like that since his mother had died. Not without any sexual intent, not casually or just because they'd wanted to. Not even the succession of nannies who'd brought him up had done so. They'd been given strict orders not to touch him or to comfort him—no reassurance or support had been allowed. Because he'd had to learn self-sufficiency, to find consolation in detachment and isolation, since that would be his life as king.

It had been a very hard lesson, but he'd learned it in the end. And it had taken Catherine to finally hammer it home. Since then he hadn't missed it—hadn't wanted the comfort of another person's touch. He'd had lovers to meet his physical needs and that was all he'd required.

Until Charlotte. Until her cool fingers had touched his cheek. Her touch delicate, tentative. Gentle.

He'd guarded himself against *her* vulnerability; he had just never dreamed she would discover something vulnerable in *him*.

What was clear was that he couldn't let that happen. He couldn't let her take that power from him. Which meant he had to show her where the power truly lay: with him.

She'd already given him the acknowledgement that she wanted him, and it clearly wasn't a stretch for her to obey him as she dropped to her knees on the soft rugs of the tent floor.

She was breathing very fast, the sound of it was audible in the tent, so he reached down and grasped her chin, tilting her head back so he could see her face, look into her eyes. They were very dark, the silver blue of a daytime sky turning to midnight. It was immensely satisfying to see how badly she wanted him.

'Open your mouth.' He pressed his thumb to the centre of her bottom lip for emphasis. 'Take me inside.'

'I… I haven't done this before.' Her cheeks were pink and she sounded breathless, a little uncertain. 'I'm not sure what to do.'

'That is why I will instruct you.' He stroked the softness of her lips, admiring her courage, because this time he couldn't see any apprehension in her at all. 'Do as you are told.'

She took a little breath, then opened her mouth obediently.

Ah, she made such a pretty picture, kneeling before him, naked and wet, her nipples pink and hard, her thighs spread, giving him a tantalising glimpse of the nest of blonde curls between them.

He was aching as he took himself in hand, guiding himself to her mouth. He gritted his teeth as she leaned forward, touching him with her tongue, tentative and hesitant. And then heat wrapped around him, slick warmth, as she took him into her mouth, and his heartbeat was as loud as a drum in his head, pleasure licking like a velvet whip up his spine.

He growled, unable to help himself, shoving his fingers in her hair and holding her, guiding her, as she began to suck him. She was inexpert and uncertain, but there was an eroticism to her inexperience that made pleasure burn like hot coals inside him. And knowing that he was the first man she'd ever done this to made it even more intense.

The first man. The *only* man.

His lips pulled back in a snarl as the thought hit him, and as her tongue curled around him it came to him all of a sudden that perhaps he'd made a mistake. Perhaps what had been intended to put her at a distance had only served to draw her closer. Because she had the power to undo him—

he knew that now. With her hot mouth and her innocence, with her hesitant tongue and her cool fingers.

She could undo him completely right where he stood—and that was not what he'd intended at all.

Tariq tightened his grip, pulling her head away.

Her eyes widened in surprise. Her mouth was full and pink and slick from taking him.

'Did I—?' she began.

But he didn't let her finish, hauling her to her feet and kissing her hard and deep and territorial. She gave a little moan, shuddering in his hands, arching her body into his.

Ah, but he had to take control. He needed her to be the one desperate for him, not the other way around. He couldn't allow her to get to him any more than she had already.

He picked her up, holding her warm body against him. Her skin was still cool and damp from the oasis, but now she was starting to warm up. Silky little woman. He was going to have to go slowly and carefully if he wanted this to last.

Crossing the few steps to the bed, he lowered her onto the mattress and followed, coming onto his hands and knees over her, watching the expressions across her face shift like the wind on the surface of a lake.

She was panting, her breasts rising and falling fast, her pretty nipples were tight and the flush in her cheeks had spread down her neck and over her chest. Her thighs had fallen open, baring her sex to his gaze: slick pink skin and a cluster of silver-blonde curls.

Beautiful. Delicate.

Yours.

He looked into her eyes, watching her as he lifted a hand and brushed her throat with his fingertips, then ran them lightly down the centre of her body, stroking her satiny skin. She shuddered, goosebumps rising in the wake of his touch, her breasts and stomach quivering. He didn't stop, and he didn't look away as his fingers brushed the soft curls between her thighs and then the slick, hot folds beneath them.

She gasped, her hips rising to his hand, her eyes going wide. Her pleasure was obvious. The musky, sweet scent of her arousal was like a drug, turning his hunger sharp as knife. But it wasn't his desire he wanted to sharpen. It was hers. So he parted her gently with his fingers, finding the hard bud that would give her the most pleasure and teasing it lightly. She groaned and jerked, panting.

'Arms above your head,' he ordered softly. 'And do not take them down until I say.'

'T-Tariq, I don't know if I—'

'Trust me, *ya amar*.'

She took another shuddering breath, then slowly raised her arms and let them rest on the pillows behind her head. Her gaze was on his, as if he was the centre of the entire universe, and he liked that. Liked the way she trusted him. Liked it far, far too much.

'Yes,' he murmured, stroking and teasing her. 'Look at me. Keep looking at me.'

She shook, gasping as he slid his fingers over her slickness, her hips lifting restlessly. 'Tariq…' Her voice was thick and desperate. 'Oh… I can't… This— This is…'

He lowered his head and stopped her words with his mouth, kissing her hard and deep. She groaned, letting him in. The taste of her was the same as it had been in the baths, achingly sweet, and it made him feel wild, made his restraint feel thin and tenuous.

But he was used to testing himself, so he kissed her harder, letting his fingers find the slick entrance to her body and circling it, tantalising her, before gradually easing inside. She was tight, her body clamping down on his fingers, and the hot, wet heat of her pulled hard on the leash he'd placed on his control.

She arched beneath him, moaning, her hands gripping onto the pillows above her head and twisting. He took his mouth from hers and kissed down the delicate arch of her neck, tasting the salt in the hollow of her throat, and then further, between her breasts. He covered one nipple with his lips and sucked, teasing it with his tongue as he stroked his fingers in and out of her.

She called his name, gasping. Her eyes were closed, her head thrown back, her silver hair sticking to her forehead and neck.

Beautiful. Desperate. His.

He moved his mouth to her other breast and at the same time pressed his thumb down on that small bud between her thighs, sliding his fingers deep. She cried out, her body stiffening as the climax washed over her.

Her taste was in his mouth and her scent was all around, the sound of her pleasure loud in his ears.

And his control hung by a thread.

He could not wait any longer.

Pulling his fingers from her body, he knelt between her thighs and slid his hands beneath the shapely curve of her bottom, lifting her, fitting himself to the entrance of her body.

He put one hand down on the pillow beside her head and leaned over her, looking down into her eyes.

Then he thrust deep and hard inside her.

CHAPTER NINE

Charlotte gasped, arching against the deep, firm, relentless push of Tariq inside her. The sensitive tissues of her sex stretched around him, taking him. Then she cried out, shuddering. Because it was overwhelming and strange and yet somehow so good she didn't have words for it.

He was stretched out above her, his golden eyes burning down into hers, and for a moment an intense sense of wonder was all there was. Her friends, whenever they'd talked about sex, had mentioned that the first time could be painful, but that it was in the end very pleasurable. But they'd never mentioned this sense of...closeness. Of connection. The intense intimacy of having another person inside you.

She didn't feel pain right now, only that sense of connection blazing through her and into him, joining them together in a way that wasn't possible at any other time, in any other way.

It wasn't anything like she'd expected. She'd had a glimpse of it as she'd knelt at his feet, taking him into her mouth, the taste of him rich and salty on her tongue. His expression had been so fierce, and she'd loved the pleasure she'd seen flare in the golden depths of his gaze. But then he'd pulled away, and she'd thought that perhaps she'd done something wrong—until he'd taken her on the bed and put his hands on her. And then she hadn't thought at all, completely lost as he'd touched her…made the world explode behind her eyes.

But this was different—this was mutual. Giving to each other.

He held her gaze—held it so completely that it felt as if he was touching her both inside and out—and then he shifted, gripping her wrists and holding them down on the pillows above her, adjusting himself so he could push even deeper.

She couldn't speak—didn't have the breath…didn't have the words either. All she could do was look up at him in amazement that this was happening between them, that it could feel like this.

And it wasn't frightening. It wasn't frightening in any way.

Strange and a little uncomfortable, yes, but not scary.

He began to move, drawing his hips back and then pushing in again, the slide of him inside her making her gasp. She could feel her body adjustiing to him, and soon it wasn't uncomfortable or strange as pleasure began to radiate, curling through her. She began to move with him, responding to an instinct that felt as if it had always been there, and it made the light in his eyes blaze brighter.

He murmured something in his beautiful language, the liquid whisper of sound almost a caress in itself. She wanted to touch him, run her hands all over him, feel the hard strength of his muscles and taste his skin, but the way he was holding her down and the movement of him inside her made that impossible.

She moaned as the pleasure gathered strength, urging him to move faster, and he did, going deeper, harder, and it was so good. So very, *very* good that even the thought of how afraid she'd been of this was impossible to imagine.

This wasn't shouting or bitterness. This wasn't anger or pain. This was wonder and joy and connection.

Careful. Be careful.

But she couldn't think about that now. She couldn't think at all as pleasure spiralled higher and higher, gathering inside her, tighter and tighter.

She wound her legs around Tariq's lean hips and moved with him, becoming demanding, getting desperate, calling his name and not caring, giving herself up to the relentless build of sensation.

And then he shifted, lifting one hand from her wrist and slipping it down between her legs, touching her where all the pleasure seemed to centre at the same time as he thrust one last time, deep and hard. And the world exploded into flames around her, making her scream his name as the molten gold of his eyes seemed to consume her whole.

She lost herself after that, dimly aware of him suddenly moving hard and fast, and then the stiffening of his body and the sound of her name as he found his own pleasure.

Then he was on top of her, heavy as a mountain falling, his breath hot in her ear, and the heat of his body was burning her alive. He remained like that for a couple of breathless seconds and she didn't mind at all. His weight and the hard muscle against her was making her feel safe. Bringing her back to earth and anchoring her.

Then his arms came around her and she was held fast against him as he turned over onto his back, taking her with him so she was at last resting on his broad chest. And they remained like that for long minutes, not speaking, with the silence of the desert filtering through the thin tent walls.

'Did I hurt you?' he asked after a long moment, his fingers trailing in a long caress down her back.

His chest was so warm, his skin so smooth, with a light prickle of hair, and he smelled salty and musky and absolutely delicious. She couldn't stop herself from pressing her mouth to his skin.

'No, not at all.' She kissed him again, then glanced up, smiling a little shyly. 'It was amazing.'

He didn't smile back, the set of his mouth grim. Yet she could see the after-effects of pleasure glowing like hot coals in his eyes. Something tight collected inside her. Had he not enjoyed it? It had seemed as if he had, and yet his expression said the opposite.

'It wasn't amazing?' She swallowed, searching his face. 'I tried not to disappoint—'

She broke off as his fingers tangled abruptly in her hair and he lowered his head for a hard kiss, his mouth ravaging hers with an intensity that left her breathless.

'You did not disappoint,' he growled, releasing her.

Panting slightly, she stared at him, bewildered. 'Then why are you looking like you'd never had a worse experience in your life?'

His eyes glittered, the expression in them still impossible to read. 'You are dangerous, *ya amar*. Do you know that?'

'Dangerous?' she repeated blankly, not understanding. 'How am I dangerous?'

'A king is supposed to be isolated. He should remain detached or else face having his judgement impaired.' He untangled his fingers from her hair, and one thumb stroked the back of her neck in an absent movement, as if he couldn't help himself. 'I cannot risk my judgement being impaired.'

She leaned back into his hand, loving his caress, yet remaining puzzled by his words. 'What's that got to do with me being dangerous?'

'You are a threat to my detachment.' His voice had got lower, rougher, and the fierce glow in his eyes was burning bright. 'And to my judgement. So you need to understand that this marriage will be a physical one only. Is that clear?'

Something in her gut twisted, as if in distress. Which was strange, because she hadn't expected anything from this marriage at all. But this didn't sound bad. In fact, if sex was like that every time, then there didn't appear to be a down side. It was good, even. If it was only sex, then there was no risk of feelings entering into the mix—no risk of it turning poisonous like her parents' marriage.

'Yes,' she said, folding her hands on his chest and resting her chin on them. 'I understand.'

'Good.'

The starkly beautiful lines of his face relaxed and he ran the backs of his fingers down her cheek in a light caress that made goosebumps erupt everywhere.

'Now, tell me why such a passionate woman has remained a virgin so long.'

She let out a long breath. It didn't feel so bad to be telling him—not here, not with his big muscular body spread out beneath hers.

'I told you that my parents had a very bitter divorce? Well, their relationship was…uh…volatile, to say the least. Lots of shouting at each other. Lots of screaming. Especially towards the end.' She rubbed her thumb across his skin, tracing a little circle. 'I thought if that was what a relationship was all about, then I didn't want anything to do with one.'

'Understandable. You can have sex without a relationship, however.'

'I know.' She lifted a shoulder. 'I just never met anyone I wanted enough.'

His gaze was very focused, very intense. 'Never met anyone you let yourself want, you mean.'

Charlotte sighed. 'I suppose you're right. I didn't want to risk getting involved with anyone, considering how bad it had been with Mum and Dad. And it's probably a good thing—especially now.'

'Why especially now?'

She could feel her cheeks redden. Did she really have to explain it to him? Surely he would know?

'Well, sex is pretty amazing, isn't it? I mean, I don't know how you could experience that and not get involved with someone.'

Something flickered in his eyes, and again she couldn't read it.

'You say that like it is always that way. It is not, Charlotte.'

She waited for him to elaborate, but he didn't. And suddenly she understood. What she had felt between them—that sense of connection—he must have felt too. And it wasn't usual.

That's why you're dangerous to him. And that's why he is dangerous to you too.

'Oh…' she said faintly, the tangle of emotions in her gut knotting tighter. 'I didn't know.'

'Of course you did not.' His expression didn't change, his focus remaining on her. 'But it is a good thing that you do now. And it is also a good thing for us that we have such physical chemistry.'

She could hear what he didn't say.

Because there will be no one else for either of us.

Knowing that didn't upset her—not as she'd thought it might. The fact was that she didn't want anyone else. Even the thought of having another man touch her, be inside her the way Tariq had been, made her feel cold.

But that connection you felt with him will only ever be in bed.

Of course it would. That was fine, though. She didn't need to have that sense of connection anywhere else.

She met his gaze and smiled. She ignored the small kernel of ice that sat in the pit of her stomach. 'You didn't mind that I was inexperienced?' she asked.

'No, *ya amar*. Not in the slightest.'

'Why do you call me that? I'm not your "most beautiful".'

'Yes, you are,' he disagreed. 'Now you are my wife you will always be my most beautiful. And because your hair is silver, and you are so pale, you are like the moon, Charlotte.'

The words made something warm glow in the centre of her chest. She'd never been given an endearment like that before. She'd never been given an endearment at all, and she liked it. Especially the idea of being his moon when he was the sun.

'What about you?' She stared up at him, suddenly curious. 'What were your parents like?'

A shadow crossed his face, gone so quickly that if she hadn't been looking she might not have seen it at all.

'My mother died when I was very young, so I did not know her. And my father was…very strict.'

Her curiosity tightened at this odd hesitation, which seemed uncharacteristic for him. 'Oh? How so?'

But he only shook his head, reaching for her again. 'Not now.' His hand cupped the back of her head and exerted pressure, urging her towards him. 'Now I need to make certain that my people get the heir I promised them.'

And then her mouth was on his and there was no more talking.

He kept her in the tent for a few more hours after that, making her desperate for him over and over, making her forget about everything but her frantic need to have him inside her.

And after that, when twilight had begun to fall, he arranged her outside on the divan beneath the palms, and made her sit there with a glass of wine while he prepared the food that had been delivered by palace staff.

Solar-powered lighting strung around the palms gave the oasis a soft illumination and later, after they'd eaten a delicious meal and the darkness had closed in, Tariq lit a fire with capable hands, then wrapped her in a blanket that he'd brought from the tent, making her lean back in his arms as they talked.

He was not forthcoming about his family, but he was passionate about his people and his country, talking at length about his plans to keep Ashkaraz thriving. There was no doubting his conviction or his vision, and his drive to protect his people was incredibly attractive.

He was incredibly attractive full stop.

'Why do you keep the borders closed?' she asked after a small lull in the conversation, with her hands wrapped around a mug of the most delicious hot chocolate she'd ever tasted. 'And why do you give the outside world the impression of being a narrow and vicious ruler?'

He'd risen to put more wood on the fire, wearing only a pair of loose black trousers. The flames played over his impressive chest, making her fingers itch to touch him again, but the answer to this was important. Too important to be distracted from.

Crouching, he added another stick to the flames from the pile beside him. Firelight limned the fierce planes and angles of his face in gold, making him look like a hero of old, bringing fire from the gods for the good of mankind.

'You have not read our history, then?' he asked, not looking up from what he was doing. 'That is what you were told to do.'

She flushed. 'I know—and I did. But I started way back,

when Ashkaraz first became Ashkaraz. I haven't got to any recent history yet.'

'All you need to know will be in the books.'

There was a note of warning in his tone, an edge that made her gaze narrow. 'You don't want to tell me yourself?'

'No.' The word was flat and hard. The command of a king.

Puzzled, Charlotte gazed at him. Recent history seemed a strange thing to be recalcitrant about, but she was reluctant to push it since they'd reached a pleasant equilibrium. Perhaps she should leave it. She was enjoying sitting out here with him, watching him do things for her and talking with him about all kinds of trivialities. He had a dry sense of humour that appealed to her, and he knew far more about the outside world and its politics than she'd thought he would.

Pushing him would definitely make things tense, and she did hate that. Then again, he'd been constantly pushing her since she'd arrived in Ashkaraz, and much to her own surprise she hadn't backed down. So why should she now? He'd made her reveal her father's disappointment in her—why shouldn't he give a little in return?

Why should you care?

Not wanting that particular thought, Charlotte shoved it away.

'Why not?' she asked carefully. 'If I'm going to find out sooner or later, I'd much rather hear it from you first.'

THE FIRE GLOWED in the darkness, radiating heat, casting a warm light over Charlotte, wrapped in a blanket. Her hair lay loose over her bare shoulders and he was very aware that she hadn't bothered to dress. That she was naked underneath that blanket.

It would be easy to go over to her, pull away the blanket and lay her down before the fire. Make her scream his name to the stars above their heads the way he had in the tent earlier. But there was a danger in that too—as he'd discovered the minute he'd pushed inside her. When he'd looked down into her eyes and read the wonder and amazement in them as she'd looked back at him. Staring at him as if he'd given her all the secrets of the universe.

'Dangerous' he'd called her, and she was.

But at least in bed he could keep it all about physical pleasure. Out here by the fire, with her lovely face lit by the flames, her gaze level and very direct, there were no such comforting lies.

Why are you so reluctant to tell her the truth? Why does it matter?

He didn't know. What he did know, however, was that he could not allow his reluctance to win. He had to be very careful with her around, to ensure his detachment was solid—especially considering how she threatened it.

Which meant, of course, that he had to tell her.

Ignoring the strange reluctance that pulled at him, Tariq straightened up. 'What is there to say? My father had an American lover whose family was very keen on knowing the secret of our wealth, so she tried hard to get that secret from him. But he would not tell her.'

He looked at Charlotte over the flames.

'So she turned her sights on me. I was seventeen and... angry with my father for various reasons. So I let her seduce me. And when she asked where our country got its wealth from I told her about the oil reserves in the north.'

Charlotte frowned. 'You meant to tell her?'

'I was in love with her.'

You were not. You told her because you wanted to punish your father.

The thought was a whisper in his head, highlighting the

lie he'd just told Charlotte. The lie he'd always told himself. But it wasn't really a lie, was it?

His father had denied him something he'd wanted passionately and desperately and he'd been *so* angry. So he'd allowed Catherine to seduce him. Allowed her to get under his skin. Allowed himself to give away his country's secrets. Because he could blame it all on love.

Except it hadn't been love. It had been selfishness—his own needs put before his country's.

Sympathy glowed in Charlotte's eyes, and an understanding he didn't deserve.

'Oh, Tariq,' she murmured. 'I'm so sorry.'

'What are you sorry for?' he said brusquely. 'It is not your fault.'

'No, but you think it's yours, don't you?'

'It *is* mine.' More than she knew.

'You were only seventeen.'

'Old enough to know better.'

He knew he sounded cold, but he couldn't afford to make it any different. Nor could he afford to lean into that sympathy and understanding he saw in her face.

'I sold my country out for love.' Which was not entirely untrue. 'It will not happen again.'

The flames played over her pretty face, lighting her pale with a golden glow, and the searching way she was looking at him made him want to push her back on the sand and take her hard, to distract her.

'That's not all there is, though, is it?' she said quietly. 'There's more to the story.'

How she knew that, he wasn't quite sure. But it wasn't anything he'd share with her. She didn't need to know the true extent of his pettiness.

Why should it matter what she thinks anyway?

He ignored the thought. 'There is nothing that you cannot find out from the books in the library,' he said, and stepped around the fire, coming over to where she sat, her hands still wrapped around the mug of hot chocolate he'd made for her.

She tilted her head back, looking up at him. 'Why won't you tell me?'

The question was so simple, so honest and open. And something within him wanted to respond. To tell her the truth about the aching loneliness of his childhood. The need he'd had for someone—anyone—and how that had always been denied him. Until one day he'd broken.

You cannot tell her. A king must be self-sufficient. Detached. Alone.

He knew it—had learned his lesson and learned it well. Catherine had been his teacher in that, even though she hadn't realised it herself. She'd given him what his father had never allowed: someone to talk to, confide in. And he *had* confided in her, and part of him had known his error even as he'd told her about the oil. Known and yet he'd done it anyway. Because he had been angry.

Because you couldn't bear to be lonely and you hated your father for the way he kept you isolated. You were a selfish boy and you nearly destroyed your country because of it.

Charlotte frowned, and he had the strange impression that she could read every thought in his head, because she put her mug down in the sand and rose to her feet, her blanket caught awkwardly around her. She stepped forward and put her arms around him, leaning her head on his chest.

There was nothing sexual in it. It was merely a hug.

He'd never been hugged before. Not by his father, nor by the nannies who'd brought him up. So the feel of Charlotte's arms around him shocked him. Made him freeze in place. He felt as if there was an animal inside him, struggling to get free of a cage, and as if any move he made would spring the cage door wide open.

He didn't know what would happen if that animal got free. *You know what happens.*

Yes, he did. Disaster.

His instinct was urging him to shove her away, but that would hurt her, and for some reason the thought of hurting her caused him actual pain. So he was forced to stand there and endure the hug she was giving him, even though he didn't want it.

'I'm sorry,' she said, her voice muffled against his chest. 'You don't have to tell me if it's painful.'

He had no idea how he'd given himself away. And no idea of what to say to her now either. Earlier that day she'd told him about the way her father had treated her and he'd seen how painful that had been for her. How her parents' bad marriage had made her afraid of getting involved with anyone.

He'd thought initially that was a good thing, that her fear would prevent her from getting too close. But the way she was holding him now made it clear that it wasn't as simple as that.

She wasn't afraid to ask him about the things he didn't want to talk about. Or to offer him comfort. She wasn't afraid to show him she cared. And she wasn't thinking of herself or her fear right now. She was only thinking of him.

His heart ached, raw and painful in his chest.

He wanted to tell her his secrets. Wanted to share those hours he'd spent in the desert at a young age, taken out and left there alone so he could develop self-reliance. Those days of silence in the palace, when he had been forbidden company so he could learn how to deal with loneliness. Days of not seeing anyone. Not speaking to anyone.

Sometimes he would hear laughter, the shouts of children in the courtyards outside, and he'd wanted so much to go out and play. But he had never been allowed.

Alone, his father had told him. *A king always stands alone. Because he is stronger that way.*

She was warm against him, all soft, silky bare skin and the sweet scent of her body.

Telling her the truth only means something if you let it.

And it didn't have to, did it? After all, it had happened a very long time ago. He was making amends for his mistake now. He wouldn't let it rule him. So what did it matter if she knew about what he'd done? It might even be a lesson to her to keep her distance. He'd told her back in the tent that they would never have a normal marriage, but it wouldn't hurt to drive that message home.

Tariq could feel his body already responding to her nearness, but all he did was raise his hands and gently put her from him. He would not make this about sex now. Not yet, at least.

She frowned and opened her mouth, but he laid a finger on her soft lips, silencing her.

'I was not entirely truthful,' he said quietly. 'I did love Catherine. But...that was not the reason I told her about my country's wealth.'

Puzzlement flickered over Charlotte's features. 'Oh?'

'My father had...set ideas on how a ruler should be brought up. He believed that a king must always stand apart, and that is how he raised me. Always apart. I was not allowed friends, or companions of any kind, and no comfort from any of the nannies who looked after me. A king has to be used to loneliness, so he made sure I got used to it from a very early age.'

Charlotte stared at him in obvious shock. 'No friends? None?'

'No.' He refused to allow the expression on her face to

affect him. 'It was not so bad as a child. But as I got older I found it more…difficult. My father had always stressed the importance of a good education, so I thought I could at least get a taste of what life would be like if I was not a king and go to university. I applied to Oxford, unbeknownst to my father, and was accepted. But…'

He'd thought his anger long since blunted by now, but it wasn't. Even after so many years he could still feel its sharp edge. It deepened his voice to a growl.

'My father would not let me go. I argued with him, shouted at him, but he would not be moved. He even put guards on my door in case I tried to sneak away.' Tariq looked down into Charlotte's pale face. 'I was so angry. So very, *very* angry. And when one night I saw Catherine, weeping beside a fountain in the gardens, I knew I'd found an opportunity to get back at him. She wanted me and I let her seduce me. And when she asked me about Ashkaraz's secret, I told her.'

'Oh, Tariq…' There was nothing but sympathy in Charlotte's expression.

'I told her because I was angry,' he went on, so she fully understood. 'Because I was petty. Because I was selfish. I told her because I had not learned the lessons my father had tried to teach me about detachment. About not letting my emotions control me or affect my judgement. I did what a ruler is never supposed to do, and that is to put his own feelings before his country.'

There was no judgement in Charlotte's eyes, only distress. She reached out and put a hand on his chest.

'Of course you were angry. You wanted some time to be a normal teenager.'

But he didn't want her pain on his behalf. Didn't want her sympathy. Not when he didn't deserve any of it.

'That is no excuse. I should have listened to what he

was trying to teach me, yet I did not. I was just a spoiled boy who wanted something his father would not give him.'

'No!' Charlotte shot back, suddenly fierce. 'You weren't spoiled, Tariq. You were lonely. Terribly, desperately lonely.'

'I betrayed my country, Charlotte.' He made it explicit, because it was clear that she did *not* understand. 'Out of nothing more than selfishness. There can be no excuses for that. No forgiveness. There is only atonement and my dedication to make sure it does not happen again.'

She closed her mouth, but the distress in her eyes lingered and he didn't like it, didn't want her to feel it—because it made that animal inside him claw at the cage, wound the tension in his shoulders even tighter. Made him want to take her in his arms and hold her, take the distress away.

But he couldn't allow himself that. And there was one way he could get rid of that look in her eyes. One way to ease her distress.

Tariq put his palm over hers on his chest, then lifted his other hand, tugging the blanket from around her. She made no move to grab it, standing there warm and naked in the firelight.

'Tariq…' she whispered.

But whatever else she'd been going to say was lost as he reached for her, gathering her up in his arms. And then he stopped her mouth entirely with his, and made them both forget about history and pain and loneliness.

At least for a little while.

CHAPTER TEN

Charlotte sat in the palace library on one of the low couches near the window, with the sound of the fountain drifting in from the garden outside. The early-evening air was warm and full of the smell of flowers, and she could hear a couple of the gardeners out amongst the rose bushes, talking in low voices.

Her Arabic wasn't good enough yet for her to be able to tell what they were talking about, but she recognised the odd word here and there. Something about football.

It reminded her of her flatmates in England and made her smile—at least until a wave of homesickness hit her. Strange to feel that way about a place where she hadn't much enjoyed living anyway, but she did. And it didn't help that she'd spent the last couple of weeks since getting back from the oasis on her own. Tariq had disappeared into the endless meetings and official business that took up a lot of his time, and she barely saw him at all during the day.

It wasn't as if she'd been completely left to her own devices, though. She had her own royal duties as sheikha, and that was taking some getting used to, plus she had a lot of study to do in order to get up to speed on the customs and history of Ashkaraz, as well as more language and protocol classes.

She might have been fascinated by all this, and certainly

she would have enjoyed it a lot more, if her head hadn't been quite so full of her husband.

Ever since those three days at the oasis he was all she could think about. What he'd told her about his childhood had shocked her. To be kept alone and apart from everyone, denied friendship and even simple human comfort, must have been horrific.

It made her wonder about the ferocity that burned in his eyes and the sense of volcanic emotions simmering just below the surface, kept tightly leashed and locked down. How would such loneliness have affected such a passionate man?

Well, she didn't need to wonder. He'd told her. He'd been broken and the consequences had been awful. And so terribly unfair. Because it wasn't his fault he'd been pushed to breaking point.

Her throat tightened, her eyes prickling with unexpected tears. That night at the oasis he'd told her about it so flatly, so emotionlessly, and yet she'd seen the rage that burned bright in his eyes. Rage that was still there even all these years later. And not only that, it seemed to her that he was still punishing himself for that youthful mistake, denying himself the emotional outlet that he so clearly needed.

Why do you care so much about this?

Charlotte pushed the book she'd been reading off her lap and stood, pacing over to the windows and back to the couch again, restless.

She cared because she knew what it was like to be pushed into making a mistake that you wished you could take back. And she cared because he was her husband. Because he was a kind man, no matter that he said he wasn't, and he believed in what he was doing. Because he was passionate.

Pacing back to the windows, Charlotte looked out sightlessly at the rose bushes and the fountains, her heart beating far too fast for comfort. She couldn't stop thinking about him. Couldn't stop thinking about those three days she'd spent with him.

It hadn't been the same after that first night, though the sex had been incendiary. It hadn't been the same since they'd returned to the palace either, with them seeing each other only when Tariq needed her physically. Their bed the only place where it felt as if they communicated fully with each other. Where they were joined and words weren't needed…where their pasts were irrelevant.

What would it be like if they had that feeling outside the bedroom too?

Ah, but there was no point thinking about that. It was impossible. He'd told her their marriage would only be a physical one, that he couldn't give her any kind of emotional connection. She'd thought she'd have no problem with that, but maybe she did.

You never wanted a marriage like your parents', but what if that's how yours ends up?

A cold thread wound through her, making her fingers feel icy. That could happen, couldn't it? Tariq might strive for detachment, but she would always be able to sense the hidden currents that shifted beneath his hard, merciless surface. She could feel his anger and his passion, see it in his eyes, sense it burning him alive.

And then it would be like it had been at home, with her parents' bitterness and animosity battering her, surrounding her. With her wanting to take away their anger and pain but not knowing how. Until the day she'd broken away and run from it all, and made everything ten thousand times worse.

You can't run away now, though.

No, she couldn't. She was married to a king and she couldn't leave even if she'd wanted to. But she didn't want to. She wanted to stay, to help him, to turn her marriage into something good for both of them.

Except what could she do when he was determined to stay detached?

Carefully, she went over what he'd told her out at the oasis again—about the dreadful childhood he'd had, with no one and nothing to ease his loneliness.

Lonely, that was what he was. So maybe all he needed was a friend. Someone to talk to, to confide in. Someone who wouldn't make any emotional demands on him.

She could do that, couldn't she?

She could be his friend?

'I have been looking for you.'

There was no mistaking the dark, deep voice that echoed through the room, making her jump.

She turned, looking towards the double doors that were standing open. Tariq's tall, muscled frame was filling the doorway. His hot golden stare found hers and her mouth dried, her cheeks heating.

She knew that look. He had it when he wanted her. And he often did during the day, coming to find her wherever she was and taking her by the hand, leading her to his rooms or to somewhere secluded, where he would strip her bare and take her, with that familiar ferocity molten in his eyes.

He didn't speak afterwards, just left her burned to ashes where she stood while he turned away and went back to doing whatever it was he'd been doing before he'd come to find her, apparently satisfied.

She had the sense that he wanted something from her in those moments, that it wasn't simply sex, but she never knew what it was.

Perhaps she might have an answer to that now.

He was in dark charcoal suit trousers and one of his exquisitely cut business shirts, this one in dark blue, making his bronze skin seem richer and highlighting the gold of his eyes. She was struck, as she always was, by the raw, stark beauty of him. By how amazing it was that a man like this was hers.

He is not yours, though. And he never will be. Just as you will never be his.

The sliver of glass sitting inside her twisted—a sharp, unexpected pain that seemed to radiate out from the centre of her chest.

Which was ridiculous. She'd never thought he would be hers and she'd never wanted him to be. So where this pain was coming from she had no idea, and it was best she simply ignored it.

He turned and locked the doors, then turned back, his stare becoming even hotter. 'Come here,' he ordered darkly.

She could feel her own need start to rise, ignited by the way he looked at her. It didn't take much to set her burning these days—not when he was around. But she couldn't let it get to her, not right now. She needed to say something first.

'Wait.' She took a steadying breath. 'I have something to say.'

His gaze narrowed. 'What?'

Okay, good. He was prepared to listen. 'I've been thinking about what you said at the oasis. About your childhood.'

His inky brows pulled down in a scowl. 'That has nothing to do with you.'

'Yes, it does. You're my husband. You told me once that everything about me is your business, which also must mean that everything about you is mine.'

A certain kind of energy was gathering about him now, dark and electric and absolutely mesmerising. His golden stare held her fast, frozen where she stood, and the warning glitter in it made it obvious that he didn't like what she'd said.

But that was too bad. She hadn't let herself be intimidated by him since she'd arrived here and she wasn't about to start.

'I do not want to hear about this now,' Tariq growled, advancing on her. 'I have other needs first.'

But she knew what those needs were, and she had a suspicion that they weren't only to do with sex. That it was the forbidden connection he came in search of whenever he was in this mood. He would accept it if she offered it without strings. Without any need for him to return it.

'Or we could sit and talk.' She lifted her chin, looking him in the eye. 'Conversation, Tariq. You remember how to do that?'

He didn't stop, his lean-hipped hunter's stride closing the distance between them, his tiger's gaze on hers. 'I do not want to talk.'

She didn't have any time to evade him. One minute he was nowhere near her, the next he was gripping her hips and pulling her close.

She flung up her hands, pressing her palms against his hard chest, holding him away. 'I'm not trying to take anything from you or make you give me something in return,' she said, trying to master her own helpless physical response to him. 'I'm not going to demand anything from you. Just… If you need a friend, I can be one for you.'

He went very still, staring down at her, his eyes glittering. 'A friend?' He said the word as if he had no idea what it meant. 'Why would I need a friend?'

'Everyone does.' His chest was hot beneath her palms, his muscles like iron, stiff with tension. 'Even kings.'

'You are mistaken.' His fingers tightened on her. 'I have no need of a friend. Ever.'

But she could see behind the desire in his eyes and she knew what drove him. Because she felt it in herself. He wanted a connection just as badly as she did.

'How would you know?' she asked softly. 'When you've never had one?'

He made a deep, dismissive sound, pulling her closer, fitting her hips against his so she could feel the hard, demanding length of him through the silk of her robes.

'I have Faisal. And I have other advisors.'

Her heart clenched tight. Was that what he truly thought friends were? His royal advisors? An old family servant? But of course he would. He had no other reference, did he?

'They're not friends, Tariq.' She pressed her fingertips to the warm cotton of his shirt. 'They are employees. And that's not the same thing.'

He ignored her, taking her mouth in a hot, hard kiss that left her breathless and unsteady on her feet.

'You should sit down,' he growled. 'And stop talking.'

The kiss left her lips tingling, with the dark, rich taste of him on her tongue, and it would have been easy to let him keep going. To stop pushing him, to let him do what he wanted and make her mindless with pleasure right here in the library.

But that, in essence, would be running away again. That would be hiding under the table the way she'd used to do, or running into the woods. Curling around her pain like a wounded animal and keeping it inside, not letting it leak into the atmosphere and make everything worse.

Yet running hadn't solved anything. It had only caused her even more pain. She couldn't do that again. She had to make a stand.

Her hand slid from his chest and up, to cup his strong, beautiful face. 'You do know what a friend is, don't you?'

The gold of his eyes was like a sword spearing through her, full of sharp edges. 'Of course I do not,' he snapped.

'As you said before, I have never had one.' He pulled away from her suddenly and gestured to the low couch nearby. 'Sit down, Charlotte.'

Another order. And calling her 'Charlotte' meant he was displeased with her.

She studied the look on his face. He was angry, that was clear, and he didn't want her pushing him. Didn't want her reminding him of the past that still so obviously hurt him and the mistake he'd made because he was human, because he'd been a boy who'd desperately wanted someone.

She could show him that, couldn't she? She could show him what it was like to have someone. A friend and a lover. A wife. A support. It would mean opening herself up and not demanding anything from him. But that was what you had to do when you wanted to tame a beast, wasn't it?

Slowly and carefully you fed it your heart.

'Charlotte,' he repeated, low and dark. 'I gave you a command.'

His eyes glittered like golden flames burning behind glass and she was reminded of what she'd thought weeks ago: this man was a volcano. Harsh and cold on the outside, while underneath he seethed, molten with rage and passion, burning up inside because all those emotions had nowhere to go.

Well, maybe she would give them an outlet. That was what a friend would do.

'Your father was wrong, by the way,' Charlotte said steadily, moving over to the couch Tariq had indicated. 'He shouldn't have brought you up the way he did.'

She sat down, arranging her robes around her and folding her hands in her lap. Then she looked up at him.

'No one can live in a vacuum, let alone a child. They'd suffocate.'

His face was impassive as he moved to where she sat,

standing in front of her, hard and cold as granite. Yet the heat in his eyes was as unyielding and merciless as the desert sun.

'This conversation, wife, is over.' His voice was rough and hot, full of lava and gravel. 'Spread your legs for me.'

TARIQ'S HEART WAS beating far too fast, and it felt as if the hungry animal in his chest, the one he kept caged and leashed, was sinking its claws into him once again. If he wasn't careful it would claw him to pieces entirely—and who knew what would happen then?

He remembered the disgust in his father's eyes as he'd looked at Tariq from across his desk...

'You are a disgrace,' Ishak had said angrily over the constant ringing of the phone, with the consequences of Tariq's betrayal already reverberating through Ashkaraz. *'After everything I have taught you, you have learned nothing.'* His father's expression had twisted. *'You are unworthy, Tariq. Unworthy of being my heir. Unworthy of being my son.'*

The memory shuddered through him and he shoved it aside, concentrating instead on the woman sitting calmly on the couch in front of him, her blue gaze steady on his.

His chest ached, and a strange and molten anger was seething inside him. He didn't know what she was talking about. A friend? That was nonsense. What did he need a friend for? He'd never had one, it was true, but then, he'd never needed one.

He didn't need anyone.

A lie. You need her.

But only for sex. In fact, since coming back from the oasis it seemed as if sex with his wife was all he thought about. He couldn't concentrate on his duties, on the work he needed to do. Instead he found himself stalking the corridors of the palace in search of her, hard and aching.

She would always give him what he wanted. And yet afterwards, when he should have been well sated, all he felt was hollow. Empty. Like Tantalus, for ever drinking and for ever thirsty.

It was inexplicable.

He felt it now as he looked down at her, sitting on that couch in a spread of sky-blue silk. An aching emptiness. A hunger. A thirst.

She was wrong about suffocating in a vacuum. You'd only suffocate if you needed air to breathe, and he didn't. He'd trained himself to live without it. In fact, he'd prove it to her.

'You heard what I said.' His voice was too low and too rough. 'Do as you are told.'

She didn't protest, spreading her knees, her blue eyes full of the same understanding he'd seen in the firelight that night at the oasis.

'Did you know that one night I ran away from home?' she said quietly. 'My parents had been arguing more than usual and I couldn't stand it. I stayed out all night and they ended up calling the police.'

Tariq ignored her, dropping to his knees in front of her. He put his hands on her thighs and pushed them apart, spreading her wider.

'They searched for hours,' Charlotte went on. 'I heard them calling my name but I didn't answer. I didn't want to go back home and listen to all that shouting. They found me, though, and dragged me back.'

Why was she telling him this? He didn't want to hear it. He wanted to hear nothing but her gasps of pleasure and her sighs. The way she called his name just as she was about to come.

He took the hem of her robes in his fists.

'My parents were so angry. And my mother decided that

I was too much trouble to fight over, so she let Dad have custody of me.' Her voice wavered slightly. 'Even though he didn't really want me.'

The material was soft in his hands, the scent of her body sweet. His hunger was pulsing in time with his heartbeat and he didn't know why he'd stopped. Didn't understand why that tremble in her voice had made his chest ache.

'I know you may not want me either,' she continued. 'Not for anything more than sex. But if you need someone to talk to or just…be with, I will be that person for you.'

The words hurt—sticking inside him like thorns, piercing him right through. Which was ridiculous.

He didn't want someone to talk to or 'be with'—whatever that meant. He had Faisal. He had his council. And as for her—well, he needed her for one thing and one thing only.

'Be silent,' he growled.

Understanding glowed in her eyes, as if she could see those thorns in his heart. As if she knew how much they hurt and how hard he was fighting them.

She said nothing, only looked at him. And for some reason her silence made him feel even worse, so he jerked her robes up to her waist, uncovering her, not caring if the fabric ripped.

He had to do something to take away the terrible understanding on her lovely face. To strip it from her, turn her pretty eyes dark, make her blind to everything but pleasure. Make her need him.

Prove that you do not need her?

Yes, and that too. Because he didn't. He needed nothing from her but her body.

Under her robes was a pair of loose trousers in the same fine silk, and the material parted without any resistance as he tore them from her, along with the lacy knickers she wore underneath.

She didn't stop him, but he felt her tremble as she was finally bare under his hands, her skin warm and as fine as the silk he'd ripped from her.

His heart was beating so loudly he couldn't hear a thing, and the edge of hunger inside him was made sharper by the scent of her arousal.

He looked down at the soft, damp nest of curls between her thighs, her skin pink and slick. His hands on her pale flesh looked rough and dark—as if they would tear her as he'd torn the fabric of her robes.

You are unworthy. A disgrace.

He growled again, shoving her thighs wide, wanting to look at her and not listen to his father's voice in his head.

She was so pretty. So delicate. And this was all he needed from her—nothing more. Certainly not friendship. Nothing that would threaten the walls he'd built around himself. Nothing that would threaten his detachment. He was perfectly fine, here in his vacuum.

He slid his hands up her thighs, losing himself in the feel of her beneath his fingertips. Then higher still to the heat that lay between. She sighed as he touched her, parting her wet flesh gently, and the soft, needy sound shivered through him.

Yes, this was how it should be. Her needing him. Her desperate for him. Not the other way around. Never that.

Yet his hands were shaking as he held the soft folds apart, and he was breathing so fast it was as if he couldn't get enough air. And he was ravenous, suffocating in his vacuum, and she was the air he needed to breathe.

He should have stopped then—if only to prove to himself that he could hold himself apart from her. But he couldn't. The hunger was too much to bear.

Leaning forward, he bent his head between her thighs, running his tongue directly up the centre of her sex, desperate for a taste.

She jerked, a soft cry escaping her, but he didn't stop, The hunger was sinking its claws deep into him. He slid his hands to her hips and held her still as he began to explore her, the taste of her exploding in his head, a salty-sweet burst of flavour that made him even harder and more desperate.

'Tariq…' she gasped, twisting in his grip. 'Oh…'

The pleading note in her voice was exactly what he'd been hoping for, so he didn't stop then either, teasing the hard little bud with his tongue and then dipping down, circling the entrance to her body, before pushing inside to taste her deeper.

He wanted her as hungry as he was. As desperate. As frantic. He wanted that terrible knowledge in her eyes gone. She looked at him as if she'd seen inside him and seen the lonely little boy he'd once been. The boy who'd broken under his father's lesson.

The boy who was unworthy, a disgrace to his name.

He would never let himself be that boy again.

She cried out, her fingers tangling in his hair, her grip on him bordering on pain. But that only sharpened everything deliciously, making him growl yet again against her wet flesh and loosen his grip on her hip, sliding his hand beneath the soft curve of her buttocks. Then he tilted her so he could taste her even deeper, making her groan and arch in his hold.

A dark satisfaction at the sound of her cries unwound inside him, along with a deep possessiveness that he couldn't hold back. He would make her forget all this friendship nonsense. Make her forget so completely she'd never think of it again. Yes, and he'd make her forget that her father hadn't wanted her, that her mother hadn't fought for her. He'd make her forget about everything but him and what he could give her. She wouldn't need anything else and neither would he.

He pushed deeper with his tongue and she writhed, her body trembling harder as he brought her to the brink. And then he pushed her over with another wicked lick, holding her tightly as she sobbed and twisted between his hands, the climax riding her hard.

Her scent was all around him, her taste on his tongue, her heat so close, and abruptly his own need tightened its grip around his throat, threatening to choke him.

He let her go, pushing himself back from her. She made a glorious picture, leaning against the back of the couch with her face a deep rosy colour, her eyes glittering and dark with the after-effects of pleasure. Her legs were spread wide, there was the sheen of moisture on her inner thighs, and her sex was open and wet and ready for him.

He reached for the rest of her robes, pulling them away from her until she was sitting there naked, surrounded by blue silk, like a jewel in the middle of fine tissue paper.

'Lie down,' he ordered hoarsely, and rose to his feet, not taking his gaze from her as she did as she was told, lying back on the couch, naked and beautiful and ready for him.

He couldn't wait to undress. He simply undid his trousers and freed himself, then joined her on the couch, settling himself between her spread thighs. She reached for him but he pushed her hands away, guiding himself to the entrance of her body and thrusting home.

Charlotte gasped and arched beneath him, her silky thighs closing around his hips, her breasts lifting. Her silvery lashes came down, lying on her cheeks, her mouth was slightly open. For a second he couldn't move. Could only gaze down at her beneath him, the grip of her sex around him and the heat of her body blanking his mind utterly.

And it should have been enough. It shouldn't have made him feel so hollow, as if there was something more. Something so close he could almost touch it.

'Look at me,' he demanded roughly, before he could stop himself. 'Look at me, Charlotte.'

Her lashes lifted at his command, her gaze meeting his, and a hot, intense electrical charge pulsed straight through him. For a moment it felt as if he held something in his hands, something ineffable and beautiful, that would break if he gripped it too hard.

There was tenderness in Charlotte's eyes, a warmth that had nothing to do with sexual heat, and she put out a hand, cupping his cheek as if he was the precious thing, the thing that might break.

His chest ached, a heavy weight pressing on it. The consequences of the vacuum in which he'd been trying to breathe for so long. The vacuum that seemed to be suffocating him, after all.

Yet not when she touched him. The contact of her fingers on his cheek, the clutch of her sex around his, the heat of her body and the warmth in her silver-blue eyes were all lifelines containing oxygen.

It felt as if they were the only things keeping him alive.

He took a shaken breath, then another, and when her fingers trailed along his jaw the pressure on his chest lifted. He took another breath, right down deep into his lungs, and it felt like the first breath he'd ever taken.

And when he moved inside her, deep and slow, it felt as if the pleasure was another lifeline too, another strand connecting him to her.

Her lovely mouth curved, her darkening gaze holding

him as fast as the grip of her sex around his shaft, and he couldn't look away.

She could see him. She could see who he was deep down inside. She could see that lonely little boy and she was reaching out a hand to him. She was pulling away the barriers around his heart as if they were nothing but paper. Putting out her hands and holding him.

Holding him as if he was worth something.

He couldn't stop her. Couldn't stop himself from wanting that touch, craving the way she held him, reaching to grasp all the lifelines she was throwing him.

He moved faster, harder, holding on tight to her as he drove into her, their shared breathing fast and ragged in the room. And her hands were on him, stroking him lightly and easily as he drove her down into the cushions. As he felt the pleasure beginning to take him apart.

'Charlotte...' He hadn't meant to say her name—not like that. Not so deep and dark and desperate. 'Little one...'

Her arms were coming around him, her thighs tightening, embracing him in a way no one had ever held him before. The immensity of his hunger was a tidal wave of need washing up inside him, all the years he'd spent alone crashing down on him.

But he wasn't alone. Not now. Because now he had her. She was his wife and she could never leave. She was safe.

The thought stayed with him as he tore her hands from his body and pushed them up and behind her head, holding them down with his own. And it glowed brightly as he thrust harder into her, the couch shaking with the force of it, burying all the heat and desperation inside her with every flex of his hips.

And she met every thrust, panting and as wild as he was, his name on her lips as she arched and moved beneath him, the pleasure becoming more intense, more raw with every movement.

It was too much to look at her. The wild blue of her eyes ripped him apart. And he only had time to shove his hand between them, stroking her sex hard and sure, feeling the wave of her climax hit as she convulsed beneath him.

Then he was following her, his own hitting him, stealing every breath from his body and every thought from his head.

Minutes or maybe hours later, the feel of her hands drifting down his back returned him to himself and he tried to shift his weight off her. But she made a little protesting sound, her nails digging into his hips, clearly wanting him to stay where he was. So he did, propping himself up on his elbows instead and looking down at her.

She didn't speak, and neither did he, and for long moments he simply let himself be lost in the endless blue of her eyes.

'My father wanted to disown me when he found out what I had told Catherine,' he heard himself say, giving her the final piece of himself—the piece he'd told no one else about. 'He called me a disgrace…said I was unworthy.'

There was tenderness in her eyes, and sympathy too. 'Your father was wrong about a lot of things, Tariq. And most especially that.'

He wanted to disagree with her, but that was a question for another day. Right now there were more important things to do. Like picking her up and carrying her to his bed. And then maybe, after they had sated themselves again, they could even have a conversation.

'I am not letting you leave, *ya amar*,' he said. 'You understand that, do you not? You are mine.'

Something in her face relaxed—a tightness he hadn't

noticed before. 'I know. You've said that before, believe it or not.'

'I am not joking.'

One fair brow rose. 'Were you joking before?'

'Let us just say that I did not know that I was in a vacuum.' He paused, holding her gaze. 'And that I needed air in order to breathe.'

CHAPTER ELEVEN

Charlotte was in the middle of yet more language lessons with Amirah when one of the palace servants knocked on the door of her suite, issuing a summons to Tariq's study.

It had been a week since he'd taken her in the library, when it had felt as if the earth had shifted beneath her and something had changed between them. She hadn't been able to stop thinking about how he'd said he needed air to breathe, and had looked at her intently, as if *she* was the air. He hadn't said it outright, but she'd felt it. As if he'd finally discovered the connection that had been forged between them back in the oasis.

He was such a lonely man—a man desperate for someone—and she'd tasted desperation in his kiss. Felt it in the way he'd taken her. It had made her heart twist in her chest, made her want to give whatever she could, coax his rare and beautiful smile from him. Make him laugh. Take the loneliness from him and give him comfort instead.

So she'd spent time over the past week doing things with him that weren't based either around sex or his duties as ruler. Things that friends did together. A relaxed dinner by the fountains, talking about nothing in particular. Watching a movie in the palace's own cinema. An outing into the city, where he'd shown her a few of his favourite places. A horse ride into the southern hills.

They had been special moments. When he hadn't been the king and she hadn't been his queen. When they'd simply been Tariq and Charlotte, enjoying each other's company.

She didn't know why she wanted to do this for the man who was keeping her from her family and friends and who'd pretty much forced her to marry him. But she didn't let herself think too deeply about it. Being with him made her feel less lonely, and that was enough. In fact, for the first time in her life she felt wanted—and not only that but needed too. Needed by a king.

That fact alone had given her a courage and strength she'd never known possible.

After the summons arrived she let Amirah go for the rest of the day, then made her way through the palace corridors to Tariq's study.

He was sitting behind his vast desk as she came in and closed the door behind her, glancing up from his computer screen as she approached.

This past week she'd been the lucky recipient of quite a few of his smiles, but not today. His expression remained grim and a sense of foreboding stole through her, making her feel cold. Then he stood and came around the side of the desk, and abruptly she felt even colder.

'What is it?' she asked as he approached.

'I've just had word that your father had a heart attack last night and has been taken to hospital.' His voice was level and matter-of-fact as he stopped in front of her, reaching for her hands and taking them in his own.

Shock echoed through her. 'I don't...' She tried to get her brain working. 'Dad's in hospital?'

Tariq's fingers were warm as they wrapped around hers, and when he drew her to him she didn't resist, needing the strength of his tall, muscular body, because suddenly she was afraid she might fall.

'Yes.' His deep voice calmed her somewhat. 'As I said, he had a heart attack.'

'How bad is it?'

'They're not sure. I spoke to your father's doctor myself, and it appears that it may take some time to see how severe the damage is. But it's entirely possible that he'll make a full recovery.'

Charlotte swallowed. Tariq's warmth surrounded her, and the heat of his skin burning against her numb fingers comforted her.

Her father wasn't perfect, but he was her father all the same, and although he hadn't exactly made her feel wanted, he *had* taken care of her after her mother had left. He'd fed and clothed her, given her a roof over her head and ensured she'd got a decent education. He'd never been actively cruel or abused her. But now he was sick. Now he was alone...

She couldn't bear the thought of that. He might not be the world's greatest dad, but that didn't mean she could leave him in hospital with no support. He had no other family except her. Besides, she wasn't like her mother—she couldn't simply walk away when someone needed her.

Charlotte lifted her head and stared up into the hard gold of her husband's eyes. 'I have to go to him. I have to go back to England.'

There was sympathy in Tariq's expression, but his voice when he spoke was firm. 'The borders are closed, *ya amar*. You may not leave.'

'This is different. Dad's ill.'

Yet he only shook his head. 'It does not matter. I cannot let you go.'

'Why not?' She frowned, not understanding. 'Surely this is allowed? He's sick. And there's no one else to take care of him.'

The planes and angles of Tariq's fiercely beautiful face

hardened, the warmth that had been there before fading. 'That is what a hospital full of doctor and nurses is for, is it not?'

'But…he's my father, Tariq. And it won't be for long, I promise.' She squeezed his hand in reassurance. 'I'll just see that he's okay and then—'

'No.' Tariq's voice was flat, and all sympathy drained abruptly from his expression.

She blinked at his tone, instinctive anger licking up inside her, and opened her mouth to tell him he was being unreasonable.

Then she caught a glint of what looked like fear in his golden eyes.

Her anger disappeared as quickly as it had risen.

'What's wrong?' she asked quietly, because it was clear something was. 'This isn't just about Dad, is it?'

His features had turned forbidding, as if she'd seen something he didn't want her to see.

'You are my sheikha. You cannot simply leave the country whenever the mood takes you.'

'This is not a "mood", Tariq.'

The glint in his eyes blazed unexpectedly, his grip on her hand tightening. 'I do not care. You are my sheikha and your place is by my side.'

Her heart clenched at the intensity in his face and the fierce note in his voice. At how much he needed her. And part of her didn't want to push him or argue, because she liked it that he did.

But this was important to her. And, anyway, she would come back. It wasn't as if she was going for good.

'I know,' she said, trying to sound calm. 'But it won't be for long, I promise. Only until I know what's happening with Dad and then I'll be back.'

The ferocity in Tariq's expression didn't lessen. 'You

have no idea how long it will be. And what if he needs long-term care? What if he is hospitalised for good? What will you do then?'

'I'll work something out. It won't be an issue.' She reached up to touch his cheek, wanting to soothe him. 'Please don't—'

But he didn't wait for her to finish, releasing her all of a sudden and turning away so that she touched nothing but empty air.

Charlotte stared after him as he stalked back to his desk, her heart beating faster. Something was wrong and she didn't know what it was.

'What is it?' she asked into the tense silence. 'You know I'll come back. I will, Tariq. I promise.'

He was standing with his back to her, looking out over the gardens through the window, the line of his powerful shoulders stiff with tension. 'I have been promised things before. Promises mean nothing.'

'But, I can—'

'No.' He turned sharply, pinning her with that fierce, hot stare. 'If I let you go, what will bring you back? Me?'

She stared at him, bewildered. 'Of course. You're my husband.'

'A man you were forced into marrying. A husband who keeps you here against your will.'

'Yes, you've done those things, but it's different now. I said I'd stay and I meant it. I'm your wife, not to mention your friend. I would never walk out on you.'

'No,' he said flatly. 'I cannot risk it.'

'Tariq—'

'My father kept everything that was good from me when I was growing up and I told myself that I did not need it. But you have made me see things differently, Charlotte. This week you have made me see what I have been missing. You have made me see what I need. And now I have that I do not want to give it up.' Fire burned in his eyes, a deep, fierce amber. 'I told you that you were mine and so you are. And I do not give up what is mine. I will not.'

He *was* afraid—she could see it in his eyes. He was afraid she wouldn't return.

'You can trust me,' she said, trying to calm him. 'I give you my word.'

Anger flashed across his intense features. 'Do you think that I am a skittish horse that needs soothing? I have been lied to before, so do not think that your "word" will work.'

Of course. Catherine and her promises to him. But, no, this went deeper than Catherine. This was about his father. This was about himself.

Automatically, she opened her mouth to say something that would ease his anger, and then stopped.

Why? Why are you always placating him? When you know he's being unreasonable?

That was a very good question. And it was a question she didn't have the answer to. But, no, that was wrong. She did have the answer. She just didn't want to acknowledge it. She wanted to pretend it didn't exist.

Except it did exist.

It was staring her in the face and had been for weeks.

She always wanted to soothe him and comfort him because he mattered to her. Because she loved him. She'd been in love with him since the moment he'd taken her in that tent at the oasis.

Charlotte's chest tightened as the knowledge swept through her, overwhelming her, making it hard to breathe, making her feel dizzy.

Her mouth was as dry as the desert and she was afraid. Because she knew all about love. Love was pain. Love was listening to her parents scream at each other over her head. Love was watching her mother give up on her and walk away. Love was the ache that cut deep inside every time her father looked at her as if she was nothing but a nuisance to him.

Love was giving everything and getting nothing in return.

She stared at her handsome husband, her heart roaring in her ears. Stared at the man to whom she was slowly, little by little, giving away the pieces of her soul. And he was taking it. He was keeping it for himself and giving her nothing back.

And you've done that before, haven't you?

Of course she had. With her father. Being quiet and good for him…not causing a fuss as a child. Helping him with his career and being his dogsbody as an adult. Trying and trying to get him to look at her with something more than impatience and frustration. To see her as his daughter and not the millstone around his neck that she suspected he thought she was.

You tried to make him to care. But he never did. And now you're doing the same with Tariq.

'You're very clear about what you want,' she said suddenly, hoarsely. 'But what about what I want? Does that not matter at all?'

His expression was hard. Cold. The mask of the sheikh.

'What has that got to do with anything?'

'Answer the question.'

Something flickered across his face and then it was gone. 'That is not a requirement.'

An empty, hollow feeling opened inside her. He didn't care what she wanted, which meant he didn't care about her.

Did you expect that he would?

Maybe she'd hoped. Maybe that was why she'd never looked too closely at her own feelings. Because she knew she wouldn't be able to bear the disappointment if he didn't feel the same way. But he'd told her in the tent at the oasis that theirs would only be a physical marriage, and she'd been okay with it back then. She hadn't expected or wanted more.

Except things had changed. He'd given her physical pleasure, made her feel beautiful, and then, over the past week together, he'd given her his friendship. He'd made her feel interesting and special. Desirable, sexy and brave. He'd made her feel needed.

And that was the problem.

He'd made her want more.

He'd made her want to be loved.

'It's a requirement for me,' she said, her voice cracking.

And just like that the fierce expression on his face closed, like the door of a furnace shutting, depriving her of all its light and all its heat.

'In that case perhaps you are not as suited to life here as I expected.'

His voice was hard as stone, his gaze as pitiless as it had been that day she'd fainted in front of him.

'Perhaps it would be better if you returned to England, after all.'

Somewhere deep inside her she felt a tearing pain.

So much for all your hopes. If he can give you up so easily, then he really doesn't care.

He stood on the other side of the desk and the distance between them felt vast, cavernous. He was so isolated, and so lonely, and there was a part of her that wanted more than anything to bridge that gap.

But she wasn't the same woman she'd been a couple of weeks ago. She'd found a strength inside her she hadn't thought possible. And she was tired of giving everything of herself to someone who would never give anything back. She didn't want to do it any more.

So if he expected her to soothe and placate him, to beg him to let her stay, he was in for a surprise. Because she wasn't going to. She wasn't going to demand he tell her why he'd changed his mind either. If he wanted to sit here in splendid isolation, in his arid life in a vacuum, then he could.

She wouldn't stop him, not this time.

Charlotte drew herself up, looking him in the eye even as her heart shredded itself in her chest. 'Fine,' she said. 'Then you can arrange for me to fly out tonight.'

A fleeting look of shock crossed his face before it was quickly masked. 'Charlotte—'

'No,' she interrupted, furious and heartbroken, everything hot and raw. 'You will damn well listen to what I have to say. I'm not choosing to leave because I want to. I'm choosing to leave because you haven't given me one single reason to stay.'

She found she was shaking.

'You made it clear what our marriage was. Right from the beginning you told me, and I thought I was okay with it. I thought I didn't want more. But I've changed my mind.'

She met his gaze head-on.

'I've decided I do want more. I want a real marriage, Tariq, emotional as well as physical. I want love. Give me that and I swear no power on earth will make me leave you.'

He was suddenly still, as if she'd turned him to stone. And the silence deepened, lengthened.

'I cannot,' he said at last, roughly, as if it had been dragged from him. 'That is the one thing I cannot give you.'

It wasn't a shock. It wasn't even a surprise. And maybe that was what hurt most of all. She knew he couldn't. And whether it was a case of him not being able to or simply not wanting to, it didn't matter.

The outcome was still the same.

Charlotte ignored the desert that had taken the place of her heart. She didn't plead with him, didn't beg. Didn't ask him why. All she said was, 'Then I have to leave.'

The mask of the sheikh had settled back over his strong features once again, and there was no emotion at all in his eyes. 'I will have Faisal handle your travel arrangements,' he said, without any discernible emotion. 'You will, of course, let me know if you discover you are pregnant.'

That hurt—as he must have known it would.

But she didn't let it show.

She turned on her heel and left him there.

TARIQ STOOD IN front of the window for a long time after she'd gone, staring out at his beautiful gardens and the fountains playing, desperate for the peaceful scene to calm the sudden and terrible rage that clawed up inside him. Desperate to find his detachment, the black silence of his vacuum.

But it was nowhere to be found, so he stayed where he was, unmoving. Because if he moved even a muscle he wasn't sure that he wouldn't go running after Charlotte, pick her up and toss her over his shoulder, carry her into his bedroom, lock the door, throw away the key.

He couldn't do that, though. No matter how much he wanted to. No matter how much the pain in her silver-blue eyes had felt like glass sliding under his skin. Or how her request for love had made that glass slice through his soul. Or how her leaving had made him feel suffocated, left to bear the crushing weight of his isolation alone.

No, he couldn't go after her. Couldn't give her the one thing—the only thing—she'd ever asked of him.

He couldn't give her love.

He'd worked too hard, borne too much, to give in to those terrible betraying feelings. Being true to his father's teachings, keeping himself isolated—that was all he could do now. And if he felt as if he was dying inside, then that was his own fault. He'd been the one to think he could have friendship and pleasure, that he could have her smile and her laughter—all the things he'd been missing in his life and all without consequence.

Little by little she'd got past his walls and he should have stopped her days ago. He'd let her get too far and this was the result: his detachment, the thing he needed to be a good king, cracked and broken.

'Does what I want not matter at all?'

Tariq stared sightlessly at the fountain, her voice and the break in it replaying in his head. He'd told her that she was his, that he would never let her go, but the moment she'd said those words and he'd felt something inside him twist and crack he'd understood.

She had to leave. She made him feel too much. She made him *feel*, full stop. And that was a very bad thing. It compromised the very foundation he'd built his life upon, not to mention his reign, and that he wouldn't allow. He couldn't put himself and what he wanted first because he was responsible for an entire nation. And keeping it safe was his primary objective.

Even if that meant keeping it safe from himself.

He'd put his country at risk once before because he'd been too much a slave to his emotions. He couldn't do it again.

'I want love, Tariq. Give me that.'

No, not even for her.

It was a long time before he permitted himself to move. A long time before he turned away from the window, forcing himself to make a few calls, arranging the travel details for her himself.

Then, once that was done, he shut himself in his office, leaving instructions with his guards that he was not to be disturbed under any circumstances.

And he threw himself into work.

A WEEK LATER and he still hadn't granted anyone an audience or interview. He'd refused meetings. Even requests for casual conversation had been ignored.

Everyone had been turned away from his door.

He didn't want to see anyone. He didn't want to talk to anyone.

He had to shore up the cracks in his armour that Charlotte had created and he could only do that alone.

The week turned into two and then three.

Faisal came at least once every day, demanding admittance, but Tariq ignored him.

Yet he still couldn't find any peace.

One evening he headed to the palace baths, as he had every night since Charlotte had left, unable to sleep and tortured by a warmth that wasn't there. By memories of soft curves and hair like moonlight. Of deep blue eyes that had looked at him as if there was something worthy in him when he knew there wasn't.

He flung himself into the water, driving his hands through it as if he was digging himself out of a hole, or pulling himself up a sharp cliff, swimming on and on. Driving himself into the spurious peace of exhaustion.

That exhaustion never lasted, though, and once it had passed the ache would return, bringing with it the intense longing and the sense of suffocation. As if the air he needed to breathe was being depleted and he was slowly choking and by inches dying.

You need air. You need her.

He forced that thought from his head, driving himself harder through the water.

No, he'd been fine before she came to him and he would be fine again. All he needed to do was hold fast to his detachment and these sensations would pass. They had after Catherine and they would again—he was sure of it.

His hand hit the end of the pool again, but this time, sensing someone standing there, he stopped and stood up, pushing his hair back from his eyes.

Faisal stood at the edge, his expression impassive.

'How did you get past the guards?' Tariq demanded gracelessly. His temper these days was on a hair trigger. 'No one is permitted to enter.'

'I knocked them out.' Faisal's tone was short. 'You need new guards.'

Tariq scowled. He didn't want Faisal here. He didn't want to talk. He wanted to continue swimming until his muscles ached and he was exhausted, the feeling of being suffocated gone.

'What do you want?' he asked. 'Tell me, then get out.'

Faisal stared at him a moment, then said with unexpected savagery, 'You're a fool, Tariq. Sulking in your palace alone. Why did you send her away?'

Tariq felt his hands clench into fists and he had to force the anger away, get himself under control. 'I do not recall asking for your opinion, Faisal. And be careful what you say—'

'Your father was a fool too,' the old man interrupted harshly. 'He closed himself down completely after your mother died—did you know that? He never got over it. He isolated himself and then he did the same to you.'

Tariq went still.

'I told him it was wrong,' Faisal went on. 'That just

because he had lost his wife it did not mean that his son should not find happiness and companionship. But he ignored me. And now look what has happened.' The old advisor virtually spat the words. 'You have closed the borders of your country and your heart. You are him in everything but name.'

Abruptly the weight sitting on Tariq's chest increased, like a vice crushing him, the vacuum pressing in. He should command Faisal's silence, tell him to get out, but he couldn't speak.

'Do you know what happens to a tree with its roots cut?' Faisal asked, suddenly quiet. 'Or to a fire starved of oxygen? It dies.' There was a pause. 'Your insistence on your father's outdated lessons may not end up killing this country, Tariq. But it will certainly end up killing you.'

The water was cool, but suddenly he was burning up. The emotions inside him, the anger and desperation and longing, were too strong and too powerful. They were inescapable and there was nowhere for them to go but inward. And now they were eating him alive.

'Perhaps,' he heard himself say roughly, 'that should have happened years ago. Before I betrayed Ashkaraz in a rush of foolish temper.'

Faisal was silent, but Tariq couldn't look at him. He couldn't bear to see what was on the old man's face.

'No,' Faisal said at last. 'No, that is not true. It was your father who betrayed Ashkaraz. If he had brought you up with love, rather than harshness, you would not have been so lonely. And if you had not been so lonely you would not have been angry with him. You would not have turned to Catherine.'

'You cannot say that—'

'I can and I will,' the old man interrupted. 'You are a good king, Tariq. But you could be a great one. Better than your father ever was. Because you have what he lacked: a strong and passionate heart. You just need to use it.'

His jaw ached, along with every muscle in his body. He felt as if he was standing on the edge of a cliff, the ledge crumbling beneath him. 'Detachment is what makes a great king, Faisal. Not a strong and passionate heart.'

'That is your father talking.' Faisal's voice was uncompromising. 'And he was wrong. Love is what makes a great king.'

A few weeks ago he would have ignored the words. Now they settled into him, through the chink in his armour that Charlotte had left there.

He didn't know how long he stood in the chilly waters of the baths after Faisal had gone, watching the light filter down from the hidden windows in the ceiling, his heart beating fast and getting faster, the emotions inside him burning him alive.

If love was what made a great king, then that was something he couldn't be. Because what did he know of love? It was his father's grief and pain. It was Catherine's empty promises. His own anger and betrayal...

That's not all it is.

He caught his breath, memories coiling through him. Charlotte's gentle hand on his skin. Charlotte's smile as she looked up at him. Charlotte's arms around him, holding him close.

'I want love,' she'd said—as if she knew exactly what it was, as if it was something to be deeply desired and longed for and not something that led to pain and betrayal.

Faisal isn't wrong. If your father had even let you have one friend, one connection, would you have gone to Catherine that night?

Perhaps he wouldn't. Perhaps he wouldn't have been so lonely and so angry. So desperate for any connection that he'd let his father's mistress seduce him. Perhaps if his father had brought him up with love he'd understand what Charlotte wanted.

You can understand now.

The thought made air rush abruptly into his lungs and he found himself gasping, as if he'd forgotten how to breathe.

'You have what he lacked...' Faisal had said. *'A strong and passionate heart. You just need to use it.'*

And to do that he needed to open it. To stop fighting his emotions. To embrace them, make them part of him.

So he did. He stood in the water, his hands in fists, his skin getting cold, and instead of fighting the feelings inside him he set them free, let them rush through him like oxygen down an air line.

And suddenly everything became clear.

He loved Charlotte Devereaux.

He'd loved her for weeks.

She made him better. She made him stronger. She made him compassionate and merciful and protective. She made him humble.

She made him whole.

She made him the king he should be for his people.

And if he wanted to be that king he needed her at his side.

Give her a reason to be there, then.

His heart was beating far too fast and his hands were shaking—because there was only one thing he could offer her and that was himself, and he was honest enough to admit that probably wasn't enough. She'd told him she'd wanted love from him, but maybe after the way she'd left, after the way he'd treated her, she had changed her mind.

But he had to go to her and offer it anyway. He needed to show her that what she wanted mattered to him. He needed to tell her that she was loved. That she was his queen, and to death and beyond would remain so.

Tariq moved to the edge of the pool and hauled himself out. It was late, and he should go to bed, but he wasn't tired. Instead he dried himself off and went straight to his office.

He worked through the night, putting various and very necessary things in motion. And then, just as dawn was breaking, he finally put through the call he'd been waiting all night to make.

'Ready my jet,' he ordered, when one of his assistants answered. 'I will be flying to London as soon as possible.'

CHAPTER TWELVE

Charlotte smoothed the blanket over her father's knees as he sat in his favourite armchair beside the fire in the living room and ignored his fussing. Luckily the heart attack had been mild, and the doctor was incredibly pleased with his progress—but he was a terrible patient. He wanted to be back in his office at the university, putting together a new lecture or organising a new dig, not sitting 'mouldering' at home. At least, that was what he kept saying to her, as if he was expecting her to do something about it.

'I don't have my laptop,' he said peevishly, readjusting the blanket. 'How am I supposed to prepare anything when I don't have my laptop? I need you to go into my office and get—'

'No, Dad.' Charlotte interrupted, before he could get into a list of all the things he needed. 'I have a job interview tomorrow, so you'll have to wait.'

It was for an office job, doing administrative tasks, and she'd been surprised she'd got an interview, given her lack of work experience. But she'd felt a vague sense of satisfaction that she'd managed to score it. Now her father was better, and would be returning to work in the next week or so, her own life could resume. Not that she knew quite what that life was going to look like.

One thing was clear, though: it wasn't going to be what she'd had before.

When she'd come back to England she'd been caught up in her father's illness and looking after him, too busy to think about what her next move might be. But since he'd been released from hospital, and she'd had to move into her father's mews house in order to look after him, she'd had time to make a few decisions. And one of those was that she wasn't going to be returning to work for him.

She was done with men who did nothing but take.

She was going to do what *she* wanted for a change.

'You don't need a job.' He fussed with his blanket yet again. 'You can be my assistant. The new one isn't working out as well as I'd hoped.'

Once upon a time Charlotte might have leapt at the opportunity. But not now.

Not since Tariq.

The thought of the man she'd left behind made the wound deep inside her soul ache, but she shoved the pain away. She'd made her choice and she didn't regret it. And if sometimes at night, when she couldn't sleep, she wished she'd confronted him when he'd told her he couldn't give her love, then what of it? It didn't change what had happened, and it was far too late to confront him now anyway.

The borders of Ashkaraz were closed to her and so was its sheikh's heart.

'Thanks, Dad, but, no,' Charlotte said firmly. 'It's time I started living my own life, making my own choices.'

Her father scowled. 'The new girl doesn't do things the way I like them.'

'Then I'm afraid that's your problem, not mine.'

'Charlotte...'

'What?' She gave him a very direct look. 'I'm your

daughter, not your servant. Not your dogsbody. Not any more. I have things *I* want to do.'

He was silent a moment. Then, 'You've changed. What happened in Ashkaraz?'

It was the first time he'd asked her, and Charlotte debated for a moment whether or not he deserved an explanation. But perhaps it would be good for him to hear a few home truths.

'I had my heart broken,' she said flatly. 'And I realised that for years I've been trying to prove myself to a man who took what I had to give him and never saw me as anything more than a nuisance. And even though I gave up a piece of my soul to come back and help him recover, he hasn't even said thank you. Not once. Is that enough of an explanation for you?'

Her father at least had the grace to look ashamed of himself.

There was a long, uncomfortable silence. Then he said, 'I'm sorry. I know I haven't been the…best of fathers. But, well… You look at lot like her. Your mother, I mean. And sometimes I forget that you're not her.'

Charlotte's throat closed. He'd never talked to her like this.

'It was never about you,' he added gruffly. 'You were a good girl. A good daughter. And I…missed you while you were gone.'

It was as close as her father would ever come to an explanation for his behaviour, and maybe an apology as well. But she didn't need his approval to make her feel good about herself—not these days—so all she said was, 'Good. I'm glad you did.'

He didn't say much after that, and a bit later, discovering that there was no milk for their tea, Charlotte decided that she'd have to brave the rain in order to get some.

She grabbed an umbrella from the stand in the hallway and headed out.

The cobbles in the mews outside her father's house were shiny and slippery, and it was cold. And as the hand clutching the handle of the umbrella went numb Charlotte found herself wishing she was somewhere hot. Where the sun was merciless and the sand was burning. Where neither were as hot as the passion of the man she'd left there.

Her heart squeezed and she had to grit her teeth against a wave of pain. Why was she thinking of Tariq again? Leaving had been the right thing to do. The *only* thing. Thinking of him hurt. Besides, she'd find herself someone else. He wasn't the only fish in the sea.

Except you will never love anyone as you loved him.

The thought was so bleak that she had to stop, because her vision was swimming with tears and it hurt to breathe. Then, as she collected herself and prepared to go on, she noticed someone standing in the mews ahead of her.

And everything in her went quiet and still.

It was a very tall man and he was holding a black umbrella. He was dressed in what looked like a shockingly expensive dark suit, with sunglasses over his eyes despite the rain. But even the suit and the glasses couldn't disguise the sense of authority and arrogance he radiated.

Except Charlotte didn't need that to know who it was.

She would have known him anywhere.

Tariq.

Her poor, shattered heart seized in her chest and she blinked—because surely he wasn't here. This had to be a mirage. Yet despite the blinking he didn't disappear, and, yes, it seemed that he really was here, in London. Standing in the road near her father's house.

Then he was coming towards her, moving with the same

fluid grace she remembered, and just like that rage filled her, making her shake.

How dared he come here? After she'd made the horrifically painful decision to leave him. After her heart had torn itself to pieces as she'd walked away. After she'd wept all the way back to London and for days afterwards, missing him so acutely it had felt like being stabbed.

After all that he'd come here. Why? What did he want from her? Was it to hurt her again? Taunt her with what she could never have?

Charlotte didn't wait for him to reach her. She stormed up to him instead, meeting him in the middle of the lane. Then she reached up and tore the glasses from his face so she could see him, holding the familiar intensity of his golden stare with her own.

He didn't move. Didn't speak. Only stared at her.

'What are you doing here?' she demanded, her voice breaking, even though she tried not to let it. 'How dare you? How dare you come here to—?'

It was only then that he moved, throwing away his umbrella as if he didn't care about the rain that was falling around them and stepping under hers. Then he reached for her, taking her face between his hands, and the warmth of his skin was like a bolt of lightning, rooting her to the spot.

He bent and kissed her, his mouth hot and desperate, and the taste of him was so achingly familiar that tears rushed into her eyes, the deep hunger inside her stirring, waking.

Oh, God, how could he do this to her?

She stiffened, ready to push him away, but he'd already lifted his head, the look in his eyes blazing.

'Oh, *ya amar*,' he said fiercely. 'I have been such a fool. I have done such stupid things. Said things I should not have. And all I can say is that I am sorry.' His thumbs moved caressingly over her cheekbones. 'I should have let you go to your father. I should have trusted you to return. And most important of all I should have given you a reason to come back to me.'

She was trembling and unable to stop. Unable to pull away from him either. All she could do was stand there and look up into the blazing gold of his eyes.

'What reason?' she asked, trying to hold herself together.

The lines of his beautiful face took on a familiar intensity. 'You asked me to give you love. So I am here to offer it.'

Her umbrella didn't protect him from the rain and his black hair was getting wet, his suit damp, water was trickling down the side of his face. But he didn't seem to notice. His attention was on her as if he was suffocating and she was the lifeline he needed.

Except it was she who couldn't breathe.

'Be clear, Tariq.' She barely sounded like herself. 'What are you saying?'

'I am saying that I love you, Charlotte Devereaux,' Tariq said in his dark, deep voice. 'I love you, my wife. I have spent the past three weeks telling myself that sending you away would stop these feelings inside me. That once you were gone I could stay detached. Be the kind of king my father wanted me to be. But I could not do it. I could not escape what I feel for you. And I found out that…*you* are what makes me the king I need to be.'

His gaze searched her face, unhidden desperation in it.

'You make me compassionate and merciful. You make me humble. You make me strong. You make me a better man, a better king. And I want to give you back everything that you have given me.'

She felt cold, and then hot, as if she was dying and then coming back to life. 'Tariq…'

His name was the only thing she could say.

Luckily she didn't need to speak, because he went on, 'I want you, *ya amar*. I want to give you all the love you need. And I would leave Ashkaraz if I could, be with you here in London if you wanted me to. But I cannot leave my country. So all I can do is beg you to return with me.'

Her heart felt both heavy and light at the same time, at the ferocity in his eyes, at his desperation and his anguish.

She looked up at him, drinking in every line of his beloved face. 'Then I will,' she said simply. Because this was what she'd been wanting her entire life.

And something blazed in his beautiful eyes—heat like the sun, burning there. 'You would do that? After everything that I did to you? Kept you prisoner…made you marry me? Gave you ultimatum after ultimatum—?'

Charlotte reached out and put a shaking finger on his mouth, silencing him. 'After you gave me pleasure and friendship. Showed me how brave I could be and how strong. After you helped me figure out my own worth.' She pressed harder, feeling the heat of his skin beneath her fingertip. 'Yes, you fool. Of course I would do that.'

'I am not a good man, *ya amar*. And there is much I do not understand. I will make mistakes and I will need you to help me. I am also very possessive of what is mine, and that might be…annoying for you. Are you sure you want to commit yourself to that?'

She blinked back sudden tears, her throat aching with an intense joy. 'I've had some experience of dealing with difficult men, believe me. I think I can handle it.'

His expression turned even fiercer. 'Then you have my word that I will do everything in my power to make you happy for the rest of our lives.'

There was rain on her cheeks, though some of the moisture might have been tears, because the iron band that had been around her heart since she'd left him burst open and her chest filled, her lungs filled. Her heart filled.

And then her umbrella was on the ground too, and she was in his arms. His mouth was on hers, tasting of rain and heat and the volcanic passion that was part of him.

'Tell me,' he said roughly when she finally pulled away.

'Tell you what? About my dad?' God, how she loved to tease him. 'About the job interview I have tomorrow?'

'No.' That dark intensity was back in his face. 'Do not play with me, *ya amar.*'

Charlotte relented. 'You mean tell you that I love you?'

'Yes,' he said fiercely. 'That.'

'Well, I do. I love you. And I—'

He kissed her yet again, hard, cutting off the words, stealing all her breath and then giving it back to her, so that when he raised his head again, she felt light-headed and dizzy.

'I have a hotel nearby,' he murmured. 'Come with me, wife. I need you.'

'Wait.' She pressed her hands to his hard chest, warm despite the fact that they were both soaking wet. 'You need to tell me what changed your mind.'

And, wonderfully, a fleeting magical smile crossed his face. 'A friend.'

She stared at him in surprise. 'I thought you didn't have any?'

'Turns out I have one at least. Faisal. He told me that the reason that my father brought me up the way he did was because he never got over my mother's death. That he cut himself off and did the same to me.' Tariq pushed her damp hair back from her face. 'Faisal also told me that my father was wrong. That it isn't detachment that makes a great king. It's love.' He searched her face. 'I think I am starting to see what he meant. But perhaps you can show me the rest?'

Her heart was bursting, everything she felt for him flooding out. She reached up on tiptoes and kissed him yet again, because all the kisses in the world wouldn't be enough.

'Yes. Yes, I can.'

And she did.

And even though getting lost in the desert might have been the stupidest thing she'd ever done, it had also been the best.

Because in getting lost she'd found her home.

She'd found her for ever.

She'd found herself.

In the strong and passionate heart of a king.

EPILOGUE

The knock came on the door of Tariq's office, and he'd barely had a moment to acknowledge it before it opened and his wife came in.

She was dressed in a deep pink robe today, and it brought a delightful blush to her pale cheeks as well as highlighting her silvery hair.

He smiled, his heartbeat quickening, her presence already brightening his day. 'What is it, *ya amar*?' He pushed back his chair and raised one brow. 'It had better be good. I have a very important report to read.'

'Oh, it is, don't worry.'

She gave him a secretive smile in return, then moved over to his desk and, ignoring the fact that it was the middle of the day and there were other people around, came around it and sat on his lap as if she belonged there.

Which she did.

'This is highly irregular,' he murmured as she settled back against his shoulder and lifted her mouth for his kiss. 'Perhaps we should lock the door?'

Because he was hard and getting harder and—

His thoughts broke off and he went quite still. She was looking at him with a very particular kind of focus.

'Charlotte? What is it?'

Her smile this time was breathtaking. 'What's "Daddy" in Arabic again? I feel our child will want to call you something.'

Everything in him became bright, burning. 'Charlotte…' he said again.

She touched his cheek, and everything he'd ever wanted was right there in her blue eyes.

'Are you going to faint, dear heart?' she asked.

But he didn't faint. He laughed instead, and kissed her, filling himself up with her heat, and her brightness, and all the love she'd brought into his life so far.

And all the love she had yet to bring.

* * * * *

The Spaniard's Wedding Revenge

MILLS & BOON

DEDICATION

To Justin Alastair, Duke of Avon, and
Leonie de Saint-Vire. Thanks for the inspiration!

CHAPTER ONE

The last thing Cristiano Velazquez—current duke of an ancient and largely forgotten dukedom in Spain, not to mention playboy extraordinaire—wanted to see at two in the morning as he rolled out of his favourite Paris club was a gang of youths crouched in front of his limo as it waited by the kerb. He wanted to hear the distinctive rattle and then hiss of a spray can even less.

God only knew where his driver André was, the lazy *bastardo*, but he certainly wasn't here, guarding his limo like he should have been.

The two women on Cristiano's arm made fearful noises, murmuring fretfully about bodyguards, but Cristiano had never been bothered with protection and he couldn't be bothered now. Quite frankly, some nights he could use the excitement of a mugging, and at least the presence of a gang of Parisian street kids was something out of the ordinary.

Although it would have been better if they hadn't been spray-painting his limo, of course.

Still, the youths were clearly bothering his lady-friends, and if he wanted to spend the rest of the night with both of them in his bed—which he fully intended to do—then he was going to have to handle the situation.

'Allow me, ladies,' he murmured, and strolled unhurriedly towards the assembled youths.

One of them must have seen him, because the kid said something sharp to the rest of his friends and abruptly they all scattered like a pack of wild dogs.

Except for the boy with the spray can, currently graffiting a rude phrase across the passenger door.

The kid was crouched down, his slight frame swamped by a pair of dirty black jeans and a huge black hoodie with the hood drawn up. He didn't seem to notice Cristiano's approach, absorbed as he was in adding a final flourish to his artwork.

Cristiano paused behind him, admiring said 'artwork'. 'Very good. But you missed an "e",' he pointed out helpfully.

Instantly the kid sprang up from his crouch, throwing the spray can to the right and darting to the left.

But Cristiano was ready for him. He grabbed the back of the boy's hoodie before the kid could escape and held on.

The boy was pulled up short, the hoodie slipping off his head. He made a grab for it, trying to pull it back up, but it was too late. A strand of bright hair escaped, the same pinky-red as apricots.

Cristiano froze. Unusual colour. Familiar in some way.

An old and forgotten memory stirred, and before he knew what he was doing he'd grabbed the boy's narrow shoulders and spun him around, jerking his hood down at the same time.

A wealth of apricot-coloured hair tumbled down the boy's back, framing a pale face with small, finely carved features and big eyes the deep violet-blue of cornflowers.

Not a boy. A girl.

No, a woman.

She said something foul in a voice completely at odds with the air of wide-eyed innocence she projected. A voice made for sex, husky and sweet, that went straight to his groin.

Not a problem. Everything went straight to his groin.

The grip he had on the back of her hoodie tightened.

She spat another curse at him and tried to wriggle out of his hold like a furious kitten.

Cristiano merely tightened his grip, studying her. She was quite strong for a little thing, not to mention feisty, and he really should let her go. Especially when he had other female company standing around behind him. Female company he actually wanted to spend time with tonight.

Then again, that familiarity was nagging at him, tugging at him as insistently as the girl was doing right now. That hair was familiar, and so were those eyes. And that lush little mouth…

Had he seen her before somewhere?

Had he slept with her, maybe?

But, no, surely not. She was dressed in dirty, baggy streetwear, and there was a feral, hungry look to her. He'd been in many dives around the world, and he recognised the look of a person who lived nowhere but the streets, and this young woman had that look.

She had the foul mouth that went along with it, too.

Not that he minded cursing. What he did mind was people spray-painting his limo and interrupting his evening.

'Be still, *gatita*,' he ordered. 'Or I'll call the police.'

At the mention of police she struggled harder, producing a knife from somewhere and waving it threateningly at him.

'Let me go!' she said, and added something rude to do with a very masculine part of his anatomy.

Definitely feisty, and probably more trouble than she was worth—especially with that knife waving around. She was pretty, but he wasn't into expending effort on a woman who was resistant when he had plenty of willing ones who weren't.

Then again, his tastes were…eclectic, and he liked difference. She was certainly that. A bit on the young side, though.

'No,' he said calmly. 'Your customisation of my car I could have ignored. But you have interrupted my evening and scared my friends, and that I simply won't stand for.'

She ignored him, spitting another curse and slashing at him with her knife.

'And now we're dealing with assault,' Cristiano pointed out, not at all bothered by the knife, since it managed to miss him by miles.

'Yes,' she snapped. 'You assaulting me!'

He sighed. He didn't have a lot of patience for this kind of nonsense and now, since it was late—or early, depending on your point of reference—he wanted to get to bed, and not alone. He really needed to handle this unfortunate situation.

So let her go.

Well, he should. After he'd figured out why she was so familiar, because it was really starting to annoy him now.

Though that was going to be difficult with her still swinging wildly at him with a knife.

Amongst the many skills he'd become proficient in on his quest to fill the gaping emptiness inside him was a certain expertise in a couple of martial arts, so it wasn't difficult for him to disarm her of her knife and then bundle her into his limo.

He got in after her and shut the door, locking it for good measure so that she was effectively confined.

Instantly she tried to get out, trying to get the doors to open. It wouldn't work. Only he could open the doors from the inside when they were locked.

He said nothing, watching her as she tried futilely to escape. When it became clear to her that she couldn't, she turned to him, a mix of fury and fear in her big cornflower-blue eyes.

'Let me out,' she demanded, breathless.

Cristiano leaned back in the seat opposite her and shoved his hands into the pockets of his expertly tailored black dress pants. It might have been a stupid move, since it wasn't clear whether she had another knife on her somewhere, but he was betting she didn't.

'No,' he said, studying her face.

Her jaw went rigid, her small figure stiff with tension. 'Are you going to rape me?'

He blinked at the stark question, then had a brief internal debate about whether he should be annoyed she'd even had to ask—especially since the latter part of his life had largely been spent in the pursuit of pleasure, both his own and that of any partners he came into contact with.

But in the end it wasn't worth getting uptight about. If she was indeed on the streets, then not being assaulted was likely to be one of her first concerns. Particularly when she'd been bundled into a car and locked in by a man much larger and stronger than she was.

'No,' he said flatly, so there could be no doubt. 'That sounds like effort, and I try not to make any effort if I can possibly help it.'

She gazed at him suspiciously. 'Then why did you shut me in this car?'

'Because you tried to stab me with your knife.'

'You could have just let me go.'

'You were graffitiing my car. And it's an expensive car. It's going to cost me a lot of money to get it repainted.'

She gave him a look that was at once disdainful and pitying. 'You can afford it, rich man.'

Unoffended, Cristiano tilted his head, studying her. 'It's true. I am rich. And, yes, I can afford to get it repainted. But it's inconvenient to have to do so. You have inconvenienced me, *gatita*, and I do so hate to be inconvenienced. So, tell me, what are you going to do about it?'

'I'm not going to do anything about it.' She lifted her chin stubbornly. 'Let me out, *fils de pute*.'

'Such language,' Cristiano reproved, entertained despite himself. 'Where did you learn your manners?'

'I'll call the police myself. Tell them you're holding me against my will.'

She dug into the voluminous pockets of her hoodie, brought out a battered-looking cellphone and held it up triumphantly. 'Ten seconds to let me out and then I'm calling the emergency services.'

Cristiano was unmoved. 'Go ahead. I know the police quite well. I'm sure you'll be able to explain why you were crouching in front of my car, spray-painting foul language all over it, and then pulling a knife on me when I tried to stop you.'

She opened her mouth. Closed it again.

'What's your name?' he went on. That nagging familiarity was still tugging at him. He'd seen her before—he was sure of it.

'None of your business.'

Clearly she'd thought better of calling the police, because she lowered her hand disappearing her phone back into her hoodie.

'Give me back my knife.'

Cristiano was amused. She was a brave little *gatita*, asking for the knife he'd only just disarmed her of after she'd tried to stab him with it. Brave to stand up to him, too—especially considering she was at a severe disadvantage.

Not only physically but, given her dirty clothes and feral air, socially, too.

Then again, when you lived at the bottom of life's barrel you had nothing to left to lose. He knew. He'd been there himself—if not physically then certainly in spirit.

'Sadly, that's not going to happen.' He shifted, taking his hands out of his pockets and very slowly leaning forward, his elbows on his thighs, his fingers linked loosely between his knees.

A wary look crossed her face.

And that was good. She was right to be wary. Because he was losing his patience, and when he lost patience he was dangerous. Very dangerous indeed.

'I'll ask one more time,' he said, letting a warning edge his voice. 'What's your name, *gatita*?'

THE MAN SITTING opposite Leonie—the rich bastard who'd scooped her up and put her in his limo—was scaring the living daylights out of her, and she wasn't sure why.

He wasn't being threatening. He was simply sitting there with his hands between his knees, eyes the same kind of green as deep, dense jungles staring unblinkingly at her.

He was dressed all in black, and she didn't need to be rich to know that his clothes—black trousers and a plain black cotton shirt—had been made for him. Nothing else explained the way they fitted him so perfectly, framing wide shoulders and a broad chest, a lean waist and powerful thighs.

He reeked of money, this man. She could virtually smell it.

And not just money. He reeked of power, too. It was an almost physical force, pushing at her, crowding out all the air in the car and winding long fingers around her throat and squeezing.

There was another element to that power, though. An element she couldn't identify.

It had something to do with his face, which was as beautiful as some of the carved angels on the tombs in the Père Lachaise Cemetery. Yet that wasn't quite it. He seemed warmer than an angel, so maybe more like a fallen one. Maybe a beautiful devil instead.

Night-black hair, straight brows and those intense green eyes...

No, he wasn't an angel, and he wasn't a devil, either. He seemed more vital than a mythical being. More...elemental, somehow.

He was a black panther in the jungle, watching her from the branch of a tree. All sleepy and lazy... Until he was ready to pounce.

That frightened her—but it didn't feel like a threat she was familiar with. Sleeping on the streets of Paris had given her a very acute sense of threat, especially the threat of physical violence, and she wasn't getting that from him.

No, it was something else.

'Why do you want to know my name?'

She wasn't going to just give it to him. She never gave her name to anyone unless she knew them. Over the past few years she'd developed a hearty distrust of most people and it had saved her on more than one occasion.

'So you can call your friends in the police and get them to throw me in jail?'

She shouldn't have vandalised the car, since as a rule she liked to keep a low profile—less chance of coming to anyone's notice that way. But she'd been followed on her way to the little alley where she'd been hoping to bed down and, since being a woman on her own at night could be a problem, she'd attached herself to the crowd of homeless teenagers she'd been with earlier. They'd been out vandal-

ising stuff and she'd had to prove herself willing to do the
same in order to stay in their company. So she hadn't hesi-
tated to pick up the spray can.

To be fair, she hadn't minded targeting this man's limo.
The rich never saw the people on the streets, and she rather
liked the idea of forcing her existence to at least be acknowledged in some way. Even if it did involve the police.

'No.'

His voice was very deep, with a warmth curling through
it that made a part of her shiver right down low inside.
There was a lilt to it, too...a faint, musical accent.

'But you were vandalising my car. Your name is the least
you can give me in recompense.'

Leonie frowned. What had he done with her knife? She
wanted it back. She didn't feel safe without it. 'Why? Don't
you want money?'

He raised one perfect black brow. 'Do you have any?'

'No.'

The man shrugged one powerful shoulder in an elegant
motion and she found her gaze drawn by the movement.
To the way his shirt pulled tight across that shoulder, displaying the power of the muscles underneath.

How odd. She'd never looked at a man that way before,
so why was she doing so now? Men were awful—especially
rich men like this one. She knew all about them; her father
was one of them and he'd thrown her and her mother out
on the streets. So no wonder she'd taken an instant dislike
to this guy—though maybe it was more hate than dislike.

Hate was the only word strong enough to describe the
disturbingly intense feeling gathering inside her now.

'Then, *gatita*,' he said, in his dark, deep voice, 'your
name it will have to be.'

'But I don't want to give you that.'

Her jaw tightened. Resistance was the only thing she

had on the streets and she clung to it stubbornly. Resistance to anything and everything that tried to push her down or squash her, grind her into the dirt of Paris's ancient cobbles. Because if she didn't resist then what else did she have? How would she even know she existed?

By spraying rude words on a limo?

Yes, if need be. It was all about the fight. That was all life was.

He gave another elegant shrug, as if it was all out of his hands. 'Then sadly I must be recompensed for my inconvenience in other ways.'

Ah, of course. She understood this, at least. 'I'm not paying you in sex. I'd rather die.'

His mouth twitched, which she found disconcerting. Normally men got angry when she refused them, but he didn't seem angry at all. Only…amused.

For some reason she didn't like it that he found her amusing.

'I'm sure you wouldn't,' he said lazily. 'I happen to be very good at it. No one has died having sex with me yet, for example.'

Leonie ignored the way her stomach fluttered. Perhaps that was hunger. She hadn't eaten today, and although a day without food was fairly normal for her, she didn't usually find herself chucked into a limo and kept prisoner by… whoever this man was.

'But,' he went on before she could argue, 'I know what you're talking about, and rest assured my recompense won't be in the form of sex. Though I'm sure you are, in fact, very desirable.'

She gave him a dark look. 'I am, actually. Why do you think I carry a knife?'

'Of course. What man wouldn't want a feral kitten?'

His mouth curved and she found herself staring at it. It had a nice shape, firm and beautifully carved.

She shook herself. Why was she staring at his mouth?

'You'd be surprised what men want,' she said, dragging her gaze to meet his, though quite frankly that wasn't any better.

His amusement abruptly drained away, the lines of his perfect face hardening. He shifted, sitting back against the seat. 'No. I would not.'

Leonie shivered, the interior of the car feeling suddenly cold. 'What do you want, then? I can't pay you, and I'm not telling you my name, so all you can do is call the police and have me prosecuted. And if you're not going to do that, then isn't it easier to let me go?'

'But then how would I be recompensed for my inconvenience?' He shook his head slowly. 'No, I'm afraid, *gatita*, I can't let you go.' He paused, his green eyes considering. 'I think I'm going to have to put you to work instead.'

CHAPTER TWO

The little redhead treated this suggestion without obvious enthusiasm—which Cristiano had expected.

He still didn't know why exactly he'd said it. Because she was right. He could afford the paltry amount it would take to get his limo repainted. And as for his supposed inconvenience...

He glanced out through the window to the two lovely women he'd wanted to join him for the night. They were still out there, waiting for him to give them the word, though for once he felt a lessening of his own enthusiasm for their company.

It was a bit mystifying, since he never said no to anything or anyone—still less two beautiful women. Nevertheless, he found himself more interested in the little *gatita* sitting opposite him. She was a puzzle, and it had been too long since he'd had a puzzle.

He wanted her name. And the fact that she wouldn't just give it to him was irritating. Especially when that familiarity kept tugging on him, rubbing against his consciousness like a burr in a blanket.

Women never denied him, and the fact that she had was annoying.

And then she'd muttered that thing about men, and he'd realised that letting her go meant letting her go back on the streets at two in the morning. Admittedly she'd been with a crowd earlier, but they'd all vanished, so she'd be on her own.

That she was used to looking after herself was obvious, but it didn't mean he was going to let her. He wasn't a gentleman, despite the fact that he came from an ancient line of Spanish nobility. Not in any way. But he was enough of a man that he couldn't leave this young woman alone in the middle of the night.

Because, no, he wouldn't be surprised at what men wanted from such a delectable little morsel such as herself. He was one of those men after all.

That left him with only one option: to keep hold of her in a way she'd accept.

He could, of course, simply ignore her protests and take her back to his Paris mansion and keep her there. But, again, dealing with the protests that would no doubt entail would be tiresome, and he preferred to avoid tiresome things. Things that left less time to do the things he liked doing. His own personal pleasure always took priority.

It would be easier all round if she agreed, therefore work it was.

If only he had something for her to do…

He had estates and a *castillo* back in Spain—which he avoided going to whenever possible—and numerous companies he'd invested his considerable fortune in. But he already had a number of staff managing all those things—and besides, they weren't the kinds of things a Parisian street urchin could manage, no matter how feisty she was.

No, the only work he could conceivably give her was domestic, by adding her to his housekeeping staff. He already had a large contingent, but one more wouldn't hurt. House-cleaning, at least, required no extensive training, and it would keep her close until he'd uncovered her mysteries.

Which he was going to do, since he currently had a dearth of mysteries in his life.

'What kind of work?' she asked, still suspicious.

'I need someone to clean for me.' He tilted his head, studying her. 'I have a house in Paris that's very large and needs attention. You may work out what you owe me for the car and my personal inconvenience there.'

'But I—'

'Did I mention that I have rooms set aside for my staff? You will be required to live on-site for the duration.'

'Don't guys like you already have a lot people doing your dirty work for you?'

'Yes.' Her scorn didn't bother him. He tried not to let anything bother him, since it was very dangerous for all concerned when he was bothered. 'But I could always do with one more. Plus, I pay my staff very well for doing my "dirty work".'

At the mention of pay, something changed. Her eyes lost that wary look, and a calculating gleam sparked in their depths.

He knew that gleam and he knew it intimately. It was hunger. And not in the physical sense, of needing food, but in the sense of wanting something you could never have and wanting it desperately.

Money—she wanted money. And who could blame her when she didn't have any? Money was power, and she didn't have any of that, either, he'd bet.

Sure enough, she said, 'Pay? You pay them?'

'Of course. That's why they're my staff and not my slaves.'

She leaned forward all of a sudden, losing her wariness, all business now. Her violet eyes were focused very intently on him. 'Would you pay me? Once I earned back for the car? Could I have a proper job?'

Something shifted in Cristiano's gut. Something that, again, he was intimately familiar with.

She was lovely. And he could imagine her looking at him just like that, with a pretty flush to her pale cheeks and a flame in her eyes and all the beautiful hair spread over his pillow. Hungry for him as he buried himself inside her...

A nice thought, but a thought was what it would stay. She'd never be one of his partners. Apart from the fact that the distance between them in power, money and just about everything else could not have been more vast, she was also much younger than he was.

And he was betting she'd either had some bad experiences with men or she avoided men completely.

Again, dealing with all that sounded like work, and he tried to avoid work whenever he could. He didn't want anything hard, anything difficult, and he avoided complications like the plague.

This small *gatita* was certainly a complication, but he found he was willing to expend a bit of effort on figuring out why she was so familiar to him. After all, it had been a while since he'd let himself be interested in something other than physical pleasure. It certainly couldn't hurt.

'Do you want a job?' he asked, teasing her a little just because he could.

'Yes, of course I want a job.' Her gaze narrowed further. 'How much do you pay?'

A good question—though he was sure she couldn't afford to turn anything down.

'My staff are the best and I pay them accordingly,' he said, and named a sum that made her pretty eyes go round.

'That much?' All her earlier wariness and suspicion had dropped away. 'You really pay people that much just to clean your house?'

'It's a very big house.'

'And you'd pay me that?'

It wasn't a lot of money—at least it wasn't to him. But for her it was clearly a fortune. Then again, he suspected that a five-euro note left on the street would be a fortune for her.

'Yes, I'd pay you that.' He paused, studying her. 'Where do you live? And what are you doing on the streets at two in the morning?'

Instantly her expression closed up, the light disappearing from her face, the shutters coming down behind her eyes. She sat back on the seat, putting distance between them and glancing out of the window.

'I should go home. My…mother will be worried.'

Which didn't answer his direct question but answered the ones he hadn't voiced. Because she was lying. Her slight hesitation made him pretty certain she didn't have a mother and neither did she have a home.

'I think not,' he said, watching her. 'I think you should come directly back to my house and spend the night there. Then you can start work first thing tomorrow morning.'

'I don't want to come back to your house.'

'Like I said, I have quarters for my staff and there will be more than enough room.'

'But I—'

'There will be no argument.' Because he'd decided now, and once he made a decision he stuck to it. 'You have two choices. Either you come back to my house tonight or you spend the night in a police cell.'

'That's not much of a choice,' she said angrily.

'Too bad. You were the one who decided spray-painting my car was a good idea, so these are the consequences.' He liked her arguing with him, he realised. Probably too much—which was an issue. 'So what's it to be, *gatita*?'

She folded her arms. 'Why do you keep calling me that?'

'It means kitten in Spanish.'

'I'm not a kitten.'

'You're small and feral and you tried to scratch me—of course you're a kitten. And a wild one at that.'

She was silent a moment, not at all mollified. Then, 'Why Spanish?'

'Because I'm Spanish.'

'Oh. What are you doing in Paris?'

He stared at her, letting her see a little of his edge. 'That's a lot of questions for a woman who won't even give me her name.'

'Why should I? You haven't given me yours.'

That was true—he hadn't. And why not? His name was an ancient and illustrious one, but one that would soon come to an end. He was the sole heir and he had no plans to produce another. No, the Velazquez line, the dukedom of San Lorenzo, would die with him and then be forgotten. Which was probably for the best, considering his dissolute lifestyle.

Your parents would be appalled.

They certainly would have been had they still been alive, but they weren't. He had no one to impress, no one to live up to. There was only him and he didn't care.

'My name is Cristiano Velazquez, Fifteenth Duke of San Lorenzo,' he said, because he had no reason to hide it. 'And you may address me as Your Grace.'

A ripple of something crossed her face, though he couldn't tell what it was. Then she frowned. 'A duke? Cristiano Velazquez…?' She said his name very slowly, as if tasting it.

He knew she hadn't meant to do it in a seductive way, but he felt the seduction in it all the same. His name in her soft, sweet husky voice, said so carefully in French… As if that same sense of familiarity tugged at her the way it tugged at him.

But how would she know him? They'd never met—or

at least not that he remembered. And he definitely hadn't slept with her—that he was sure of. He might have had too many women to count, but he'd remember if he'd had her.

'You've heard of me?' he asked carefully, watching her face.

'No… I don't think so.' She looked away. 'Where is your house, then?'

Was she telling the truth? Had she, in fact, heard of him? Briefly he debated whether or not to push her. But it was late, and there were dark circles under her eyes, and suddenly she looked very small and fragile sitting there.

He should get her back to his place and tuck her into bed.

'You'll see.' Moving over the seat towards the door, he opened it. 'Stay here.'

Not that he gave her much choice, because he got out and shut it behind him again, locking it just in case she decided to make a desperate bid for freedom.

He made excuses to the two patiently waiting women, ensured they were taken care of for the evening, then went to find his recalcitrant driver, whom he eventually found in a nearby alley, playing some kind of dice game with a couple of the kids who'd been standing around his car.

How fortunate.

Getting his wallet out of his pocket, Cristiano extracted a note and brandished it at one of the youths. 'You,' he said shortly. 'This is yours if you tell me the name of the woman with the pretty red hair who was spray-painting my car.'

The kid stared at the note, his mouth open. 'Uh… Leonie,' he muttered, and made a grab for the money.

So much for loyalty.

Cristiano jerked the note away before the boy could get it. 'You didn't give me a last name.'

The kid scowled. 'I don't know. No one knows anyone's last name around here.'

Which was probably true.

He allowed the boy to take the money and then, with a meaningful jerk of his head towards the car for his driver's benefit, he turned back to it himself.

Leonie. Leonie…

Somewhere in the dim recesses of his memory a bell rang.

LEONIE BLINKED AS a pair of big wrought-iron gates set into a tall stone wall opened and the car slid smoothly through them.

On the rare occasions when she'd ventured out of the area she lived in she'd seen places like this. Old buildings surrounded by high walls. Houses where the rich lived.

She'd once lived in a house like this herself, but it had been a long time ago and elsewhere, when she'd been a little kid. Before her father had kicked her and her mother out of their palatial mansion and life had changed drastically.

She still remembered what it had been like to have money, to have a roof over her head and clean clothes and food. Nice memories, but they'd been a lie, so she tried not to think about them. It was better not to remember such things because they only made her want what she could never have—and wanting things was always a bad thing.

She stared distrustfully out into the darkness, where the silhouette of a massive old house reared against the sky.

The driver came around the side of the car and opened the door. The duke gestured at her to get out.

She turned her distrustful attention to him.

A duke. An honest-to-God duke. He didn't look like one—though she had no idea what dukes were supposed to look like. Maybe much older. Although, given the faint lines around his eyes and mouth, he was certainly a lot older than she was. Then again, his hair was still pitch-black so he couldn't be *that* old.

His name had sounded faintly familiar to her, though she couldn't think why. The fact that he was Spanish had given her a little kick, since she'd been born in Spain herself. In fact maybe she'd met him once before—back in Spain, before her father had got rid of her and her mother and her mother had dragged her to Paris.

Back when she'd been Leonie de Riero, the prized only daughter of Victor de Riero, with the blood of ancient Spanish aristocracy running in her veins.

Perhaps she knew this duke from then? Or perhaps not. She'd been very young, after all, and her memories of that time were dim.

Whatever he was, or had been, she didn't want to remember those days. The present was the only thing she had, and she had to be on her guard at all times. Forgetting where she was and what was happening led to mistakes, and she'd already made enough of those since ending up on the streets.

If she hadn't been so absorbed in getting the lettering just so as she'd graffitied his car, she wouldn't be here after all.

You certainly wouldn't have had a bed for the night, so maybe it wasn't such a mistake?

That remained to be seen. Perhaps she should have fought harder to escape him. Then again, she hadn't been able to resist the lure of a job—if he actually meant what he'd said, that was.

The duke lifted that perfect brow of his. 'Are you going to get out? Or would you prefer to sit here all night? The car is quite comfortable, though I'm afraid the doors will have to stay locked.'

She gave him a ferocious glare. 'Give me back my knife

first.' She liked to have some protection on her, just in case of treachery.

He remained impervious to her glare. 'I'm not going to hurt you, *gatita*.'

Kitten. He kept calling her kitten. It was annoying.

'I don't trust you. And I don't want to sleep in a strange place without some protection.'

His jungle-green gaze was very level and absolutely expressionless. 'Fair enough.' Reaching into the pocket of his jacket, he extracted her knife and held it out, handle first.

She took it from him, the familiarity of the handle fitting into her palm making her feel slightly better. Briefly she debated whether or not to try and slash at him again, then bolt into the darkness. But she remembered the high walls surrounding the house. She wouldn't be able to get over those, alas. She could refuse to get out and sleep in the car, but she didn't like the idea of being locked in. No, it was the house or nothing.

With as much dignity as she could muster, Leonie pocketed her knife then slid out of the car. Behind her, the duke murmured something to his driver and then he was beside her, moving past her up the big stone steps to the front door of the mansion.

Some member of his staff was obviously still up, because the door opened, a pool of light shining out.

A minute later she found herself in a huge vaulted vestibule, with flights of stone steps curling up to the upper storeys and a massive, glittering chandelier lighting the echoing space. Thick silk rugs lay on the floor and there were pictures on the walls, and on the ceiling far above her head was a big painting of angels with white wings and golden haloes.

It was very warm inside.

She was used to being cold. She'd been cold ever since

she was sixteen, coming home after school one day to the rundown apartment she'd shared with her mother only to find it empty, and a note from her mother on the rickety kitchen table informing Leonie that she'd gone and not to look for her.

Leonie hadn't believed it at first. But her mother hadn't come home that night, or the next, or the one after that, and eventually Leonie had had to accept that her mother wasn't coming home at all. Leonie had been evicted from the apartment not long after that, and forced to live on the streets, where she'd felt like she'd become permanently cold.

But she hadn't realised just how cold until now. Until the warmth from this place seeped up through the cracked soles of her sneakers and into her body, into her heart.

Immediately she wanted to go outside again—to run and never stop running. She couldn't trust this warmth. She couldn't let her guard down. It wasn't safe.

Except the big front door had closed, and she knew it would be locked, and the duke was gesturing at her to follow the older woman who stood next to him, regarding her with some disgust, making her abruptly conscious of the holes in her jeans and the stains on the denim. Of the grimy hoodie that she'd stolen from a guy who'd taken it off to fight someone in the alleyway where she'd been sleeping one night. Of the paint stains on her hands.

She was dirty, and ragged, and she probably smelled since she hadn't found anywhere to clean herself for weeks. No wonder this woman looked disgusted.

Leonie's stomach clenched and she gripped the handle of her knife, scowling to cover the wave of vulnerability that had come over her. Never stop fighting. Never show weakness. That was the law of the streets.

'Go with Camille,' the duke said. 'She will show you—'

'No,' Leonie said. 'Just tell me where to go and I'll find my own way there.'

Camille made a disapproving sound, then said something in a lilting musical language to the duke. He replied in the same language, his deep, rich voice making it sound as if he was caressing each word.

Leonie felt every one of her muscles tense in resistance. She couldn't like the sound of his voice. She had to be on her guard at all times and not make any mistakes. And she didn't want to go with this Camille woman and her disapproving stare.

Much to her surprise, however, with one last dark look in Leonie's direction, the woman turned and vanished down one of the huge, echoing hallways that led off the entrance hall.

Without a word, the duke turned and headed towards the huge marble staircase. 'Follow me,' he said over his shoulder.

He didn't pause and he didn't wait, as if expecting her to follow him just as he'd said.

Leonie blinked. Why had he sent the other woman away? Was he just leaving her here? What if she somehow managed to get out through the door? What if she escaped down one of the corridors? What would he do? He wasn't looking at her. Would he even know until she was gone?

Her heartbeat thumped wildly, adrenaline surging through her—both preludes to a very good bolt. And yet she wasn't moving. She was standing there in this overwhelming, intimidating entrance hall, not running, watching a tall, powerful rich man go up the marble stairs.

He moved with economy and a lazy, athletic grace that reminded her even more strongly of a panther. It was mesmerising, for some reason. And when she found herself moving, it wasn't towards the doorway or the corridor, it was towards him, following him almost helplessly.

Was this what had happened in that fairy-tale? Those children following the Pied Piper, drawn beyond their control by the music he made. Disappearing. Never to be seen again.

You're an idiot. You have your knife. Pull yourself together.

This was true. And nothing had happened to her so far. Yes, he'd kept her locked in the car against her will, but he hadn't hurt her. And apart from the moment when he'd grabbed her, he hadn't touched her again.

She didn't trust him, or his offer of a job, but it was either follow him or stay down here in the entrance hall, and that seemed cowardly. She wasn't going to do that, either.

There was a slim possibility that he was telling the truth, and if so she needed to take advantage of it. If she was going to achieve her dream of having a little cottage of her own in the countryside, away from the city, away from danger, then he was her best chance of that happening.

Slowly Leonie moved after him, going up the winding marble staircase, trying to keep her attention on his strong back and not gawk at all the paintings on the walls, the carpets on the parquet floors, the vases of flowers on the small tables dotted here and there as they went down yet another wide and high-ceilinged corridor.

Windows let in the Parisian night and she caught glimpses of tall trees, hinting at a garden outside. She wanted to go and look through the glass, because it had been a long time since she'd seen a garden, but she didn't dare. She had to keep the duke's tall figure in sight.

Eventually, after leading her through a few more of those high-ceilinged corridors, he stopped outside a door and opened it, inclining his head for her to go on through.

He was standing quite near the doorway, and she wasn't sure she wanted to get that close to him, but she didn't want him to know it bothered her, either, so she slipped past him as quickly as she could. But not quickly enough to avoid catching a hint of his aftershave and the warmth of his powerful body as she brushed past him.

It was only an instant, but in that instant she was acutely aware of his height looming over her. Of the width of his broad shoulders and the stretch of the cotton across his muscled chest. Of the way he smelled spicy and warm and quite delicious.

A strange ripple of sensation went through her like an electric shock.

Disturbed, Leonie ignored it, concentrating instead on the room she'd stepped into.

It was very large, with tall windows that looked out on to trees. A thick pale carpet covered the floor, and up against one wall, facing the windows, was a very large bed, made up with a thick, soft-looking white quilt.

The duke moved past her, going over to the windows and drawing heavy pale silk curtains over the black glass, shutting out the night. The room was very warm, the carpet very soft under her feet, and she was conscious once again of how dirty she was.

She was going to leave stains all over this pretty pale bedroom. Surely he couldn't mean for her to stay here? It didn't look like a cleaner's room. It was far too luxurious.

'This can't be where you put your staff,' she said, frowning. 'Why am I here?'

He adjusted the curtains with a small, precise movement, then turned around, putting his hands in his pockets. 'Not usually, no. But Camille didn't have a room ready for you, so I thought you could use one of my guest bedrooms.'

'Why? Why are you doing this?'

He tilted his head, gazing at her from underneath very long, thick black lashes. 'Which particular "this" are you talking about?'

'I mean this room. A job. A bed for the night. Why are you doing any of it? Why should you care?'

She hadn't meant it to come out so accusingly, but she couldn't help it. Men like him, with money and power, never did things without wanting something in return. Even charity usually came with strings. There were bound to be strings here, if only she could see them.

But the duke merely gave one of those elegant shrugs. 'What else does one do with a feral kitten but look after it?'

'I'm not a kitten,' she said, for the second time that night.

His mouth curved and once again she felt that electric ripple of sensation move through her. It came to her very suddenly that this man was dangerous. And dangerous in a way she couldn't name. He wasn't a physical threat—though those strange little ripples of sensation definitely were—but definitely a threat of some kind.

'No,' he murmured, his gaze moving over her in a way that made heat rise in her cheeks. 'You're not, are you?'

She lifted her chin, discomfited and not liking it one bit. 'And I didn't ask you to look after me, either.'

'Oh, if you think I'm doing it out of the goodness of my heart you are mistaken.' He strolled past her towards the door. 'It's entirely out of self-interest, believe me.'

'Why? Just because I vandalised your car?'

Pausing by the door, he gave her a sweeping, enigmatic glance. 'Among other things. The bathroom is through the door opposite. A shower or a bath wouldn't go amiss, *gatita*.'

'Don't call me that,' she snapped, annoyed that he'd obviously noticed how dirty she was and how she must smell, and then annoyed further by her own annoyance—since why should she care if he'd noticed?

'What else am I to call you?' His eyes gleamed. 'Especially since you won't give me your name.'

Leonie pressed her lips together. He might have strong-armed her into staying in his house, but her name was the one thing he wouldn't be able to force out of her. That was hers to give.

Again, he didn't seem offended. He only smiled. 'Then *gatita* it will have to be.'

And before she could say another word he walked out, closing the door carefully behind him.

CHAPTER THREE

The late-morning sun poured through the big windows of Cristiano's study, flooding the room with light and warmth, but he didn't notice. He wasn't interested in the weather.

He'd got up early that morning, despite not having slept much the previous night, and gone straight to his study to see if the memory that learning Leonie's name had generated was correct. After a couple of calls and a few strongly worded orders he'd had his confirmation.

She was exactly who he'd suspected she was.

Which should have been impossible, considering she was supposed to be dead.

He leaned back in his big black leather chair and stared at the computer screen on the desk in front of him. At the photo it displayed. An old one, from years and years ago, of a tall, dark-haired man, holding the hand of a little girl with hair the distinctive colour of apricots. At the side of the little girl stood a lovely slender woman with hair exactly the same colour.

It was a loving family portrait of the ancient and illustrious de Riero family—Spanish aristocrats who'd fallen on hard times and lost their title a century or so ago.

Leonie had turned out to be Leonie de Riero, Victor de Riero's prized only daughter, who'd disappeared along with her mother fifteen years earlier, rumoured to have died in an apartment fire in Barcelona not long after she'd disappeared.

It was a scandal that had rocked Spain for months and he remembered it acutely. Especially because Victor de Riero, whose family had been blood enemies of Cristiano's, had become his mentor.

Victor had been grief-stricken about the loss of his wife and child—at least until he'd found himself a new family. *Your family.*

The deep, volcanic rage that Cristiano had thought he'd excised from his life shifted in his gut, hot enough to incinerate anything in its path, and he had to take a minute to wrestle it back into submission. Because he couldn't allow himself to feel that—not any more. He couldn't allow himself to feel anything any more.

It had taken him years to put that rage behind him, but he had. And he'd thought he'd found some measure of peace. Until Leonie had appeared.

Cristiano pushed his chair back and got to his feet, walking over to the bookshelves opposite his desk before turning and pacing back to the desk again, needing movement to settle himself.

His thoughts tumbled about in his head like dice.

Of course Leonie had been familiar to him. He *had* met her. But it had been years ago, and she'd been that little girl in the photo—a kid of around two or three, initially, when her father had first approached him.

He'd been seventeen at the time, and had just lost both his parents in a car accident. Victor de Riero had paid him a visit not long after the funeral, ostensibly to bury the hatchet on the ancient feud the Velazquez and de Riero families had been pursuing for centuries.

Cristiano had been only too happy to do so, having no interest in old feuds and still grappling with the deaths of his parents and the shock of suddenly having to take on the responsibility of a dukedom. He'd welcomed Victor's interest in him gratefully, listening to the older man's advice and accepting his help, thinking the other man was doing it out of the goodness of his heart.

But he hadn't known then that there was no goodness in Victor's heart, or that the flames of vengeance for the de Riero family still burned in him hot and strong.

In fact it hadn't been until Cristiano had married, three years later, that he'd discovered the truth about Victor de Riero's interest.

In that time, though, he'd met Victor's wife and his small, sparky daughter. Cristiano hadn't taken much notice of the daughter—kids hadn't been on his radar back then—but then Victor's wife had disappeared, taking the girl with her, only for both to be discovered dead in a fire a week or so later.

Cristiano had tried to be there for Victor the way Victor had been for him, after his parents had died, but he'd been in the throes of first love, and then early marriage, and hadn't paid as much attention as he should have.

He hadn't paid attention a year or so after that, either, when he'd gone to Victor for advice when his marriage to Anna had run into trouble. If he had, he might have noticed how much his wife had enjoyed Victor's company—how, at social occasions, she'd spent more time talking to him than she had to Cristiano.

He might have become aware that Victor had never planned on burying the hatchet when it came to their family feud but had only been lying in wait, lulling Cristiano into a false sense of security, waiting for the right time to take advantage of a vulnerable young man.

And finally he had found that advantage in Cristiano's wife. Because it had been his lovely wife Anna that Victor had wanted, and in the end it had been his lovely wife that he'd taken—Cristiano's already pregnant wife.

Along with Cristiano's son.

Cristiano paced to the bookshelves again, memories he'd long since suppressed flooding like acid through him.

Victor turning up at Cristiano's Barcelona penthouse, flanked by bodyguards and cloaked in triumph, revealing the final piece of his plot like a pantomime villain. Rubbing salt into Cristiano's wound by telling him that his seduction of Anna had all been part of their blood feud, and then rubbing glass into that same wound by telling him that Anna was pregnant and the child was Cristiano's.

He would bring up Cristiano's child as his own, Victor had said. He would take something precious from a Velazquez after a Velazquez had ruined the de Riero family a century earlier, by stealing the dukedom from them.

Cristiano had barely heard the man's reasoning. He'd been incandescent with rage and betrayal. It had been wise of Victor to have brought bodyguards, because he hadn't been at all sure he wouldn't have launched himself at the other man and strangled him.

Your anger has always been a problem.

Yes, and he'd been on fire with it.

For two years he'd used almost the entirety of his fortune trying to get his son back, but Victor had falsified the paternity tests Cristiano had demanded, paid any number of people off, and Cristiano hadn't had a leg to stand on.

Eventually he'd crashed a party of Victor's, intent on stealing back his son from the man who'd taken him—but when he'd approached the boy, the child had run from him in fear. Straight to Victor.

'This is the reason, Cristiano,' Anna had flung at him, as she'd tried to calm the hysterical child in Victor's arms.

'This is the reason I left you. You're dangerous and you only end up scaring people. Why can't you leave us alone?'

Well, she'd got her wish in the end. After that—after seeing the fear in his son's green eyes—he'd left the party. Left Spain, vowing never to return.

For his own sanity he'd excised all knowledge of his son from his heart, scoured all thoughts of revenge from his soul. He had found other ways to kill the pain lodged inside him like a jagged shard of broken glass. Pleasure and lots of it had been the key, and soon enough the edges of that piece of glass had dulled, making him look back over the years and marvel at how it had ever been sharp enough to hurt.

But it was hurting now. Because of her.

He came to the bookshelves and turned around, pacing back to the desk once more.

If he'd had any sense he'd have got rid of her the moment that sense of nagging familiarity had hit him, but he hadn't, and now she was here. In his house. And he was certain it was her.

A member of his staff had managed to track down the man who'd told Victor that Leonie and Hélène de Riero had died in a fire, and the man—once some money had been waved in his face—had admitted he'd lied. That Hélène de Riero had paid him to report her and her daughter's death to her ex-husband for reasons unknown.

Of course Cristiano would need DNA confirmation, which he'd get easily enough, but he was sure already. No other woman he'd ever met had had hair that colour or those jewel-bright violet eyes.

He had Victor de Riero's daughter in his grasp.

Tension gathered inside him and a vicious anticipation twisted through it, the rage he'd never been able to conquer entirely burning in his heart. Whether it was fate that had brought her to his door, or merely simple chance, it didn't matter.

What mattered was that here was an opportunity. A very unexpected opportunity.

Isn't revenge a dish best served cold?

After his parents had been killed, the old family feud with the de Rieros had seemed like something out of the Middle Ages. A hold-over from a different time. But he'd been young back then, and naive. He hadn't yet learned that people lied and that they couldn't be trusted. He hadn't yet learned just how far the depths of grief and loss could go.

He'd learned eventually. Oh, yes, he'd learned that lesson well.

And now here was his chance to pay that lesson back in kind.

Tension crawled through him, making his jaw ache as he came to the desk and turned around to the bookshelf again.

He couldn't deny that he liked the thought. Relished it.

Victor de Riero had taken his son, so wouldn't it be the sweetest revenge of all if Cristiano took his daughter? The daughter who'd been presumed dead for fifteen years?

An eye for an eye keeps the feud alive.

Perhaps he wouldn't have considered it if Leonie hadn't turned up. Perhaps he'd have gone through his life pretending he didn't have a son and that he'd never been married for the rest of his days. But she had, and now he could think of nothing else.

It seemed the old Spanish warlord in him wasn't as dead as he'd thought.

Maybe he'd make her his duchess. Invite de Riero to the wedding. He'd pull up her veil and then there she'd be—the daughter de Riero had thought was dead, marrying the man he'd once thought he could humiliate in front of the entire world.

And maybe to really pay him back Cristiano would have an heir with her after all. Pollute the pure de Riero bloodline with Velazquez blood.

After all, if de Riero could do it, why couldn't he?

He stopped mid-pace, his fingers curling inside his pockets, vicious pleasure pulling tight in his gut.

And then you can move on.

Not that he hadn't moved on already, but that jagged shard of glass was still embedded deep inside his heart, ensuring it could never heal. Perhaps if he took the revenge he was owed it finally would.

Certainty settled inside him like the earth settling after an earthquake, forming a new landscape.

First on the agenda would be Leonie—because she was vital to his plan and would have to agree to it. Which might be a problem when she was so stubborn, wary and distrustful. Not so surprising, given the circumstances under which he'd found her, but not exactly conducive to his plan. Then again, money seemed to motivate her. She could consider being his bride part of her job, for which she'd receive a very healthy bonus.

Revealing that he knew who she was could be a concern, however. She hadn't given him her name for a reason, and everything hinged on how she felt about her father. Had she ever wanted to return to him? Did she even know she was supposed to be dead?

He frowned at the wall opposite. Perhaps telling her about his discovery immediately would be a mistake. Now she was here, within his grasp, he couldn't afford for her to run, and he'd be at risk of scaring her away if he wasn't careful. No, maybe it would be better to gain her trust before he let her in on his secret—an easy enough task to accomplish with a beautiful woman. All it would require was a bit of careful handling.

Galvanised in a way he hadn't been for years, Cristiano turned towards the door, heading out of his study and going in search of the newest member of his staff.

He found her, as he'd expected, in the big library that faced onto the walled garden at the rear of the house. She was kneeling on the floor before one of the big bookshelves with her back to him. Her dirty clothes were gone—clearly Camille had found her something else to wear—and she now wore the staff uniform of plain black trousers and a fitted black T-shirt. Nondescript clothes that should have made her blend in, and yet the skein of silken hair that fell down her back in a sleek ponytail effectively prevented that. The colour glowed against her black T-shirt, a deep red-gold tinged with pink.

Beautiful.

His hands itched with the urge to run his fingers through it, to see if it felt as soft as it looked. To touch that vibrant colour, wind it round his wrist, examine the contrast against his own skin...

Except that was not what he wanted from her. Her name, yes. Her body, no. He might find her more attractive than he'd expected, but he could get sex from any of the women in his extensive little black book. He didn't need to expend any effort on a skittish, homeless, much younger woman, no matter how pretty her hair was.

But what about your plans for an heir?

Ah, yes, but there would be time for that later.

He hitched one shoulder up against the doorframe and gazed at her.

It was clear she wasn't actually cleaning, since her cloth and polishing spray were sitting next to her. Her head was bent, as if she was looking at something, and it must be very absorbing since it was clear she hadn't heard him and he hadn't exactly been quiet.

That was what had got her into trouble the previous night, hadn't it? She'd been totally caught up in the 'art' she'd been creating on his limo door and hadn't run when she should have.

What would that attention be like it bed? Would she look at you that way? Would she touch you like—?

Cristiano jerked his offending thoughts out of the gutter, irritated with himself. Perhaps he needed to contact those two lovely women he'd been going to take home the previous night and finish what they'd started. Certainly he'd have to do something with his wayward groin—especially if he kept having thoughts like these about Leonie.

He shifted against the doorframe and said finally, 'Find some interesting reading material, *gatita*?'

THE DUKE'S DEEP, rich voice slid over Leonie's skin like an unexpected caress, making her jump in shock, then freeze in place, the book she'd been reading still clutched in her hands. She stared at the shelves in front of her, every sense she had focused on the voice that had come from behind her.

A small cold thread wound its way through her veins.

Her employer had caught her reading on the job on her very first day. Not a good look. Ugh—what had she been thinking?

Everything had been going extremely well since he'd left her the night before, too. She'd availed herself of the shower, even though everything in her had wanted to spend hours soaking in the vast white marble bath. But it had been very late and she'd needed some sleep. So she'd given her body and hair a decent scrub before falling into that outrageously comfortable bed naked, since she hadn't been able to bear putting on her filthy clothes again—not when she was so clean.

Her sleep had been fitful, due to the comfortableness of the bed—she was used to sleeping on hard surfaces covered with nothing but pieces of cardboard or, if she was lucky and had managed to get a night in a shelter, a hard mattress covered by a thin blanket—and she'd kept waking up. Her sleep was always light, in case of threats, but even so she'd felt okay when she'd woken this morning.

There had been a set of clothes left outside her door, which she'd snatched up and put on, glorying in the feel of soft, clean cotton against her skin. Coffee and a fresh warm croissant had been left along with the clothes, and she'd devoured both in seconds. She had still been hungry, but then Camille had come, a little less scornful than she'd been the night before, and given her an introduction to her duties.

There'd been no time for more food.

She was supposed to have spent no more than half an hour in the library—concentrating on dusting the shelves, since the duke was most particular about them—before moving on to the formal sitting room next door. But she had a horrible suspicion that she'd been in here longer than half an hour. And she hadn't even touched the shelves yet.

She'd just got very interested in some of the books, and hadn't been able to resist taking one off the shelf and opening it up.

Back when she'd been smaller, when her mother had still been around, she'd used to love going to the library and reading, and books were something she'd missed on the streets. And back further still, when she'd been very young, her father had read to her—

But, no, she wasn't going to think of her father.

She needed to be more alert to her surroundings, that was what she needed to be, because this wretched duke was always sneaking up on her.

Quickly, she closed the book and put it back. 'I wasn't

reading,' she said, picking up her cloth and polish. 'I was just polishing the shelf.' She ran the cloth over the already gleaming wood a couple of times. 'It's very dirty.'

'Which book was it?'

Again that voice—a deep, dark purr that felt like soft velvet brushing against her skin. It made her shiver and she didn't like it…not one bit.

Clutching her cleaning equipment, Leonie got to her feet and turned around, only to have the words she'd been going to say die in her throat.

The duke was leaning one powerful shoulder casually against the doorframe, his hands in his pockets. He was in perfectly tailored black suit trousers today, and a pristine white shirt with the sleeves rolled up to his elbows, revealing strong wrists and sleekly muscled forearms. It was plain, simple clothing that set off his sheer physical beauty to perfection, accentuating the aristocratic lines of his face, the straight black brows, the sharply carved mouth and the deep emerald glitter of his eyes.

He seemed different from the man he'd been the night before. There was an energy about him that hadn't been present the previous evening. It was oddly compelling and that made her wary.

Everything about this man made her wary.

He raised a brow in that imperious way he had. 'You were going to say something?'

Leonie was irritated to feel a blush rising in her cheeks, because she had a feeling he'd noticed her reaction to him and was amused by it.

'No,' she said, wishing she had her knife on her. Because although he hadn't made a move towards her, she felt the threat he presented all the same. 'Is there anything you need…uh…*monsieur*?' She couldn't quite bring herself to say *Your Grace*.

A smile curled his mouth, though it didn't look like an amused smile. More as if he was...satisfied.

'Not at all. Just coming to see how my newest staff member is settling in. Is everything to your liking?'

'Yes, thank you.' She kept a tight grip on her cloth and polish. 'Camille said she would find me another room to sleep—'

'I think not,' he interrupted, with the casual arrogance of a man who was used to his word being law. 'You'll stay in the room you're in.'

Leonie wasn't unhappy with that—especially when she hadn't had a chance to use that amazing bath yet, and also didn't like being in close proximity to a lot of people—but she didn't like his automatic assumption that she could be told what to do.

And your need to fight is what gets you into trouble.

This was very true. And there was also another problem. A problem she'd foreseen the night before and yet had dismissed.

In accepting a bed for the night, and now a job, she'd had a tiny taste of what her life might be like off the streets.

Having a shower whenever she wanted it...having clean sheets and clean clothes. Having food brought to her and having something to do that wasn't figuring out how to shoplift her next meal or begging for coins. Being safe behind walls and locked doors.

Just a tiny taste. Enough to know she didn't want to give it up—not just yet.

This is how they suck you in. You should have run...

She swallowed, clutching her cleaning implements even tighter. It was too late to run now—too late to decide that life on the streets was better than being in this house and working for this duke. Like Persephone from the myth, she'd had a bite of the pomegranate and now she was trapped in the Underworld.

Which makes him Hades.

And a very fine Hades he made, too. No wonder she found him dangerous. He was the snake in the garden, offering temptation…

'I don't need a special room,' she said, because her need to fight was so ingrained she couldn't stop herself. 'I'm happy to sleep wherever the other employees—'

'As I said, you will stay in the room you've been given.'

'Why?'

'Because I said so,' he replied easily. 'I'm the duke and what I say goes.' That smile was still playing around his fascinating mouth. 'Which reminds me—I usually have a formal job interview with my employees, and since you didn't have one, I suggest we schedule one for tonight. Over dinner.'

Instantly all her alarm bells went off at once. A job interview over dinner? That didn't sound right at all. Not that she had any experience with job interviews, but still…

She gave him a suspicious look. 'Job interviews are usually in offices during the day, not over dinner.'

'Astute, *gatita*. If being in an office would make you more comfortable, I can have dinner served to us there.'

Leonie scowled. 'I'm not sleeping with you.'

He raised both brows this time. 'Have I asked you to sleep with me?'

'No, but when a man asks a woman to dinner he expects certain things. Men always do.'

'You appear to have a very poor opinion of men—though I suppose that's understandable. We're not especially good examples of the human race.' His eyes glittered strangely. 'It's also true that I'm a particularly bad example. But I don't have any sexual designs on you, if that's what you're worried about.'

She *had* been worried about it. The threat of sexual violence was ever-present for a woman on her own on the streets. So why did him telling her that he had no sexual designs on her make her feel almost…disappointed?

'That's all very well,' she said, ignoring the feeling, 'but I don't trust you.'

He shifted, drawing her attention to his powerful body, making her aware of him in a disturbingly physical way.

'Fair enough. We've only just met after all. Bring your knife with you. And if I try anything romantic feel free to cut me with it.'

'Or you could just decide we don't need to have an interview,' she suggested. 'After all, you've already employed me.'

'It's true—I have. But the process is the process. I can't just let anyone into my house. Security checks need to be done…reference checks, et cetera. It's all very tiresome but absolutely necessary.' He paused, his gaze sharpening on her. 'Especially when said employee hasn't even given me her name.'

Leonie took a silent breath. She should have given it to him last night when he'd asked. What did it matter if he knew? She'd only wanted to retain a little bit of autonomy, but now she'd turned it into a big deal and maybe he thought she was trying to hide something, or that she was on the run from something.

Not the actual truth, which was that she was only a girl who'd been discarded by both parents. A girl nobody wanted.

Her gut tightened. He certainly didn't need to know that. And, anyway, her name was her own and it was hers to give. No one had the right to know it.

Why don't you give him a fake one, then?

She could. But that would be giving in, regardless of whether it was a fake name or not, and something inside her wouldn't let her do that.

What was it about him that had her wanting to fight him all the time? She'd never had such strong reactions to a man before. Admittedly, she hadn't come into contact with a lot of men, since it was better safety-wise to avoid them, but the few she'd had run-ins with hadn't endeared themselves to her. But this man…

He made her want to fight, to stand her ground, kick back. He also made her feel physical things she hadn't felt before in her entire life. A kind of shivery ache. A prickly restlessness. The stupid desire to poke at him just to see what he'd do. What on earth was that?

You know what it is.

But Leonie didn't want to think about it. She couldn't afford to—not when she was seconds away from catastrophe. Who knew how long this job would last? Or when she'd be turned out back on to the streets again?

She'd got herself into this situation, and if she was very lucky it would mean good things for her. So the most logical thing to do now was to be careful with the dangerous panther that lounged on the branch above her head. To keep her head down and perhaps not present herself as so much prey. Keep a low profile and not struggle. If she did that well he might even forget she existed and leave her alone.

So she said nothing, dragging her gaze away from him and looking at the ground instead.

'Ah, so that's how it's to be, hmm?'

Again, he sounded just like that panther—all low and purring and sleek.

'Come to my study when you finish up today. I'll tell Camille that you're expected.'

She nodded silently, and when she finally looked up the doorway was empty.

He'd gone.

CHAPTER FOUR

Cristiano frowned at the clock on the mantelpiece, an un-expected impatience gathering inside him. Leonie was late and he suspected it was intentional, since Camille wouldn't have kept her working if she was expected to attend a meeting with him.

And she was definitely expected to attend.

He supposed he could have had the conversation with her in the library earlier that day, rather than make a performance of it over dinner. But trust was a difficult thing. You couldn't compel it and you couldn't buy it—it could only be given.

Which made him a liar in some respects, because he was absolutely planning a seduction. Except sex wasn't the goal. He was planning on seducing her curious mind instead.

He found himself energised by the prospect. It had been a long time since he'd had to exert himself for a woman—for anyone, for that matter—and the idea was more exciting than he'd anticipated. Lately his life of unmitigated pleasure had begun to pall, and it made a nice change to have to put his brain to good use instead of his body.

The thought of de Riero's shock as his daughter was revealed was...

The feeling of satisfaction was vicious, hot, and he had to force it back down—hard. He couldn't let emotion rule him.

Not given the mistake he'd made the last time he'd tried to confront de Riero, blundering around in a blind rage, sending his son straight back into the other man's arms.

This time he needed to be casual, detached. Keep his revenge cold.

Mastering himself once more, Cristiano checked the time again, allowing himself some amusement at his own impatience, then crossed over to his desk. Since she was late, he might as well do something. It wouldn't do for her to find him cooling his heels and watching the clock for her arrival; he wasn't a man who waited for anyone, still less looked as if he was.

There were a few business matters he had to attend to, a few calls to make, and he made them, keeping an ear out for the door. And sure enough, ten minutes later, while he was in the middle of a conversation with a business acquaintance, he heard a soft knock.

'Enter,' he said, then turned his chair around so his back was to the room, continuing with his call.

It was petty, but he'd never been above a little pettiness. It would do her good to wait for him—especially since he'd spent the last ten minutes waiting for her.

He carried on with his call in a leisurely fashion, in no hurry to end it since his acquaintance was amusing, and only when the other man had to go did he end the call and turn his chair back around.

Leonie was standing near one of the ornate wooden shelves he kept stocked with his favourite reading material—business texts, philosophy, sociology and a few novels thrown in the mix—staring fixedly at the spines. She held herself very tense, her shoulders and spine stiff, that waterfall of beautiful hair lying sleek and silky down her back.

He had the sense that she wasn't actually looking at the books at all. She was waiting for him. Good.

'Good evening, *gatita*,' he said lazily, leaning back in his chair. 'You're late.'

Slowly, she turned to him, and his gaze was instantly drawn to the dark circles beneath her eyes. Her pretty face looked pale, her big violet-blue eyes shadowed. One hand was in the pocket of her black trousers—clutching that knife, no doubt.

A feeling he wasn't expecting tightened in his chest. He ignored it, raising a brow at her. 'Well? Any particular reason you're late to your job interview?'

Her determined little chin lifted. 'Because you distracted me in the library I didn't get my work done on time, so I had to make it up at the end of the day.'

He almost laughed. She did like testing him, didn't she? 'I see. Nothing whatsoever to do with the fact that I caught you reading, hmm?'

Colour bloomed across her delicate cheekbones. 'No.'

Which was an outright lie and they both knew it.

Highly amused, he grinned. 'And you took some time to go back to your room for you knife, also, I think?'

Her forearm flexed above where her hand disappeared into her pocket, as if she was squeezing her fingers around the handle of something. But this time she didn't deny it.

'You said I could bring it.'

'It's true. I did.'

He got up from the chair and came around the side of his desk, noting the way she tensed at his approach. She was very wary of him. As wary as she'd been the night before. Understandable, of course, and it was an obvious sign of distrust. In fact, he could probably gauge her progression in trusting him through the way she acted around him physically.

It made him wonder, though, exactly what had happened to her out there on the Parisian streets. How she'd managed to survive. What had happened to Hélène? Why hadn't she gone to her father and told him she was still alive…?

So many questions.

If he wanted answers, he had some work to do.

He moved over to the fireplace against one wall, opposite the bookshelves. He'd had one of his staff light a fire even though it wasn't particularly cold, mainly because it made the room feel more welcoming. The fire crackled pleasantly, casting its orange glow over Leonie's beautiful hair.

She watched him as if he was a dangerous animal she had to be cautious about, yet her gaze kept flicking to the fire as if she wanted to get close to it. As if she was cold.

'You're afraid of me,' he said, and didn't make it a question. 'I can assure you that you have no need to be.'

Her gaze flickered. 'I'm not afraid.'

But the response sounded as if it had been made by rote—as if that was always her answer, whether it was true or not. It made sense, though. When you were small and female you were viewed as prey by certain people, which meant fear wasn't something you could afford. Fear was weakness. Especially when there was no one to protect you.

Had she ever had anyone to protect her? Or had she had to do it herself?

That tight feeling in his chest shifted again. It had been such a long time since he'd felt anything remotely resembling pity or sympathy that he wasn't sure what it was at first. But then he knew. He didn't like the idea of her being on her own. He didn't like the idea of her not being protected. How strange.

'Then come closer.' He thrust his hands in his pockets so he looked less intimidating. 'You want to be near the fire. Don't think I hadn't noticed.'

She didn't like that—he could see the tension ripple

through her. Perhaps he was wrong to test her. But if he wanted her trust he had to start somewhere, and having her be less wary around him physically was certainly one way of doing it.

He remained still, not moving, keeping his hands in his pockets, silently daring her. She was brave, not to mention stubborn, and he suspected that if he kept challenging her she'd rise to it.

Sure enough, after a couple of tense moments, she gave a shrug, as if it didn't matter, and then came slowly across the room to stand on the opposite side of the fireplace. Her expression was carefully blank, and when she got closer to the flames she held out her hands to warm them.

Ostensibly she looked as if nothing bothered her and she was perfectly comfortable. But she wasn't. He could feel the tension vibrating in the air around her.

She was like a wild animal, ready to start at the slightest sound or motion.

'There,' he murmured. 'That's not so bad, is it?'

She flicked him an impatient look. 'I'm not afraid of you. I have a knife.'

'Good. Keep that knife about your person at all times.' He turned slightly, noting how she tensed at his movement. 'So, nameless *gatita*. I suppose my first question to you is why on earth were you spray-painting my limo at two in the morning?'

Her attention was on the flames, but he suspected she was still very aware of him. 'Why shouldn't I be spray-painting your limo at two in the morning?'

'That's not the correct answer,' he reproved mildly. 'Don't you think I'm owed an explanation, considering it was my property you vandalised?'

Irritation crossed her features. 'Fine. The people I was with dared me to. So I did.'

'And if they dared you to jump off the Eiffel Tower you'd do the same?'

'Probably.' She gave him a sidelong glance. 'You can't back down—not even once. Not if you don't want to be a target.'

Ah, so now they were getting to it. 'I see. And these people are your friends?'

He thought not. Not considering how a one-hundred-euro note had been enough to pay for her name.

She shook her head. 'Just some people I was hanging around with.'

'At two in the morning? Didn't you have somewhere else to go?'

Her lashes fell, limned in gold by the firelight. 'It's… safer to be around other people sometimes.'

The tight thing coiled in his chest shifted around yet again, because even though she hadn't said it outright he knew. No, she didn't have anywhere to go, and she didn't want to admit it.

Proud *gatita*.

'I'm not sure those people were very safe,' he murmured. 'Considering how your night ended.'

She gave a shrug. 'Could have been worse.'

'Indeed. You could have spent another night on the streets.'

There was no response to that, though he didn't expect her either to confirm or deny it—not given how reluctant she was to give him any information about herself. Clearly telling her that he knew who she was wouldn't go down well, so he definitely wasn't going to reveal that in a hurry.

A small silence fell, broken only by the crackling of the fire.

'Will you sit down?' he asked after a moment. 'The

chair behind you will allow you to stay close to the fire if you're cold.'

She gave him another sidelong glance, then made a show of looking around the room, as if trying to locate the chair. Then, without any hurry, she moved over to it and sat down, leaning back, ostensibly relaxed, though she'd put her hand in her pocket again, holding on to her knife.

There was another armchair opposite hers, so he sat down in that one. A low coffee table was positioned between them, which should present her with a safety barrier if she needed it.

'So what now?' she asked, staring at him, her chin set at a stubborn angle.

'Tell me a little about yourself. If not your name, then at least a few things that will give me an idea about the kind of person I've just employed.'

'Why do you want to know that?'

He smiled. 'This isn't supposed to be a debate—merely a request for information.'

'Why do you need information?'

Persistent, wasn't she? Not to mention challenging. Good. His life had been without any challenges lately, and he could use the excitement.

'Well, since you won't give me your name, I need some indication of whether you're likely to make off with all the silverware.' He paused, considering whether or not to let her know just how much leeway he was allowing her. Why not? If she was testing him, he could test her. 'I do a background check on all employees who are granted access to my house, in other words. For safety reasons, you understand?'

A little crease appeared between her red-gold brows. 'How can you be unsafe? Here?'

Of course she'd find that surprising. Especially if she

was living on the streets. She no doubt thought nothing could harm him here, and to a certain extent she was right. Physically, he was safe. But four walls and bodyguards—even if he employed any—didn't equal safety. You could have all the physical protection in the world and still end up broken and bleeding.

Luckily for him, his wounds had healed. And no one could see the scars but him.

'You can be unsafe anywhere,' he said dryly. 'In my experience you can never be too careful.'

'And what is your experience?'

He almost answered her. Almost. Sneaky kitten.

Cristiano smiled. 'It's supposed to be your job interview, *gatita*, not mine. I already have a job.'

'And so do I. You gave it to me, remember?'

'I do. Which means I can take it back whenever I like.'

She sniffed, glancing over to the fire once more. 'I might be more inclined to answer your questions if you answered some of mine.'

Well, this was an interesting tactic…

'That's not how a job interview works,' he said, amused by how she kept on pushing. 'Also, if you'll remember, I gave you my name last night.'

An irritated expression flitted across her face. She shifted in her seat and he didn't miss how her hand had fallen away from the pocket where her knife was kept.

So. Progress.

'I don't know why you keep asking.' Her sweet, husky voice had an edge to it. 'Not when you could just threaten me and be done with it.'

'Threats are effective, it's true. But ultimately they're not very exciting.' He watched her face. 'Not when it's much more fun to convince you to give it to me willingly.'

She flushed. 'You're very sure of yourself.'

'Of course I'm sure of myself. I'm a duke.'

'Duke of what?'

Good question. And because he was enjoying himself, and because it had been a long time since any woman had provided him with this much amusement, he answered it.

'Weren't you listening last night? I'm the Fifteenth Duke of San Lorenzo. It's a small duchy in Andalusia.'

She gave him a measuring look. 'What are you doing in Paris?'

'Business.' He smiled. 'Catching vandals spray-painting rude words on my limo.'

She gave another little sniff at that, but the colour in her cheeks deepened—which was a good thing considering how pale she'd been.

'You didn't sleep well, *gatita*,' he observed quietly. 'But I did tell Camille to let you sleep in a little this morning.'

She blinked and looked away, shifting around in her seat. 'The bed was...uncomfortable. And I'd had a long shower—too long.'

Well, he knew for a fact that the bed wasn't uncomfortable, since he had the same one in his room here. And as for the shower...that may have been the case. But he suspected she hadn't slept well because she wasn't used to having a bed at all.

'What do you care anyway?' she added irritably.

'I care because I like my employees to do a good job. And they can't if they're not well rested.'

'Or well fed,' she muttered.

He thought she probably hadn't meant him to hear that, but unfortunately for her he had excellent hearing. So she was hungry, was she? Again, understandable. If she lived on the streets, decent food must be hard to come by.

How lucky, then, that he'd organised a very good dinner. Right on cue, there was a knock at the door.

She sat up, tension gathering around her again, instantly on the alert.

'Enter,' he said, watching her response as several staff members came in, bearing trays of the food he'd ordered.

Her eyes went wide as he directed them to put the food on the coffee table between them, including cutlery and plates, not to mention a couple of glasses and a bottle of extremely good red wine from his cellar.

'I told you there would be dinner,' he murmured as his staff arranged the food and then quietly withdrew.

Leonie had sat forward, her gaze fixed on the food on the table. It was a simple meal—a fresh garden salad and excellent steak, along with some warm, crusty bread and salted butter. All her earlier wariness had dissipated, to be replaced by a different kind of tension.

Her hands were clasped tightly in her lap.

She was hungry.

He became aware that her cheeks were slightly hollow, and her figure, now it wasn't swamped by that giant hoodie, was very slender. Probably too slender.

No, she wasn't just hungry—she was starving.

That tightness in his chest grew sharp edges, touching on that dangerous volcanic anger of his. Anger at how this lovely, spirited woman had ended up where she had. On the streets. Left to fend for herself with only a knife.

Left to starve.

Hélène had taken her and disappeared, letting Victor de Riero think she and his daughter were dead, but what had led her to do that? Had de Riero treated them badly? Was there something that had stopped Leonie from seeking him out?

A memory trickled through his consciousness…a small green-eyed boy running into de Riero's arms in fear…

Fear of you.

Red tinged the edges of Cristiano's vision and it took a massive effort to shove the rage back down where it had come from, to ignore the memory in his head. He had to do it. There would be no mistakes, not this time.

But her challenging him so continually was dangerous for them both. It roused his long-dormant emotions and that couldn't happen. Which meant she had to give him the answers he needed. Tonight. Now.

As she reached out towards the food Cristiano shot out a hand and closed his fingers around her narrow wrist. 'Oh, no, *gatita*. I've given you enough leeway. If you want to eat, you must pay me with some answers first.'

LEONIE FROZE, HER heart thudding hard in her ears, panic flooding through her. When his fingers had tightened her free hand had gone instantly to her knife, to pull it out and slash him with it.

'No,' he said, very calmly and with so much authority that for some strange reason her panic eased.

Because although his grip was firm, he wasn't pulling at her. He was only holding her. His fingers burned against her skin like a manacle of fire—except that wasn't painful, either. Or rather, it wasn't pain that she felt but a kind of prickling heat that swept up her arm and over the rest of her body.

She felt hypnotised by the sight of his fingers around her wrist. Long, strong and tanned. Competent hands. Not cruel hands.

'You'd stop me eating just to get what you want?' she asked hoarsely, not looking at him, staring instead at that warm, long-fingered hand gripping her wrist.

'No,' he repeated, in that deep, authoritarian voice. 'But I've given you food and a bed. A job that you'll be paid for. I haven't touched you except for twice—once when I grabbed you last night, and once now. I've given you my name and told you a few things about me. I have let you into my home.'

He paused, as if he wanted those words to sink in. And, as much as she didn't want them to, they did.

'I'm not asking for your date of birth or your passport number, or the number of your bank account. I'm not even asking for your surname. All I want is your first name. It's a small thing in return for all that, don't you think? After all, it was you who decided to deface my car, not me.'

Then, much to her shock, he let her go.

Her heart was beating very fast and she could still feel the imprint of his fingertips on her skin. It was as if he'd scorched her, and it made thinking very difficult.

But he was right about one thing. He wasn't asking for much. And he hadn't hurt her or been cruel. He *had* given her a bed and a job, and now there was food. And he hadn't withheld his name from her the way she had withheld hers from him.

She didn't trust him, but giving him this one small thing wouldn't hurt. After all, there were probably plenty of Leonies around. He couldn't know that she was Leonie de Riero, the forgotten daughter of Victor de Riero, the rich Spanish magnate, who'd tossed her and her mother out because he'd wanted a son. Or at least that was what her mother had told her.

'Leonie,' she said quietly, still staring at her wrist, part of her amazed she didn't have scorch marks there from his hand. 'My name is Leonie.'

There was a silence.

She glanced up and found his green gaze on hers, deep and dark as forests and full of dangerous wild things. She couldn't look away.

There was a kind of humming in the air around them,

and the prickling heat that had swept over her skin was spreading out. Warming her entire body. Making her feel restless and hot and hungry. But not for food.

'Thank you,' the duke said gravely.

He was not triumphant or smug, nor even showing that lazy amusement she'd come to associate with him. It was as if her name had been an important gift and he was receiving it with all the solemnity that entailed.

'Pleased to met you, Leonie.'

Just for a moment she thought he might reach out and take her hand, shake it. And, strangely, she almost wanted him to, so she could feel his fingers on her skin again. How odd to want to touch someone after so long actively avoiding it.

But he didn't take her hand. Instead he gestured to the food.

'Eat.' His mouth curled. 'Not that I was going to stop you from eating.'

Leonie decided not to say anything to that. She was too hungry anyway.

Not wanting to draw his attention, she didn't load her plate with too much food and she tried to eat slowly. It was all unbelievably delicious, but she wanted to pace herself. It had been a while since she'd eaten rich food and she didn't want to make herself sick. But it tasted so good—especially the fresh vegetables.

The duke poured her a glass of wine and she had a sip—and her toes just about curled in the plain black leather shoes she'd been given. Everything tasted amazing. She wanted to eat and drink all of it.

He didn't eat—merely sat there toying with a glass of wine in a leisurely fashion and studying her. It was disconcerting.

'You're not hungry?' she asked, feeling self-conscious.

Had she been gorging herself? She didn't want to give away how starving she was, wary of him asking more questions that she wasn't prepared to answer.

What does it matter if he knows you're homeless?

Perhaps it didn't matter. Perhaps it was only instinct that prevented her from revealing more, the long years of being wary and mistrustful settling into a reflex she couldn't ignore. Then again, there were reasons for her mistrust and wariness. She'd seen many young women in the same situation as herself fall victim to unscrupulous men because they'd trusted the wrong person, revealed the wrong thing.

Easier to keep to oneself, not let anyone close and stay alive.

It was a habit her wary, bitter mother had instilled in her long before she was on the streets anyway, and she'd seen no reason to change it.

Then again, although trusting this particular man might be a bridge too far, it was clear he wasn't here to hurt her. He'd had ample opportunity to do so and hadn't, so either he was saving it for a specific time or he wasn't going to do anything to her at all.

Maybe she could relax a little. Perhaps part of her reluctance to tell him anything had more to do with what he'd think of her, a dirty Parisian street kid, than whether he'd harm her. Not that she cared what he thought of her. At all.

'No, not hungry right now.' He leaned back in his chair, his wine glass held between long fingers. 'Did Camille not feed you enough?'

Despite all her justifications, she could feel her cheeks get hot. When she'd been turned out of the dilapidated apartment she'd shared with her mother, after her mother hadn't ever returned home, she'd had to fend for herself. And that hadn't allowed for such luxuries as pride. So why she was blushing now because he'd spotted her hunger, she had no idea.

'Just hungry today,' she muttered, not willing to give him anything else just yet. Mainly because she'd been doing nothing but resist for so long she couldn't remember how to surrender.

'I think not.' His tone was casual. 'I think you're starving.'

She tensed. Had the way she'd been eating given her away? 'I'm not—'

'Your cheeks are hollow and you're far too thin.' His gaze was very sharp, though his posture was relaxed. 'You're homeless, aren't you?'

Did you really think you could keep it from him?

Damn. Why did he have to be so observant? Why couldn't be like all the other rich people in the world who never saw the people living on the streets? Who were blind to them? Why couldn't he have simply called the police when he'd grabbed her the night before and got her carted away to the cells?

Why do you even care?

She had no answer to that except to wish it wasn't true. Sadly, though, it was true. She did care. She didn't want him to know that she was homeless—that she had no one and nothing. And she especially didn't want him to know that she'd once been the daughter of a very rich man who'd left her to rot on the streets like so much unwanted trash. Her mother had been very clear on that point.

Except, all the wanting in the world wasn't going to change the fact that he'd picked up on a few things she'd hoped he wouldn't see and had drawn his own conclusions. Correct conclusions. So was there any point in denying it now? She could pretend she had a home and a family, but he'd see through that pretty quickly. He was that kind of man.

So, since pretending was out, Leonie decided on belligerence instead. She stared back at him, daring him to pass judgement on her. 'And if I am?'

His gaze roamed over her face, irritatingly making the heat in her cheeks deepen even more. 'And nothing,' he said at last. 'It was merely an observation.'

'Don't you want to know where and why and how it happened? Whether I'm a drug addict or an alcoholic? Why haven't I found somewhere to go or a shelter to stay in?'

'Not particularly.' His green eyes gleamed. 'But if you want to tell me any of those things I'm happy to listen.'

That surprised her. She'd been expecting him to push for more information since he'd been so emphatic about her name before. Yet apparently not.

A strange feeling settled in her gut. Almost as if she'd wanted him to ask so she could tell him and was disappointed that he hadn't.

To cover her surprise, she reached for another piece of bread, spreading it liberally with the delicious butter and eating it in slow, careful bites.

'I'll have Camille make sure you get enough to eat,' he said after a moment. 'I won't have you going hungry here.'

She swallowed the last bit of bread. 'Don't tell her—'

'I won't. Your secret's safe with me.'

She didn't want it to be reassuring, yet it was. Not that she cared about what Camille thought, but still… Questions would be asked and she didn't want questions. She didn't want to have to explain her situation to anyone—including this powerful, yet oddly reassuring duke.

He could protect you.

The thought was a discomforting one. She'd protected

herself well enough for nearly six years, so why would she need him?

You need someone, though.

No, she didn't.

She picked up her wine and took another sip, allowing the rich, dark flavour to settle on her tongue. It made her a little dizzy, but she didn't mind that.

He began to ask her a few more questions, though these were solely about how she'd found the work today and whether she had what she needed to do her job, so she answered them. Then they had a discussion about what other tasks she might like to tackle and how she'd prefer to be paid—cash, since she didn't have a bank account.

The conversation wasn't personal, his questions were not intrusive, and he didn't make any more of those unexpected movements. And after maybe another half an hour had passed his phone went. Since it was apparently urgent, he excused himself to answer it.

Leonie settled back in the chair and finished her wine. It was very warm in the room, and she was very full, and since they were both sensations she had almost never felt she wanted to enjoy them for a little while.

The deep, rich sound of his voice as he talked to whoever he was talking to was lulling her. There was warmth and texture to that voice, and it was comforting in a way she couldn't describe.

Maybe it was that voice. Or maybe it was the wine and food. Maybe it was fire crackling pleasantly in the fireplace. Or maybe it was simply the fact that she'd barely slept a wink the night before, but she found her eyes beginning to close.

It took a lot of effort to keep them open.

Too much effort.

She closed them, all her muscles relaxing, along with her ever-present vigilance.

And then she fell asleep.

At some point she became aware that she was in someone's arms and was being carried somewhere. Normally that would have been enough to have her struggling wildly and waking up. But a familiar warm and spicy scent wound around her, and a comforting heat against her side was easing her instinctive panic.

And instead of struggling she relaxed. Letting the heat and that familiar scent soothe her. Feeling those arms tighten around her.

Where she was being carried, she didn't know, and a minute or so later she didn't care.

She was already asleep again.

CHAPTER FIVE

Cristiano made an effort over the next week to keep an eye on Leonie in an unobtrusive way, stopping by wherever she was working to exchange a few words with her. Sometimes it was just that—a few words—and sometimes it was more of a conversation.

And slowly she began to relax around him. She no longer tensed when he appeared, and during the last two visits, she hadn't even scowled.

He counted it a victory.

Of course the real victory had been that night in his study, when she'd finally given him her name.

Reaching out to grab her wrist had been a gamble, but she'd had to learn that he meant business and that he had his limits. He wasn't a man to be toyed with. Besides, he hadn't been asking for much—just her name.

She'd seemed to understand and the gamble had paid off. She hadn't given him anything else, but he hadn't pushed. He knew when to insist and when to back off. She'd eventually give him what he wanted—he was sure of it.

He'd been even more sure when he'd finished his phone call and turned around to find that she'd fallen asleep in her chair. He hadn't wanted to wake her, since the shadows under her eyes had been pronounced, but nor had he wanted to leave her sleeping in an uncomfortable position.

So, compelled by an instinct he hadn't felt in years, he'd gathered her into his arms and carried her up to her room.

Another gamble, considering how hyper-vigilant she was. But she hadn't woken. Or at least she hadn't panicked. Her lovely red-gold eyelashes had fluttered and her muscles had tensed, and then, just as quickly, she'd relaxed against him. As if she'd decided she was safe.

A mistake on her part, because he wasn't safe—not in any way—but he'd liked the way she'd felt in his arms. Liked the way she'd relaxed against him as if she didn't need to fear him. Liked it too much, truth be told.

Anna had never nestled sleepily in his arms. She'd never been comfortable with his displays of affection. But he was a deeply physical man and that was how he expressed it. She had also known his darkest secret, known the damage he was capable of, and although she'd never said it outright he knew she'd always judged him for it.

He'd tried to contain himself for her, change himself for her, but it hadn't been enough in the end. Victor de Riero had offered her what Cristiano hadn't been able to, and so she'd left him.

But it was dangerous to think of Anna, so he'd shoved his memories of her away and ignored the way Leonie had felt in his arms.

Leonie hadn't mentioned it the next day when he'd stopped by the room where she was dusting, so he hadn't mentioned it, either, merely giving her a greeting and then going on his way.

Which was what he'd done the next couple of days, too, only stopping for longer on the subsequent days after that. And the day before, not only had he not had a scowl, but he thought he might have had a smile. Or at least the beginnings of one.

It was very definitely a start.

But he needed to do more.

He wasn't normally an impatient man, since he never wanted anything enough to get impatient about it, but the thought of revenge had definitely put him in an impatient mood. He needed to gain her trust and then either get her to tell him who she was or reveal that he already knew in a way that wouldn't frighten her off.

After that, he had to ascertain her feelings about her father and find out whether she'd agree to let him widen her job description, as it were. In return for a sizeable bonus, naturally.

It was a good plan, and one he was sure would work, but it would require a certain delicacy. So far he'd done well, but more needed to be accomplished—and faster.

It was a pity trust wasn't one of those things that could be compelled.

He was reflecting on that as he arrived back home late one night the following week. He'd come from a party that had started out as tedious, only to descend into unpleasant when he'd heard Victor de Riero's name being bandied about in a business discussion.

Normally that wouldn't have caused him any concern. He'd detached himself so completely from what had happened fifteen years ago that he could even have attended the same party as the man and not felt a thing.

Yet tonight even the sound of that name had set his anger burning so fiercely that some disconnected part of him had been amazed at the intensity of his emotions when for so long he'd felt nothing. It had been disturbing, and it had made him even more certain that he must move his revenge plan on faster—because the quicker he dealt with it, the easier it would be to put out the fire of his anger once and for all.

He'd left the party early, full of that intense directionless anger, and was still in a foul temper now, as he arrived home. He'd been intending to sit in the library alone, with a very good Scotch, so his mood was not improved when he found that the library was already occupied by Leonie, kneeling on the floor in front of the bookshelves once again.

She was still in her uniform, and there were cleaning implements next to her, even though it was nearly midnight and she should be in bed, asleep. Something jolted in his chest at the sight of that familiar red-gold skein hanging down on her back.

He remembered carrying her to bed that night—how that hair had brushed against his forearm and then drifted over the backs of his hands as he'd bent over to lay her down on the mattress. It had felt very silky, and the urge to touch it, to sift his fingers through it, had gripped him once again. She'd felt light in his arms, but very soft and warm and feminine, and she'd smelled subtly of the rose-scented soap her bathroom had been stocked with.

He'd been very good at not paying attention to his physical reactions around her. Very good at not thinking about that moment of chemistry in his study that night when he'd put his fingers around her wrist, touched her soft skin. And it had been soft, her pulse frantic beneath his fingertips.

It hadn't been a problem before. He was always in complete control of himself, even when it looked to the rest of the world as if he wasn't. Yet right now, looking at her kneeling there, that control seemed suddenly very tenuous.

There'd been enough beautiful women at the party tonight for him to take his pick if it was sex he wanted. He didn't have to have her. She'd be a virgin, too—he'd bet his dukedom on it—and he wasn't into virgins. They were complicated, and the last thing he needed was more complications.

Yet that didn't put a stop to the hunger that gripped him, and his temper, already on a knife-edge, worsened.

Meirda, what was she doing here? Hadn't she finished her work? There were plenty of chairs around. Why wasn't she sitting on one of them? But, most importantly, why wasn't she safely in bed and out of his reach? And why did he always find her poring over a book?

He prowled up behind her, where she knelt, but she didn't look around, once again absorbed in whatever she was reading.

'You can take that upstairs if you want,' he said, unable to keep the growl out of his voice. 'You don't have to sit on the floor.'

She gave a little start, then sprang to her feet, turning around quickly. Her violet-blue eyes were very wide, and one hand automatically went to her pocket—as if her knife was still there and not where he'd seen it last, on her bed-side table.

And then, as she took in his presence, her posture relaxed as quickly as it had tensed. 'Oh…' she breathed. 'It's you.'

He should have been pleased by how quickly she'd calmed, since it indicated more progress towards her trusting him. But tonight he wasn't pleased. Tonight it rubbed against his vile temper like salt in a wound. She was the daughter of his enemy and he was going to use her to get his revenge on that *hijo de puta*. She should be afraid of him. He was dangerous—and most especially when he was angry.

Hadn't Anna always told him that he frightened her? She'd been right to be scared. He was capable of such destruction when he let his emotions get the better of him. This little kitten should be cowering, not relaxing as if she was safe.

'Yes, it is,' he agreed, his temper burning with a sullen heat. 'What are you doing in the library at this time of night?' It came out as an accusation, which wasn't helpful, but he didn't bother to adjust his tone. He wasn't in the mood for adjusting himself for anyone tonight. 'You should go to bed.'

'I was working late.' Her forehead creased, her violet-blue gaze studying him. 'Are you all right?'

A dart of something sharp he couldn't identify shot through him. Was his temper that noticeable? Maybe it was. He hadn't exactly been hiding it after all. Still, he hadn't been asked that question in a very long time. Years, possibly. Not by his staff, not his few close friends, not his lovers. And the fact that this homeless girl should be the first one to have even a fleeting concern for his wellbeing annoyed him all the more.

He smiled without humour. 'Of course. Why would you imagine I'm anything other than all right?'

'Because you're...' She made a gesture at him.

'Because I'm what?' He took a leisurely step towards her. 'Have you been watching me, *gatita*?'

Her cheeks flooded with telltale colour. 'No, I haven't.'

A lie. She *had* been watching him. How interesting.

You should order her upstairs. Away from you. Nothing good comes from your temper—you know this already.

Oh, he knew. He knew all too well. But he was tired of having to do what he always did, which was to shove that temper away. Beat it down so no one would ever know it was there. Tired of having to pretend he didn't feel it, of having to restrain himself all the time.

Dios, she was the one who'd brought all this to the surface again. This was her fault if it was anyone's.

So what are you going to do? Punish her?

He ignored the thought, taking another step towards her. 'I think you have. I think you've been watching me. And why is that?' He let his voice drop to a low purr. 'Do you see something you like?'

Something flickered through her eyes, though he couldn't tell what it was. It wasn't fear, though, and he didn't understand. She was normally wary, and yet she wasn't wary now, which was strange. Had he done his job already? Did she trust him?

Silly *gatita*. Perhaps he should show her what she had to be afraid about.

He closed the distance between them, crowding her very purposefully back against the bookshelves, and this time obvious alarm rippled across her pretty face. He was standing close enough to feel the warmth of her body and inhale the faint, sweet scent of roses. Close enough to see the pulse beating fast beneath the pale skin at the base of her throat.

Fool. Giving in to your temper will undo all the progress you've made, and you swore you wouldn't make any more mistakes this time.

Cold realisation swept through him—of what he was doing and how badly he'd allowed his control to slip. She was supposed to trust him, supposed to feel safe with him—that was the whole point. And he wasn't supposed to make any more mistakes.

'You should leave,' he forced out, trying to handle the fury that coursed through him. 'I'm not fit company right now.'

She gave him another of those wary looks, but didn't move. 'Why not?'

'Too much wine, too many women, and not enough song.' He tried to hold on to his usual lazy, casual demeanour, baring his teeth in what he hoped was a smile, but probably wasn't. 'Leave, Leonie. I'm not in the mood to be kind.'

Yet again she made no move, only studied him as if he

was a mystery she wanted to unravel and not a man she should be afraid of. A man whose passions ran too hot for anyone's comfort.

'Why?' she asked again. 'What happened?'

His fury wound tighter. He didn't want to talk about this with her and he didn't know why she was even interested. She shouldn't be wanting to know more; she should be running back upstairs to the safety of her room.

'I commend your interest in my wellbeing, *gatita*. But I think it is a mistake.' He moved closer since she wasn't getting the message. 'I'm telling you to leave for a reason.'

She was still pressed up against the bookshelves behind her but, strangely, her earlier alarm seemed to have vanished. Instead she was frowning slightly, searching his face as if looking for something, her gaze full of what looked like…concern, almost.

You've done nothing to deserve it.

No, he hadn't. Not a single damn thing.

Her scent wrapped around him and he was aware that the black T-shirt of her uniform was very fitted, outlining to perfection the soft curves of her breasts. They were round and full, just the right size for his hands. Would they be sensitive if he touched them? If he put his mouth to them? Kissed them and sucked on her nipples? Some women were very sensitive there, the slightest touch making them moan, while others needed firmer handling…

'What reason is that?' Leonie asked, and her sweet husky voice did nothing to halt the flood of sexual awareness coursing through him.

There was no alarm in the question, and her gaze was direct. Almost as if she was challenging him. Which would be either very brave, or very foolish, especially when he was in this kind of mood.

'You don't want to know,' he said roughly. 'It might frighten you.'

A spark glowed suddenly in the depths of her eyes. 'I'm not scared of you.'

It was fascinating, that spark. It burned bright and hot and he couldn't drag his gaze from it. Yes, this time it was definitely a challenge, and all he could think about was the fact that Anna had never looked at him that way. Anna had never challenged him—not once.

'You should be.' His voice had deepened, become even rougher, and his groin tightened in response to her nearness. 'I've told you before. I'm not a kind man.'

'That's a lie.' She gave him another searching look, apparently oblivious to the danger. 'You've been nothing but kind since I got here.'

Naturally she'd think that. She wasn't to know that he was being kind only because he wanted something from her. That he wasn't doing this out of the goodness of his heart, but to appease his own desire for vengeance.

Tell her, then. Tell her so she knows.

But if he told her she might run, and he couldn't afford for her to do that. Not yet.

She might run from you anyway if you keep on like this.

It was true. Which meant he needed to pull himself together—perhaps call one of those women who'd indicated interest tonight. It had been a while since he'd taken anyone to bed, so maybe it was that getting to him. Sex had always been his go-to when it came to working out his more primitive emotions. That was why he revelled in it.

'My kindness has a threshold,' he said instead. 'And you're approaching it.'

Her head tilted, her gaze still bright. Almost as if she was pushing him.

'Why? What have I done? You're not very good at answering questions, are you?'

He should have moved—should have stepped away. Should definitely not still be standing there, so close to her, now he'd decided he was going to find some alternative female company.

Yet he couldn't bring himself to move. He was caught by the bright spark in her eyes and by her sweet scent. There was colour in her cheeks still and the pulse at the base of her throat was beating even faster. Her mouth was full and red. Such temptation.

He could kiss that mouth. He could stop her questions and her ill-considered challenges simply by covering it with his own. Would she taste sweet? As sweet as she smelled?

'You haven't done anything but be where you shouldn't be.' He lifted his hand before he could stop himself and gently brushed her bottom lip with his fingertips. 'Which is a mistake, *gatita*.'

Her mouth was as soft as he'd thought it would be, and velvety like rose petals. She stilled, her eyes going wide. But she didn't pull away.

Aren't you going to find yourself another woman?

He was. So why he wasn't—why he was standing here and touching *this* woman he had no idea. It shouldn't matter which woman he touched, and since Anna he'd made sure it didn't. He didn't need someone who was his—not again.

Not when you can't be trusted with them.

The thought should have made him move away. But it didn't. Instead, he put one hand on the bookshelf behind her head, leaning over her while he dragged the tip of his finger across the softness of her skin, tracing the line of her lower lip.

She shivered, taking another audible breath, her gaze

never leaving his face. Her body was stiff with tension and yet she didn't move, the spark in her eyes leaping higher.

'Why are you touching me?' Her voice had become even huskier than normal.

'Why do you think?'

Every muscle in his body had tightened; his groin was aching. His anger had dulled. Physical desire was smoothing the sharp edges and making it less acute. Replacing it with another, safer hunger.

'This is the reason you should have left, Leonie.' He dragged his finger gently over her bottom lip once more, pressing against the full softness of it. 'Because you're a lovely woman and I'm a very, *very* bad man.'

LEONIE COULDN'T MOVE. Or rather, she probably could—it was more that she didn't want to. And she didn't understand why, because what the duke was doing to her should have sent her bolting from the room in search of her knife.

A week ago it would have.

But that had been before she'd spent a whole week in his house, cleaning the rooms she'd been assigned to. A whole week of a comfortable bed and good food, of being clean and dry and warm. A whole week of being safe.

A whole week of him stopping by every day to visit her—sometimes just to say hello, sometimes to chat.

She hadn't realised how much she liked his little visits until the fourth day, when he hadn't stopped by the room she was cleaning and she'd begun to feel annoyed, wondering if she'd missed him. Wondering if she'd been forgotten.

If she'd still been the Leonie of a week ago being forgotten would have been preferable. But she wasn't that Leonie. Not since she'd fallen asleep in his study that night and he'd gathered her up in his arms and put her to bed.

She'd woken the next morning disorientated and restless,

panicking slightly when she'd realised what had happened. But when she'd jerked back the quilt she'd found she was still fully clothed. Only her shoes had been removed. She'd been asleep, at her most vulnerable, and all he'd done was tuck her into bed.

Perhaps that was why she felt no fear now, even though he was definitely touching her and threatening her into the bargain. But it wasn't a threat like those she'd experienced before, that promised only violence and pain. No, this was different. This promised something else, and she wasn't at all sure she wouldn't like whatever it was he was promising.

Especially if it was this prickling kind of heat sweeping over her, making her mouth feel full and sensitive. Making something inside her pulse hard and low, with that same hunger she'd felt the night he'd gripped her wrist.

Unfamiliar feelings. Good feelings.

She didn't want to move in case they vanished, as everything good in her life always seemed to do.

She tipped her head back against the bookshelf, staring up him, right into those intense green eyes. There was a flame burning there, giving out more heat than the fire that night in his study, and she wanted more of it. More of the heat of his tall, powerful body so close to hers.

Men had never been anything but threatening to her before, and sex something only offered as a transaction or taken with violence. She knew that there was more to it than that, because she'd watched couples holding hands in the streets. Couples hugging. Couples kissing.

She'd once been interrupted by a well-dressed man and woman slipping into the alley she'd been sleeping in at the time, and had watched unseen from behind a pile of boxes as the man had gently pressed the woman to the brick wall of the alley and lifted her dress. The woman had moaned, but not in protest. Her hands had clutched at the man, pulling him to her, and when she'd cried out it hadn't been in pain.

Leonie had wondered what it would be like to be that woman, but she knew she never would be. Because to be that woman she'd have to be clean and wear a nice dress. To be that woman she'd have to be cared for, and the only person who'd ever cared for her was herself.

So, since physical pleasure was not for people like her, she'd had to settle on invisibility instead. Blending into the background and never calling attention to herself, staying unnoticed and unseen, the way her mother had always taught her.

Except she wasn't unseen now. The duke had seen her, and continued to see her, and with every brush of his finger he made her more and more visible. More and more aware of how she liked that touch, how she wanted it. How cold she'd been before, and also how lonely.

And now he was here, with his hot green eyes and his hard, muscular body, and he was touching her.

He was turning her into that woman in the pretty dress in the alley and she liked it. She didn't want to run away. She wanted to be that woman. The woman who deserved pleasure and who got it.

'I don't think you're bad.' She held his gaze, every nerve-ending she had focused on the touch of his finger on her mouth. 'If you were that bad you wouldn't have told me to leave.'

'I don't think you know bad men, in that case.'

His gaze was all-consuming, a dark forest full of secrets, making her want to journey into it, discover what those secrets were.

'Of course I do.' Her mouth felt achingly sensitive. His touch was so light it was oddly maddening. 'I see them all the time on the streets. And I avoid them whenever I can.'

'So why aren't you running now?'

He shifted, leaning a fraction closer, bracing himself on the bookshelf behind her while his fingers moved on her mouth, his thumb pressing gently on her lip as if testing it.

'Or perhaps it's because you can't see past a warm bed and good food.'

That could be true. He might have lulled her into a false sense of security. She'd been wrong a couple of times before. But she didn't think she was wrong now. He'd had plenty of opportunity to touch her, to take what he wanted, and he hadn't. He had no reason to do so now.

Yes, so why now?

Good point. His obvious sexual interest was rather sudden. Perhaps he didn't want her the way she thought he did. Perhaps he was only trying to frighten her away.

After all, he'd been in a strange mood when he'd come in, with a sharp, raw energy to him, his eyes glittering like shards of green glass. Anger, she was sure, though she wasn't sure why.

Perhaps he'd come into the library hoping for some time to himself and found her there instead, intruding. Ignoring him when he told her to leave. And now he'd had to take more drastic steps to scare her off.

He doesn't want you, idiot. Why would he?

Her stomach dipped, an aching disappointment filling her. There was no reason for him to want her. She was just a homeless person he'd rescued from the streets and for some reason been kind to. And because she hadn't taken the hint and left when he'd asked her to he'd had to be more explicit. All this touching and getting close to her wasn't actually about *her*, and she'd be an idiot to think otherwise.

She tore her gaze away, not wanting him to see her disappointment or the hurt that had lodged inside her. 'Perhaps you're right. Perhaps you're really not all that kind after all.' She tried to sound as level as she could. 'If you want me to go, you'd better move.'

Yet the hard, masculine body crowding her against the bookshelves didn't move. She stared at the fine white cotton of his shirt—he was in evening clothes tonight, so it was obvious he'd been to some fancy party or other—her heartbeat thudding in her ears, a sick feeling in her gut.

Then the finger stroking her mouth dropped, as did the arm near her ear, and the duke straightened up, giving her some room.

The feeling of disappointment deepened.

She pushed herself away from the bookshelf, wanting to get away now, to get some distance from him. But before she could go past him, his fingers closed around her upper arm.

Her bare upper arm.

Leonie froze. His fingers burned against her skin the way they had that night in his study, making her breath catch and that restless heat sweep over her yet again.

She didn't look at him, staring straight ahead, her pulse racing. 'I thought you wanted me to go?'

'I thought I did, too.' His voice was dark, with threads of heat winding through it. 'You're really not scared of me, are you?'

'Does it matter?' She tried not to shiver in response to the sound of his voice, though it was difficult. 'I'm sorry I was here when you came in. I know you wanted to be alone, and I shouldn't—'

His fingers tightened around her arm abruptly and she broke off.

'Why did you think I wanted to be alone?' he demanded.

'You looked angry, and I shouldn't have been in here.'

'You're fine to be in here. Also, yes, it does matter.'

His fingers felt scorching. 'You should let me go.' She

kept her gaze on the wall opposite, trying to ignore his heat and the delicious scent of his aftershave. 'I know you were trying to scare me away—but, for the record, it won't work.'

There was a tense silence, full of the same humming tension that had surrounded them last week in his study.

'It won't, hmm…?'

Unexpectedly, his thumb stroked the underside of her arm in a caress that sent goosebumps scattering all over her skin. 'That's something you shouldn't have told me.'

'Why not?'

'Because it only makes me want try harder to scare you, of course.'

The sound of her heart hammered in her ears. She stared blindly across the room, every sense she possessed concentrated on the man standing beside her, holding her.

Was that another warning? And if it was, why was he still holding her? If he really wanted her to leave he only needed to open his hand and she'd be free.

Yet he hadn't.

She tried to process what that meant, but it was difficult when his thumb was pressing against the sensitive flesh of her under-arm, caressing lightly.

You could pull away. You don't have to stand here.

That was true. She didn't need to stand there being reminded of how empty and cold her life was, of all the good things she was missing out on. She didn't need to be reminded of how unwanted and unneeded she was.

Anyway, she had a warm bed, and food, and a job. Wanting more than that was just being greedy. She should be happy with what she had.

'All this talk of scaring me and being bad—yet you're not doing anything but hold on to me.' She kept her gaze resolutely ahead. 'I know you don't really want me. So why don't you just be done with it and let me go?'

There was a moment of silence and then she was being tugged around to face him, his glittering green gaze clashing with hers.

'What on earth makes you think I don't want you?' he demanded.

'Why would you?' She lifted her chin, prepared for the truth, ignoring the hurt lodged deep inside her. 'I'm just some poor homeless woman you picked up from the streets. No one else has ever wanted me so why should you?'

The hot flame in his eyes leapt, an emotion she couldn't name flickering over his handsome face. *'Gatita...'*

He looked as if he might say something more, but he didn't. Instead he jerked her suddenly towards him.

Not expecting it, she flung up her hands, her palms connecting with the heat and hardness of his broad chest. His fingers had curled around both her upper arms now, keeping her prisoner, and he'd bent his head, so his green eyes were all she could see.

'You are very foolish indeed if you think that,' he said, in a soft, dangerous voice.

Then, before she could say anything more, his mouth covered hers.

She froze in shock. She'd never been kissed before—had never wanted to be. Although sometimes, when the nights were very dark and she was especially cold, she'd remember that man and woman in the alleyway. Remember how the woman had cried out and how the man had kissed her, silencing her. And she'd wonder what it would feel like to have someone's mouth touching hers. Kissing her...

Now she knew. And it became very clear why that woman had clutched at the man kissing her.

The duke's lips were warm, so much softer than she'd expected a man's lips to be, and the subtle pressure and implicit demand were making a river of unfamiliar heat course the length of her spine.

She trembled, curling her fingers into the warm cotton of his shirt, her own mouth opening beneath his almost automatically. And he took advantage, his tongue pushing inside, tasting her, coaxing her, beginning to explore her.

A low, helpless moan escaped her. The delicious flavour of him was filling her senses and making her want more. She clutched at his shirt tighter, pressing herself closer. The heat of his kiss was melting all the frozen places inside her. All the lonely places. Lighting up all the dark corners of her soul.

Her awareness narrowed on the heat of his mouth, the slow exploration of his tongue, the dark, rich flavour that was all him and the iron-hard body she was pressed against.

It was overwhelming.

It was not enough.

It was everything she'd missed out on, all the good things she'd never had, and now she'd had a taste she wanted more.

She wanted them all.

'Cristiano…' she murmured against his mouth. And the name he'd given her, that she'd only used once before now, came out of her as easily as breathing. 'Please…'

CHAPTER SIX

He shouldn't have kissed her. Yet now her mouth was open beneath his, the sweet taste of her was on his tongue and the slender heat of her body was pressed against him, he couldn't stop.

She was right in thinking he'd been trying to scare her. And he'd expected it to be easy—that a blatantly sexual touch would have her jerking away from him and leaving the room.

But she hadn't run as he'd anticipated. Because it seemed she never did the thing he anticipated.

Instead she'd only stayed where she was and let him touch her. Let his fingers trace her soft mouth, looking up at him, her eyes darkening with what could only be arousal.

He should have let her go. He hadn't needed to keep holding on to her and he wasn't sure why he had. He certainly shouldn't have compounded his mistake by covering her mouth with his—not when he'd already decided that he wasn't going to have her.

But something in his heart had stopped him. Because the way she'd looked so defiantly up at him, telling him that no one had ever wanted her before and why should he... Well, he hadn't been able to stand it.

A kiss to prove her wrong—that was all it was supposed

to be. A kiss to ease the hurt she hadn't been able to hide.
And maybe, too, a kiss to frighten her away once and for all.

*No, you kissed her because you wanted to, because you
wanted her.*

Whatever the reason, it didn't matter. What did matter was the furnace that had roared to life inside him the
minute her mouth was under his. The very second he'd felt
her soften and melt against him, a throaty, husky moan escaped her.

And he wasn't sure why, or what it was about her that
had got him burning hot and instantly hard. Yet as she
arched against him, her fingers tugging on his shirt, the
desire that just about strangled him was as if he hadn't had
a woman in months. Years, even.

He could taste her desperation, could feel it in the way
she pressed against him, in the sound of his name whispered in her husky voice, so erotic it felt as if she'd reached
inside his trousers and wrapped her fingers directly around
his shaft.

Anna had never done any of those things during sex.
She'd never clutched at him, never moaned his name or
pressed herself against him. She'd found his brand of earthy,
physical sexuality uncomfortable, telling him he was too
demanding. He'd tried to be less so, restraining himself to
make her comfortable, turning sex from something passionate into something softer, more palatable, and thus more
acceptable. Though it still hadn't been enough for her.

Since she'd left, and since his son had been claimed by
another, he'd lost his taste for passion. Something easy,
fun and pleasurable—that was all he wanted from sex,
nothing more. His lovers could touch his body but they
touched nothing else, and that was the way he made sure
it always was.

But there was something about the way Leonie clutched

at his shirt, her mouth open and hungry beneath his, whispering his name against his lips, that reached inside him, unleashing something he'd kept caged for a long time.

Raw, animal passion.

Perhaps it was because she wasn't a random woman he'd met at a party, or some pretty socialite he'd picked up at a bar. A woman who didn't want more from him than one night and a couple of orgasms, and that was all.

Perhaps it was the wrongness of it. Because there were so many reasons why it was a bad idea. She'd been living on the streets. She was homeless. She was a virgin. She was the daughter of his enemy and he was going to use her to get his revenge. He should not be hard for her, let alone kissing her hungrily late at night in his study.

And yet when she whispered, 'Cristiano... Please...' and arched against him, the soft curves of her breasts pressing against his chest, the sound of his name spoken in her husky voice echoing in his ears, all he could think about was giving her exactly what she was begging for.

After all, who was he to deny her? He'd never been a man to refuse anyone when it came to sex, still less one bright and beautiful woman whom he wanted very much.

Besides, perhaps taking her would cement what trust there was between them rather than break it. And when desire was this strong it was always better not to fight it. Always better to take command and sate it so it was easier to control later on.

That all sounds like some excellent justification.

But Cristiano was done listening to his better self.

He dropped his hands from her upper arms to her hips, letting them rest there a second to get her used to his touch. Then he slid them higher, until his palms were gently cupping her breasts.

She gave another of those delicious little moans, shud-

dering and then arching into his hands like a cat wanting to
be stroked. He kept his mouth on hers, making the kiss teasing as he traced her soft curves with his fingertips before
brushing his thumbs over the hard outlines of her nipples.

She gasped and he wanted to devour her whole, but he
forced himself to lift his mouth from hers instead, to stare
down into her face to check if she was still with him. Her
cheeks were deeply flushed, her lips full and red from the
kiss.

'Why did you stop?' she asked breathlessly. 'Please don't.'

Oh, yes, she was with him.

Satisfaction pulsed through him and he took her mouth
again, nipping at her bottom lip at the same time as he
pinched her nipples lightly, making her jerk and shudder
against him.

His own heartbeat roared in his ears; his groin was aching. He wanted her naked, wanted her skin bare to his
touch, wanted her hands on him, clutching at him. He
wanted her desperate for him.

He'd given her food and drink. Given her a job. Given
her a bed. And now he wanted to give her pleasure, too. He
didn't pause to examine why this was important to him—
he just wanted to.

*Dangerous. You know how you get when you give in to
your passions.*

Ah, but this was only sex. It wouldn't touch his emotions in any way. He'd make sure of it.

'*Gatita,*' he murmured roughly against her hungry
mouth. 'In ten seconds I'm going to have you naked on
the floor, so if that's not what you want you'd better tell
me right now.'

'I want it.' There was no hesitation in her voice, no coy
dancing around the subject. 'Cristiano, please—I want it.'

Desire soaked through every husky word, and when

he lifted his head and looked down into her eyes a part of him was shocked by the nakedness of her desire. Because she made no effort to hide it. Everything she felt was laid bare for him to see, exposing a vulnerability he was sure she hadn't meant to expose.

He could use that against her if he chose—get her to do anything he wanted if he handled it right. Even convince her to be his wife, for example. And if he'd been a more unscrupulous man...

What are you talking about? You are an unscrupulous man.

Oh, he was. But there was something innocent about Leonie, an honesty that he found almost painful. And he could not bring himself to take advantage of it.

Though she should know better than to let herself be so vulnerable—especially with a man like him. He was dangerous and hadn't he told her that? She needed to be more wary, more on her guard.

He bent his head further, moving his mouth to her jaw, kissing down the side of her neck and nipping her again in sensual punishment. But, again, she didn't push him away, only pulled harder on his shirt instead, as if she wanted more.

It was like petrol being poured over an already blazing fire, making his own passion leap high and hot.

Without another word, he lifted her into his arms and carried her over to the soft silk rug in front of the empty fireplace. Then he laid her down on it and took the hem of her T-shirt in his hands, dragging it up and over her head.

She didn't stop him, and a wave of gorgeous pink swept down her throat and over her chest as he uncovered her. The colour turned her eyes a vivid blue and made the plain black bra she wore stand out. But not for long. He undid the catch and stripped that from her, too, leaving her upper body bare.

Instantly her hands went to cover herself, but he caught her wrists, preventing her. 'No,' he said roughly, unable to keep his voice level. 'I want to look at you.'

She swallowed, but there was no resistance in her as he pushed her down onto her back, taking her arms above her head and pinning them to the rug, gripping her crossed wrists in one hand.

Lying there stretched out beneath him, all silky pale skin, her breasts exposed, hard nipples flushed a deep pink, she was the most delectable thing he'd ever seen.

He stared down into her eyes, watching the passion that burned there burn even higher as he stroked his free hand up and down her sides.

'Cristiano...' she said breathlessly, shivering.

'What it is, *gatita*? Do you need more?' He moved his hand to cup one of those perfect breasts, felt her skin hot against his palm. 'This, perhaps?'

'Oh...' she sighed. 'That's so—'

She broke off on a gasp as he rubbed his thumb over one hard nipple before pinching it, watching the pleasure chase itself over her lovely face. Her body arched beneath his hand, her lashes half closing.

'Oh...that's so good. More...'

His little kitten was demanding.

Yours? Already?

Maybe. And why not? No one else had claimed her, so why couldn't he? She was so very responsive, so very rewarding. Making her gasp like that might even become addictive.

He pinched her again, rolling her nipple between his thumb and forefinger, making her writhe. 'You'd best be more respectful,' he murmured, teasing the tip of her breast relentlessly. 'Please and thank you are always welcome.'

'Please…' She moaned softly, arching yet again beneath him. 'Please, more…'

'So obedient.' He eased his hand lower, over the soft skin of her stomach to the fastening of her plain black trousers. 'I like that, though. I like how you beg for me.'

Flicking open the button of her trousers, he grabbed the zip and drew it down. Then he pushed his hand beneath the fabric and over the front of her underwear. She shuddered as his fingers traced her through the damp cotton, pleasure and a certain wonder making her eyes glow. She was looking at him as though he'd shown her something amazing, the most precious thing in all the universe.

'Oh…' Her eyes went very wide as he pressed a finger gently against the most sensitive part of her and then circled around it, making her hips shudder and lift. 'What are you doing?' She didn't sound alarmed, only a little shocked.

'Giving you pleasure.' His voice came out rougher than he'd intended. 'Does it feel good, Leonie? Does it feel good when I touch you?'

'Yes, oh, yes…' The breath sighed out of her and her gaze fixed to his, more wonder and amazement in her eyes. 'I never thought…it would…feel like this.'

She was so unguarded, so sincere. This woman had been denied a lot of things—warmth and comfort and safety. She'd been denied physical pleasure, too, and that was a crime. Because it was becoming apparent to him that she was a creature of passion, greedy for all the pleasure he could give her. And he had a lot of that to give.

Pleasure wasn't new to him, but for some reason introducing her to it was completely addictive. From the way she shivered under his hand to the flush in her silky skin.

From the sounds she made to the wonder of discovery as she looked at him.

It was a discovery for him as well, he realised. It had been a long time since he'd been engaged in bed. He always gave his partners pleasure, but only in so far as it affected his own reputation. It was never about the woman in particular.

But now it was about this woman. He wanted to give her something she'd never had before—wanted to show her something new. He wanted her to look at him exactly the way she was looking at him now, as if she'd never seen anything or anyone so amazing in all her life.

The way no one, not even Anna, had ever looked at him.

You can't give that up.

A dark, ferocious thing stretched out lazily inside him, flexing its claws.

Well, maybe he didn't have to give it up. Why should he? She wanted him—that was obvious—and passion like hers didn't stay sated. This needn't be a one-off thing. He was planning on marrying her anyway, so why not make it a true marriage for a time?

Are you sure that's a good idea? Look what happened last time with Anna.

Yes, but that had only been because those dangerous emotions of his had been involved, and they weren't here. He didn't love Leonie and she didn't love him. He was simply taking advantage of their intense physical chemistry, nothing more.

She might not feel that way when you tell her you've known who she is all along.

Cristiano ignored that thought, slipping his hand beneath the fabric of her underwear, then sliding his fingers over her slick, wet flesh. She gave a little cry, pushing herself into his touch, her eyes darkening as her pupils dilated.

Satisfaction deepened inside him. He could have watched the pleasure rippling over her face for ever. 'You like that, *mi corazón*? Do you like it when I stroke you here?'

He found the small, sensitive bud between her thighs and brushed the tip of his finger over and around it. She gasped, shivering.

'And here?'

He shifted his hand, put his thumb where his finger had been, then slid that finger down through the slick folds of her sex to the entrance of her body, easing gently inside.

'Do you like it when I touch you here?'

Her cheeks were deeply flushed and she moved restlessly, unable to keep still. 'Yes…' Her voice had become even more hoarse. 'Oh, yes… Cristiano… I need…'

He could become addicted to hearing his name spoken like that…husky and soft and desperate. Just as he could become addicted to the silky, slippery feel of her flesh and the hot grip of her body around his finger. To the way she shook and gasped and arched. To the obvious pleasure she was feeling and didn't hide.

His groin was aching, his own desire winding tight, and he wanted to be inside her with a desperation he hadn't thought possible.

But he wanted to watch her come even more. So he eased his fingers in and out of her, adding more pressure and friction with his thumb until her eyes went wide and her mouth opened and her body convulsed.

She cried out in shocked pleasure as her climax hit, and he leaned down and kissed her, tasting that pleasure for himself.

CRISTIANO'S MOUTH ON hers was so hot and so delicious she could hardly bear it. Waves of the most intense pleasure were shaking her, and all she could do was lie there and let them wash over her.

She'd told him the truth when she'd said she'd had no idea it would feel like this. She really hadn't. Had the woman against that wall felt the same pleasure? Was it this that had made her cry out? Because, yes, *now* she understood. Now she got it completely.

When Cristiano had touched her she'd felt as if something was blooming inside her. A flower she'd thought had died, which had turned out to be only dormant, waiting for the sun, and now the sun was shining and she was opening up to it, revelling in it.

She hadn't been afraid. His kiss had been hot but his hands gentle, and when a fit of modesty had overcome her when he'd taken her bra off he'd been very clear that he wanted to look at her. That he liked looking at her.

And so she'd let him. And the longer he'd looked, the more she'd wanted him to. Because she'd seen the effect she'd had on him, the heat burning in his eyes, and it had made her feel…beautiful. She'd never felt that before, nor ever been conscious of her own feminine power. Her ability to make him burn as much as he made her.

Then he'd touched her, and the world around her had turned to fire.

Perhaps she should be ashamed that she'd been so open with her responses. Perhaps she should have been more guarded. But the pleasure had been too intense, and she simply hadn't been able to hide her feelings.

He'd touched her as if she wasn't some dirty forgotten kid that he'd found on the streets of Paris. He'd touched her as if she was precious…as if she was worth something. He'd touched her as if he cared about her, and she realised that she wanted him to.

It didn't make any sense—not when she hadn't known

him long—yet every touch had only made her more certain. He'd given her many things she'd been missing in her life and now he was giving her another—something she'd never thought she'd want.

And, despite the fact that he'd seemed so angry when he'd come into the library earlier, he wasn't taking that anger out on her. He wasn't taking from her at all.

He was giving to her. Giving heat and a shivery desperation. A delicious need. Pleasure to chase away the cold and the dark, the fear and the loneliness. So much pleasure...

She wanted more of it.

She tried to pull her hands away from his restraining hold, but his grip only firmed as his glittering green eyes scanned her from head to foot.

'Are you okay?'

His voice was a soft, roughened caress, whispering over her skin like velvet.

'Did you like that?'

'Yes. Very much.' She didn't sound much better herself. 'But I want you. I want to touch you.'

There was no hiding it so she didn't bother.

He swept his free hand down the length of her body in a long stroke that soothed her at the same time as it excited her.

'There will be time for that. But first, you're wearing far too many clothes.'

With practiced, careful hands he stripped the rest of the clothing from her body, finally baring her.

She'd thought she might feel terribly vulnerable and exposed, being naked in front of a man. Being naked in front of anyone, really. But she didn't feel either of those things. Only strangely powerful as he pulled the fabric away from her and she saw the look on his face became hungrier, sharper, as if the sight of her was something he'd been waiting lifetimes for.

And when she was finally naked, lying back on the rug, he knelt over her, his gaze roaming all over her body, and she felt for the first time in her life as if maybe there was something worthwhile about her after all.

What it was, she didn't know. But it was certainly something that had this powerful duke looking at her as if she was the Holy Grail itself.

He ran his fingertips lightly all over her, inciting her, watching her face as he did so, gauging her every response as if there was nothing more important in the world than discovering which touches made her shiver and which made her moan. Which ones made her pant his name.

She'd long since lost any shyness by the time he pushed apart her legs, brushing his mouth over her trembling stomach before moving further down. And then all she could do was thread her fingers in his hair as he put that clever mouth of his between her thighs.

Pleasure exploded through her as he began to explore, his fingers delicately parting her wet flesh while his tongue licked and caressed, driving her higher and higher. Making her cry out as the most delicious ecstasy threaded through her.

She'd never thought this feeling would be hers. Never thought that sex could be something so intense, so incredible, that it would feel so good. She'd never thought it would make her feel treasured and desired rather than dirty and worthless, but with every flick of his tongue and stroke of his hand that was what he made her feel.

She pulled on his hair, crying his name as he pushed his tongue inside her and she shattered for a second time, her climax so all-consuming that all she could do was lie there with her eyes closed as it washed over her, feeling him stroke her gently as he moved away.

Then there came the rustle of clothing and the sound of a zip being drawn down, the crinkle of foil. And then the brush of hot skin on hers, setting every nerve-ending to aching life once again.

She opened her eyes.

The duke was kneeling between her spread thighs, tall, powerful and extremely naked. And somehow he seemed even more intimidating without his clothes on, because all that lazy amusement, the studied air of ennui, had vanished completely as if it had never been.

It was a smokescreen, she realised. A distraction. A disguise hiding the true nature of the man beneath it.

She'd imagined him as a panther, lazily sunning himself on a branch, and he was that. But a panther was a predator—and that was what she was looking at now, not the lazy cat.

He was all velvet tanned skin drawn over sharply defined muscle, broad and powerful and strong. A work of art. A Greek statue come to life. As hard as the bronze from which he'd been fashioned yet not cold, but hot. Heated metal and oiled silk.

And his beautiful face was drawn tight with hunger and intent. His eyes had narrowed; hot emerald was glittering from between silky black lashes. The panther ready to pounce. The predator ready to feast.

A delicious shiver chased over her body and she allowed herself to look down to where he was hot and hard and ready for her. She'd never thought that could be beautiful as well, but it was. She pushed herself up on one hand and reached to touch him, and he made no move to stop her, letting her fingers brush along the velvet-smooth skin of his shaft.

She looked up at his face as she did it, wanting to see what effect her touch had on him, and was thrilled to see a muscle jump in the side of his impressive jaw.

'No playing, *gatita*,' he murmured, his rich voice dark and thick with heat. 'Like I said, my patience is limited.'

'I want to touch you, though.' She closed her fingers around him, marvelling at how hard he was and yet how soft and smooth his skin felt. 'You're so hard...' She squeezed experimentally.

He hissed, and then suddenly everything was moving very quickly. He pulled her hand away and pushed her down on her back, his long, muscular body settling over hers. She protested, but he shook his head, the smile he gave her sharp and edged.

'You can touch me later. Seems I have limited patience where you are concerned.'

She liked that. Liked the way her touch could incite him the way his could incite her.

She wanted to help him with the protection, too, but he gave a sharp shake of his head, dealing with it himself. And then his hands were sliding beneath her bottom, gripping her tight and lifting her, and he was positioning himself so he was pressing gently at her entrance.

'Are you ready for me?'

His jaw was set and hard, every muscle in his body drawn tight and ready. All that strength and power was held back, and not without effort. But it was definitely held back. For her.

'Answer me. I'm not made of stone.'

What a lie. He *was* made of stone. Not bronze after all, but hard, living rock that she couldn't stop touching. Enduring and powerful. She could shelter beneath him right here and nothing would touch her.

The feeling was so intense she put her hands on his chest

and spread out her fingers, stroking up over all that hard muscle to his strong shoulders. Holding on.

'I'm ready,' she whispered.

And he didn't hesitate, his fingers tightening as he pushed into her. She gasped as she felt her flesh part for him, in an intense yet delicious stretch, and tensed, ready for pain, because this was supposed to hurt. Yet apart from a slight pinch there was nothing. Only more of that sensual stretch that had her panting and twisting in his arms as she tried to adjust to the sensation.

'Look at me,' he ordered. 'Look at me, Leonie.'

So she did, staring straight up into his eyes, and suddenly everything clicked into place. She was made for him. Her body was made especially for him—for his hands and his mouth, for the hard, male part of him, and he was where he was supposed to be. He might be holding her, but she was also holding him.

'Cristiano…' She lingered over the sound of it, loving how it felt to say it. Loving, too, the way his eyes flared as she said it. So she said it again, digging her nails into his skin, lifting her hips, because she was ready for him to move. Ready for him to take her on another journey.

'Demanding, *gatita*,' he growled. 'You are perfect.'

Then he covered her mouth in a kiss so hot and blinding she trembled and he began to move, the long, lazy glide of him inside her making more of that intense, delicious pleasure sweep over her.

She tried to press herself harder against him, because it wasn't quite enough and she didn't know how to get more, and then he reached down and hooked one hand behind her knee, drawing her leg up and around his hip, allowing him to sink deeper, and she moaned in delight against his mouth.

He felt so good. The glide of his hips, the silk of his skin, the flex and release of all those powerful muscles as he thrust in and out. The warm spice of his scent was cut through with the musk of his arousal. It was delicious.

She sank her teeth into his lower lip, hardly aware of what she was doing, only knowing she wanted even more of him and this insanely pleasurable movement. He growled in response—a deep rumble in his chest that sent chills through her.

Yes, she wanted the panther. The raw untamed part of him, not the lazy, civilised man he was on the outside. Not the smokescreen. Did anyone else know he was this way? Was he like this when he made love to other women?

She didn't like that thought—not at all. She wanted him to be like this with her and only her.

She bit him again, scratching him with her nails, thrilled when he grabbed her hands and held them down on either side of her head.

He lifted his mouth from hers and looked into her eyes as he thrust hard and deep. 'You like showing me your claws, don't you?' He sounded breathless. 'What's that all about, hmm…?'

'You're not the only one who's bad.' She put a growl of her own into her voice as she pulled her hands away, running her nails down his back in a long scratch, lifting her hips to meet his thrust. 'You're not the one who's dangerous.'

'Is that so?' He thrust harder, pushing deeper, making her gasp and arch her back, her nails digging in. 'Show me how bad you are, then, *leona*. Show me your teeth.'

Pleasure twisted inside her and she turned her head, bit his shoulder, tasting the salt and musk of his skin, loving how he gave another growl deep in his throat and moved faster.

She clung to him, licking him, biting him, scratching him as pleasure drew so tight that she didn't think she could bear it. She called his name desperately and he answered, shifting one hand down between them and stroking her where she needed it most. And then she had to turn her face against his neck as everything came apart inside her. Tears flooded her eyes and she was sobbing his name as ecstasy annihilated her.

She had a dim sense of him moving faster, harder, and then she heard his own roar of release, felt his arms coming around her and holding her, his big, hot body over her and around her, inside her.

Protecting her.

CHAPTER SEVEN

Cristiano pulled a shirt on, slowly doing up the buttons, then methodically starting on the cuffs. He stood at the window of his bedroom while he did so, his attention on the garden below, though he wasn't looking at the view.

He was too busy thinking about what he was going to say to the woman still asleep in the bed behind him. His little *gatita*. Though she wasn't really a kitten. Not after last night. Last night he'd discovered she was a lioness, and he had the scratches down his back to prove it.

It would have made him smile if he'd been in a smiling mood, but he wasn't.

There were a number of things he wanted to do, and he couldn't do any of them until he'd told her that he'd known who she was from the moment he'd taken her home. And that he intended to marry her to take his revenge on her father.

She probably wasn't going to take either of those things well.

Are you sure it's wise to tell her now?

He frowned at the garden for a moment, then turned around.

Leonie was curled up in the centre of his bed, her hair a scatter of brilliant red-gold across his white pillows. She was fast sleep, with the sheet falling down off her shoulders a little, revealing pale, milky skin.

Last night she'd felt like pure joy in his hands, passionate and generous and honest. Pleasure had been a discovery and she a fascinated explorer. She'd denied him nothing, taken everything he'd given, and now all he could think about was doing it again. And again and again.

He hadn't had sex like that in years—if ever.

Leonie hadn't found his passion frightening or uncomfortable, the way Anna had. No, she'd demanded it. And then, when he'd given it to her, she'd demanded more.

His groin hardened, and the decision he'd made in the early hours of the morning, when he'd had to get up and have a cold shower so he could sleep, was now a certainty.

He'd take her back to San Lorenzo, his ancestral estate. There he would have her all to himself. He could certainly tell her about his plans here, but perhaps it would be better if she was at home in Spain. Where he could keep an eye on her.

The chances of her running away or not wanting anything to do with him once she found out about his plans were slim—or so he anticipated—but it was better to be safe than sorry.

Plus, marrying her in the ancient Velazquez family chapel would no doubt rub further salt in the wound for Victor de Riero. A further declaration of Cristiano's possession.

And if she refuses to marry you?

He would just ensure that she wouldn't. Everyone had a price, and no doubt so did she.

Finishing with his cuffs, he moved over to the bed and bent, stroking his fingers along one bare shoulder, smiling as she shivered. Her red-gold lashes fluttered and then she let out a small sigh, rolling over onto her back. The sheet fell all the way to her waist, exposing those small, perfect breasts and their little pink nipples.

He was very tempted to taste one of them, to make her

gasp the way he had the night before. But that wouldn't get them any closer to San Lorenzo, and now he'd decided to go he saw no reason to linger in Paris.

'Wake up, sleepy *gatita*,' he murmured, unable to stop himself from brushing his fingers over one pert nipple, watching as it hardened, feeling his own hunger tighten along with it.

She sighed and lifted her arms, giving such a sensual stretch he almost changed his plans right there and then in favour of staying a few more hours in bed with her.

Her eyes opened, deep violet this morning, and she smiled. It took his breath away.

'Good morning.' Her gaze dropped down his body before coming to his face again. 'You're dressed. That's unfortunate.'

He smiled, the beast inside him stretching again, purring in pleasure at her blatant stare. 'Hold that thought. I have plans for us today.'

'What plans?' Her eyes widened and she sat up suddenly. 'What's the time? Am I late for work? Where are my—?'

'There will be no work for you today. Or perhaps any other day.'

He saw shock, hurt and anger ripple across her lovely face. 'Why not? I thought I—'

'Relax, *mi corazón*. I have another position in mind for you.' He sat on the side of the bed and reached for her small hand, holding it in his. 'I'm planning to return to my estate in Spain.'

'Oh.' Her expression relaxed. And then she frowned. 'Why?'

Naturally she would have questions. She was nothing if not curious.

'I have some things that need attention and I haven't been back for a while.'

Years, in reality. Fifteen of them, to be exact. But she didn't need to know that.

He turned her hand over in his, stroking her palm with his thumb. 'It would please me very much to take you with me.'

She glanced down at her hand, enclosed in his. 'But what about my job here? Camille wouldn't like it if I suddenly left with no word.' Another troubled expression crossed her face. 'She wouldn't like it if she knew what I…what we…'

'Leave Camille to me.' He stroked her palm reassuringly, noting how she shivered yet again. 'And, like I told you, I have another position in mind for you.'

She looked up at him, her gaze very direct. 'What position? Your lover?'

There was a challenging note in her voice and he couldn't help but like how unafraid she was to confront him. She was strong, that was for certain, and although she might have been an innocent when it came to sex, she wasn't an innocent in anything else. She'd lived for years on the streets. She would have seen all kinds of cruel things, seen the basest of human nature. She knew how the world worked and knew that it was not kind.

If you tell her the truth she'll understand. She, more than anyone, will know what it's like to lose everything.

It was true. And if she didn't—well, there was always the money option. Either way, it wouldn't be an issue.

'Is there a problem with that?' he asked casually. 'You seemed to enjoy it well enough last night.'

She glanced down once again at her hand resting in his, at his thumb stroking gently her palm. 'So will that now be my job?'

The question sounded neutral, but he knew it wasn't.

'To be your whore?' The word was like a stone thrown

against glass, jagged and sharp. 'Will you pay me more to be in your bed, Cristiano?'

The question sounded raw in the silence of the room. It wasn't a simple challenge now, because there was something else in her tone. She sounded...vulnerable, and he had the sense that he'd hurt her somehow.

You have hurt her.

Anger twisted sharply inside him and he dropped her hand and pushed himself off the bed, striding restlessly over to the window, trying to get his thoughts in order and his ridiculous emotions safely under control again.

The issue, of course, was that she was right. That was exactly what he'd been planning to do. Pay her to be his wife. And since he was also thinking their marriage would include sex, essentially he was paying her to sleep with him.

'Would that be so very bad?' he asked harshly.

There was a brief silence, and then she said in a small voice, 'So that's all last night was? Just a...a transaction?'

Ah, so that was what this was about. She thought the sex had meant something.

It did.

No—and he couldn't afford it to. His emotions had to remain detached, and already they were more engaged than he wanted them to be. His anger was far too close to the surface and she had an ability to rouse it too easily. He had to make sure he stayed uninvolved—that his feelings for her didn't go beyond physical lust.

'I thought last night was all about mutual pleasure,' he said, keeping his tone neutral. 'Though if there was anything transactional about it I apologise.'

'Oh.' Her voice sounded even smaller. 'I see.'

Cristiano's jaw tightened. He hadn't thought about her feelings and he should have. Because of course the sex for her wouldn't simply have been physical. It had been her first time, and she didn't have the experience to tell the difference between great sex and an emotional connection.

Are you sure you do?

He shoved that thought away—hard. Oh, he knew the difference. He wasn't a boy any more. But he couldn't have her thinking that the sex between them had meant more than it had. He also couldn't have her getting under his skin the way she was currently doing.

Which left him with only one option.

He would have to give her the truth.

It would hurt her, but maybe that would be a good thing. Then she would know exactly what kind of man he was. Which was definitely not the kind of man she could have sex that meant something with.

She might not want to have anything to do with you after that.

His chest tightened with a regret and disappointment he didn't want to feel, so he ignored it, placing his hands on the sill and staring sightlessly at the rooftops of Paris.

'I was married years ago,' he said into the silence. 'Both of us were very young—too young, as it turned out. She found me…difficult. And I *was* difficult. But I didn't know that she was so unhappy.' He paused, the words catching unexpectedly in his throat. 'At least not until she left me for someone else.'

Leonie was silent behind him.

'That someone else was an old enemy of my family's,' he went on. 'Someone who befriended me after my parents died and became a mentor to me. I told him about my marriage difficulties in the hope that he'd give me some advice, and he did. All the while using what I said to seduce my wife away from me.'

His grip on the sill tightened, his nails digging into the paintwork.

'And that's not all. I didn't realise that Anna was pregnant when she left me for him. In fact, I only found out when he came to tell me that not only was the baby mine, but he'd organised it so that legally he was the baby's father. I could never claim him.'

There was a soft, shocked sound from behind him, but he ignored it.

'This enemy was a powerful man,' he said roughly, 'and even though I tried to uncover what he'd done I was unable to. I was young and had no influence, no power and no money.'

He paused yet again, trying to wrestle the burning rage that ate away at him under his control again.

'I felt I had no choice. If I wanted my son I would have to take him by force. And so I planned to do that. I crashed a party they were giving and tried to confront the man who'd taken my child. But I was…angry. So very angry. And I ended up frightening my son. He ran straight into my enemy's arms—'

His voice cracked and he had to fight to keep it level.

'I knew then I had to let him go,' he went on, more levelly this time. 'That I had to let everything go. And so I did.'

Even though it had cut him in half. Even though it had caused his heart to shrivel up and die in his chest.

'I cut my marriage and my son out of my life, out of my memory. I pretended that it never happened, that he never existed. And then…then I found a woman in the streets. A woman who was defacing my car. I found out her name. Leonie de Riero. The long-lost, much-loved daughter of Victor de Riero.'

Cristiano let go of the windowsill and turned around to face the woman in the bed.

'Victor de Riero is the man who first stole my wife and

then stole my child from me. And he owes me a debt that I will collect.' He stared at her, let her see the depth of his fury. 'With you.'

LEONIE CLUTCHED THE sheet tight in her hands, unable to process what Cristiano had just told her.

He stood with the window at his back, his hands at his sides, his fingers curled into fists. His beautiful face was set in hard lines, the look in his emerald eyes so sharp it could cut. The smokescreen had dropped away entirely. He looked fierce, dangerous, and the fury rolling off him took her breath away.

What little breath she had, given that apparently all this time he'd known who she was. Known *exactly* who she was.

That's why he picked you up off the streets. That's why he gave you a job. You were never anything to him but a means to an end.

Pain settled inside her, though she ignored it. As she ignored the cold waves of shock and the sharp tug of pity because there was so much to take in.

He'd been married. He'd had a child. A child that had been taken from him. God, she could still hear his voice cracking as he'd told her what had happened, and that pity tugged harder at her heart.

But she didn't want to feel pity for him.

'You knew,' she said thickly, focusing on that since it was easier than thinking about the rest. 'All this time, you knew.'

His expression was like granite. 'Yes. I went to get my driver and found him playing a dice game with one of your friends. I gave the kids a hundred euros to tell me what your name was.' His mouth quirked in a humourless smile. 'Everyone has their price.'

She felt cold. But it was a cold that came from the inside,

something that no amount of blankets or quilts could help. 'But...how could you know who I was from my first name?'

His gaze went to her hair, spilling down her back. 'You were familiar to me and I couldn't put my finger on why. But the colour of your hair gave it away. Anna and I used to go to many events hosted by your father and you attended some of them.'

Her stomach dropped away. Her memories of that time were so dim they were only blurry impressions. A pretty dress. A crowd of adults. Nothing more.

But Cristiano had been there. She must have seen him and clearly he'd remembered her.

She stared at him, her heart pounding. Before, she'd noted that he was older, certainly much older than she was, but she hadn't thought about it again. She hadn't thought about it last night, either—had been too desperate for him.

There had been a vague familiarity to his name when she'd first heard it, but she hadn't remembered anything. She'd been too young.

'Why...?' She stopped, not sure which question to ask first since there were so many.

'Why did I bring you here? Why did I not tell you I knew?' He asked them for her. 'Because you were familiar and I wanted to know why. And when I discovered who you were I didn't tell you because I wanted you to tell me. I wanted you to trust me.'

A sudden foreboding wound through her. 'What do you want from me?'

He smiled again, his predator's smile, and it chilled her. 'What do I want from you? I want you to help me get my revenge, of course.'

Ice spread through her.

Did you think he wanted you for real?

She fought to think, fought her pity for him and for what had happened to him.

'How? I don't understand.'

'I'm going to marry you, Leonie. And I'm going to invite your father to our wedding, to watch as a Velazquez takes a precious de Riero daughter the way he took my son.'

The ferocity on Cristiano's face, gleaming in his eyes, made the ice inside her deepen, yet at the same time it gave her a peculiar and unwanted little thrill.

'You will be mine, Leonie. And there will be nothing he can do to stop it.'

You want to be someone's.

The thought tangled with all the other emotions knotting in her chest, too many to sort out and deal with. So she tried to concentrate only on the thing that made any kind of sense to her.

'It won't work,' she said. 'My father doesn't care. He left me to rot in the streets.'

Something flickered across Cristiano's intense features. 'No, he didn't. He thought you were dead. Didn't you know?'

Her stomach dropped away. Dead? He thought she was dead?

'What?' she whispered, hoarse with shock. 'No, my mother told me he got rid of us. That he'd wanted a son, and she couldn't have any more children. And he…he…' She trailed off, because it couldn't be true. It couldn't.

Maybe it is and your mother lied to you.

This time the expression on Cristiano's face was unmistakable: pity.

'He didn't get rid of you,' he said quietly. 'I know. I was there. Your mother left him, and took you with her, and you both disappeared. A week or so later he got word that you'd both died in a fire in Barcelona.'

'No,' she repeated pointlessly. 'No. We came to Paris. Mamá had to get a job. I wanted to go home, but she told me we couldn't because Papá didn't want us. She couldn't give him the son he'd always wanted so he kicked us out.' Leonie took a shaken breath. 'Why would she say that if it wasn't true?'

Cristiano only shook his head. 'I don't know. Perhaps she didn't want you to find out that he'd been having an affair with my wife.'

Does it matter why? She lied to you.

The shock settled inside her, coating all those tangled emotions inside her, freezing them.

'All this time I thought he didn't look for me because he didn't care,' she said thickly. 'But it wasn't that. He thought...he thought I was dead.'

Cristiano's anger had cooled, and a remote expression settled over his face. 'I wouldn't ascribe any tender emotion to him if I were you. He didn't demand proof of your deaths. He merely took some stranger's word for it.'

A lump rose in Leonie's throat. There was a prickling behind her eyes and she felt like crying. Okay, so not only had her father thought she'd died, and hadn't much cared, but her mother had lied to her. Had lied to her for years.

Does knowing all that really change anything?

No, it didn't. She was still homeless. Still in this man's power. This man who'd known who she was all this time and hadn't told her. Who was planning to use her in some kind of twisted revenge plot.

It made her ache, made her furious, that all the heat and passion and wonder of the night before had been a lie. The joy she'd felt as he'd touched her as if she mattered was tainted.

He'd lied to her the way her mother had lied to her.

Bitterness and hurt threatened to overwhelm her, but she

grabbed on to that thread of fury. Because fury was easier than pain every single time.

'So that's why you slept with me?' She fought to keep the pain from her voice. 'To make sure I'd do what I was told?'

Something flickered through his green eyes, though she didn't know what it was.

'No, sleeping with you was never the plan. I was going to make sure you trusted me and then I was going to put it to you as a business proposition. If you'd agree to marry me I would pay you a certain amount, and then in a few years we would divorce.'

'I see.' Carefully she drew the sheet around her, though it didn't help the numbness creeping through her. 'The sex was part of building trust, then?'

A muscle flicked in his jaw. 'That wasn't the intention.'

But it was clear that he wasn't unhappy that it had happened between them.

Of course he wasn't. It was another thing for him to use. And you thought you could trust him…

The cold in the pit of her stomach turned sharp, digging in, a jagged pain. She was a fool. The last person she'd trusted had been her mother and look how that had turned out. She'd thought after that she'd be more careful about who she gave her trust to, but apparently she'd learned nothing.

Though, really, what did it matter? The sex had been amazing, but so what? It was only sex and he wasn't different. He was a liar, like everyone else. And one thing was certain: he would never touch her again.

'Then what was your intention?' She was pleased with how level her voice was.

He stared at her for a long moment, his gaze unreadable. 'You're beautiful, Leonie. And I thought—'

'You thought, *Why not? A girl from the streets could be fun? Something a bit different.*'

Bitterness was creeping in now, which wasn't supposed to happen, so she forced it out.

'It doesn't matter,' she went on dismissively. 'It was a nice way to pass the evening.'

Shifting, she slid out of the bed, keeping the sheet wrapped around her as she took a couple of steps towards him, then stopped.

'You didn't need to bother, though. If you'd asked me the night you picked me up if I wanted to help you get revenge on my father I would have said yes. Especially if you're going to pay me.'

Cristiano didn't move, but the line of his shoulders was tense, his jaw tight. His gaze was absolutely impenetrable.

'You have no loyalty to him, then?'

'Why should I? I barely remember him. Money is what I need now.'

There was silence as he stared at her and she couldn't tell what he was thinking.

'For what it's worth,' he said quietly, 'I slept with you last night because you're beautiful and I wanted you, Leonie. Because I couldn't stop myself.'

She hated him a little in that moment, and part of her wanted to throw it back in his face. But that would give away the fact that their night had mattered to her, and she didn't want him to know that. She didn't want him to know *anything*.

Last night she'd trusted him, but she certainly wasn't going to make that mistake again. His money, on the other hand, was a different story. She could buy herself a new life with money like that. Buy that little cottage in the country, where she'd live with the only person she trusted in the entire world: herself.

So all she did was lift a shoulder as if she didn't care and it didn't matter. 'Fine—but I want the money, Cristiano.'

His features hardened. 'Name your price.'

She thought of the most outrageous sum she could and said it out loud.

'It's yours,' he replied without hesitation.

'There's a condition,' she added.

His granite expression didn't change. 'Which is?'

'You can never touch me again.'

The muscle in the side of his jaw flicked, and there was a steady green glitter in his eyes. 'And if I don't like that condition?'

'Then I'll refuse to help you.'

He said nothing, and didn't move, but she could sense the fury rolling off him in waves. He didn't like her condition. Didn't like it one bit.

'I could make you change your mind.'

The words were more a growl than anything else, and the fighter in her wanted to respond to that challenge, relished it, even.

'Could you?' She gave him a very direct look. 'Why would you bother? I'm just a girl from the streets. You could get better with a snap of your fingers.'

'It's true, I could.' His gaze clashed with hers. 'But I don't want better. I want you.'

That shouldn't have touched her own anger, shouldn't have made it waver for even a second. But it did. Not that she was going to do anything about it. He was a liar, and even though that nagging pity for him still wound through her anger she ignored it.

'That's too bad.' And then, because she couldn't help herself, 'Feel free to try and change my mind if you can. But you won't be able to.'

The flame in his eyes blazed and he pushed himself

away from the window, straightening to his full height. A wild thrill shot straight down her spine. Oh, yes, challenge accepted.

'You shouldn't say things like that to men like me,' he murmured. 'But, fine, you'll have your money. You'll have to come to San Lorenzo with me if you want it, though. We'll be married in my family chapel.'

Leonie didn't think twice. She wanted the money—what did she care if she had to return to Spain to get it?

Are you sure it's a good idea to be near him?

Why wouldn't it be? She didn't care about him—not now. She didn't care about her father, either. Now all she cared about was the money, and she had no problem with using Cristiano the way he'd used her.

'Fine,' she said, shrugging. 'I don't care.'

'Good.' He moved, striding past her to the door of his bedroom without even a glance. 'Prepare to leave in an hour.'

And then he went out.

CHAPTER EIGHT

Cristiano filled the flight to Spain with business. It was the only way to distract himself from the fact that Leonie was right there, sitting casually in one of his jet's luxurious leather seats, leafing through a magazine as if the night before and the morning after had all been just a passing encounter for her.

It was a performance worthy of himself.

It also drove him mad enough that he stayed on the phone even as the car they'd transferred to from the small airport where they'd landed wound its way through the sharp crags of the mountains on the road to San Lorenzo.

He could think of no other way to handle having her in his vicinity and not touching her.

Since she had no other clothes, she wore the black T-shirt and black trousers of his staff uniform, the small bag at her side containing only her old clothes and her useless phone—items she'd insisted on bringing with her for no reason that he could see.

He hadn't argued. She could bring them if she wanted to. He was planning on providing her with a proper wardrobe anyway, once they'd got to his estate, since if she was going to be his duchess he would need her to look the part.

But even that plain black uniform didn't stop memories of the night before rolling through him. Of her silken skin beneath his fingers, of the cries she'd made, of how tightly she'd gripped him as he'd slid inside her, of the look in her eyes as she'd stared up at him.

He'd told himself that the sex didn't matter, that it was physical, nothing more, and yet he couldn't get it out of his head. Couldn't get the memory of her white face as he'd told her the truth that he'd known who she was all this time out of his head, either.

He'd been right. Not only had he shocked her, he'd hurt her, too. She hadn't even known that her father thought she was dead. And what had been worse was the feeling that had swept through him as those big violet eyes had stared back at him in shock and betrayal. The need to go to the bed and sweep her into his arms had been strong. To hold her. Soothe her. Comfort her.

But he hadn't allowed himself to give in to those feelings. Instead he'd watched as his little *gatita* had drawn on some hidden core of strength, her pain and shock vanishing beneath her usual stubborn belligerence and an emotion he was all too familiar with.

Anger.

He'd hoped telling her the truth would make her aware of what kind of man he was and put some distance between them, and it had. He just hadn't expected to feel quite so disappointed about that—or disappointed in her demands. The money wasn't important—it wasn't an outrageous sum— it was the fact that she didn't want him to touch her again that he cared about. Which was especially enraging since he wasn't supposed to care.

Your emotions are involved with her whether you like it or not.

Yes, which meant he had to *un*-involve them.

Difficult when touching her was all he wanted to do.

The car wound through yet another green valley, with

vineyards spread out on either side, almost to the foothills of the sharp, jagged mountains rising above them. But Cristiano wasn't watching the homeland he hadn't been to in years unroll before him. He was too busy watching the woman sitting beside him.

She had her head turned away, and was staring at the view outside. The sun was falling over the fine grain of her skin and turning her hair to fire.

Beautiful *gatita*.

He couldn't stop the sound of her voice replaying in his head, even huskier than it normally was, telling him how her mother had told her that her father hadn't wanted her, that he'd wanted a son instead.

Cristiano didn't know what to think about that, because it was certainly something that Victor de Riero had wanted. And maybe it had been true that Hélène couldn't have any more children. Maybe that had been part of the reason for de Riero targeting Anna. He'd wanted a new, more fertile wife for an heir.

'I thought he didn't look for me because he didn't care...'

A deep sympathy he didn't want to feel sat in his chest like a boulder, weighing him down. All those years she'd been on the streets, thinking herself unwanted. Where had Hélène been? Gone, it was clear, leaving Leonie to fend for herself. Alone.

He knew that feeling. He knew what it was to be alone. He'd had it all his childhood, as the only child of a man who'd cared more about his duties as duke than being a father, and a woman who'd preferred socialite parties to being a mother.

No wonder you scared Anna away. You were an endless well of need.

Cristiano dragged his gaze from Leonie and tried to

concentrate on his phone call instead of the snide voice in his head.

Another reason not to care—as if he needed one. His emotions were destructive, and he had to make sure he stayed detached from them, which meant caring about Leonie wasn't something he should do.

He shouldn't give in to this sexual hunger, either, no matter how badly he wanted to. Letting one little kitten get the better of him just wasn't going to happen.

He leaned back in his seat, shifting slightly, uncomfortable with being so long in the car. Then he noticed that Leonie had tensed. Her gaze was flicking from the window to him, her hand lifting an inch from her thigh before coming down again. Colour crept into her cheeks as she turned towards the window again.

Interesting. So she was physically aware of him, perhaps as painfully as he was aware of her, which made sense. Because she'd loved everything he'd done to her and had answered his passion with her own fierce, untutored desire. A hunger like that, once released, didn't die. It burned for ever. She wouldn't be able to ignore it the way she had on the streets.

Cristiano didn't smile, but he allowed himself a certain satisfaction, filing away her response for future reference. Then he focused completely on his phone call as the car wound its way through another vineyard and then the tiny ancient village that had once been part of his estate. They moved on up into the mountains, and from there down a rocky, twisting driveway that led at last to the *castillo* he'd been born in.

The *castillo* he'd grown up in.

The big, empty *castillo* that had echoed with nothing but silence after his parents had been killed.

And that was your fault, too.

Cristiano tensed as the car cleared the trees and Leonie sat forward as the *castillo* came into view.

'You live here?' she asked, in tones of absolute astonishment. 'In a castle?'

It was literally a castle, built into the hillside. A medieval fortress that his warlord ancestors had held for centuries. Had it really been fifteen years since he'd been back?

After Anna had gone, and he'd lost his son, it had felt too big and too empty. It had reminded him of being seventeen once again, of losing his parents and walking the halls, feeling as if the silence and the guilt was pressing in on him. Crushing him.

After Anna, he hadn't been able to get out of the place fast enough, filling up his life with music and talk and laughter. With the sound of life.

A cold sensation sat in his gut as the car drew up on the gravel area outside the massive front doors. Why had he thought coming back was a good idea? He didn't want to go inside. The whole place had felt like a tomb the last time he'd been here and nothing would have changed.

Something's changed. You have Leonie.

She was already getting out of the car, walking towards the doors, looking up in open amazement at the *castillo* towering above her.

Ah, but he didn't have her, did he? She wasn't his. She'd made that very clear.

Still, if he was going to make her his duchess he wanted it to happen on Velazquez ground, and he'd already sent messages to his PR company to let them know he'd be bringing his 'fiancée' back to his estate, and that more information would follow. They were naturally thrilled that the duke of San Lorenzo, infamous for his pursuit of pleasure, would be marrying again. The press would be ecstatic.

Gathering himself, Cristiano got out of the car and

strolled after Leonie, letting none of his unease show. He'd called his staff here before he'd left Paris, telling them to prepare for his arrival, so everything should be in place.

Sure enough, they were greeted in the huge, vaulted stone entrance hall by one of his family's old retainers. The woman spoke a very old Spanish dialect that no one spoke outside the valley, and the memories it evoked made the cold inside him deepen.

He answered her in the same language, issuing orders while Leonie wandered around, looking up at the bare stone walls and the huge stone staircase that led to the upper levels. Portraits of his ancestors had been hung there. He'd always hated them—dark, gloomy paintings of stone-faced men and women who looked as if they'd never tasted joy in their entire lives and perhaps hadn't.

Leonie had started climbing the stairs to look at them and he walked slowly after her, the familiar cold oppressiveness of the ancient stones wrapping around him, squeezing him tight.

'Are these people your family?' she asked, staring at the portraits.

'Yes. Miserable bunch, aren't they?'

'They don't look that happy, no.' She frowned. 'But… they're so old. How long has your family been here?'

He climbed up a little way, then stopped one step below her, looking at her since that was better than looking at those ghastly portraits. She was all pale skin, bright hair and deep blue-violet eyes. Life and colour. Unlike these dim, dark portraits of people long dead.

'Centuries.' He thrust his hands in his pockets, his fingers itching to touch her. 'Since medieval times, if not before.'

'Wow…' she breathed, following the line of portraits on the walls. 'And what about this one?'

She pointed at the last picture, the most recent—though it didn't look like it, given it had been painted in the same dark, gloomy style. Her earlier anger at him seemed to have faded away, and interest was alight in her face.

Cristiano didn't look at the picture. He knew exactly which one it was. 'That one? Those are my parents. They were killed in a car accident when I was seventeen.'

She flicked him a glance, a crease between her brows. 'Oh. I'm sorry.'

It sounded almost as if she really meant it—not that he needed her sympathy. It had happened so long ago he barely remembered it.

That's why you can never escape the cold of this place. That's why you carry it around with you wherever you go. Because you can't remember how you tried to warm it up...

Cristiano shoved the thoughts away. 'It was a long time ago.'

'Your mother was pretty.' She leaned closer, studying the picture. 'Your father was handsome, too. But he looks a little...stern.'

'If by "stern" you mean aloof and cold, then, yes. He was. And my mother was far more interested in parties than anything else.' He was conscious that he hadn't quite managed to hide the bitter note in his voice.

Leonie straightened and turned, studying his face. 'They weren't good parents?'

He didn't want to talk about this. 'What happened to Hélène, Leonie?' he asked instead. 'What happened to your mother?'

Her lashes fluttered; her gaze slid away. 'She left. I was sixteen. I came home from school one day and she was just...gone. She left me a note, saying she was leaving and not to look for her. But that was it.'

His fingers had curled into fists in his pockets, and that

same tight sensation that Leonie always seemed to prompt was coiling in his chest. 'She just left? Without saying why?'

'Yes.' Leonie was looking down at the stairs now. 'I'll never know why.'

So. She'd effectively been abandoned by the one person in the world who should have looked after her. At sixteen.

'What did you do?' he asked quietly.

She lifted a shoulder. 'Eventually I was evicted from our apartment. No one seemed to notice I was gone.'

He felt as if a fist was closing around his ribs and squeezing, and he wanted to reach out, touch that petal-soft cheek. Tell her that he would have noticed. That he would have looked for her.

But then she glanced up at him again, a fierce expression in her eyes. 'Don't you dare pity me. I survived on my own quite well, thank you very much.'

'Survived, maybe,' he said. 'But life isn't just survival, Leonie.'

'It's better than being dead.'

Proud, stubborn girl.

'You should have had more than that.' This time it was his turn to study her. 'You deserved more than that.'

Colour flooded her pale cheeks, shock flickering in her eyes. 'Yes, well, I didn't get it. And you didn't answer my question.'

'No,' he said. 'Mine were not good parents.'

She blinked, as if she hadn't expected him to capitulate so quickly. 'Oh. Do you have brothers or sisters?'

'No.'

'So it was just you? All alone in this big castle by yourself?' There was a certain knowledge in her eyes, an understanding that he'd never thought he'd find in anyone else.

She knew loneliness—of course she did.

'Yes.' He lifted a shoulder. 'I was alone in this big castle by myself. This mausoleum was my inheritance.'

'Is that what it felt like? A mausoleum?'

'Don't you feel it?' He moved his gaze around the soaring ceilings and bare stone walls. 'All that cold stone and nothing but dead faces everywhere. I never come here if I can help it. In fact, I haven't been here in fifteen years.'

There was silence, but he could feel her looking at him, studying him like an archaeologist studying a dig site, excavating him.

'What happened here, Cristiano?'

That was his *gatita*. Always so curious and always so blunt.

'Do I really have to go into my long and tedious history?' he drawled. 'Don't you want to see where you're going to be sleeping?'

'No. And isn't your tedious history something I should know? Especially if I'm going to be marrying you.'

He looked at her. She was so small; she was on the stair above him but she was still only barely level with him. He didn't want to talk about this any more. He wanted his hands on her instead. He wanted her warmth melting away the relentless cold of this damn tomb.

'What is there to say?'

He kept his gaze on her, hiding nothing. Because she was right. She should know his history. So she knew what to be wary of.

'It was my seventeenth birthday, but my parents had some government party they had to attend. I was lonely. I was angry. And it was the second birthday in a row that they'd missed. So I took a match to my father's library and set it on fire.'

Leonie's gaze widened. 'What?'

'You think that's the worst part? It's not.' He smiled, but

it was bitter. 'One of my father's staff called him to let him know the *castillo* was on fire. So he and my mother rushed back from the party. But he drove too fast and there was an accident. They were both killed.'

SHE HADN'T UNDERSTOOD until that moment why he so obviously hated this place, with its ancient stones and the deep silence of history. She'd thought it was wonderful—a fortress that no one could get into. A place of security and safety. She'd never been anywhere so fascinating and she wanted to explore it from top to bottom.

But it was clear that Cristiano did not feel the same. It was obvious in every line of him.

This man had used her, hurt her, and no matter that he'd said their night together had been because he'd wanted her, she couldn't forget her anger at him and what he'd done.

Yet that didn't stop the pulse of shock that went through her, or the wave of sympathy that followed hard on its heels.

There was self-loathing in his voice, a bitterness he couldn't hide, and she knew what that meant: he blamed himself for his parents' death.

No wonder he hated this place. No wonder he thought it was a tomb. For him, it was.

'You blame yourself,' she said. 'Don't you?'

He gave another of those bitter laughs. 'Of course I blame myself. Who else is there? No one else started a fire because he couldn't handle his anger.'

Her heart tightened. Although their stations in life were so far removed from each other that the gulf between them might have been the distance from the earth to the sun, they were in fact far closer than she'd realised.

He'd lost people the same as she had.

'For years after Mamá left I blamed myself,' she said. 'I thought that maybe it was something I'd done that had made her leave. Perhaps I'd asked too many questions, disobeyed her too many times. Nagged her for something once too often.' Her throat closed unexpectedly, but she forced herself to go on. 'Or…been a girl instead of a boy.'

The bitter twist to his mouth vanished. 'Leonie—' he began.

But she shook her head. 'No, I haven't finished. What I'm trying to say is that in the end I didn't know why she'd left. I'll never know, probably. And I could have chosen to let myself get all eaten up about what I did or didn't do, or I could accept that it was her choice to leave.' Leonie stared at him. 'She didn't have to leave. I didn't make her. She choose that. Just like your father chose to return here.'

Cristiano's expression hardened. 'Of course he had to return. His son had just set fire to the—'

'No, he didn't,' she interrupted. 'He could have got a staff member to handle it. He could have decided he wasn't fit to drive and had your mother drive instead. He could have called you. But he didn't do any of those things. He chose to drive himself.'

Cristiano said nothing. He was standing on the step below her but still he was taller than she was, all broad shoulders and hard muscle encased in the dark grey wool of his suit. He wasn't wearing a tie, and the neck of his black shirt was open, exposing the smooth olive skin of his throat and the steady pulse that beat there.

She didn't know why she wanted to help him so badly— not after he'd hurt her the way he had. But she couldn't help it. She knew loneliness and grief, and she knew anger, too, and so much of what had happened to him had also happened to her.

'You are very wise, *gatita*,' he said at last, roughly. 'Where did you learn such wisdom?'

'There's not much to do on the streets but think.'

'In between all the surviving you had to do?' A thread of faint, wry amusement wound through his beautiful voice.

You deserved more than that…

A shiver chased over her skin. He'd said it as if he meant it, as if he truly believed that she had. But why would she trust what he said about anything?

'Yes,' she said blankly, her gaze caught and drawn relentlessly to the pulse at the base of his throat once again. 'In between all that.'

She'd put her mouth over that pulse the night before. She'd tasted his skin and the beat of his heart, had run her hands over all that hard muscle and raw male power.

A throb of hunger went through her.

She'd spent most of the day trying to ignore his physical presence. She'd thought it would be easy enough to do since he'd ignored her, spending all his time on the phone. She'd been fascinated by all the new sights and sounds as they'd left Paris and flown to Spain, so that had made it easier.

But despite that—despite how she should have been concentrating on her return to her long-forgotten homeland—all she'd been conscious of was him. Of his deep, authoritative voice on the plane as he'd talked on his phone. Of his hard-muscled thigh next to hers in the car. Of the spice of his aftershave and the heat in his long, powerful body.

And she'd realised that she might ignore him all she liked, but that didn't change her hunger for him, or her innate female awareness of him as a man. It couldn't be switched off. It pulsed inside her like a giant heartbeat, making her horribly conscious that her declaration of how she wasn't going to let him touch her again had maybe been a little shortsighted.

That was another thing she hadn't understood before, yet did now. Sexual hunger hadn't ever affected her, so she'd imagined that refusing him would be easy. But it wasn't, and she felt it acutely now as he stood there staring at her, his jungle-green eyes holding her captive. As if he knew exactly what she was thinking.

Her heartbeat accelerated, the ache of desire pulsed between her thighs, and she knew her awareness of him was expanding, deepening.

He wasn't just a powerful and physically attractive man. He was also a man who seemed not to care about very much at all on the surface, yet who burned on the inside with a terrible all-consuming rage. And a rage like that only came from deep caring, from a man with a wounded heart who'd suffered a terrible loss.

At least after the deaths of his parents he'd been able to grieve. But how could he grieve a child who wasn't dead? Who was still alive and who had no idea that Cristiano was his father?

He hasn't grieved. Why do you think he's so angry?

'You'd better stop looking at me that way, *gatita*,' he murmured. 'You'll be giving me ideas.'

She ignored that, feeling her own heart suddenly painful in her chest. 'I'm sorry about your parents,' she said. But she wanted him to know that although his son might not be aware of Cristiano, she was. And that she acknowledged what the loss had meant for him. 'And I'm so sorry about your son.'

A raw emerald light flared in the duke's eyes. That wry amusement dropped away, his whole posture tightening. 'Do not speak of it.' His voice vibrated with some intense, suppressed emotion.

She didn't want to cause him pain, yet all of a sudden she wanted him to know that she understood. That she felt for him. And that to a certain extent she shared his loss—because she, too, had lost people she'd once felt something for: her mother and her father.

So she lifted a hand, thinking to reach out and touch him, having nothing else to give him but that.

'No, Leonie,' he ordered.

The word was heavy and final, freezing her in place.

'I have respected your wishes by not touching you, but don't think for one moment that it doesn't go both ways. Not when all I can think about is having you on these stairs right now, right here.'

Her heart thudded even louder. He had respected her wishes. He hadn't made one move towards her. And she... Well, she'd never thought that even though he'd broken her fledgling trust she'd still want him—and quite desperately.

So have him. It doesn't have to mean anything.

It didn't. And now there were no secrets between them, no trust to break, it could be just sex, nothing more. After all, she'd been denied so many good things—why should she deny herself this?

He'd told her she deserved better and he was certainly better than anything she'd ever had. So why couldn't she have him?

She lifted her hand and, holding his gaze, very deliberately placed her fingertips against the line of his hard jaw, feeling the prickle of hair and the warm silk of his skin.

'Then take me,' she said softly.

He was completely still for long moments, unmoving beneath her hand. But his eyes burned with raw green fire.

'Once you change your mind there will be no coming back from it, do you understand me?' His voice was so deep, so rough. The growl of a beast. 'This is the place of my ancestors, and if I have you here that makes you mine.'

He was always trying to warn her, to frighten her. Letting her see the fire burning in the heart of the man he was beneath the veneer of a bored playboy. But Leonie had never been easily frightened. And the man behind that veneer, with his anger, his passion and his pain, was far more fascinating to her than the playboy ever had been.

She wanted that man. And she wasn't frightened of him. After all, she'd always wanted to be someone's. She might as well be his.

'Then I'll be yours,' she said simply.

Cristiano didn't hesitate. Reaching out, he curled his fingers around the back of her neck and pulled her in close, his mouth taking hers in a kiss that scoured all thought from her head. He kissed her hungrily, feverishly, his tongue pushing deep into her mouth and taking charge of her utterly.

But his wasn't the only hunger.

Desire leapt inside her and she put her hands on his chest, sliding them up and around his neck, threading her fingers in the thick black silk of his hair and holding on tight. She kissed him back the way she had the night before, as hard and demanding as he was, showing him her teeth and her claws by biting him.

He growled deep in his throat. His hands were on her hips, pushing her down onto the cold stone of the stairs so she was sitting on one step while he knelt on the one below her.

He didn't speak, making short work of the fastenings of her trousers and then stripping them off her, taking her underwear with them. The stone was icy under her bare skin, but she didn't care. She was burning up. Everywhere he touched felt as if it was being licked by flame.

His mouth ravaged hers, nipping and biting at her bottom lip before moving down her neck to taste the hollow of her throat. She sighed, her head falling back as he cradled the back of it in his palm. His hand slid between her bare thighs, stroking and teasing, finding her slick and hot for him.

Leonie moaned, desperate for more pressure, more friction. Desperate for more of him.

And it seemed he felt the same, because there were no niceties today, no slow, gentle seduction. He ripped open the front of his trousers, his hands falling away from her as he grabbed for his wallet and dealt with the issue of protection. Then his hot palms were sliding beneath her buttocks, lifting her, positioning her, before he pushed into her in a hard, deep thrust.

The edge of the stair above her was digging into her back. She didn't care, though, was barely conscious of it as she gasped aloud, staring up into his face. Again, he was nothing but a predator, his eyes glittering with desire, his sensual mouth drawn into a snarl as he drew his hips back and thrust again.

All she could see was that hot stare and the possessive fire in it, and it twisted the pleasure tighter, harder. She wanted to be possessed. She wanted to be taken. And she wanted to take in return. Because, as much as he wanted her to be his, she wanted something to call her own.

He could be that for you.

Her heart slammed against her ribs and she curled her legs around his lean waist, holding him tightly to her, forgetting how he'd hurt her, how he'd lied to her in that moment.

'You could be mine, too,' she whispered hoarsely as he thrust into her again, making her gasp in pleasure. 'You could be, Cristiano.'

He didn't reply, but the fire in his eyes climbed higher. His fingers curled into her hair, protecting her head from the hard stone of the stairs, but he gave her no mercy from the brutal thrust of his hips. As if he could impress himself into her. As if he was trying to make her part of the stones of the castle itself.

And beneath the passion she could feel his need, could sense it in some deep part of her heart. The need for touch and warmth and connection. So she gave it to him, wrapping herself around him, and he took it, holding tight to her as he gave her the most intense pleasure in return.

It didn't take long.

He grabbed one her hands and guided her own fingers between her thighs, holding it down over that tight, aching bundle of nerves. And then he thrust again, deeper, harder, as he held her fingers there until the desperation inside her exploded into ecstasy and the entrance hall rang with the sounds of her cries.

She was hardly aware of his own growl as he followed her, murmuring her name roughly against her neck.

For long moments afterwards she didn't want to move, quite happy to sit on the cold stone of the stairs, with Cristiano's heat warming her through. But then he was shifting, withdrawing from her, dealing with the aftermath. Only after that was done did he reach for her, gathering her up into his arms and holding her close against his chest as he climbed the rest of the way up the stairs.

He carried her down a long and echoing stone corridor and into a room with a massive four-poster bed pushed against one wall. There he stripped her naked, put her down on it, and proceeded to make her forget her own name.

CHAPTER NINE

Cristiano finished up the phone call he was on with his PR people then leaned back in the old hand-carved wooden chair that sat behind his father's massive antique desk, reflecting once again on how hideously uncomfortable it was.

His father had liked the chair—his father had liked all the heavy old wooden furniture in the ducal study—but Cristiano had already decided that the chair had to go. Especially if he was going to make his home here—and he was certainly considering it.

The *castillo* was different with Leonie in it. She'd spent the past week investigating every corner of the ancient stones, exclaiming over things like the deep window seat in the library that could be enclosed when the heavy velvet curtains were drawn. Like the big bathroom that had been modernised to a point, but still retained a giant round bath of beaten copper. The cavernous dining room, where he'd had many a silent dinner with his parents, now filled up with Leonie's questions about the history of the estate and the *castillo* itself. Like the tapestries on the walls and the huge kitchen fireplace that was large enough to roast a whole cow in and probably had. The courtyard with the overgrown rose garden, the orchard full of orange trees, and the meadow beyond where he'd used to play as a child, pretending he had brothers and sisters to play with him.

But those memories seemed distant now—especially now he'd created new ones. Memories that were all about her laughter, her husky voice, her bright smile. Her cries of pleasure. Her bright hair tangled in his fingers and her warmth as he took her in yet another of those old, cold rooms.

He'd even taken her in that window seat in the library, and the memories of books flaming and shelves burning as bright as his anger were buried under flames and heat of a different kind.

It was better—much better. And the castle didn't feel so cold any more, or so silent. In fact, it felt as if summer had come to stay in the halls, making the place seem warmer and so much brighter than he remembered.

He was even considering staying on here with her after the wedding—and why not? She would be his wife, after all, and now they were spending every night, not to mention quite a few days, exploring the chemistry between them, it seemed only logical to indulge in a honeymoon, as it were. Maybe even beyond that.

He'd thought about the possibility of having an heir with her and tainting that precious de Riero bloodline even before they'd left Paris, and the idea certainly still held its appeal. He could create a home here with her. Create a family the way Victor de Riero had created a family.

You really want to have another child?

Something jolted inside him, a kind of electric shock, and he had to push himself out of his chair and take a couple of steps as restlessness coiled tight through his muscles.

Another child…

Intellectually, the idea was a sound one, and it would certainly make his revenge all the sweeter—so why did the thought make him feel as if ice was gathering in the pit of his stomach?

'I'm so sorry about your son...'

The memory of Leonie's voice on the stairs drifted back to him, the sound husky with emotion, her eyes full of a terrible sympathy, bringing with it another hard, electric jolt.

It had felt as if she was cutting him open that day, and he'd told her not to speak of it before he'd been able to stop himself. Before he'd been able to pretend that the thought of his child no longer had the power to hurt him.

So much for detachment.

His hands dropped into fists at his sides and he took a slow breath.

Yes, he could recognise that the thought of having another child was difficult for him, but he also had to recognise that this situation was different. Any child he had with Leonie would be born in pursuit of his revenge, nothing more. It would not be for him. Which meant it was perfectly possible for him to remain detached.

He would simply choose not to involve himself with any such child, and that would be better for the child, too. Certainly he wouldn't love it—not when love led to nothing but pain and destruction. The cost of love had been too high the first time; he wouldn't pay it again.

At that moment the heavy wooden door of the study burst open and he turned to find Leonie sweeping in, a blur of shimmering white silk and silvery lace, her hair in a loose, bright cascade down her back. She came to a stop in front of him, her cornflower-blue eyes alight with excitement, and put her hands on her hips.

'Well?' she asked. 'What do you think of this?'

He stared, all thoughts of children vanishing, his chest gone tight.

She was wearing a wedding gown. It was strapless, the gleaming white silk bodice embroidered with silver and cupping her breasts deliciously. Then it narrowed down to her small waist before sweeping outwards in a white froth of silky skirts and silver lace.

She looked beautiful—a princess from a fairy-tale or a queen about to be crowned.

'You forgot, didn't you?' she said as he stared at her in stunned silence. 'The designer's here with a few of the dresses we picked last week.'

He *had* forgotten. He and Leonie had sat down the previous week to choose a gown for her—not that he'd been overly interested in the details of the wedding, since it was the revenge that mattered. But Leonie had been excited, and had enjoyed choosing a gown for herself, and he'd surprised himself by enjoying helping her, too.

'So I see.' He tried to calm his racing heartbeat, unable to take his eyes off her. 'I'm not supposed to see the final gown before the wedding, am I?'

'Well, it's your revenge. I thought you might want to make sure the dress is...' she did a small twirl, the gown flaring out around her '...revengey enough.'

Her excitement and pleasure were a joy, and yet they only added to that tight sensation in his chest—the one he hadn't asked for and didn't want, and yet had been there since the night he'd picked her up off the street.

He fought it, tried to ignore it. 'You like it, don't you?'

She smiled, her expression radiant, her hands smoothing lovingly over the silk. 'I love it. I've never had anything so pretty or that's felt so lovely.'

She'd been like this over the past couple of weeks as he'd bought clothes and other personal items to add to her meagre stock of belongings, greeting each new thing with a thrilled delight that was immensely gratifying. And it didn't matter whether it was expensive or not—the fact that she had something of her own seemed to be the most important thing.

It made sense. She'd literally had nothing when he'd found her that night on the streets of Paris except for a very old cellphone and some dirty clothes. Now she had a wardrobe full of items she'd chosen with great care herself and a new phone, not to mention shoes and underwear and perfume and lots of other pretty girly things.

But he hadn't felt like this when he'd given her those things and she'd smiled at him. Not like he did now, with her so radiantly lovely in a wedding gown, full of excitement and joy. He hadn't felt as if he couldn't breathe... as if the world was tilting on its axis and he was going to slide right off.

All he could think about was the day they'd arrived here and how he'd told her that once he took her here, in the place of his ancestors, she'd be his. And how she'd surrendered to him as if she'd never wanted to be anyone else's, all the while whispering to him that he was hers, too.

You want to be hers.

No, he didn't. He couldn't be anyone's—just as he couldn't have anything that was his. Not any more. Not when he couldn't trust himself and his destructive emotions. And this tight feeling in his chest, the way he couldn't breathe...

You're falling for her.

Absolutely not. He had to stay detached and uninvolved. Keep it all about revenge. Because that, in the end, was the whole point of this charade: a cold and emotionless revenge against the man who'd taken his wife and son from him.

Which meant he had to keep his emotions out of it.

Yet still he couldn't stop himself from touching her, reaching out to brush his fingers over the lace of her bodice, watching as her eyes darkened with the passion that always burned so near the surface. She was always ready for him. She never denied him.

'You are beautiful, *gatita*,' he murmured. 'You are perfect in every way.'

She flushed adorably, giving him a little smile. 'Thank you.' Then that smile faded, a look of concern crossing her face. 'Are you all right?'

How she'd picked up on his unease he had no idea, because he was sure he'd hidden it. Then again, she was incredibly perceptive. Too perceptive in many ways.

'What? I can't give my fiancée a compliment without my health being questioned?' he asked, keeping his voice casual. 'Whatever is the world coming to?'

She didn't smile. 'Cristiano…'

The tight thing in his chest tightened even further, like a fist. 'You know this will be a proper marriage, don't you?' They hadn't had this conversation and they needed to. It might as well be now. 'You'll be my wife in every way?'

'Yes,' she replied without hesitation. 'You made that clear.'

'I will want children, too.'

This time her gaze flickered. 'Oh.'

'It makes my revenge even more perfect, *gatita*. Don't you see? He took my son and I will have another with his daughter.'

An expression he couldn't catch rippled over her face, then abruptly her lashes lowered, veiling her gaze. 'I do see, yes.' Her tone was utterly neutral.

He stared down at the smooth, silky curve of her cheek and the brilliant colour of her lashes resting against her pale skin. She seemed a little less bright now, her excitement dimming, disappearing.

'You don't like the idea of children?' he asked.

'No. I just…just hadn't thought of them before.'

He couldn't blame her. She was young, and probably hadn't considered a future with a family. But still, he didn't think it was surprise she was trying to hide from him—and she was definitely hiding something.

Reaching out, he took her chin between his thumb and forefinger and tilted her face up so he could look into her eyes. 'This bothers you. Why?'

She made no attempt to pull away, her violet gaze meeting his. 'You'd really want another child? After what happened with your son?'

Ah, she never shied away from the difficult questions, did she?

'It will be different this time.' He stroked her chin gently with his thumb, unable to resist the feel of her satiny skin. 'Because the child won't be for me. The child will be for the pleasure of seeing Victor de Riero's face when I tell him he will have a Velazquez grandchild.'

That way he could retain his distance. He'd never have to feel what he'd felt for his son for another child again. Never have to experience the pain of another loss. Anger was the only emotion he could allow himself to have.

Some expression he couldn't name shifted in her eyes. 'That's a terrible reason to have a child, Cristiano.'

The flat note of accusation in her voice burrowed like a knife between his ribs, making him realise how cold and callous he'd sounded.

He let go of her chin, felt the warmth of her skin lingering against his fingertips. 'Too bad. That's the only reason I'll ever have another.'

Cold and callous it would have to be. He couldn't afford anything else.

'Revenge…' The word echoed strangely off the stone walls of the room, her gaze never leaving his. 'Don't you want more than that?'

Something inside him dropped away, while something else seemed to claw its way up. Longing. The same kind of longing that had gripped him the day he'd taken her on the staircase of this *castillo*. The need for her touch, for the feel of her skin and the taste of her mouth. The heat of her body burning out the cold.

The need for *her*.

He couldn't allow that. Need had caused him more pain than anything else ever had, so he'd cut it out of his life. Successfully. He had no desire to let it back in again.

'No.' He kept his voice cold. 'I don't.'

But she only looked at him in that direct, sharp way. Seeing beneath the armour of the playboy duke that he wore, seeing the man beneath it. The desperate, lonely man...

'Yes, you do,' she said quietly. 'Would it really be so bad? To let yourself have more?'

Ah, his *gatita*. She couldn't leave well enough alone, could she? She should really learn when to stop pushing.

'I had more once,' he said. 'And I lost it. I do not want it again.'

Those big violet eyes searched his. 'Because of your son? Because of Anna?'

He should have laughed. Should have lifted a shoulder and made a joke. Should have closed the distance between them and put his hands on her, distracted her the way he knew so well how to do.

But he didn't do any of those things. He turned away from her instead and moved around his desk. 'I told you before—do not speak of them. They have nothing to do with our wedding.'

He sat down in his father's uncomfortable chair, ignoring the way his heart was beating, ignoring the pain that had settled in his heart for absolutely no reason that he could see.

'Now, if there's nothing else, I have some work to do.'

Except Leonie didn't move. She just stood there in the

lovely gown, looking at him. Sympathy in her eyes. 'It wasn't your fault, Cristiano. What happened with my father and Anna…with your son.'

The knife between his ribs sank deeper, pain rippling outwards, and he found he was gripping the arms of the chair so hard his knuckles were white. 'I told you. Do not—'

'You were young and you didn't know.' Leonie was suddenly standing right in front of his desk, that terrible piercing gaze of hers on him. 'You were used. You were betrayed by someone you thought you could trust.' There was blue flame burning in her eyes, conviction in her voice. 'And you had every right—*every right*—to be angry.'

'No,' he heard himself say hoarsely, and then he was on his feet, his hands in fists, fury flooding through him. 'Maybe I did have every right, but I should have controlled it. Controlled myself. I barged into that party, shouting like a monster, and I scared my son, Leonie. I *terrified* him. And he ran straight to Victor as if I was the devil himself.'

His jaw ached, his every muscle stiff with tension, and he wanted to stop talking but the words kept on coming.

'I would have taken him, too. I would have ripped him from Victor's arms if Anna hadn't stopped me. If she hadn't thrown herself in front of Victor and told me that this was why she'd left me. Because I terrified her.'

Leonie was coming, moving around the side of the desk towards him, and he shoved the chair back, wanting to put some distance between them. But she was there before he could move, reaching out to cup his face between her small hands.

'You're *not* to blame,' she insisted, her voice vibrating with fierce emotion. 'That man—my *father*—' she spat the word as if it were poison '—took your son from you. He seduced your wife from you. He had no right. And it was *not* your fault. Just like the deaths of your parents weren't your fault.'

The fire in her eyes was all-consuming, mesmerising.

'Just like it wasn't my fault my mother left and my father just accepted I was dead and never once looked for confirmation.'

Her grip held him still, her conviction almost a physical force.

'You were angry because you cared about him, Cristiano. And, yes, caring hurts—but wouldn't you rather have had the pain than feel nothing for him? Than for all of that to have meant nothing at all?'

He couldn't move. He was held in place by her hands on him. By the passion and fierce anger that burned in her lovely face. Passion that burned for *him*.

His world tilted again and he was falling right off the face of it. And there was no one to hold on to but her.

Cristiano reached for her, hauled her close. And crushed her mouth beneath his.

LEONIE WAS SHAKING as Cristiano kissed her, sliding her hands down the wall of his rock-hard chest, curling her fingers into his shirt, holding on to him.

She hadn't meant to confront him. Hadn't meant to hurt him. But she knew she *had* hurt him. She'd seen the flare of agony in his green eyes as she'd mentioned his son, had heard the harsh rasp of it in his beautiful voice as he'd told her that he'd lost what he'd had. And so, no, he didn't want more.

But he'd lied. Of course he wanted more. She felt his longing every time he touched her, every time he pushed inside her. It was there in the demanding way he kissed her, in the brutal rhythm of his hips as he claimed her, stamping his possession on her. In the way he said her name when he came, and in the way he held her so tightly afterwards, as if he didn't want her to get away.

That was fine with her; she loved the way he wanted her. But she hadn't understood why he kept denying that was what he wanted until now. Until he'd tried to end the conversation.

It had all become clear to her then.

Of course he didn't want more. Because he blamed himself for the loss of his wife and child and he thought he didn't deserve more.

She'd told him that day on the stairs that he wasn't responsible for his parents' death, but it was clear that he hadn't taken that on board. That the guilt he was carrying around extended to the loss of his son.

And she didn't know why, but his pain had felt like a knife in her own heart.

She hadn't been able to stop the fierce anger that had risen inside her on his behalf, the fierce need to make him understand that he didn't have to take responsibility for what had happened because it wasn't his fault. None of it was.

He might act as if he was frightening, as if he was bad, but he wasn't. There was nothing about him that was cruel or mean or petty. That was violent or bullying. He was simply a man whose emotions ran fathoms deep and so very strong. A man who'd lost so very much.

She couldn't bear to see him hurt.

He gripped her tight, lifting her, then turning to put her on the desk, ravaging her mouth as he did so. She spread her legs, dropping her hands to his lean hips to pull him closer, the fall of her skirts getting in the way.

'Leonie,' he said hoarsely against her mouth. 'Not like this, *gatita*. Not again.'

'But I—'

He laid a finger across her mouth and she was stunned to feel it tremble lightly against her lips. His eyes had darkened, the green almost black.

'I want to savour you, *mi corazón*. I don't want to be a beast today.'

'I like the beast,' she murmured.

But that was all he gave her a chance to say, because then his mouth was on hers again, his hands moving down the bodice of the beautiful wedding gown, his fingers shaping her through the fabric, cupping her breasts gently in his palms.

She shivered, because there was something reverent in his touch that hadn't been there before. As if she was a work of art that he had to be careful in handling.

You're not a work of art. You're dirt from the streets—don't forget.

No, she didn't believe it. And she didn't feel it, either—not as his kiss turned gentle, teasing.

The passion between them that normally flared hot and intense had become more focused, more deliberate, settling on delicacy and tenderness rather than mastery.

He tasted her mouth, exploring it lightly before brushing his lips over her jaw and down the side of her neck in a trail of kisses and gentle nips that had her shuddering in his hands. He didn't speak but he didn't need to; the reverent way he touched her made it clear. He'd said he wanted to savour her and that was exactly what he was doing.

He unzipped the gown and slid it down her body, lifting her up so he could get it off her, then laying it carefully over the desk. He turned back to her and pushed her down over the polished wood, so she was lying across the desk next to her gown.

Slowly, carefully, he stripped her underwear from her, his fingers running lightly over every curve, and with each touch she felt something inside her shift and change. She had become something else…something more. Not the dirty, unwanted girl from the streets but someone treasured. Someone precious.

His hands swept down her body, stroking, caressing, as if she was beautiful, wanted, worth taking time over. And, perhaps for the first time in her life, Leonie actually felt that. Tears prickled behind her lids, her throat was tight, but she didn't fight the sensations or the emotions that came along with them, letting them wash through her as he touched her, as if his hands were sweeping them away for good.

He kissed his way down her body, teasing her nipples with his tongue, then drawing them inside the heat of his mouth, making her arch and gasp. His hands stroked her sides and then moved further down, along her thighs. With each caress the dirt of the streets fell away, and with it the cold loneliness and the isolation.

She would have let him touch her for ever if she could, but soon her entire body was trembling and she wanted more from him than gentle touches. She sat up, pushed her hands beneath his shirt, stroking the hard, chiselled muscles of his stomach, glorying in the heat of his skin. Glorying too in the rough curse he gave as she dropped one hand to the fastenings of his trousers and undid them, slipping her hand inside, curling her fingers around his shaft.

'Ah, *gatita*…' he murmured roughly, letting her stroke him. 'You should let me finish proving my point.'

'Which is…?' She looked up into his green eyes, losing herself in the heat that burned there. 'That you're not a beast? I know that already.'

'No. My point is that you're worth savouring.'

'Well, so are you.' She ran her fingers lightly along the

length of him, loving how he shuddered under her touch. 'You're not the only one worth taking time over.'

His gaze darkened. *'Mi corazón...'*

He didn't believe her, did he?

'Here,' she said thickly. 'Let me show you.'

And she pushed at him so he shifted back, then slid off his desk to stand before him, going up on her tiptoes to kiss the strong column of his neck and then further down, tasting the powerful beat of the pulse at his throat. Then she undid the buttons of his shirt, running her fingers down his sculpted torso, tracing all those hard-cut muscles before dropping to her knees in front of him.

Her hands moved to part the fabric of his trousers, to grasp him and take out the long, hard length of him. And then she closed her mouth around him.

His hands slid into her hair and he gave a rough groan, flexing his hips. He tasted so good, a little salty and musky, and she loved the way she could make his breath catch and his body shake. But she also loved giving him pleasure—because if she deserved to feel wanted and treasured, then he did, too.

So she showed him, worshipping him with her mouth until he finally pulled her head away, picking her up in his arms and taking her over to the butter-soft leather couch under the window. He laid her down on it, dealt with protection, then spread her thighs, positioning himself. And when he pushed inside her it felt like a homecoming, a welcome rather than something desperate and hungry.

He didn't move at first, and she lost herself in the green of his eyes and the feel of him inside her, filling her. There was a rightness to this. A sense of wholeness. As if she'd been waiting for this moment, for him, her entire life.

You're in love with him.

Something shifted in her chest, a heavy weight, and it

made her go hot and cold both at the same time. Made her dizzy and hungry, bursting with happiness and aching with despair all at once.

Was what she felt love? How would she know? No one had ever given her love. She'd never even contemplated it before.

Yet the hot, powerful thing inside her, pushing at her, was insistent, and she had no other name for it. And it was all centred on him. On his beautiful face and the heat in his eyes. On his smile and the dark, sexy sound of his laughter. On the way he touched her, the way he made her feel. As if she wasn't broken or dirty, but beautiful and full of light. A treasure, precious and wanted.

He began to move inside her and she couldn't look away. The feeling suffusing her entire body was making her ache. She'd never known till that moment that pain could have a sweet edge.

Words stuck in her throat. Part of her wanted to tell him. Yet something held her back.

'I had more. And I lost it.'

And she was simply a replacement for what he'd lost, wasn't she? A handy vehicle for his revenge. He pitied her and wanted her, that was clear, but that was all she was to him.

Why don't you just ask him?

But she didn't want to ask him. She would lose this moment, and the moment was all she'd ever had. The moment was all there was.

So she ignored the heavy feeling in her heart, in her soul, and pulled his mouth down on hers. Losing herself to his heat and his kiss and the pleasure he could give her and letting the future take care of itself.

CHAPTER TEN

Cristiano waited in a small side room in the ancient chapel that had once been part of the Velazquez estate. Many of his ancestors had been christened and married in this same place, before making their final journey from there to the small cemetery at the back.

He'd waited for a bride here before, his heart beating fast with happiness and excitement as he'd watched through the window for her arrival.

Today, although he was waiting for another bride, it wasn't her he was watching for, and he felt neither excitement nor happiness. He felt cold, and a bone-deep anger was the only thing warming him as he watched for de Riero.

Initially there had been some doubt as to whether the man would accept the invitation, but curiosity and perhaps a chance to gloat had clearly won out, because he'd passed on his acceptance to one of Cristiano's staff.

Guests were already streaming in, and journalists were gathering as per his instructions to his PR people. He wanted as many news media people there as possible to record the moment when he would lift Leonie's veil and reveal her for the first time. To record Victor's face when he realised that it was his daughter standing at the altar.

The daughter who was supposed to be dead.

The daughter who was now his hated enemy's bride.

The daughter who doesn't deserve this pettiness.

Cristiano gritted his teeth, shifting restlessly as he watched the guests enter the chapel.

It wasn't pettiness. It was necessary. How else was he to deal with losing everything that had ever meant something to him?

Doesn't she also mean something to you?

The memory of Leonie's touch wound through him. Not her mouth on him, but her hands cupping his face. That fierce, passionate gaze staring up into his, telling him that none of it was his fault. As if it was vitally important to her that he understand that. As if *he* was important to her.

His hands closed into fists as he gazed sightlessly through the window.

No, he couldn't think about this—about her. It was vital his emotions stay out of it. The important thing was that he was very close to finally getting the satisfaction he craved from de Riero—payback for the agony he had caused him—and nothing was going to stop him from getting it.

And after that?

Cristiano ignored the thought, focusing instead on the long black car that now drew up in the gravel parking area outside the chapel and the tall man that got out of it.

De Riero.

Cristiano began to smile.

And then de Riero turned as another person got out of the car. A tall, gangly teenager with a shock of black hair. De Riero said something and the boy straightened up, looking sullen. Then he reached to adjust the boy's tie, and he must have said something else because the boy lost his sullen look, grinning reluctantly.

An arrow of pure agony pierced Cristian's heart.

His son.

He couldn't move, couldn't tear his gaze away. He purposely hadn't looked at any pictures of the boy, or read any news stories about him. He'd simply pretended that the child had never existed.

But he did exist. And now he was here. And he was tall, handsome. He'd grow into those shoulders one day, just as he'd grow into his confidence, and then the world would be his oyster. He'd be a credit to his parents...

But Cristiano would not be one of those parents.

Pain spread outwards inside him, a grief he wasn't prepared for. Why had de Riero brought the boy? To gloat? To rub salt in the wound? As a shield? Why?

And then another person got out of the car—a woman with dark hair in a dark blue dress. Anna.

She came to stand by her son, smiling up at him, saying something to both him and de Riero that made them laugh. De Riero put a hand at the small of her back and leaned in to kiss her cheek while Anna's hand rested on her son's shoulder.

Something else hit Cristiano with all the force of a quarrel shot from a crossbow.

They were happy.

His son was happy.

You will destroy that. Publicly.

Realisation washed over him like a bucket of ice water and he found himself turning from the window and striding into the middle of the room, his hands in fists.

Anger was a torch blazing inside him. Of course de Riero had brought the boy. Yes, he *was* here as a shield— to protect de Riero against anything Cristiano might do. The coward. Well, he was mistaken. This wedding would go ahead, and Cristiano would parade his daughter in front of him, and...

In front of your son.

Cristiano took a breath, then another, adrenaline pumping through him, anger and bitterness gathering in his throat, choking him.

He couldn't stop thinking about it—about what would happen when Leonie was revealed. What de Riero would do and, more importantly, what his son would do. Did he know he had a stepsister? If he did, how would he react to the knowledge that she wasn't dead, but alive? And if he didn't what would he think about the fact that his so-called father hadn't told him?

That happiness you saw outside... You will destroy it. In front of the world.

The breath caught in his throat, an arrow reaching his heart.

He couldn't do it.

He couldn't destroy his son's happiness.

He'd already done it once before, when the boy had been small, frightening him and sending straight into de Riero's arms. He couldn't do it again.

And all the revenge in the world wouldn't give him back what he'd lost. That was gone. For ever.

Love. That was the problem. That had *always* been the problem.

He'd loved his parents and, no matter what Leonie said, that love had destroyed them. He'd loved Anna once, and had nearly destroyed her. And this love he had for his son— well, now he was on the brink of nearly destroying him, too.

This revenge wasn't cold. It burned like the sun and that was unacceptable.

Love. He was done with it.

And Leonie? What about her?

Yes, she was another casualty of his caring. He'd drawn her into his orbit and kept her there—a tool he could use, a weapon he could wield against Victor de Riero.

Lovely, generous, passionate Leonie, who didn't deserve the use he'd put her to.

Who deserved so much more than being tied to man who only saw her only as something he could use.

He was selfish and he'd hurt her. And he would keep on hurting her. Because that was all he knew how to do.

Hurting people was all he ever did.

Certainty settled down inside him, along with a bone-deep pain and regret. He should never have picked her up off the street and taken her home. Or at least he should have found her a place to live and a job far away from him, where she would have been able to create the kind of life she wanted, not be dragged into his own self-centred plans.

Anna was right to be afraid of you.

His hand was shaking as he grabbed his phone from his pocket and called one of his assistants to get Leonie's location. Luckily she was still a few minutes away, so he ordered the assistant to get the driver to bring the car around to the back of the chapel instead of the front. He'd get another member of staff to intercept her and bring her here, where he could talk to her, tell her what he intended to do.

He paced around for ten minutes, conscious that the moment when they were supposed to exchange vows was getting closer and closer, and that the sooner he made an announcement the better. But he needed to tell her first. She deserved that from him at least.

Finally the door opened and Leonie was ushered in.

His heart shuddered to a complete halt inside his chest.

She was in that gorgeous wedding dress, a princess out of a fairy-tale. The veil that covered her face was white lace, densely embroidered with silver thread, and all that could be seen was the faint gleam of her red-gold hair. In one hand was a spray of simple wildflowers, gathered from the meadow near the castle, while the other held her skirts out of the way so she could walk.

His beautiful *gatita*.

She will never be yours.

He hadn't thought that particular truth would hurt, but it did, like a sword running through him. He ignored the pain. He wouldn't be the cause of any more hurt for her. She'd had enough of that in her life already.

'What's happening?' Leonie pushed back her veil, revealing her lovely face, her cornflower-blue eyes wide and filling with concern as they saw his face. 'What's going on, Cristiano? Are you okay? You look like you've seen a ghost.'

The deep violet-blue of her eyes was the colour that he only ever saw on the most perfect days here in the valley. The warmth of her body was like the hot, dry summers that were his only escape from the silence and the cold. Her rich, heady scent was like the rose garden hidden in the courtyard, where he'd used to play as a child.

She was everything good. Everything he'd been searching for and never known he'd wanted.

Everything he could never have—not when he'd only end up destroying it.

He stood very still, shutting out the anger and the pain, the deep ache of regret that settled inside him. Shutting out every one of those terrible, raw, destructive emotions.

'I'm sorry, *gatita*,' he said. 'But I'm going to have to cancel the wedding.'

LEONIE STARED AT the man she'd thought she'd be marrying today, shock rippling through her. She'd been nervous that morning as a couple of Cristiano's staff had helped her prepare for the ceremony, doing her hair and make-up, preparing her bouquet and finally helping her into the gown.

But she wasn't nervous about finally seeing her father after all these years. In fact, she'd barely thought about him, and even when she had it had only been with a savage kind of anger. Not for herself and what he'd done to her, but for what he'd done to Cristiano.

No, it was marrying Cristiano that she was nervous about. And she was nervous because she was hopelessly in love with him and had no idea what that was going to mean. Especially when she was certain he didn't feel the same about her.

She'd had a battle with herself about whether or not to tell him about her feelings and had decided in the end not to. What would telling him achieve? Who knew how he'd take it? Perhaps things would change, and she didn't want that.

Anyway, she knew that he did feel something for her, because he showed her every night in the big four-poster bed in his bedroom. It was enough. She didn't need him to love her. She'd survived for years without love, after all, and she'd no doubt survive the rest of her life without it, too.

Of course there had been a few nagging doubts here and there. Such as how he'd mentioned having children, but said they wouldn't be for him. They'd only be in service to his grand revenge plan. That had seemed especially bleak to her, but then she couldn't force him to care if he didn't want to. She would just love any children they had twice as much, to make up for his lack.

What was important was that now she had her little cottage in the countryside—although the cottage had turned out to be a castle and she had a genuine duke at her side. She had more than enough.

More than the homeless and bedraggled Leonie of the streets had ever dreamed of.

Except now, as she stood there in her wedding gown, staring at the man she'd been going to marry, whose green eyes were bleak, she suddenly realised that perhaps all of those things hadn't been enough after all.

'What do you mean, cancel the wedding?' Her voice sounded far too small and far too fragile in the little stone room. 'I thought you were going to—?'

'I thought so, too,' he interrupted coolly. 'And then I changed my mind.'

She swallowed, trying to get her thoughts together, trying not to feel as if the ground had suddenly dropped away beneath her feet. 'Cristiano—' she began.

'De Riero has arrived,' he went on, before she could finish. 'And he has brought my son and my ex-wife with him.'

Leonie stared at him. 'You...weren't expecting them?'

'I didn't even think about them.' He was standing so still, as if he'd been turned to stone. 'Until I saw them get out of the car. And then there he was—my son. And Anna. De Riero's *family*.'

He said the word as if it hurt him, and maybe it did, because it was definitely pain turning his green eyes into shards of cut glass.

'They are happy, Leonie. My son is happy. And going through with this will hurt him. Publicly. I have no issue with doing that to de Riero, but I cannot do that to my child.' He paused a moment, staring at her. 'And I cannot do that to you, either.'

She blinked. 'What? You're not hurting me. And as for my father—'

'It won't bring my son back,' Cristiano cut her off, and the thread of pain running through his voice was like a vein of rust in a strong steel column. 'It won't make up for all the years I've missed with him. And I've already hurt him once before, years ago. Revenge won't make me his father, but...' A muscle ticked in his strong jaw, his eyes glittering. 'Protecting him is what a father would do.'

Something twisted in her gut—sympathy, pain.

How could she argue with him? How could she put herself and what she wanted before his need to do what was right for his son?

Because that was the problem. She wanted to marry him. She wanted to be his.

'I see,' she said a little thickly. 'So what will happen? After you cancel the wedding?'

He lifted a shoulder, as if the future didn't matter. 'Everyone will go home and life will resume as normal, I expect.'

'I mean what about us, Cristiano? What will happen with us?'

But she knew as soon as the words left her mouth what the answer was. Because he'd turned away, moving over to the window, watching as the last of the guests entered the chapel.

'I think it's best if you return to Paris, Leonie,' he said quietly, confirming it. 'It's no life for you here.'

Why so surprised? He was only ever using you and you knew that.

No, she shouldn't be surprised. And it shouldn't feel as if he was cutting her heart into tiny pieces. She'd known right from the beginning what he wanted from her, and now he wasn't going to go through with his revenge plan he had no more use for her.

He'd told her she was his. But he'd lied.

Her throat closed up painfully, tears prickling in her eyes. 'No life for me? A castle in Spain isn't as good as being homeless on the streets of Paris? Is that what you're trying to say?'

He glanced at her, his gaze sharp and green and cold. 'You really think I'd turn you back out onto the streets? No, that will not happen. I'll organise a house for you, and a job, set up a weekly allowance for you to live on. You won't be destitute. You can have a new life.'

She found she was clutching her bouquet tightly. Too tightly. 'I don't want that,' she said, a sudden burst of intense fury going through her. 'I don't want *any* of those things. I'd rather sleep on the streets of Paris for ever than take whatever pathetic scraps you choose to give me!'

He looked tired all of a sudden, like a soldier who'd been fighting for days and was on his last legs. 'Then what do you want?'

She knew. She'd known for the past few weeks and hadn't said anything. Had been too afraid to ask for what she wanted in case things might change. Too afraid to reach for more in case she lost what she had.

But now he was taking that away from her she had nothing left to lose.

Leonie took a step forward, propelled by fury and a sudden, desperate longing. 'You,' she said fiercely. 'I want you.'

His face blanked. 'Me?'

And perhaps she should have stopped, should have reconsidered. Perhaps she should have stayed quiet, taken what he'd chosen to give her and created a new life for herself out of it. Because that was more than enough. More than she'd ever dreamed of.

But that had been before Cristiano had touched her, had held her, had made her feel as if she was worth something. Before he'd told her she deserved more than a dirty alleyway and a future with no hope.

Before he'd told her that she was perfect in every way there was.

'Yes, you.' She lifted her chin, held his gaze, gathering every ounce of courage she possessed. 'I love you, Cristiano. I've loved for you for weeks. And the kind of life I want is a life with you in it.'

For a second the flame in his eyes burned bright and hot, and she thought that perhaps he felt the same way she did after all. But then, just as quickly, the flame died, leaving his gaze nothing but cold green glass.

'That settles it, then,' he said, with no discernible emotion. 'You have to leave.'

She went hot, then cold, an endless well of disappointment and pain opening up inside her.

You always knew he didn't want you. Come on—why would he?

She ignored the thought, staring at him. 'Why?' she demanded.

His eyes got even colder. 'Because I don't love you and I never will. And I have nothing else but money to give you.'

The lump in her throat felt like a boulder, the ache in her heart never-ending. She should have known. When he'd told her that any children they had wouldn't be for him, it had been a warning sign. If he had no room in his heart for children, why would he have room for her?

'So everything you said about me deserving better?' she said huskily. 'That was a lie?'

An expression she couldn't interpret flickered over his face.

'You do deserve better. You deserve better than me, Leonie.'

'But I don't want better.' Her voice was cracking and she couldn't stop it. 'And what makes you think you're not better anyway?'

'What do you think?' His face was set and hard. 'I hurt the people I care about. I destroyed my parents, I nearly destroyed Anna, and I almost destroyed my son.' There was nothing but determination in his gaze. 'I won't destroy you.'

Her heart shredded itself inside her chest, raw pain filling her along with a fury that burned hot. She took a couple of steps towards him, one hand crushing the stems of her bouquet, the other curled in a fist.

'Oh, don't make this about protecting me,' she said, her voice vibrating with anger. 'Or your son. Or Anna. Or even your parents.' She took another step, holding his gaze. 'This is about you, Cristiano. You're not protecting us. You're protecting yourself.'

Something flickered in the depths of his eyes. A sudden spark of his own answering anger. 'And shouldn't I protect myself?' he demanded suddenly, tension in every line of him. 'Shouldn't I decide that love is no longer something I want anything to do with? Losing my son just about destroyed me. I won't put myself through that hell ever again.'

Her throat closed up, her heart aching. She had no answer to that, no logical or reasonable argument to make. Because she could understand it. He had been hurt, and hurt deeply, and that kind of wound didn't heal. Certainly she couldn't heal it.

You will never be enough for him.

Her anger had vanished now, as quickly as it had come, leaving her with nothing but a heavy ache in her chest and tears in her eyes. But still she tried, reaching out to him, trying to reach him in some way.

He caught her by the wrist, holding it gently. 'No, *gatita*.'

His touch and that name. It hurt. It hurt so much.

Her heart filled slowly with agony as tears slid down her cheeks, but she refused to wipe them away. Instead she tugged her hand from his grip and stepped away.

She wouldn't beg. She had her pride. He might not want her, but that didn't change what she felt for him, and she wouldn't pretend, either.

Leonie drew herself up, because to the core of her aching heart she was a fighter and she never gave up. 'I love you, Cristiano Velazquez, Duke of San Lorenzo. I know

I can't change the past for you. I can't ever replace what you lost. And I can't heal those wounds in your soul. And I know you don't love me back. But…' She lifted her chin, looked him in the eye. 'None of that matters. You made me see that I was worth something. You made me want something more and you made me think that I deserved to have it. I think we both do.'

A raw expression crossed his face and she couldn't help it. She reached up and touched one cheek lightly, and this time he didn't stop her.

'I just wish… I just wish you believed that, too.'

But it was clear that he didn't.

She dropped her hand and stepped away.

Her poor heart had burned to ash in her chest and there were tears on her cheeks, but her spine was straight as she turned away.

And when she walked out she didn't falter.

CHAPTER ELEVEN

Cristiano didn't arrive back at the castle till late that night. Stopping a wedding certainly took less time than planning one, but still it had taken hours of explaining and arranging things until everyone's curiosity had been satisfied.

It would be a scandal, but he didn't care.

He'd told everyone that his bride had taken ill unexpectedly and that the wedding would have to be postponed.

He would naturally cancel everything once the fuss had died down.

The first thing he'd done on arriving back was to see where Leonie was. He'd given orders that she was to be granted anything she wanted, and he'd expected that she'd probably have holed herself up in one of the *castillo*'s other guest rooms.

But what he hadn't expected was to find that she had gone and no one knew where she was. She'd come back from the chapel, disappeared into the bedroom to change and then had apparently vanished into thin air.

When he found out he stormed upstairs to the bedroom, to see if she'd taken anything with her, and was disturbed to find that she hadn't. Not even the new handbag and purse he'd bought her, with all the new bank cards he'd had set up for her.

In fact, she hadn't taken anything at all.

She'd simply…gone.

He got his staff to check every inch of the castle, and then the grounds, and then, when it was clear she wasn't anywhere on the estate, he called his staff to start searching the entire damn country.

He wanted her found and he wouldn't rest until she was.

Why? She's gone and that's how you wanted it. You threw her heart back in her face. Did you really expect her to stick around?

Something tore in his chest, a jagged pain filling him.

He could still feel the imprint of her skin on his fingertips as he'd taken her wrist in his, still see the pain in her eyes and the tears on her cheeks. See her courage as she'd lifted her chin and told him that it didn't matter if he didn't love her. That she loved him anyway.

Dios, she was brave. It wasn't her fault he didn't deserve that love and never would. That he never wanted anything to do with love and the pain it brought, the destruction it wreaked, not ever again.

It's not her fault you're a coward and ended up hurting her anyway.

The tearing pain deepened, widened, winding around his soul.

He shoved himself out of his uncomfortable chair and paced the length of his study, his fingers curled tight around his phone, ready to answer it the second someone called, telling him they'd found her.

He didn't want to think about what she'd said. He only wanted to think about whether or not she was safe. And she would be, surely? She could look after herself. After all, she had for years before he'd taken her from the streets, so why wouldn't she be safe now?

Yet he couldn't relax. Couldn't sit still. Couldn't escape the pain inside him or the cold feeling sitting in his gut.

It's too late. Too late not to love her.

He stopped in the middle of his study, staring out at the darkness beyond the window as the cold reached into his heart.

Because he knew this feeling. It was familiar. He'd felt it once for Anna and for his son. Fear and pain, and longing. An all-consuming rage. An endless well of need that no one could ever fill.

She can. She did.

Cristiano froze, unable to breathe.

Leonie, her face alight with passion as she took his face between her small hands…

Leonie, touching him gently, as if he was precious to her…

Leonie, filling his *castillo* with sunshine and warmth, with her smile and her laughter.

Leonie, whose love wasn't destructive or bitter, despite the long years she'd spent on the streets. Whose love was open and generous and honest, with nothing held back or hidden.

Leonie, who loved him.

She's what you need. What you've always needed.

Everything hurt. It was as if every nerve he had had been unsheathed, sensitive even to the movement of air on his skin.

Love was destructive, but hers wasn't. Why was that?

You know.

Cristiano closed his eyes, facing a truth he'd never wanted to see.

It wasn't love that was destructive, because there had been nothing destructive about the way Leonie had looked at him. Nothing cruel in the way she'd touched him gently as he'd thrown her love back in her face. Nothing angry.

Because it was anger that destroyed. Anger that frightened. Anger that made him bitter and twisted and empty inside.

Anger that made him a coward.

Anger that had hurt her.

He took a shuddering breath.

His proud, beautiful *gatita*. He'd hurt her and she'd simply touched his cheek. Told him that she wished he could see what she saw when she looked at him.

His brave Leonie. Walking away from him with a straight back, unbowed. A fighter in every sense of the word. But alone. Always alone.

Not again.

It was the only thought that made sense. He'd made mistakes in his life—so many mistakes—but the one mistake he'd made, that he kept making over and over again, had been to let his anger win. And he couldn't let it.

Once…just this once…he would let love win.

And he loved her.

Perhaps he had loved her the moment he'd picked her up from the street, seen her staring at him with wide blue eyes, her hair a tangled skein down her back.

He'd tried to deny the emotion, tried to ignore it. Tried to squash it down and contain it because his love had always been such a destructive thing. But he couldn't stop it from pouring through him now, intense and deep. A vast, powerful force.

He remembered this feeling—this helpless, vulnerable feeling. And how he'd fought it, tried to manage it, to grab control where he could. The anguish of wanting something from his parents that they were never going to give, and their instinctive withdrawal from him and his neediness. The pain of it as he'd tried to hold on to Anna. As his son had slipped through his fingers.

The vulnerability that he'd turned into anger, because that was easier and he'd thought it more powerful.

But it wasn't. This feeling was the most powerful. It was everything and he let it pulse through him, overwhelm him, making everything suddenly very, *very* clear.

He had to find her. She thought that they both deserved more. He wasn't sure that was true for him. But she definitely did. And though he had nothing to give her but his own broken, imperfect heart, it was all he had.

He just had to trust it was enough.

Cristiano turned and strode out of the study, his heart on fire, his phone still clutched in his hand.

LEONIE WAITED OUTSIDE in the garden of the tiny hotel in San Lorenzo, hiding in the darkness. She'd gotten good at it in Paris, and it seemed she still had the gift since no one had spotted her.

It was a long wait. But she had nowhere to go, and nowhere to be, so she stood there until at last the door to the wide terrace opened and a man came out to stand there, gazing out over the garden.

De Riero.

She really didn't know why she was here, or what she intended to do by coming—maybe just see him. Her memories of him were very dim, and they were still dim now. She didn't recognise his face. He was a stranger.

After she'd left the castle, walking to the village in the dark, she'd thought she'd probably have to hitchhike or stow away in a truck or something in order to leave San Lorenzo. The thought hadn't worried her. She just wanted to get as far away from Cristiano and his cold green eyes as she could.

But then, outside the small village hotel, she'd spotted a tall boy with vaguely familiar features and vivid green eyes and she'd known who it was. And who the tall man beside him must be, too.

And she hadn't been able to go any further.

She hadn't wanted to go into the hotel, so she'd slunk into the gardens and skulked in the shadows, watching the hotel terrace.

Waiting for what, she didn't know, but she hadn't been able to leave all the same.

De Riero reached into his jacket and took out a cigarette, lit it, leaning on the stone parapet of the terrace.

She could step out of the shadows now, reveal herself. Show him that she was still alive—though at the moment 'alive' was relative. Especially when she felt so hollow and empty inside.

What do you want from him?

She didn't know that, either. An apology? An acknowledgement? To be welcomed into his family with open arms?

Her father leaned his elbows on the parapet, his cigarette glowing.

Would he be disappointed if he found out she wasn't dead after all? Would he be angry with her for disrupting his family? Or would he be grateful? Happy?

Does it matter?

Her throat closed and her chest ached. And she knew the truth. It wouldn't change a thing. Because her heart was broken and it had nothing to do with her father. Nothing to do with his acknowledgement of her or otherwise. She felt nothing for him. Nothing at all.

Because her heart wasn't with him. It was with another man. A man who didn't want it and yet held it in his strong, capable hands anyway.

Whether her father wanted her or not, it wouldn't change that feeling. Wouldn't alter it. Which meant it wasn't this man's acceptance that would make her whole.

Only Cristiano could.

The boy came out onto the terrace, tall and already broad, joining the man. Cristiano's son.

The sounds of their voices carried over the garden, and then their laughter. There was happiness in their voices, an easy affection, and Leonie knew she wasn't going to reveal herself. That she would stay out of it.

That wasn't her family. Not any more.

It felt right to melt away into the shadows and leave them behind.

Her future wasn't with them.

A certain calmness settled inside her, along with determination.

She would find her own family and her own future. She would carve it with her bare hands if she had to, but find it she would. Her future wasn't as a de Riero and it wasn't as a Velazquez, but she would find something else.

She wasn't lost. She'd found herself.

Slowly she walked down the tiny street of San Lorenzo, alone in the dark. And then a car came to a screeching halt beside her and a man leapt out of it.

'Leonie!' a dark, familiar voice said desperately. 'Stop!'

She stilled, staring as Cristiano came towards her, his hair standing up on end, his wedding suit rumpled, the look on his face as raw and naked as she'd ever seen it.

He stopped right in front of her, staring at her, breathing hard. 'Don't leave,' he said hoarsely before she could speak. 'Please don't leave me.'

Shocked tears pricked her eyes, her heart aching and burning. What was he doing here? He'd been very clear on what he'd wanted and it wasn't her, no matter what he was saying now.

Resisting the urge to fling herself into his arms, she drew herself up instead, lifting her chin. 'What are you doing here, Cristiano?' Her voice was hoarse, but she was pleased with how calm she sounded.

'What you said in the chapel…' The look in his eyes burned. 'About deserving more.'

'What?'

'You told me that we both deserved more and that you wished I could believe it, too.' He stared at her. 'I want to know why.'

She blinked her tears back furiously. 'Does it matter?'

He moved then, taking her face between his big, warm palms, his whole body shaking with the force of some deep, powerful emotion. 'Yes,' he said fiercely. 'It matters. It matters more than anything in this entire world.'

His touch was so good. The warmth of it soothed all the broken edges of her soul, making her want to lean into his hands. Give him everything she had.

But he didn't love her, did he? And he never would. And that wasn't enough for her any more. It just wasn't.

'Why?' She forced away the tears. 'Why does it matter to you?'

The street lights glossed his black hair, made his eyes glitter strangely. 'Because you matter, *gatita*. You matter to me.'

Her breath caught—everything caught. 'What?' The question came out in a hoarse whisper.

'I came back and you were gone, and no one knew where you were.'

There was something bright and fierce in his expression. 'I couldn't rest and I couldn't sit still. I was afraid for you. And I knew it was too late. I've been trying not to love you, my little *gatita*. I've been trying not to care, trying to protect myself. But you're so easy to love, and I fell for you without even realising that I'd fallen.'

His thumbs moved gently over her cheekbones, wiping away tears she hadn't known were there.

'I resisted so hard. Love is so destructive, and I've hurt so many people. But it was you who showed me another way. You made me see that it wasn't love that destroyed things, it was anger. My anger.'

He loved her? He really loved her?

Everything took on a strange, slightly unreal quality, and she had to put her hands up and close her fingers around his strong wrists to make sure he was real.

'How?' she asked hoarsely. 'I didn't do—'

'You've spent years on the streets. Years fighting for your survival. Years with nothing and no one. And, yes, you're angry—but you haven't let it define you. You haven't let it make you bitter. No, it's your love that defines you. Your joy and your passion. And that's what I want, *mi corazón*. I want you to teach me how to love like that... teach me how to love *you* like that.'

She was trembling, and she didn't want to look away from him in case this wasn't real. In case he disappeared, as all the good things in her life seemed to do.

'You don't need me to teach you,' she whispered in a scratchy voice. 'You already know how to love, Cristiano. You just have to let go of your anger.'

He said nothing for a long moment, staring down into her face, holding her as if he was afraid of exactly the same thing she was: that this thing they were both within touching distance of would vanish and never come back.

'Is that what you see?' he asked roughly. 'When you look at me? How do I deserve anything if anger is all there is?'

His face blurred as more tears filled her vision and she had to blink them away fiercely. 'That's not all there is. You're a good man, a kind man. A man who feels things deeply and intensely. A protective man desperate for something to protect.'

She slid her hands up his wrists, covering the backs of his where they cupped her face.

'A man who wants someone to be his—and you deserve that, Cristiano. More, I think you need it.'

'I don't know that I did to deserve it. But I'm willing to spend my life trying.' His eyes burned with an intense green fire. 'Will you be mine, Leonie?'

'You don't have to try,' she said thickly. 'And I'm already yours. I've never been anyone else's.'

'Then please come back to me, *gatita*.' He searched her face as if he couldn't quite believe her. 'Please come home.'

But she didn't need him to plead. She'd already decided.

She went up on her toes and pressed her mouth to his, and when his arms came around her and held her tight she became whole.

With him she would never be homeless.

Because he was her home.

EPILOGUE

Cristiano paid the bill and pushed back his chair, standing up. The restaurant was very crowded and no one was looking at them, too involved with their own conversations to pay attention to the tall man with green eyes and the other, much younger man opposite him, who also stood, and who also had the same green eyes.

The lunch had gone surprisingly well, but it was too soon for an embrace so Cristiano only held out his hand, looking his son in the eye. 'It was good to meet you, Alexander.'

His son frowned, looked down at his extended hand, and then, after a moment, reached out and took it, shaking it firmly. 'I can't call you Papá—you know that, right?'

'Of course not,' Cristiano said easily. 'You already have one of those.'

De Riero—which wasn't what Cristiano had either wanted or chosen, but he couldn't change what had happened twenty years ago. All he could do was let go of his anger and accept it.

It hadn't been easy, but he'd done it. With a little help from Leonie, naturally enough.

In fact, that he'd made contact with his son at all had been all down to her. After a few years—after their lives had settled down and his son had become an adult in his own right—she'd encouraged Cristiano and supported him to reach out.

De Riero hadn't liked it, but something must have mellowed him over the years, because when Alexander had asked him about his parentage he apparently hadn't denied that Cristiano was his father.

He'd even tried to make contact with Leonie, when word had got out about the identity of Cristiano's wife. She hadn't wanted to take that step yet, but Cristiano knew she would one day. When she was ready.

As for Alexander... Cristiano didn't know what de Riero had told the boy about him, but clearly nothing too bad, since he had eventually agreed to meet him.

It had been tense initially, but Alexander had eventually relaxed. As had Cristiano.

'I'd like to meet with you again,' Cristiano said after they'd shaken hands. 'Lunch? Once a month, say?'

The young man nodded, looking serious. 'I think I'd like that.' He paused, giving Cristiano another measuring look. 'You're not what I expected,' he said at last.

Cristiano raised a brow. 'What did you expect?'

'I don't know. You're just...' Alexander lifted a shoulder. 'Easier to talk to than I thought you'd be.'

Something in Cristiano's heart—a wound that hadn't ever fully healed—felt suddenly a little less painful.

He smiled. 'I'll take that.'

Ten minutes later, after Alexander had left, he stepped out of the restaurant and onto the footpath—and was nearly bowled over by two small figures.

'Papá!' the little boy yelled, flinging himself at his father, closely followed by his red-haired sister.

The pain in Cristiano's heart suddenly dissolved as if it had never been. He opened his arms, scooping both children up. They squealed, his daughter gripping onto his hair while his son grabbed his shirt.

It was soon apparent that both of them had been eating ice cream and had got it all over their hands.

'They're too big for that,' Leonie said, coming up behind them, her face alight with amusement. 'And look what Carlos has done to your shirt.'

Cristiano only laughed. 'That's what washing machines are for.'

She rolled her eyes. She'd lost nothing of her fire and spark over the past five years, coming into her own as his duchess. Not only had she proved adept at helping him manage the San Lorenzo estate, as well as becoming the driving force behind various charities aimed at helping children on the streets, she'd also proved herself to be a talented artist. Luckily she used oils and canvas these days, rather than spray cans and cars.

She was looking at him now in that way he loved. Sharp and direct. Seeing through him and into his heart. 'How did it go?' she asked.

He grinned. 'It went well. Very well indeed.'

Her eyes glinted and he realised they were full of tears. 'I'm so glad.'

His beautiful, beautiful *gatita*. She had worried for him.

Cristiano put down the twins and ignored their complaints, gathering his wife in his arms. 'He wants to meet again. Lunch, once a month.'

'Oh, Cristiano.' Leonie put her arms around his neck and buried her face in his shirt.

He put his hands in her hair, stroking gently, his heart full as he soothed his wife while two of his children tugged at his jacket, oblivious, and the third…

The third he'd find out more about soon.

It was enough. It was more than he'd ever thought he'd have.

After winter there was summer.

And after rain there was sunshine.

After anger and grief and loss there was love.

Always and for ever love.

Cristiano kissed his wife. 'Come, Leonie Velazquez. Let's go home.'

* * * * *

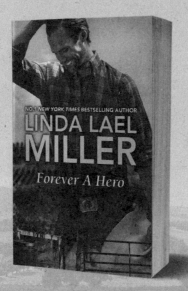

MILLS & BOON

Want to know more about your favourite series or discover a new one?

Experience the variety of romance that Mills & Boon has to offer at our website:

millsandboon.com.au

Shop all of our categories and discover the one that's right for you.

MODERN

DESIRE

MEDICAL

INTRIGUE

ROMANTIC SUSPENSE

WESTERN

HISTORICAL

FOREVER
EBOOK ONLY

HEART
EBOOK ONLY

f @millsandboonaustralia 🐦 📷 @millsandboonaus

Subscribe and fall in love with a Mills & Boon series today!

You'll be among the first to read stories delivered to your door monthly and enjoy great savings.

WE SIMPLY LOVE ROMANCE